Facing our destiny
Standing on shaking knees
But we won't go quietly
Can we hold the line?
Can we hold the line?

Yeah, this is where we rise.

-Where We Rise, Neoni

To the little girl who held onto her dreams
even when they seemed impossible.

We love things that seem impossible.
You got this.

SAVAGE

Sierra Prynne

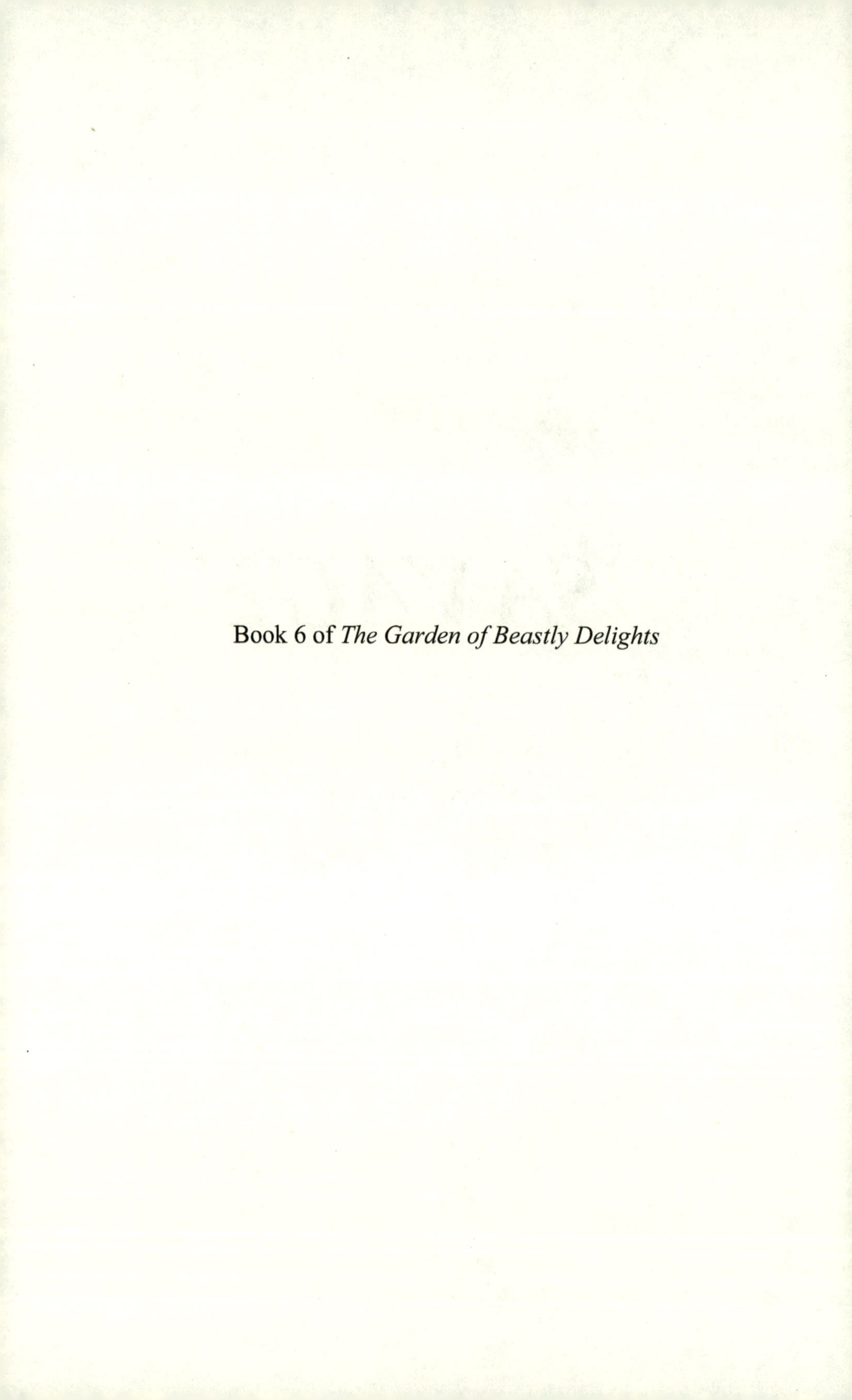
Book 6 of *The Garden of Beastly Delights*

CHAPTER 1

A game.

This standoff in a great library at the bottom of a mountain surrounded by the bodies of our fallen friends is a game to him.

That was the first thought that went through my head as Rav settled into his position at the entrance to Idalia's library and began his torturous waiting game for me to…simply fall asleep. He genuinely seemed to think that was how I would lose this standoff.

No, I realized he wanted me to *surrender*. He wanted me to give in. Either physically—when I couldn't keep my eyes open any longer and my creatures currently holding him back blipped out of view like an electric fence slowly losing its charge. Or emotionally—by finally admitting that the lengths he'd gone to find me were proof of his love for me.

That wasn't how this was going to go, but it was cute that he thought it would.

If this was a game, I wanted to play too.

"Why are you smiling?" he asked after the silence between us grew long. "Undressing me with your eyes? You know we can do all of that and more in the comfort of our own home, *min skat*."

That was as good a way to pass the time as any. I let my eyes roam south, from his beautiful face, dancing across his Adam's apple, to the little notch between his neck and chest, and farther down, remembering the tattoos that were arranged like faded calligraphy across his skin, in blue ink with a bright spark of orange magick on top.

I'd always liked his hands; they were firm, yet soft to the touch, and well-manicured. And they were one of the few parts of his body not covered in tattoos.

His legs were lovely robust columns, guarding that pillar of marble between that seemed to be waking up to greet me the longer I left my gaze to roam across the stretched landscape of him.

"Goddess, I cannot wait to capture you," he purred, as if he couldn't help himself, and my gaze snapped back to his eyes, unsurprised to find heat and amusement in them.

"You haven't captured me yet," I teased. "And you won't."

"We'll see," he hummed.

"You're going to leave disappointed," I sang.

"Since I'll have you across my knees, I doubt it," he sang back, reveling in the chuffed low laughs of his men.

I wished I could chuckle too, since he clearly hadn't realized what I was doing yet. But I resisted the temptation.

"Natalie, you should *just go*."

My eyes jerked to Fern wishing I could speak directly into her mind and soothe away the fear that had her body tight and coiled. She hadn't yet realized what I was doing either, and there'd been no time to tell her before Rav's forces had stormed down the tunnel to the library and bottlenecked in this unfortunate way.

But she would understand soon enough.

So would he.

"Natalie's not going anywhere, Lady Saeli," Rav said with a smartass smirk on his face. "She can't. You're here. She'd never leave you to die. Isn't that right, *min skat*?"

He thought he knew me so well. He *did*. That *was* one of the reasons I was still standing there and not flying through the tiny tunnels in the rock overhead and out into the Italian Alps beyond. I couldn't leave Fern to die like our other friends. Not with Idalia and Asterios's bodies at my feet, gone too soon from the world because of me.

But it wasn't the only reason.

"My lady, plea—"

"Hush, Fern," I said calmly. "There's no point arguing about this."

"I disagree," Rav said. "I'd love to discuss the terms of your surrender while we have the time."

"Like I said, there's no point," I said, smiling.

"No?"

"I already know the terms of this surrender," I said. "You want to take me back to Denmark. To marry me."

"Among other things."

I pursed my lips playfully at that, buying time. I only needed time.

“Let me guess, you want to trap me in Hrafnagud,” I teased again, relishing in the bolt of anger I saw flash across his eyes.

“No, I swore I would *never* do that again,” escaped him in a hiss. “*Our home*. It’s repaired and waiting for you. For us.”

“And we’ll what? Rule the world from there?”

That dazzling smile of his returned, delighting in the thought. “Yes.”

“Together?”

“Yes.”

I raised an eyebrow at that. “Even though I “lack the experience?””

“As I’ve told you before, that experience will come in time.”

“How? You gave away my kingdom.”

At that he sneered dismissively. “Archer’s nothing. He’s keeping the seat warm for you.”

“And Ulric?”

“He’s a good guard dog satisfied with the small yard he roams.”

“And Idalia?” I asked, motioning to where one of his soldiers was practically standing on her body. “Asterios?”

“I already have their replacements picked, *min skat*.” He said the words as if he was trying to reassure me everything would be okay. *He would handle it*.

“Everyone’s just so easily replaceable?” I asked.

“Not you,” he swore. “Never you.”

But therein lied the rub. I was “irreplaceable” because I was literally one of a kind. Not because I had worth beyond my utility.

“On a scale of one to ten, Rav, how excited were you the moment the cult announced me as their ruler?”

A low chuckle escaped him. “Infinite.”

“Even though they only chose me?”

“Once we mate, they’ll have both of us. Together, we will be formidable. The world will have two pillars on which to build its new future. We’ll give them more than they ever dreamed possible, *min skat*.”

Oh Rav. He said so many things that almost sounded promising.

Some part of me wanted to give him the benefit of the doubt, believing that if we were in private, talking one-on-one, the conversation would be…deeper. Richer. And maybe it would have been.

But I’d only ever been trying to buy us time.

And as I stood there pretending to consider his offer, a tiny flicker of movement caught out of the corner of my eye, and I knew our latest "negotiation" was coming to an end.

There, just above the jumpy man to Rav's right, was a spider. As I watched, it let itself down its impossibly fine silk and crawled into the man's collar.

"Unfortunately, Rav, I don't think you've done enough to earn me yet," I said, stepping toward Fern and taking her hand, squeezing.

"I have time, *min skat*."

"Not as much as you think."

"S-S-SPIDER! SPIDER! SPIDER!"

There was a single moment, when the jumpy man began to flail and claw at his clothing, that I thought I might have jumped the gun a little bit on saying our time was coming to an end. For a moment, it was *only* him squirming, drawing Rav's annoyed attention like a child screaming for his mother.

But all at once, in a terrible tremble that sent tiny bits of rock falling to the floor around us, the wall above our would-be conquerors—and those of the passage itself—began to move, chitter, *skitter*.

And a tsunami of spiders poured into the tunnel, eager to meet their king.

CHAPTER 2

The good thing about spiders, especially in the midst of an ambush, was that almost none of the soldiers thought to use their guns. Why would they? Their targets were tiny. Crawly. Bitey. The soldiers needed their hands to smack and swat and claw.

Only one soldier's hand was on the trigger of his weapon when hundreds of spiders launched themselves at his eyes and ears and open screaming mouth. The gun was pointed at me, and I heard the roaring *BOOM* of the bullet firing, saw the bright blinding flash—

—and two things happened simultaneously.

So coordinated you might have thought it was planned, rather than pure instinct.

Rav yanked the muzzle of the gun skyward a second before the rest of the soldier's bullets fired…

And Cass, my silent ghostly protector, caught the silver bullet inches from my heart.

Dropped it as his hand began to smoke. Glanced down at his sizzling palm with curiosity and annoyance instead of pain.

Even in the midst of danger, the urge to kiss it to make it better was so strong, I would have laughed at myself, if there'd been time for any of that.

No there was none. Not before my dark garnet dragon darted his head out and chomped down on the shooter's neck before flinging him away into a far wall.

Rav backed up as much as he could with his screaming men around him, but the bottleneck in the tunnel left him nowhere to go. His options were the passageway full of flailing, panicking men or my *wall* of animal forms. My dragon's vicious teeth. My bear's striking claws. My raven's mind. My wolf's protective spirit.

And the spiders that were at every second swarming across his body like a nightmare. He crushed a few; the bites healed as quickly as they appeared on his skin. But the rest, he simply ignored.

And when my dragon saw an opening and darted his head and long neck out in Rav's direction, Rav landed a single brutal punch to my dragon's nose that almost knocked me off my feet. Pain flared for a bright second between my eyes.

"Ow, Rav!" I barked.

He staggered in surprise, glancing between me and my dragon, who was rubbing-rubbing-rubbing at his wounded nose.

Cass, too, glanced between us before he disappeared.

"*Min skat*," Rav said apologetically, pulling my attention back as the bodies of his men began to fall around him, swollen with venom and choked with too many creepy-crawly limbs. "I didn't mean to—"

"My lady!" Fern barked, cutting him off. "Can you hear that?"

As if someone spun a dial in my head, my wolf's hyper-hearing kicked in, and a sound reached me as beautiful as it was triumphant. Helicopters. Shouted commands.

Gunfire.

The narrow opening of the library amplified the noise until the world beyond the tunnel sounded apocalyptic, drawing Rav's attention away.

I knew it was my only chance.

I knew it was now or never.

So quietly in my mind, I gave the order, "*Stampede*."

And just as Rav turned his startled face back to me, he was knocked off his feet by my speeding wolf. She *barreled* into him, almost *through* him, carrying him away, up the tunnel and out of sight. My bear followed. Then my dragon crawled up onto the ceiling of the tunnel and slithered away into the dark, purr-growling like some great hungry beast.

Technically he was.

"Ready?" I asked Fern.

Off her nod, we pushed. We *ran*. Or tried to. Up the tunnel. Over the bodies of fallen men, kicking and punching any that tried to reach for us as we made our way past.

I'd never asked Idalia how long the library tunnel actually was, but it must've been a mile of bodies. At least. More than that, it was a mile of *feeling* my animals fight for me. I couldn't split my attention through the slog up the tunnel to watch their fights through my viewing windows, so instead, I *felt* strange textures against my teeth and a ghostly metallic tang on my tongue, and phantom cuts and scrapes and jams on my feet and between my fingers. Bruises appeared on my body as I ran. A headache struck my right ear and left it ringing. And I felt the cruel sting of something slamming into the back of my leg, leaving me to hobble.

My body was a haunted battlefield.

But it got me to the basement, then up the stairs past more bodies. Then to the ground floor of Arachne's Revenge where the battle filled every room and threatened danger around every corner. It was loud and brash and violent and overwhelming.

And Cass was…blinking in and out around me so fast it was hard to follow him with my eyes as he…fielded…attackers. There were so many. So many, but I knew there would have been more without him there.

Didn't mean we were safe, though. He couldn't be everywhere at once.

A man spotted me and charged; I bent at the last second, slammed my shoulder into his groin, and used his own momentum to toss him over my aching back before Fern brought a hard foot down on his head, one I could tell had an elephant's strength behind it.

Another forced me back into defensive footwork before he made one accidental advance that gave me the advantage and I struck his face with the heel of my palm, utterly shattering his nose and damaging his eyes.

A third hit me with a taser from behind. It was like an electric painful version of the spider's venom that had once paralyzed me. It made my teeth vibrate, as if they were on the verge of exploding. But the second Fern wrenched the woman's arm away from my body, I turned and sent a high kick right into her chest; she crashed through a glass display case and didn't get up again.

There was no time for anything like discretion.

I didn't know how to "only hobble."

I didn't think I even should. I was outnumbered. I was outstrengthed. They were coming *for me*. This wasn't a fight between life or death; this was a moment between freedom and slavery and that seemed worse. So much worse.

It felt like it meant more.

And if they hadn't come for me, they wouldn't have died.

That was the only thing I could think as I fought. *If they hadn't come for me, they wouldn't have died.*

The men and women Fern and I encountered as we forced our way outside were mostly only maimed, but the taste of blood on my tongue became impossible to mistake for anything other than death. The sound of approaching choppers told me more were coming; who knew if they were friend or foe? And there were *bodies everywhere* by the time I saw Brodie fighting across the plaza near the Celestial Temple, slicing through people with a bowie knife the size of his forearm.

I took a single step in his direction and froze as the choir of my animals screamed in my head, "*No! Mountains*."

"We have to get out of here," I told Fern, pointing to the Alps.

"This way, my lady!" Fern shouted, grabbing my arm.

She dodged for the unassuming gate that led away from the battle, but our advance was cut off by a sudden row of Rav's giant men. Their blue eyes locked on me with icy calculated focus half a second before they *sprinted* at me in a way that *horrified* my senses. Twice my height. Twice my build. Hands on guns and tasers and rope. No humanity in their eyes.

One I could take.

Two I could wound.

Three, four, and five? My mind splintered at the inevitable loss I faced, watching those enormous men sprint toward me like a zombie horde.

But I couldn't focus on that. Not if I wanted to remain free.

No, the only thing I could focus on was Eike, of all things. Those rounds and rounds of early morning ambushes at Hamingja she'd used as training. How she'd taught me to improvise. How she'd warned me to anticipate behaviors.

It wasn't so much a trip down memory lane as it was a bright burst of traumatic stress.

I took in everything around me at once—the layout of the plaza and the realization that the fighting was happening too close at our backs to turn and run, the temple, my allies, my animals. I saw my wolf and dragon turn toward me a fraction too late to stop all but the last man from advancing. I felt Fern's hand land on my chest at dead-center and attempt to tuck me behind her, to protect me for half a second longer.

I saw the stone wall that separated this property from the mountains and forest. There was a drop off on the other side, but if I could find ten seconds to open my wings and launch before someone caught me, I could fly Fern across that gap and land on the slope beyond.

But I didn't have ten seconds. I had two.

And then the first man reached us, and Fern crippled him with a kick between his legs. The second she shoved away to gain more room, and I saw Cass dash him away in a blur before the third was there in front of us.

She managed to land half a dozen blows to his body, splitting his lip, cracking a rib, but it only incensed him. Until he pulled something glinting from his side that I realized was a knife after he swung.

A horrendous *slicing* sound—*at Fern*—was followed by a scream I heard in my soul. A splatter across my face I knew was blood before I smelled it. Before my body registered the texture that wasn't quite water.

He'd sliced through her cheek with a knife the size of a trowel. *Deep.* Through the tissue into her mouth. I could see her teeth. *Horrible.*

But I couldn't focus on that.

He turned for me. Still holding that knife, now coated in Fern's blood.

Then he swung at me.

And *not* as if he was merely attempting to wound or capture. He swung with his whole chest as if he intended to decapitate me if he could.

And Eike came back to me. A lesson she'd showed me once upon a safer time. How to use the momentum of a much stronger, much larger opponent against them.

As he swung at my head, I ducked and grabbed his arm in passing, *adding my own speed and power behind it* as it swung around and sliced right into the throat of his nearest comrade.

He was so surprised. *So surprised.*

Guilt froze him.

And I didn't hesitate. I swung my arm down at his elbow, "collapsing it" at the same moment I wrapped my other hand around his wrist and plunged the knife he was holding into his own throat.

"I'm sorry," I whispered, trying to catch my breath, even though I wasn't sure I was sorry.

There was no time for anything else.

By the time I turned, the first man was on his feet again, clutching that spot between his legs, his face red with hatred and pain.

And all I thought to say was, "You should've stayed down."

He roared at me and charged. Hit me with a closed fist so hard I saw stars. But he swung again…with *just enough momentum* that when he missed, I grabbed his face, pulled it in and *bit* into his cheek. Blood sprayed into my mouth, *disgusting*, as he shoved me away, tearing his own cheek off in the effort.

I landed hard on the ground.

And he landed on me half a second later in a body slam that stole the breath from my lungs.

"How many pieces could I break you into before the king couldn't put you back together again?" he asked, rubbing his hand on his cheek and smearing more of his blood across my face.

"I don't know. How many balls do you have?" I asked, kicking up as hard as I could.

I felt his body crumple like a struck car above me as he yelped in pain and I shoved him off just in time for my dragon to appear, snap his jaws around the man's entire head and shake him like a ragdoll before hurling him away into the Celestial Temple's belltower, reducing it to brick and clanging bell noises.

"*Injured?*" my dragon asked, sniffing at the blood on my face.

"*No. Defend.*"

He turned and *pounced* for another man in a blur of jewel tones.

I rose to my feet and helped Fern to hers. I didn't have much to give her as she clutched her face, except for a piece of my shirt. I tore the sleeve off at the shoulder and offered it to her.

"Let's get out of here," I said. "I have my azurite. We can use it to heal you once we're—"

"Ducpmf!" she shouted too late.

A boot struck her chest, knocking her back.

A hand latched onto my hair, clawing. Yanking me around to face—*the other viper twin*. Gaspar? Marcelo? Whichever one it was it was the insane one. There was a twisted smile on his face, caught between enraged joy and devastation. I'd never seen insanity this close, but that's what it was, as he wrapped a hand around my throat, sucker punched me, and then took an extra second and a half to carefully tuck a piece of hair behind my ear as I tried to pull air into my lungs.

But it wasn't just him there. A circle of armed men had come with him, all but blocking the rest of the fight from view, as they turned their backs on us, as if to give us privacy. Faintly, I registered my animals coming to fight. Attempting to break through to me amidst a barrage of gunfire. Faintly, I registered a flash of saffron orange fighting too.

I didn't know if they'd make it in time.

My instinct was to go for his insane gray eyes. To scratch them out. To get away.

But I didn't make it that far. Another pair of hands wrapped around me from behind and took hold of my wrists, stopping me.

It was one of Rav's men. Young. Boyish.

But only in looks.

"You crazy bitch!" he yelled at me so loudly, I flinched away. "You must want to die."

"That privilege belongs to me," the viper said, tightening his grip on my neck and pulling me toward him.

Rav's boyish soldier didn't like that. He yanked back on my wrists, accidentally twisting until I felt a strain in the muscles of my arms. A *tearing* that lanced pain into my throat so sour I wanted to vomit and cry. "She killed my friends!"

"She killed my brother!" the viper roared back, tightening his grip again.

I wished I could've said some last clever thing, but with the pain and the closing throat, there was nothing clever *to* say.

I was running out of time. I was running out of air. My vision was graying around the edges as the men continued to bicker over who'd get to hurt me first.

So, I went with a classic. I kicked between the viper's legs hoping it would at least get him to drop me. At least get him to stagger.

It didn't.

At all.

He huffed with annoyance, surprising both me and Rav's soldier.

The viper smirked. "Nothing to kick." Off our mutual confusion, he added, "That's not where my *cojones* are."

Right before his grip tightened around my throat again and he *thrust* my head backward into the skull of the boyish soldier holding me from behind. The back of my head hit the front of his so hard, it didn't even hurt; it just made my vision swim, and the world went sideways.

The boy fell back like a stone...and as his grip on me released, I realized whatever he'd done to my arms had left them dangling by my sides, useless.

Worse, caught in the viper's grip, my azurite was dangling away from my body, unreachable.

I didn't know where my animals were. I didn't know where Cass was.

I wanted to cry.

I wanted to scream for the fear that crawled into my heart, at how vulnerable I knew I was. Especially when the viper opened his smiling mouth a little wider, revealing a forked tongue…and inch-long fangs.

And I knew I had only one option remaining. One I'd used before a long time ago.

"Just do it already," I croaked at him.

He lunged forward and sank his fangs into my neck, pouring hot, acidic, bubbling venom into my body. It wasn't like the vampire that had attacked me in London; that bite had been almost pleasant and numbed by the heady cocktail of…whatever…was in his fangs. This was just pain. I could feel my veins *tensing* as my blood began to coagulate. I could feel the *burn* as the venom coursed farther away from that primary touch.

But I could also feel…the buzz of my azurite where it was touching my body between us, pressed to me as he'd tightened his hold.

And when that blue stone asked me if I wanted to transform, the yes was so instinctual it wasn't even a word in my mind, only a *surrendering* to the chance that one more blinding burst of unraveling pain would free me from the pain of everything else.

It *was* blinding.

It was brutal.

But then it was over and the pain—all of it—vanished in the blink of an eye. Many eyes.

I had…many eyes. A dozen of them suddenly, giving me a wide, *wide* view.

And many legs. Eight of them—well, six of them, along with my two arms—which were suddenly strong and working again. My legs were pressed awkwardly to the ground beneath me. I realized why as I rose to stand, easily stepping out of the viper's grasp.

I was tall. *Shockingly* tall. Standing precariously on the very narrow ends of my legs where tiny claws had replaced my feet.

I also had a giant abdomen the color of deepest darkest pink that jutted out behind me like a Victorian-era skirt bustle.

And as I glanced down at the viper, frozen in awe below me, I saw my own reflection in his wide gray eyes.

I wasn't a spider. I was a spiderlady, like the one I'd met down in the Archives re-creating beautiful historical scenes from spider silk. Like the one I'd met under the Domus Aurea in Rome.

"*Monster*," the viper whispered, right before he screamed, "Monster! Monster! Monster!"

The fight almost paused around me. At least, it looked like it did, for a split second anyway. Confusion mixed with fear as hundreds of eyes turned toward me…

…and guns pivoted in my direction.

But it wasn't the guns I focused on. There were two people moving through the frozen crowd—one silent, the other roaring, "RUN! NATALIE, RUN!"

Cass. Rav. Running for me.

And my animals. They reached me first, crashing into me one after the next after the next, all screaming "*RUN!*" inside my head.

Someone shouted, "Open fire!"

No one heard Rav's roared rebuke. "NO!"

No one except me. I turned as the first shot sailed over my head. Enveloped and lifted Fern in my arms. Raised my wings as they erupted out of my back and took the first hail of gunfire like a shield of feathers.

One silver bullet struck me in the leg; another grazed my abdomen. But those were bee stings compared to my eviscerated wings, which scattered feathers and blood around me as bullets ripped holes in them.

Pain tore through every part of me as I scurried to the tall wall between us and the forest. As I leapt for the slope and darted for the cover of the trees. I ran until the gunfire died behind me. Then I ran farther. Higher. As fast as I could.

It wasn't over. I knew that in my bones.

And I had to get as far away as I could before the exhaustion tied to the pain could claim me. Dragging my tattered wings behind me was like trying to drag a vampire mid-feed; every bump and pivot and branch sapped my energy with agony. I couldn't even pull my wings back into my body, they were so damaged.

I just needed a few seconds to transform to heal myself, but if I altered into my human form, I wouldn't be able to run as fast, and we hadn't covered enough distance yet.

At the very least I wanted to be able to heal Fern before…

…before…

A sound ripped my attention to the sky behind me—a helicopter. I spotted it between the pine trees. But it wasn't alone. There were two others alongside it. Armed men were in all of them.

But only one had its cabin door open. And standing right at the edge staring down at me was Rav. I couldn't read his expression from this distance, but did it really matter what he was feeling while he chased me to exhaustion through the forest?

I just kept running. Zigzagging. Seeking out the thickest trees. Looking for *anywhere* to hide. A cave for my bear. A tiny hole for my raven.

I found little more than an outcropping of stone under which to lay Fern down. But it would have to do. It was too dangerous for her to be with me.

She shivered with pain and fear, eyeing me like the monster they all thought I was.

"I'm sorry, I didn't want you to find out like this," I told Fern as I raised the azurite stone to her body. "Brace yourself. Two taps, real quick, all right?"

She nodded. Through her wounded mouth, she whimpered, "Do it."

It happened with a flash of blue light and a savage scream that ripped from her throat as a chord—first human, then elephant—as her human shell gave way to the animal within. She was a *beautiful* creature to behold. Tall as a tree with rounded ears and a color akin to radioactive volcanic ash.

But I wasted no time at all tapping her with the stone again, bringing her back into her human form.

Only then did I ask, "Are you okay?"

"Y-Yeah," she managed, still shaking, still eying me with wonder verging on panic.

"It's not what you think," I said. "I'm not dangerous, I promise. But I'm going to run now. I'm going to lead them away from you. Be careful going back to Brodie. Secure Arachne's Revenge, if you can. That library's too important to lose, okay?"

She hesitated, still deciding, but nodded her head. It had to be enough.

And I tore away across the hillside, leaving her behind.

The helicopters followed me. And at first, I was happy they did. Fern was safe. And it meant there were fewer fighters for Brodie to overcome.

But the farther I ran, the slower I ran. Soon, the buzz of the chopper wings grew incessant, almost idling above me.

I got pretty far, all things considered. I ran until the slope of the hills became the rootstalk of the mountains, tilting up and up and up, forcing me down narrowed paths where I could see peaks adorned with snow far away between the trees.

But it just wasn't far enough.

"*Lie down, min skat*," Rav's voice bellowed from the heavens. "*Surrender already. Please. So I can heal you.*"

I flipped him the bird as I staggered onward on my spider legs, my impossibly tiny claws at the end of each, which were beginning to feel like they were bleeding too.

And then, all at once, in a *fwoomph* of air, I found myself on the ground, caught in a net so heavy I could barely raise my own hand to my azurite pendant to return my human body to me, hoping it would at least end the pain. It didn't. My damaged wings fell off, thankfully, but the silver bullet wounds on my leg and stomach remained.

Rav landed on the ground a few feet away and marched toward me like some obnoxious conquering hero, and I half expected to see a self-satisfied smile on his face.

I didn't, though. He looked worried. He looked concerned.

He dropped to his knees beside me and reached for my head, gently running his fingers across my hair, as if trying to soothe me.

"*The wolf, sir*!" I heard one of Rav's men say. "*It's running away*."

Faintly, I sensed her absence in my inner sanctum. Not that I could do much about it.

"*Go after it,*" Rav said. "*See if silver bullets work on it*."

"No, Rav," I said, begging in my mind for my wolf to *run*.

"Let me handle it," he cooed at me. "We'll have to weed out disobedient forms anyway."

I felt the bite of a sedative being injected into my leg as he added, "Don't worry, you're all right. You won't be hurt for much longer, I promise."

"You should've caught me fair and square, Rav," I grumbled, as I felt the sweet lull of sleep beginning to take hold. "This is…no fair."

He smiled at that, with such a tender look of love in his eyes it pained my heart even through the atrocious agony of the rest of me. Still petting, he whispered, "Haven't you heard, *min skat*? Everything is fair in love and war."

CHAPTER 3

The moment my eyes fluttered open hours later, I knew exactly where Rav had brought me. Still, I blinked, letting the reality of the room bleed into my awareness in its own time.

Tall conical ceiling, white as snow.

A bed fit for a giant. A mullioned window high overhead, through which I could see the waning moon, glowing orange against the indigo dark.

And an enormous man clutching me like a beloved toy in his sleep.

"Fylgja Castle," I whispered. "The Pirate's Perch."

"Yes."

His whisper purred against my ear from behind, streaking sensation down into my neck. I could lie and say I felt only fear, but that wouldn't be true. Even without him pouring magick into me like before, Rav's touch tickled, teased. It wasn't like Cass's touch—it had never been like that—but it begged responses from my body that my mind struggled with anyway. That spark. That fizzing *need* in Rav's caress was a reminder; the only reason it wasn't stronger was because I was already mated to Cass. If I weren't…If I hadn't made that mistake so early, I would've felt as strongly for Rav as he clearly did for me.

The real reason I couldn't ignore that spark, though, was…both mechanical and intuitive. I was bound by rope again. Soft rope. Loose enough not to pain me but rope all the same. There was also something I could feel, tight against my neck. No doubt I was surrounded by guards, too, whose sole mission was to prevent me from escaping. And deep inside me, some whispered warning told me to feel the spark—observe the spark—without letting it blind me to the reality of my situation. I was in the most dangerous place I could be. Not just out of the pan and into the fire…but being cradled by it.

I tried to roll to face him.

"Would you like my help?" he asked.

"Yes."

His large hands landed on my shoulder and hip and gently rolled me over, right into his gravity. He lay there, not four inches away, staring at me with an expression on his face that broke my heart as much as it scared me. There was love there, in his eyes. Fear, in the downward curve of his lips. Resentment, in the set of his jaw. Longing, in his panted honey breaths. Need, in the touch of him when he slowly drew his fingers up my side, my arm, my neck, to cradle my cheek.

I didn't know what to say to him, as we stared at each other. What was there to say?

"Was all this necessary?" I asked.

"If you finally believe I love you, yes," he said.

"Chasing me across Europe doesn't prove you love me," I pointed out.

"It's a start. A grand gesture."

I rolled my eyes at that, and he smiled. *He smiled so friggen sincerely.*

"Quit smiling!"

"Sorry," he said, still doing it. I raised my eyebrow. He grabbed his own cheeks and tried to force the smile away. "I'm stopping. I'm stopping."

But as he brought his hand back to my cheek, running his thumb across it, the smile crept back in, softer this time. Just admiring me.

"What is *wrong* with you?" I couldn't hclp asking.

"Very little, now," he said, arching a brow at me. "And nothing, after tomorrow."

Tomorrow? I blinked at him, wincing. He couldn't possibly think…

"If you force me back down the aisle tomorrow, you won't like what happens, Rav." He opened his mouth to say something stupid, but I cut him off, "That's not an empty threat. I don't make those anymore."

He closed his mouth for a full five seconds before he said, "*Tomorrow*, we begin negotiations."

"Who does?"

"You and me."

"For what?"

"How we'll earn each other's trust back."

I snickered in disbelief. "*I* have to earn *your* trust back?"

"Yes."

"For what?"

"Your lack of faith."

"Huh?"

No playful smile graced his face this time. "You are my mate, and I'm yours. Blessed by the Goddess and *literally* made for each other. That isn't something you just throw away. And yet, at the first sign of disagreement, you gave up on me. Gave up on us."

"There is no—"

"I'm not perfect, but neither are you. That doesn't mean we aren't perfect for each other."

I wanted to clap back with something snarky and dismissive. Something profoundly *unromantic* just to make him an enemy from the start. To set us off on the wrong foot immediately. But I didn't. I left things unspoken. That quiet instinct inside told me to. Maybe it was my truthsayer gift. Maybe it was some new sixth sense. Maybe it was simply that life experience had slapped the snark out of my mouth enough times to know that sometimes the best offense was camouflaged as defense. You catch more flies with honey, or something like that.

I stayed quiet and let him tell me things.

"I made mistakes," he continued. "Mistakes I'll never make again, I promise you. You've made mistakes too—some you didn't even know you were making. But that's why we need each other. You're the *only one* who can make me a better man, a better animal, a better ruler. And if a ruler is what you wish to be, I can give you an education you'd never be able to get anywhere else. You know that's true, don't you?"

I stayed quiet…and nodded.

And Rav's arms swept around me, pulling me against him, swaddling me in some shiver as it ran through him.

"And if tenderness is what you want, teach me how to be what you need," he groaned, pressing his forehead to mine so sincerely. "I miss yours in a way that would scare you, if I was honest with you."

That was a new one—admitting he was deflecting to get around having to tell me the truth.

"You don't think I'm 'too sweet' anymore?" I asked.

"No," he said, almost cooing as he added, "Sweet girls don't dominate in the heat of battle."

Oh boy, did I want to dissuade him of that delusion.

Still, I stayed quiet…and sunk into him. As much as I could wrapped neck-to-toe in rope, anyway.

He sighed with relief against my ear, and I weathered another shiver as he promised, “We’ll get through this. We can get through anything together.”

“I hope so,” I said, motioning to the ropes around me.

Rav ignored the glance and kissed my nose before rolling me over so he could cuddle me again, punctuating the conversation he’d decided was over with, “I know so.”

CHAPTER 4

"Why Fylgja Castle?"

"What do you mean why?"

We were eating a late breakfast out on the patio overlooking the statue garden, a silent housekeeper spooning yogurt parfait into my mouth while I wriggled futilely against my bindings, when I asked him.

"Why not Hamingja? It's more isolated. You're more exposed here. Is the war over?"

The grounds were literally swarming with guards as far as my eye could see. I couldn't turn my head without seeing at least ten armed men from here to the far tree line in any given direction. The castle was the same, so overstuffed with muscle it looked like a 24-hour gym.

And they were all deer alters. Every single one of them.

"Eh, it remains to be seen," he admitted. "The cult hasn't reached out to me. Yet. I'm sure they will, now that you're here, but…until then, we remain vigilant."

"And Hamingja?" I asked, reminding him.

He smiled. "I can feel your power rooting around in my throat, you know."

"I know."

"Will you always use your truthtelling gift around me?"

My eyebrow rose. "Is there a reason I shouldn't?"

"We're trying to rebuild trust. We can't rebuild anything if you treat me like a liar before I've even spoken."

"And if you always told the truth, my gift wouldn't matter."

Rav let out a light, low chuff of a laugh; it sounded edged in reluctant respect.

Then he smiled shyly. "I wanted no temptation, *min skat*. That is why we did not go to Hamingja."

"Temptation to magickally sedate me again, you mean?"

He shrugged, then swore, "Unintentionally, of course."

But to that, I felt like teasing, "Are you worried you'll explode, or that the Goddess might have some things to say about what you've done to me?"

Rav grunted, not quite meeting my eye. "She's a busybody anyway. Antiquated, too, in the new order of things."

"How so?" I couldn't help asking. "Now that everybody knows about the magick; it's only a matter of time before they know about her too."

"Not necessarily," he countered. "We get to decide how our lore is released to people. What they learn and how they learn it, and when."

Even though I assumed he was already aware, I didn't volunteer the information that the Knights had opened orientation centers in cities across the continent. I also didn't point out how…entitled that single sentiment sounded coming out of his mouth.

Instead, I sat there for a long moment mulling his words over. Picking them apart. Dissecting them. Studying him and the way he sat erect as a piece of plywood, still as a monk, with just the littlest twitch telling me his leg was bouncing under the table.

We get to decide.

He gets to decide.

Antiquated busybody.

He was guarded. Choosing his words carefully. So carefully that around and between them were hidden clues to everything he was thinking, everything he was planning.

"Which lore?" I asked after a while.

"Which?"

"Will you go with the story about how Alter Supremes were given the Divine Right to rule, or something else?"

I expected surprise in his eyes; instead, they narrowed with admiration.

"You went to Idalia's Archives to read the creation stories?"

I'd only read the one, in tandem with Asterios as he explained it was a fake story—the fairytale told to Alter Supremes to hide that seven ancient rulers basically found a way to siphon power away from the collective *and* the Goddess to keep for themselves—but I nodded anyway, to see how Rav would reply.

"I could have told you that story, if you'd asked," he insisted, his tone genuine. "It is a very good fable. Potentially one fit for the young children who will join our community in the future, although we might make better ones. If things happen as they should, we could arrange a 'Princess Diana' moment for you. Have you read *The First Gathering* to a classroom of kids, once we introduce ourselves to the human world. Would you like that?"

Very good fable...although we might make better ones.

If things happen as they should.

Princess Diana moment.

Once we introduce ourselves.

"Maybe," I responded. "If they'll accept me. I mean, there are just as many old stories claiming beasts are monsters that'll destroy the world."

Rav's eyes blew wide. "The humans will never read them. Once the library is free, we can cleanse any mention of them for you."

"But the alters still believe them."

Rav's hackles rose. "Not for long."

"If you reveal what I am, they'll probably kill me."

His flat hand landed on the table with a startled *thunk*, not as if he slammed it down in anger, but in fear. "*Min skat*, no one will *ever* harm you. I swear it."

"I know you want to protect me, Rav, but—"

"No!"

My spoon-feeder retreated from my side as Rav rose abruptly from his seat, stormed toward me with his jaw clenched again, and leaned into my space. His hand slid around the base of my neck. His lips went to my forehead, pressing, before he pulled back just enough to stare me in the eye.

"Natalie, soon, you'll be untouchable. *Invincible*. Not because you marry me, although you will—of your own *free will*, mark my words. But because I command it. I can't tell you more yet but *trust me when I say* I will make you invulnerable. In this very house earlier this year, I warned you not even Death could take you from me, and I meant it."

"Meaning...?"

"There is no reason to drag the ancient past into the present. The old ways are over. We can remake this brand-new world in our image. This is what I meant when I said we can decide what we tell people. I have already begun setting the stage for our ascension. And I have been working on a path forward for the pair of us that will protect you—protect us—otherwise."

"From whom? Death?"

I meant it as a joke—I literally snarked it at him as if it was ridiculous. But he didn't laugh. No, he kissed me. *Planted* one on me in excitement and stoic joy, pressing me into the chair with his passion, zapping me with his magick.

Finally, he tore his lips away and said, “From all threats, great and small, *min skat*. Our time apart taught me lessons I know I deserved…The silence…Feeling left behind. Even this new power of yours—it taught me humility. It held up a mirror to my shortcomings in so many ways. I have worked on myself. You have worked on yourself. Now, we shall come together and become the greatness I always knew we could be.”

I blinked at him, still swirling in that snarky, disbelieving energy.

“Rav, I think we have wildly different definitions of the word ‘great.’”

He smiled again and let go of me. He backed away toward the castle, teasing, “We will have to negotiate for that as well, then,” before he walked inside and left me where I sat, still tied in the chair.

***

For whatever reason, Rav left me to the whims of my silent staff for several hours. They placed me and the chair I was tied to in the solarium, with a fiction novel a tourist had clearly left in the building by accident at some point awkwardly balanced in my lap, surrounded by more guards than there were windows.

I didn’t complain. It was time I needed—first to whisper “Cass” over and over again, until I realized that that ghostly form of him hadn’t made it to Fylgja Castle with me, and then to debrief myself after my talk with Rav.

Rav had divulged so much. Without realizing it, I think. No, I didn’t know what he was planning in specific terms, but in his excitement, he’d revealed…himself. Elements of himself that, well, didn’t surprise me *now*, but which explained why he’d been so tight-lipped with me before.

Lessons I know I deserved. Humility. Shortcomings.

It was confirmation, at least to me, that he’d thought he was better than me before the wedding. I’d thought so too once upon a time. But his ‘realization’ that he wasn’t had nothing to do with understanding how badly he’d treated me, no matter what he’d told me over the phone in Rome. He had been humbled…because the Goddess had given me the power to shift into multiple animal forms instead of him. His mistakes weren’t failings of character on his part, but fumblings. Recalibrations.

Antiquated busybody. There's no reason to drag the ancient past into the present. The old ways are over. The silence. Feeling left behind.

For some reason I didn't know, he thought we could move on without the Goddess. He *wanted* to move on without her.

How…how would that work? She existed. She simply *was*. She could appear and disappear at will. The moment an alter revealed that anyone could simply request the gift of her presence and she might blink into their awareness, she would be a busy, *busy* creature. But he wasn't putting her aside to protect her from being overwhelmed. He didn't care about her that way.

I didn't think I could ask him outright, but I had a sneaking suspicion he hadn't spoken to the Goddess since before I left him. He was obviously pissed about it. Angry at her. Resentful.

Remake the world in our image. Decide what we tell people. Ascension. Become the greatness I always knew we could be.

Rav was planning our future, and though the *grandness* of his vision didn't surprise me, the entitlement did.

What felt like ages ago now, his mom's journal had warned he didn't fix mistakes. He doubled down on them. If I'd needed more proof—which I didn't—this would be it.

He was planning to take over the position of Arch-Sovereign through me.

He was planning to shirk the old ways and remake the world—and me—in his image.

And I was in more danger than I could fully understand.

I needed to escape. That was obvious. But I needed to escape *now*. I needed to escape with an urgency I could feel in my soul.

Easier said than done, of course. For no sooner had that thought planted a flag in my mind, but movement caught in the corner of my eye. I looked up and saw someone I knew would eventually come for me.

"Good to see you again, little birdy," Eike said, tapping that horrifying curved blade of hers in her hand.

CHAPTER 5

My heart skipped a beat in warning as I stared at Eike's weapon. And at her. We hadn't seen each other since Alexandria. Not since she dove into the harbor after me and clawed at my shoulders to keep me from fleeing with Rawan. Not since Ghost Cass clawed her eyes out to pry her off me.

Her eyes were back and there wasn't a scratch to be seen, aside from that old, faded scar along her cheek that I'd never really thought about before. She was fine physically, at least; Rav or the full moon had healed her.

But emotionally? Her blue eyes were dark and cold. Full of resentment. Chill licked up my spine so frosty it made me shiver. And when I did, my head recoiled and I felt that tight, lumpy thing around my neck that I'd felt in bed the night before. What the hell was it?

Preemptively, I said, "Eike, don't."

"Don't what?" she asked, as one by one by one the deer guardsmen around the edges of the room turned to face the walls and she slowly began to pace in front of me. "I wanted to welcome you back. I wanted to greet my fair sovereign upon her less than triumphant return."

I remained quiet.

"It is good to see you," she said again, low and pointed. "To be *able* to see you."

"Eike," I risked. "I didn't take your sight."

SLAM!

It happened so fast I-I didn't even feel the pain, at first. I felt the shockwave across my body as that curved blade struck the top of my thigh and sliced through it like butter. I felt the muscle split. The blood pour. The crack as the tip hit bone…and lodged in it.

I only realized I was screaming when I stopped, when that loud deafening noise gave way to whimpers and sobs and shaking. *Excruciating*. Mind-numbing for a split second before the pain dulled to a throbbing sting as she left the weapon embedded and slowly continued pacing.

"What the hell, Eike!" I moaned, trying to focus, watching as my body healed around the blade.

"I'm going to ask you some questions, my queen," she said. "This is to be a simple conversation. You tell me the truth, and this is all the pain you'll feel. Understand?"

"I-I-I would have t-told you the truth anyway," I wheezed, trying to focus.

Her eyes shot to mine for a fleeting moment, filled with uncertainty, before she looked away. "Yes, well, you have a gift, and I have a blade. This is how we handle things."

"Fine! Questions! Go, for Goddess's sake!"

I didn't think she was expecting that response. She seemed taken aback by how I met her eye despite my shaking and breathiness.

"The cult. How long have you known of their existence?"

"W-W-What?"

"How long?"

"You were there! Rav's birthday last year!"

Again, she looked at me with doubt in her eyes. And again, I met her gaze unwavering.

"And when did you first speak to someone from the cult?"

Technically? When I was nine; William Mahon in all his stepfather glory had been the first. But I wasn't about to tell her that. *Technically*, there was a safer answer.

"Last year at Lunasa."

She did a double-take. "What are you talking about?"

"The wolf. The wolf Rav killed for me! The one who shot me with the silver arrow!"

"And the next?"

I rolled my eyes. "Uh. The one in Germany at Yule? With Rav again."

"And the next?"

"The ones that attacked Rav and me in France."

She growled at me, as if annoyed, and *flicked* the blade in my leg, sending a ripple of pain streaking through my body.

"I am *talking* about *recently*!" she barked. "Without his majesty there."

"A few weeks ago. Prisoners."

"What prisoners?"

"Prisoners from France that my people caught while defending Giselle's home."

"You hid this from the king?"

"Yes. Just like *he* hid things from me!" I snapped back.

"Where are these prisoners?"

"None of your Goddess-damned business, Eike."

This time, I anticipated the spiral of pain that radiated through my body when she slapped the blade to make it hurt. This time, I gritted my teeth through it and sneered at her willfully. It was all I could do to keep the pain from pulling me under like a tide. Spite alone kept me awake.

"I'll ask you again—"

"Ask me all you want. Every twist of that blade wedges an extra mile between me and the king."

That gave her pause.

"I am here for my own reasons," she said as if she actually believed it. "He has nothing to do with this."

And I laughed. I laughed right in her face. "Puh-*lease*. You're a lapdog, Eike. You do what the king commands. He might as well be here hurting me himself."

Fear shot across her eyes. Right before she darted forward into my space, growling. "Which of your forms clawed my eyes out? Was it the wolf? The raven?"

"Does it matter?"

"It matters to me!"

"Neither then," I almost spat. Literally, my lips were trembling and moist, tight against exposed teeth as we snarled inches from each other. "You attacked me."

"I was trying to bring you home!"

I ignored that. "Whatever happened as a result, you can thank yourself for that."

But at that, she froze. She drew strangely still above me, and for a moment I had no idea what was happening. Until she sniffed me. *Sniffed* me. Pressed her friggen nose right to my friggen forehead like a bloodhound.

"What are you *doing?*"

She sniffed and sniffed and *sniffed* until the word "*Wolverine*," escaped her like a kitten's mew.

"I know what you are, Eike," I snarked, expecting some retort. She didn't give me one. She simply studied me until I couldn't take the oppressive close attention anymore. "You wanted to hurt me for hurting you. Well, congratulations, you did it. Even though I would have just *told you* all of this willingly if you'd asked. What do you think happens between us now, huh? This is *dumb*. This was a *dumb* way to do it. You're smarter than this."

Something like temperance broke through the haze of her anger and she withdrew from me, yanking the blade out of my leg without a second thought.

She watched me scream through the pain still wearing that frozen look of fear on her face and I couldn't help it. I couldn't help but rub it in.

"Thanks, by the way," I wheezed, letting her take the bait.

"Thanks for what?"

"If you hadn't taught me how to fight, I never would have killed so many of Rav's soldiers at Arachne's Revenge. I never would've made it so far."

I kept the smile on my sweaty face as she backed away from me, still partially frozen, and abruptly left the room.

CHAPTER 6

I must've sat in my own drying sweat and blood for a full hour, thrumming with adrenaline and the echoes of trauma, before I heard heavy footsteps and looked up to see Rav barreling into the room with a haunted, shaken look on his face.

"*Min skat*!" he groaned at the sight of me, as if devastated.

Rav dropped to his knees beside my chair and his hands went to the thigh Eike had stabbed. The wound was long healed now, but the entire torn pant leg was soaked red, and he made a show of tearing the hole larger to look at the blood-stained skin underneath. Kissed it so gently in apology.

"You're shaking," he said, swearing, "She'll be punished."

I stared at him until he added, "She overstepped—she was never supposed to touch you. It will *never* happen again."

His wording. Overstepping suggested a plan taken one step too far. As in, he'd signed off on the interrogation, but not the method. It was more 'careful truth.' More 'not quite lying.' I wanted to call him on it. I wanted to say to him what I'd said to Eike, that he might as well have tortured me himself, but I stayed quiet.

His behavior kept me quiet.

His fawning.

He checked me for more wounds. Pressed his lips to my forehead again so earnestly. Demanded a tissue from a nearby guard and carefully wiped the sweat off my brow. But the "anger" wasn't real. I knew Rav. Better than most people, probably. I'd seen his genuine anger before.

This was a show.

A performance. For me. And maybe for the others. He was acting the part of the devoted partner, offended on my behalf. He wanted me to think this reaction was real. And once I noticed the artificial nature of it, it all became artificial. It broke my heart to see it, but I couldn't unsee it.

I *could*, however, play along.

I let the painful pinch of adrenaline and betrayal leak into my eyes where it wanted to go naturally. I let the tears swell. I let the sobs escape. It felt like I'd been holding my breath for ages anyway; when I finally released it, I gulped at the air like a suffocating fish.

"You said you didn't hate me," I whimpered, letting my voice go high. "Why did you let her—"

Rav's eyes widened—with some mixed emotion that suggested he'd been hoping for this reaction from me. He leapt to cup my cheeks. "I didn't. I *didn't*. She said she was just going to talk to you."

"I would have just told you all that if you'd asked," I said.

Again, his eyes widened—this time in surprise. "*We'll* do the talking from now on, okay? Just you and me."

I nodded and made a show of trying to wipe the tears from my cheeks against my shoulder. His thumb leapt to wipe my cheeks for me, and I leaned into the touch, pressing my face into his palm, watching the way his eyes brightened.

"I've always liked it when it was just you and me," I admitted. It wasn't even a lie. "I wish you did too."

At that, something soft in him broke, although I couldn't tell if it was genuine or not as he glanced away and whispered, "You don't know how happy it makes me to hear you say that."

"Why don't you?" I risked, drawing his attention back. "Why don't you feel safe to just be with me?"

"I do!" he claimed.

I shook my head gently. "You never did."

"I've felt safer with you than anyone else in my life, since my mom," he said, wiping more of my tears.

"But you still hide from me," I pushed.

"Only because I have to."

"Why?"

His response—a quick "Because!"—was entirely the result of my truthsayer ability, I could tell.

Still, I pushed, "Because?"

I watched him try to form words, watched the gears turn in his head, for a full five seconds before he said, "You wouldn't understand."

And I looked away, disappointed. "I think you're wrong."

"Maybe I am," he admitted, curling his fingers under my chin and turning me to meet his eye again. "I will be ready to share soon, I promise. It's inevitable."

Inevitable—another carefully chosen word.

"Inevitable because we're going to mate and then I won't be able to do anything *but* accept the parts of you you think are unlovable?"

Another tiny shockwave widened his eyes, as if I ate with that take.

But I pushed one more time, twisting his own words against him, "We're trying to rebuild trust, right? We can't rebuild anything if you assume I can't be trusted before you've even shared anything with me."

I wanted to tell him that he *could* trust me, but I'd already done that before.

I wanted to tell him that I could prove his fears unfounded right now, if he would just share something vulnerable and let me show him I could handle it, but I knew he wouldn't.

It had to be his decision. He had to believe he'd finally chosen to share.

So instead, I offered, "You say it's inevitable, but you keep letting chances to trust me pass you by. You told me you chose me, but it doesn't feel like it yet."

He opened his mouth to speak, but I beat him to it. Staring him right in the eye, keeping my voice calm and gentle, I said, "If you're not going to trust me, Rav, then…what are we even doing?"

I could see the barriers going up behind his eyes. It was all I could risk. So, after a moment, I tore my gaze away from his and took a deep breath, sighing.

"I need new clothes, please. Can I at least have that?"

"Of course you can," he said, rising to his feet and sweeping me into his arms. "My queen will have everything she's ever dreamed of, and so much more."

I had to bite my tongue to stop myself from saying the obvious—that what I wanted was my freedom, and he had no intention of giving me that.

***

Rav didn't remove my rope bindings until he'd carried me the forty thousand stairs up to his apartment, to the closet he'd rebuilt for me next to his, full of outfits I never would have chosen for myself.

He uncoiled the rope with an almost joke, "Just remember there's nowhere to run."

As if I didn't know that. Guards were just outside the door. I could see more on the lawn through the windows. Tidebringer Rawan's conch shell had been set on the shoe rack nearby for some reason, but we were too far from water for it to matter. And he towered over me where he stood by the chair.

"Am I allowed to get up?" I asked when I was finally unbound.

"Yes," he almost laughed. "Let me help you."

It was a command disguised as an offer. He held his hand out to me, almost daring me not to take it. I did. Of course I did. But when I rose from the chair, I was met by an unexpected sight. The original closet he'd built for me had contained a full-wall mirror; this one did too, except someone had gone along and frosted the whole thing with some sort of...gold spray paint? Normal paint? Either way, it was covered over.

And when I caught Rav noticing me notice the change, he drew attention away from it, "Here. This outfit will look lovely on you."

I wasn't surprised to see he'd selected one that matched the suit he was wearing—a sort of royal blue tartan sweater dress that went to just above my knees.

I was, however, surprised when he refused to leave the room to let me put it on.

"Rav, I'm not going to go anywhere in the ten seconds it takes to get dressed."

"You have nothing to hide from me. I can help you zip it up."

My skin *crawled* at the casual disregard for my privacy. And the fact that I didn't feel like I could tell him to leave without losing all the ground I'd earned downstairs.

But this, I couldn't fake. I didn't look at him as I took off my clothes and tried to angle my body away from him. I didn't look at him as he unzipped the dress for me and held it open for me to step into. And I didn't look at him after he'd zipped it for me.

Or when he asked, "Are you all right?"

"I'm fine," I said calmly, even though I was anything but. "I need to clean off the blood, though. Can I go to the bathroom?"

"*Min skat*, of course," he said, curling his fingers under my chin again to force me to look at him. "Why are you asking me these things as if you think I'll say no?"

I...didn't know if he was just playing coy this time. I couldn't tell when I looked him in the eye whether admitting I was his prisoner would please or anger him. So, I just offered him a shrug and turned toward the bathroom, feeling his presence behind me as he followed like a heavy shadow.

But in the bathroom, I was surprised again to see the mirror had been covered over in there too. Not with paint, this time, but with cloth.

"Scared of your own reflection?" I teased, as I reached for a washcloth and ran it under the tap.

Rav took the wet cloth from me and lifted me onto the counter. He raised the hem of my dress, and it took everything in me not to squirm, not to give away my discomfort, as he began washing the blood away from my leg.

"No," was all he offered.

"You didn't break it, did you?" I teased again. "That's seven years bad luck."

"I don't need luck either way," he replied. "I'd rather work with guarantees."

"Guarantees, like what?"

Again, he opened his mouth to tell me, and again he resisted. "Let's just say I prefer not to lose. Come on, let's get the rope back on you and go down—"

"No more rope, Rav, come on."

"Rope, *min skat*," he said, not looking at me this time.

"Why?!"

"You know why."

"Rav, I *literally can't leave*. Let me walk around my own house at least!"

"Fine, you can walk," he said, motioning me back into the closet. When we got there, he had a guard cut the rope for him and reached for my wrist.

"Is this really how you want things to be?" I asked quietly.

"No, it's not," he admitted. "And I'll happily remove the ropes the moment you promise me you'll never leave my side again."

It was my mouth's turn to open and shut. He wanted a promise. A literal promise. A *magickal* promise. One I couldn't break without exploding. One that would keep me in his gravity permanently without any effort from him whatsoever.

It hung between us like a swinging blade; one wrong move and it would cut me.

"Seems like a roundabout way of killing me," I said after a moment. "You don't want me by your side constantly. I'd annoy the hell out of you."

"Perhaps, but at least then *you* would be the one chasing *me* for a change."

Resentment ran like a current under his words. Need too. But those were the results of *his* actions, not mine.

So, I held out my wrists, and I let him wrap the rope round and round and round them until he tied it tightly.

Only once it was done did I give him one last parting take.

"Don't forget, Rav. I *did* chase you, at Hamingja. You just didn't like being caught."

***

Rav left me alone in the solarium with my silent wall of guards for the rest of the day. That was fine. More than fine. It was better than his performative public "emotions" or his private sincere ones.

Plus, it gave me what I wanted. Needed, really. It gave me "alone time" to plot.

Rav's quick beeline through Fylgja Castle with me in his arms had confirmed what I'd already seen—that barring some great catastrophe, or an outside ally realizing where I was and coming to save me, my best shot at getting out of there, getting away, lied with my animals.

If they would just come out at the right moment, if they would just kill a few guards, and give me my wings, I could be free in hours. Minutes, maybe. I could crash through one of Rav's apartment windows in the dead of night and soar away between the still blades of Fylgja's windmill before anybody but Rav knew I was gone. He might pursue me, on the wings he'd no doubt "borrowed" from me with that kiss in the solarium earlier, but that just meant I had to escape *one man*, which was far fairer than being hunted to exhaustion through the Italian Alps while injured by a swarm of helicopters and armed men.

The problem was…I couldn't reach any of my creatures.

I couldn't enter my inner sanctum either.

I sat in the solarium for *six hours* trying to force my way into my own head, calling out "*Hello, can anybody hear me?*" into my own otherwise-silent mind.

Nobody answered.

I almost felt like laughing, considering how desperate I had been to prove I wasn't crazy over the last few weeks, only to end up panicking that I suddenly couldn't contact the voices in my head.

They were in there; I was almost sure of it.

It was as if they couldn't respond.

There was something stopping them.

And there was something stopping me.

And I didn't know which new trick was keeping me separated from them, but I knew whatever it was, I only had until Rav's patience ran out to figure it out.

CHAPTER 7

Rav was a lousy negotiator. I suppose I'd always known that, given all the little snafus I'd witnessed since meeting him, and the half a dozen times I'd disagreed with him in front of the Gathering Table, only to have them prefer my methods to his and be forced to endure the consequences of his bruised ego.

The negotiations he'd promised me, regarding our mating, got pushed aside on the second day, when we had breakfast on the patio again and he mentioned there was an impromptu Gathering Table meeting happening later. Its goal was strategizing how to handle the loud, constant demands of the human public to meet this "Arch-Sovereign Natalie Damarand." They wanted reassurances. They wanted forward momentum regarding the *world-altering news* that the world and everyone in it could, in fact, be altered, if they wanted to be.

"Far more have signed up for the cult's 'classes' than any of us anticipated," Rav grumbled, his mind entirely elsewhere. "Twenty thousand in France alone. Ulric wasn't expecting so many. He is…overwhelmed."

"That's not surprising, is it?" I spoke. "Magick is real. I wouldn't be surprised if *most* people don't at least want to hear about it."

"Yes, but *we* have no infrastructure for such changes. The cult had a head start."

They hadn't just had a head start; they'd been planning this for decades. Centuries, maybe.

It was the "hold music," for me. The fact that their organization had taken the time to hire someone to produce hold music for callers to their hotline. Such a small flex. Not a priority by any stretch of the imagination, and yet they'd made time for it. They'd reached the point of preparation to fill in the gaps, to smooth down the rough edges of their organization.

"So, why not reach out to Robine?" I asked.

"Because she won't speak to me unless you're on the call," he said.

"She knows I'm here?"

His mouth opened and shut as if he hadn't meant to reveal that but nodded begrudgingly.

Interesting.

"Don't even think about it," Rav warned, trying to sound playful.

I shrugged. "I didn't think you'd let me speak to her."

"I will," he countered. "Once we're mated, you'll be there to handle all of this with me."

"Or, you can trust me now to know this is more important than either of us." He glanced away but I pushed, "The world is holding its breath, Rav. The world's biggest secret has been revealed—and they don't even know witches or the Goddess exist yet. The longer we delay, the less control you'll have over what they know or how they find out."

"I know that."

"So…?"

"No, Natalie."

"Just…no?" I almost laughed. "Giselle would probably be able to help Ulric, you know. If he's really overwhelmed; she's helped run the Wolf Court for decades—"

"It's not an option," he snipped, cutting me off.

"Why? Because she's dead or because you couldn't catch her?"

I watched him, for reaction. For a tell to gauge which it was. I couldn't, unfortunately.

"What about Rolfe?"

"I told you; it's not an option!" he snipped again.

"All right," I said. "I'm guessing Archer's also struggling—"

Rav sent his chair flying back, scraping across the marble, as he tore to his feet. "Just…let me handle it, all right?"

I think he left the patio then to avoid giving his tantrum an audience.

Which was fine with me. I wanted a moment to celebrate; Archer was struggling. I felt bad—or I tried to, at least—but I also didn't at the same time. I wanted to know whether it was because he simply couldn't handle the responsibilities of the job or because Brodie's plan to "go to ground" with all the people who recognized me as the Alter Supreme was working. Maybe Archer literally didn't have enough people willing to help him maintain his rule. Maybe the ones he did were incompetent. Maybe, since the announcement of me as Arch-Sovereign, the people in the Eighth Kingdom had rejected him as a leader at all.

Maybe I was already closer to winning my throne back than I thought.

But just as quickly, worry set in. While he'd been my teacher, Dr. Sanga had taught me a lot about successful resistance movements around the world. Employees at poorly run companies had repeatedly won wage and poor treatment fights against their employers simply by working as a collective and halting their labor. In Iceland in 1975, women won a major victory toward their equal rights under the law by going on strike—refusing to work, do domestic labor, or raise children—to show the country just how valuable their contributions to the system truly were. Iceland lost millions, entire industries including their schools, banking systems, and even airlines had to shut down for the day, and the women won without a single shot ever being fired.

However—and it was a *big* however…

Dr. Sanga warned me that those kinds of maneuvers only tended to work when they were done fast and hard. Holding the system hostage could be so damaging that if groups weren't careful, they ran the risk of angering and alienating the people they served, especially if propaganda campaigns lost their effectiveness. If too much damage was done, the groups would lose even if they won.

I needed to retake control of my kingdom before the freeze harmed too many of my people, and they forsook me as a leader anyway.

I also needed a public seat from which to "rule" as an Arch-Sovereign away from Rav. While we were figuring out what that new title even meant, and what authority I would actually have in the grand scheme of things. I needed a public position to help protect my cabinet, too. To legitimize them. It's not like I could do…whatever came next…alone. I wasn't arrogant enough to think I knew nearly enough yet. I didn't want to lead alone, either. I needed the smartest, kindest, most experienced people I could find helping me through this next phase.

To take some of the work off my plate.

To make it harder for others to take advantage of me.

To maybe give me a *little* time to…I don't know…actually *go to university* so I could serve people better? Wild concept, I know.

But most importantly, I needed a cabinet so packed with wildly different people we could ensure we actually addressed the big, global issues at their root causes rather than falling victim to the false belief that our tiny slices of experience were representative of all.

***

Someone had gone through and removed every single television and radio in the castle. I knew this because I'd eventually risen from the patio table when I realized Rav wasn't coming back and found myself surrounded by those deer guards before I'd even taken a step. I'd told them to follow and when they got over their he-man "you do what we say" nonsense, I reminded them that I was literally surrounded by an army. And bound by rope. Not to mention, "taking a walk" would be infinitely less boring for me and for everyone tasked with watching me than sitting in a chair all day. So it was, I found myself wandering Fylgja Castle with an armed escort, peeking into rooms and exploring old haunts only to discover every link to the outside world had been stripped away.

There weren't even any newspapers where there usually were in the main foyer where the tour guides greeted guests. Tours, my watchers told me, had been "suspended indefinitely." So, too, had the castle's wifi.

The only remaining link to the outside world seemed to be the slow, but consistent, loop of Rav's people who drove up in Jeeps and SUVs to deliver messages. These were spirited through the castle to Rav's office by staff who smelled of floral sugar—more of those pine marten alters like the ones at Hamingja. A guard let it slip that that was where Rav had apparently spent most of his days since I'd fled in Greece.

Obviously, Rav was isolating me.

Less obviously, he seemed to be isolating himself.

Maybe he was succumbing to paranoia? Or he genuinely feared for his safety? I mean, my team would come eventually no matter how long he hid me away.

But the part that still didn't sit quite right with me were the mirrors. Every. single. one. in the castle had been frosted over, covered, or removed. At first, I'd wondered if Rav had been…struggling with more unexpected things, like self-esteem, while I was gone…until I realized the mirror covering thing had something to do with me. I wasn't allowed anywhere near them. The moment my eyeline even drifted in the direction of a covered mirror, a guard would suggest we go somewhere else, or cough or nudge me with the butt of their rifle, as if mirrors were forbidden.

Which meant, of course, that I needed to find one, *pronto*.

***

"That's far enough, my queen."

"I just want to sit by the water and read, is that okay?"

It'd taken me several additional hours of searching the castle for any uncovered mirror—even the edge of one—before I realized Rav truly had left no reflective surface untouched. He'd even had someone scrape the metal surfaces of the toilet paper holders in the bathrooms, which impressed me as much as it annoyed me.

But he'd forgotten one.

Or rather, there was one reflective surface he *couldn't* scrape over…and I needed to use it before he figured out what I was doing.

The statue garden held a small concrete pond. It was a statue, too, technically. Stone swans and frogs and a fox dipping its nose into the water were scattered across the water's surface, lorded over by a cherub with wings that looked a little drunk, peeing into the pond. I'd never actually come to sit by it when I lived there before, but that was mostly because it stood a few hundred feet from the building, tucked away with a view of the nearby forest, and there had always been plenty of places inside and directly around the castle that worked for a reading spot instead.

Armed with that random tourist's novel Rav had left with me, I'd convinced the guards to let me go outside to read, then headed in the pond's direction before they could stop me.

"We'll have to tell his majesty," the guard warned.

"Tell him he's welcome to join me," I almost sang back, smiling pleasantly at him, as I reached the wide stone lip of the pond and picked a place to sit, leaning back against the uncomfortable pillar behind me as if I was "settling in."

I opened the book and pretended to read as he moved away to bark into his radio and the other guards moved into position around me, thickening in the direction of the forest.

That was fine. I wasn't dumb enough to try running away with a thousand eyes on me, half flesh and half firepower. No, the thing I wanted was much closer.

The dark surface of the pond rippled faintly, disturbed by the cherub's drunken relief…but not where I had chosen to sit. No, I'd watched the reflections of the other objects as we'd approached and picked my spot well.

And immediately, out of the corner of my eye, I could see why Rav was hiding my reflection from me.

It was that thing around my friggen neck—the strange smooth but lumpy thing that I could feel every time I glanced down or recoiled from someone's anger.

My mind had tossed up plenty of possibilities of what it could be. A chain. A rope. A dog collar with an electric zapper cued to an invisible fence. All seemed possible.

What I found instead…was a necklace. A tight one—a choker—of shiny polished jet-black oval beads. Beautiful, like poisonous berries. Expensive looking. Something easily mistaken for a gift. The beads were faceted and there was no space between them at all; they wrapped in a continuous loop that pinched my skin when I ran my fingers over it—

"Don't touch, my queen. Please."

It was the guard who had threatened to tattle on me saying that. This time, he didn't use the same subtly threatening tone; he sounded scared.

"Why not?"

"I don't know. He just warned us there would be consequences if you did."

I made a point of lowering my hand while he watched, to reassure him; his body visibly relaxed as I did so. Then I went back to "reading" peacefully as I studied the necklace out of the corner of my eye in the pond's reflection.

That was it, then. The rope around my wrists was just a prop; this was the real restraint holding me hostage. This pretty, pinching thing. Turned out there *was* a chain around my throat; it just didn't look like one.

CHAPTER 8

I tried scratching at my throat. I tried messing with my hair. I did half a dozen little things in the hours that followed, in an attempt to inspect the choker around my neck without triggering the guards' suspicion. To gather more information about it—whether there was a clasp holding it in place (there didn't seem to be one), whether the beads sat on a string or a chain (I couldn't tell), and whether pulling it three millimeters away from my skin changed anything (it didn't).

Until I finally found some alone-time late at night when the guards delivered me to the Pirate's Perch, shoved me inside, and slammed the door behind me. Nothing stirred. None of the lights were on. So, I let my fingers wander across the tight jewelry on my neck, feeling for give.

Ignoring the biting pinch, I managed to tuck exactly one finger inside the loop. Then I wedged in a second.

I tried twisting a single bead until the string snapped.

I tried yanking on the whole yoke until the back of my neck hurt.

I almost cut off my own blood and air supply, coaxing fingers from my second hand into the gap so I could hold on and rip the choker in separate directions. This achieved nothing and cut one of my fingers, and when I pulled away to look at the wound, I caught sight of a fleeting spark of orange magick before it disappeared and the wound healed.

At least it was confirmation that I had a threat around my neck.

What kind was anybody's guess, but so help me, I was gonna cut the blasted thing off even if I had to—

"Good evening, *min skat*."

I spun on the spot to find Rav stepping in the door with two boxes in hand. One was slender and mauve, stamped with the *Corvinus* luxury brand logo. The other…was a simple brown box.

"Come sit with me."

He motioned to the couch where we had spent so many moonlit nights meditating and slid into his old seat, patting the spot for me across from him. When I took it, he handed me the mauve garment box.

"One for you and one for me."

I...had a terrible feeling, like a spike of panic through my midsection, at the thought that it was lingerie. That fear faded a moment later, though, as I awkwardly manhandled the box with my bound hands and popped the top off to find an off-white dress instead. It wasn't a wedding gown, thank Goddess, but it was the type of thing Rav preferred me to wear which I would never have chosen for myself. Pretty, sure, but...sterile and inoffensive. The sort a modern princess or newscaster would wear.

"For our debut," he said, watching me for reaction.

I forced my face into a generous soft smile as I pulled it out and noted the details—little embroidered gold ravens along the neckline and little golden marguerite daisies along the cinched waistline.

Those, I liked.

But there were also...runes, on the dress's lining. I noticed them after the fact, because they were so faint, only a shade or two different from the main color of the fabric, that it took moving the dress around to spot them at all. Once I saw them, though, they were unignorable.

"Oh, it's lovely, thank you, Rav," I said, letting my gaze drift so he wouldn't notice where I was looking. "When will that debut be, exactly?"

"Soon. Very soon. Our lawyers are making arrangements now."

"Lawyers?" I pushed.

He shrugged. "The cult's dawn has come and gone. The next one is ours, but it's only a dawn of two. The Sovereign Supremes won't be happy, so we're negotiating terms with the broadcasters about how long after our moment they must wait before interviewing other alter leaders. That will give news of our ascension time to settle before we meet with the others separately and...use our respective gifts to determine friend from foe."

My spine tightened in warning. That was one way to do it. Dangerous, or so it seemed to me.

"Why not just talk to them about it? They understand the cult's forced our hand a little bit. Let me talk to them and tell them I had no part in it. Let's talk to all the leaders—human, witch, and alter—and make a plan before we go public with anything."

Rav shook his head as he began peeling the adhesive off the box he still held in his hand.

"You don't know Dobrynya. Or Shio Umiko. You barely know Sarab and already her danger is palpable. You don't know how many of their enemies would suddenly become dear friends with them, whispering poison in their ear about us."

"They'll do that anyway if we just *announce* ourselves as rulers."

"Not just rulers—divine sovereigns."

I blinked, surprised he admitted that. I waited to see if it was just a slip of my gift, which he planned to take back, or if he had meant to say that.

"*Min skat*, you and I have a destiny to fulfill. We can't take everyone with us."

He turned away to tear the rest of the packaging off his box when he added, mumbling, "We wouldn't want to take most anyway."

Then, as if it was a gift for me, he pulled something from the tattered pieces of cardboard in front of him and held it up for me to see. It was a necklace. A long cord of black string attached to a bobble made of brass and stone. The brass pendant was hollow, curved into a runic shape, although I didn't know which one. It was as if someone had drawn an arrow pointed straight up and then cut off the left side, and it contained a blue stone I knew all too well.

"Azurite?" I asked.

"Yes," he said, holding it up for me to see. "So I'll always have the power of transformation right at my fingertips."

Rav reached for my hand then, with his free one, and held it tenderly. His blue eyes met mine, shy and…sweet?

"See? I am learning from you. Commanding your soldiers to carry these pendants with them was an inspired bit of leadership, *min skat*."

I tried not to twist my face into a disbelieving grimace at what he seemed to think was a bonding moment. I offered him a soft flat smile and said, "Thank you."

"I honestly can't believe I never thought if it, but those little sparks of inspiration will be so invaluable as our lives grow more complex. I'm grateful my mate is so clever."

I wanted to grimace again. The attempt to flatter me about the same attributes—my intelligence, my resourcefulness—that he had once insulted back at Hamingja fell so flat inside my soul no part of me believed anything he was saying.

It wasn't a lie. He couldn't do that. Or rather, he didn't think he was lying when he *performed* making amends this way. These little bones he was throwing me, these little flatteries, were…allowances. He was admitting to tiny blips of respect as if they were some grand gesture toward me instead of the bare minimum.

He was *supposed* to respect me. And not because I was his mate. He was supposed to respect me as a friend. As a partner. As a person.

At the thought, words from long ago rose to the surface of my mind. Years ago, after William Mahon had left my mom, my grandma had flown in from the west coast to help us transition back into our old life in Pennsylvania. She'd held my mom as she cried, whispering reassurances, until she hit us both with a brutal truth that had haunted me ever since.

"He didn't respect you enough to tell you the truth about why he was leaving, sweetie," she'd said. "Respect is a foundation of love. Anyone who doesn't respect their partner is only using them."

The problem between Rav and I wasn't just that he thought he was better than me.

It wasn't that he'd admitted his honest opinions about me at Hamingja.

It wasn't even that he'd taken me hostage…for a second time.

He'd shattered the rose-colored glasses I'd worn when we were together—the ones that disguised how many red flags there actually were. Now that the lenses were broken, crimson was all I could see.

He was…performing partnership. And not even all the time, just until he couldn't do it any longer and he had to leave the room or roll me over so he could clutch me in his sleep.

Teach me how to be the tenderness you need. He was performing lines he thought would draw me deeper into the play.

She overstepped—she was never supposed to touch you. It will never happen again. He was orchestrating painful scenarios so he could look like the good guy after the fact.

The saddest part to me was that I *did* genuinely think he believed these gestures would smooth over the 'little things' that had gone wrong between us since Hamingja. He earnestly wanted them to. In his mind, there was some version of this captivity that ended with us being stronger together than we were apart. He would unbind my wrists and neck and I would stay by his side freely.

But none of these little gestures fixed the real problem—he only respected me when I posed no threat to his authority. In the moments when I acted like the 'ideal mate' he believed he deserved. He didn't like being reminded that I was my own person. Hated it, in fact.

I…decided to test it, as gently as I could.

"So, is it time to negotiate yet?" I asked, as he rose from the couch and set the azurite in a high spot near the door, obviously out of my reach.

"Negotiate for what?" he asked, motioning me up.

As I stood, he intertwined his fingers in mine and pulled me toward the bathroom.

"Negotiate how we earn each other's trust back," I said, repeating his words from the other day. "You said we'd do that."

"We already are," he replied, guiding me to a soft stop by the counter before plugging the stopper in the tub and turning on the faucet.

I eyed the tub as steam began to billow. "What are you talking about?"

"I make the mistake of sending Eike to talk with you, you forgive me for it. I remove most of your ropes, you don't try to run when you are outside reading. You offer suggestions, and I consider them. These olive branches are growing nicely, *min skat.* Tomorrow, we will exchange another."

This time, the grimace flitted across my face before I could stop it. "What's happening tomorrow?"

Rav bent quickly and planted a kiss on my nose. "You'll see. Now, raise your arms."

I froze where I stood, pulling my bound hands closer to my chest.

"Why?"

"It's time for a bath."

"I can bathe myself."

"With your wrists tied?"

"Untie my wrists."

Rav's lips twisted, amused by…something. "We both know you bathing by yourself is a hazard, *min skat.* Just let me help you—"

"I'm not taking a bath with you, Rav."

I drew the line at having to undress fully in front of him. Absolutely wasn't going to do that. I let my brow settle into a scowl; the urge to preemptively grow my claws was so *visceral* I could feel it in my gut. But…they didn't come—because of the choker or something else, I didn't know—and my spine tightened with fear. I suddenly wondered if my fingernails and teeth would be enough, if…if he tried anything.

"It's that or you stay dirty."

"Dirty then."

I expected anger. I expected a tantrum. Instead, his hands slid into place, cupping my cheeks, and he leaned in, lips still playful. "You want to be clean, don't be silly."

I didn't pull punches or moderate my voice to keep sounding polite. "Filthy. I'd rather sleep in my own shit."

"That's crass, Natalie." Rav pulled away, the playfulness fading. "It will make tomorrow quite embarrassing for you."

"Then let me take a bath by myself."

Hurt swept across his features, but there was just as much resentment, and it made my skin crawl.

"So you came here…to what? Pretend with me?" he asked after a moment…as if he hadn't been doing the very same since I got there. "How long do you intend to punish me for my mistakes?"

"Rav, it's been two days."

"It's been weeks for me," he said. "You make me feel like a villain. Do you believe I would hurt you? Is that what you're implying? I thought we could bond like we used to. I could wash you and lay you down and tease an explosion or two out of you, just to remind you how good it feels to let me love you. Nothing for me, yet. I'd just give myself to you."

It took everything in me to keep my face neutral. To keep the fear and disdain and anger from peeking through. I almost made it, too. I almost played the part until the very end.

"This isn't the way, Rav," I said, as quietly and calmly as I could. "Give me time."

But he reached for me again—to cup my face again, I think—and this time I flinched. Purely out of instinct. I flinched, exposing the internal shiver I'd managed to hide so well to that point. And I hated myself the moment the shake broke through.

But he saw it. He saw me tremble at the thought of him touching me. And his hand halted mid-air as his lips parted in surprise, and his eyebrows bent with shame and betrayal.

We stood there, frozen for a long beat, just staring at each other. I wanted to reassure him to protect myself. I wanted to deescalate the moment. I wanted a time machine, so I could go back to a few days ago before he caught me, before I knew he'd try to guilt me into doing uncomfortable things.

I was too scared to move.

Then, the moment broke and he reached for my hands. He yanked the knot free, and unspooled my bindings, and the rope fell away from my circulation-strangled wrists.

"I trust you," he grumbled, motioning to the bath without looking at it, or me. "Don't try the window, though. I'd hate to have to carry out my promise against your friends just because you fell and broke your neck."

Then he walked out and shut the door behind him.

I took the first deep breath since we entered the room. And the shake continued through my body, loosed from where I'd kept it, until I was all shaken out. I needed to escape as soon as possible. Before requests to bond became demands, or worse.

I went to the window—of course, I went to the window—but it was locked and the drop was *far*. I'd seen *In Bruges* with Scarlett; that was *no* way to go.

I tried tugging at the necklace again too, and pushed aside the cloth on the mirror to see it properly. I was both surprised and unsurprised to see runes had been carved into the beads. Got a good look at the wire on which the beads were strung too. I also searched the drawers quietly looking for something to cut it off; found nothing. Everything had been removed save for toothbrushes and some shampoo.

I took the latter to the tub, undressed and lowered myself in, letting the hot water soak my aching muscles like balm. My body might have healed after the battle at Arachne's Revenge, but my soul was tense. Coiled and brittle.

Scared. I was scared.

My eye caught on a spider web high up in the corner, and for a long while I watched the little creature. I watched it spin its web. Watched it catch and wrap a fly. Watched it let itself down its impossibly thin, impossibly strong silk to the lip of the tub, where it sat just watching me as I shivered with fear.

"Can you help me, little thing?" I asked. "Could you go for help? Find one of Idalia's snackrifices to come in here in a blaze of glory to save her ally?"

I missed Idalia. I wondered if her lover had escaped the battle unharmed…and if Scarlett and Corby and Yasmina had disappeared into the mountains uncaught. I wondered if Brodie and Fern had managed to take Arachne's Revenge in the fight.

I wondered if Idalia had told me the story about Cloelia because she *knew* Rav might capture me eventually. And suddenly, all I could think about was that spider silk tapestry on the ceiling in Idalia's library, the story of Cloelia, the brave Roman girl who had been canonized a hero by the same people who traumatized her.

I let myself accept the similarities between her story and mine. She'd escaped across a river; I'd escaped across the sea. She'd been returned to the Etruscan King who controlled her destiny; I had been recaptured by mine and was at the part in my story where my king held my fate in the palm of his hands.

Rav and I were very different; I'd always known that. I'd assumed it would make us stronger leaders over time. I'd assumed we'd find balance.

I'd given him the benefit of the doubt that he respected our differences. Now I knew better. There was an ever-present hesitation at the back of my mind every time he spoke; I let myself hear what he was really saying, rather than assuming there was more to his words than there actually was.

Talk of baths and explosions was too much. It was too much. I felt constantly on edge, sick without sickness. The implication was clear. Time was running out. *I was in danger*. Obviously. I understood that on multiple levels, but this struck a nerve in a new way that plucked at my anxiety like pliers on the strings of an electric guitar.

Had the threat of being expected to sleep with Rav again crossed my mind while I was on the run? Vaguely. In a…theoretical way. Like a terrible, terrible reality I never wanted to find myself in. Without my consent—which I couldn't give, trapped without options like this—the only way to do what he wanted would be through force. Even if I tried to justify participating for my own safety. Even if it was the price I paid for the freedom I needed to escape. It would still be against my will. I'd understood in an impersonal way that a threat of that kind would be horrible to experience. But now that it had been breathed into the very real, completely unvague air around my actual physical body? It hit different. It was one thing to imagine…it was different to *know*.

CHAPTER 9

I woke to hands on my shoulders, shaking me awake.

"Natalie. Natalie!"

"Huh?"

My eyes mutinied for a few moments until I got both to stay open long enough to see Rav looming over me. I'd slept on the couch after dressing in the robe he'd left for me by the bathroom door and not making eye contact as I veered away from the bed nook and headed for the living area instead.

Rav had let me. I could feel his heated gaze tracking my journey to the sofa, but all he'd said after a moment was, "That's far enough, *min skat*. There are guards just outside the door."

I'd made a little show of dropping onto the couch and turning my back to the door, to set him at ease about my intentions, but then we'd laid there, studying each other from across the room in silence until I finally fell asleep.

In the still of night, he'd looked disappointed, but harmless. In the morning light, by contrast, he looked *furious* and hostile.

"What's wrong?" I asked.

Rav stepped back from me, still glaring. "I've been very understanding with you. I don't know why you're testing me now. Give it back."

"Give what back?"

His brow rose sternly. "Now, Natalie. Before you force me to strip search you."

I recoiled an inch in surprise, renewing that fear from the bathroom again.

But at that, he sneered. "Don't flatter yourself. After last night, I don't want to touch you either."

"I…don't have anything, Rav."

"Natalie."

"I swear!" I yanked the linings of the robe pockets out just to show him. "Just tell me what's missing and I can—"

Hands landed on my shoulders from behind, and I yelped as if a taser had bitten me. Turning, I found a cleaning lady patting my body carefully, clinically, without looking me in the eye. Neck to ankle, her hands prodded and searched, until she stepped away and shook her head at him.

"See?" I spoke.

Rav tsked under his breath, then lunged for the couch, pushing aside cushions and pillows. I watched out of sheer curiosity and confusion.

"This was a mistake, Natalie," he said, when he found nothing. "You're only allowed one, so I hope it was worth it."

"You hope *what* was worth it?"

"I *will* find the azurite. Goddess help you, you'll have no privacy now."

"I didn't take it." I shrugged at him, glancing at the spot where he'd hung the bobble last night, far out of my reach. Sure enough, it was empty.

Rav hummed in disbelief and then stormed past me to the door and let himself out, slamming it behind him.

I kinda wished I *had* taken it, just to be worthy of all the drama. But another part of me wondered if this was more theater. If he'd taken the azurite himself so he could demand something from me and justify it as punishment for this.

***

I spent the majority of the day looking for something to cut off the choker. I wove in and out of rooms throughout the castle, keeping my eyes peeled for…literally anything of use, but particularly something for cutting through that metal or crushing one of those beads. I figured either would end the pun-intended "chokehold" this thing had over my alteration. If I could just unleash my raven—or contact my wolf, if she was still alive out there somewhere—my team could be told my location, and I'd just have to bide my time. Whether they would *want* to rescue me, now that Fern knew I was a beast, was a different fear I couldn't indulge without panicking.

No, I kept my mind to the task at hand, searching for a tool.

All while Eike chaperoned me from a barnacle's distance.

Rav had meant it when he warned I wouldn't get any privacy anymore. She had appeared at the door to the Pirate's Perch about twenty seconds after he left, and sort of took up a replacement position for Ghost Cass, watching relentlessly, saying nothing.

Well, almost nothing.

She asked where we were going when I began a slow wandering tour of every room on the castle's main floor, and grumbled when I told her we were just walking and the guard confirmed that we'd done this the day before.

She knew I was looking for a way out.

I knew the only way out was *in*.

So we found ourselves silently dancing around one another all day, until we were both frustrated and confused. Especially me, since I never found anything. Not even a butter knife. The *only* thing that even looked remotely sharp enough was that curved blade that Eike wore at the small of her back. It swayed with each step she took, taunting me. And I'd be lying if I said I didn't think about just grabbing the handle, yanking it off her body, and holding myself hostage long enough to slice the choker off.

I just didn't know how long I'd get to call out to my creatures, if I did that. I couldn't be sure she'd let me stay conscious long enough to get a word out and make the unavoidable punishment afterward worth it. Because I *would* be punished. That was a given. And after last night, threats of hunting down my family had dropped several rungs on the list of horrible possibilities.

Still, I almost let the intrusive thoughts win.

It was so tempting, with that blade just a few inches from me, catching the sunlight, winking at me…

But then…

A tiny flicker of movement caught in the corner of my eye. Barely anything. So small, I thought it was just a trick of the light. It wasn't.

There, on the cusp of the nearest staircase's top stair, I saw…a spider.

It was…

It was waving at me. *Waving* at me.

My head jerked so fast in that direction, I almost got woozy. Then when I realized I really *was* seeing what I thought I was seeing, I jerked my gaze away before Eike could notice.

"What is it?" she asked.

I thought up an excuse on the spot. "I forgot about my offices. Did Rav fix them?"

"He did."

"Can I see them?"

She sighed with disinterest but didn't stop me as I veered toward the stairs and raced up them. I hit the second-floor landing before the nearest guard did by a wide margin and let my eyes wander again, searching for the little creature.

It was there, on the wall now, waving its tiny arms for attention. And once it knew it had all of mine, it *pointed* toward a far door before scurrying away in that direction.

I turned to follow—

But Eike was there, glaring at me. "Have you forgotten where your own offices are?"

"No. I just thought I'd look for your sense of humor while we were up here."

Eike stepped in my way and motioned with annoyance back behind me. "That died in Alexandria, my queen."

I raised an eyebrow and replied, "Well, I didn't kill it."

"Would you like to tell me who did?"

"Why does it matter?" It was a genuine question.

"Because once you're mated, I will get to..." Her sentence died off with a hacking cough as she raised her hand to her throat, massaging. "Stop doing that!"

I stared at her for a good long moment, feeling my face shift into an expression of generous pity. Because I knew what she was trying to say. Once I mated with Rav, he was going to let her kill whichever of my animals blinded her in Alexandria. He'd probably claim it was just a way of "weeding out disobedient forms."

"Eike, even if one of my animals *did* blind you—which, again, they didn't—what makes you think I'd let you kill one of them?" She opened her mouth to speak, but I cut her off. "Especially over something as stupid as you losing a fight? You want revenge for something *you* did to *me*. It's so...disappointing."

She didn't want to bite. I could see her resisting, until she finally snapped, "What is?"

"You could have taken the L with grace. You could've been proud of me for besting you for the first time. You could've been impressed by my improvisation, you know? That whole teacher-student thing we had going on. I thought you were the strongest person I knew, so finding out that this is who you really are is just a little…pathetic."

I didn't wait for a retort. She'd hurt me or she wouldn't, but only one of those responses would prove me right and she knew it. Turning on my heel, I beelined for the offices, counting the doorways between it and the one where the spider had gone, trying to think of a new excuse to move that way.

But my step stuttered a few feet from the door to my rooms. Rav's office was open as I passed and I was surprised to find the front room crowded from end to end with…equipment, people, and activity.

Eike tried to nudge me on with, "Your offices, my queen—"

"What's going on?"

"Preparations."

"For?"

"Future things."

I scowled at her. "Are you getting punished by the word or something?"

"We both are."

"Seriously, that looks like recording equipment, Eike. And that portrait is new. Is that King Ivar and Queen Tenna?"

Eike reluctantly nodded, and I let my eyes linger on it for a moment longer. Ivar wore a sober, unsmiling expression—the sort too many people mistook for 'authoritative' when a man wore it and 'frigid' when a woman wore it—and a massive golden crown that looked like it weighed a million pounds. Tenna, on the other hand, looked…well… There was a soft smile on her face, but it didn't reach her blue eyes. No, those were clouded with fear, confusion, warning.

The emotion in them didn't suit the picture at all. Like, to the point I couldn't actually imagine an artist painting her that way. At least, not without being tempted to fake some sort of neutral happiness instead.

"Is that how she always looked?"

"Near the end."

I did a double-take at Eike and knew immediately that the admission had been another slip of her tongue caused by my honesty gift.

I didn't linger on it because I didn't think Eike would tell me anything else, but I guessed it was done right before Tenna escaped with Rav to Greece. Before…or after, maybe when she was forced back for some occasion. I didn't know which was sadder.

It made me wish I could talk to her…and the fact that I *could have* only a few days ago annoyed the hell out of me. At least the book with Idalia's séance ritual had been shipped to England ahead of us. If I ever escaped, I could summon her.

"And that's the bench Rav and I took meetings on at Hamingja," I said, moving on.

Eike only hummed, giving nothing away.

But I knew what this was the second I saw the largest, most unignorable thing in the room.

"Is that…a studio camera?"

I didn't need Eike's confirmation, although I'm sure she said something snide in reply. The only reason to schlep a camera the size of a small elephant that ran on one of those weird little railroad track things that let it move forward and backward into this castle was for ongoing broadcasts.

"When is he planning for us to announce ourselves?" I asked, not expecting a real answer from her.

But she gave one, and it horrified me. "Tomorrow."

"So soon?"

"A wedding planner is arriving tomorrow too. He felt quite bad about ambushing you with the first one, so this one he is leaving up to you. Told the woman to give you everything you asked for. She is quite famous, or so I hear, lucky girl. Apparently, she did the English princes' weddings."

That wasn't my gift talking. She didn't think she had anything to hide there.

But I thought she could have kept that well and truly to herself.

Tomorrow's announcement wasn't just about me, in relation to him. He was going to tell them we were engaged. He was going to turn this into a circus of some kind. A publicity stunt, maybe? What other reason could there possibly be for hiring the woman who'd done William and Harry's weddings, if not to turn ours into a spectacle too? The Royal Wedding of the Millennia. One that cemented us as the face of the entire alter population and propelled us to a level of celebrity no other Sovereign Supreme could ever fight.

Not that that mattered. I couldn't marry or mate with him…and not least of all because I didn't want to. I'd never gotten the chance to undo my accidental mating with Cass…and it was starting to feel both like some sort of cosmic gift *and* curse.

A timebomb, really.

I felt relief knowing Rav couldn't force me to mate with him, and gratitude that even without meaning to Cass was still protecting me.

But IF Rav somehow got me down that aisle and IF he somehow forced the words 'I do' out of my mouth and IF he still planned on having the Goddess officiate at all, what would happen once she revealed I was already taken?

He'd probably kill me. Just kill me right in front of everybody. I mean, what good would I be to him then?

It was a ticking clock. It was an inevitable ending to this.

More immediately, though, the prep in his office was a ticking clock for me. For my escape. I had tonight to leave. Once those words left his mouth with me beside him and every television news network on the planet spread the video, *he* would seem like the face of this. *He* would seem like the leader between us two. The world would look to *him* for guidance first.

***

It took another two hours of pretending to care about the offices Rav had rebuilt for me, and then beginning my wandering tour of the second floor, before Eike looked bored enough to risk entering the door where the spider had gone.

I half expected her to tell me it was off limits or something, but she seemed used to me randomly throwing open doors to check inside when I reached that one and did the same, tossing the door wide, anticipating another sitting room that hadn't been used in decades.

But that wasn't what I found.

The room hadn't been used in decades, but not because it was yet another useless space in an oversized palace full of them.

It was a child's bedroom. A time capsule that felt like stepping back into Tenna's apartment in Hamingja. Warm. Inviting. Cultivated with care. Unstuffy, full of toys and colors. And wholly different from the rest of the palace, painted by hand in a way that surprised me. Tenna—I had to assume she'd done it herself, or at least overseen it—had painted a lovely, impossible landscape on the walls. The half closest to the door was decorated with an old-growth temperate forest, the type that swaddled the Hamingja fjord. Halfway across the room, toward the windows, the forest gave way to a tropical beach, like the one I'd seen below Tenna's grotto in Greece, all arid and rocky twisting down to yellow sands and the green-blue of the Aegean Sea. Beautiful.

And a bit of an illusion.

No sooner had I stepped in, but movement caught in the corner of my eye, and I spotted the tiny spider waving at me again as if it had waited all that time for me to come.

It scurried toward the bed, which had been made to look like it was built in a treehouse, raised above the floor on a platform with stairs to either side, and a sort of clubhouse underneath.

I didn't ask for permission to check it out; and the fact that neither Eike nor the guards leapt to follow closely behind as I ducked into the little clubhouse told me Eike had been right all those months ago—it was possible to win a battle simply by wearing down your opponent over time.

It was also proof (to me) that curiosity was a great and powerful gift.

The second I stepped inside that room and out of sight, I hit something with my foot that I'd never expected. There, on the floor, was Rav's azurite pendant—the one he'd accused me of stealing.

As I watched, the spider raced for it, crawled under it, and carried it up the wall to the side of me, holding it out toward me. *Imploring* me to take it.

If this had happened even a week earlier, no amount of anti-psychotic meds in the world could have convinced me I wasn't going insane.

I didn't think so now.

This was real.

This tiny creature was offering me my way out.

And I took it. My fingers plucked the pendant from the spider's grip and my heart leapt with joy as that magick stone asked me if I wished to shed my human form.

I said yes in my mind before my arm had fully retracted.

I rode that wave of icy unzipping pain across my body as if it was the price of my freedom.

I cheered with delight as I felt the choker's hold on my neck loosen, then slip entirely as I found myself in my inner sanctum, a willing passenger in my raven's body.

She shed that choker with a flick of her head.

And the moment it clattered to the floor, I did the only thing I could do.

I screamed, "*GO!*"

It was mental. It was all mental. I knew that. Didn't stop me from clinging to my raven's perch anyway as she literally somersaulted in that tiny room, dove through the open doorway, soared over the heads of Eike and her guards before she could even shout, and flew into the open air of the second-floor promenade.

She sacrificed half a second to orient herself as she peered around before her head snapped to the staircase and we careened toward it, took a sharp turn right at the edge and nosedived down the central staircase well hole, veering again as she reached the ground floor.

There just ahead, we could see an open door and the garden beyond.

"CLOSE THE DOORS!"

We didn't make it before the staff shut it.

She hit a breakneck angle and sped down one of the main corridors, searching-searching.

"*Try the front door!*" I screamed.

"There! She's there!"

"Don't let her escape!"

The words chased us as we flew.

More and more guards appeared underfoot until the halls were crowded with them, and by the time we reached the tourists' foyer, the doors were shut there too.

"*Break a window*!" I begged.

And Goddess bless her, my raven pivoted on a dime. She hit the hallway and aimed for a window up ahead that faced the castle's central courtyard, then she picked up as much speed as she could.

I held my breath and braced, anticipating a little pain, or a lot, as the glass shattered around my raven's body.

I also anticipated the joy that would come as we swept up and away into the bright blue sky.

But...we never felt it.

Rav's great roaring voice bellowed, "*RESIST!*"

And a shockwave of orange magick burst ahead of us across the glass moments before we struck. Moments before our body crumpled on impact, and our neck broke.

I...had no idea how that could work.

As we fell, that's all I wondered—how Rav's single shouted command could magickally change the glass like that. But that was a question for another day.

We hit the floor like a stone. I couldn't feel a connection to my raven's body at all. What I could feel was a growing numbness. An *absence* of feeling where it should have been.

I thought I knew what it felt like to be helpless before, but this? I was trapped twice over, and it *terrified* me.

I had to accept the relief that swelled inside of me at the sight of Rav as he moved through the crowd of guards to my side. I knew he would have to change me back and I wouldn't have to feel this broken numbness for long.

But he took his time, his eyes great fiery blue marbles of disappointment looming above me as he bent down beside my raven's body.

"This is your second mistake, Natalie," he said, almost panting with anger. "What happens now is your fault."

I knew he meant it. I knew he would punish me for this.

But in what world had he imagined I'd never try to escape? In what world could he have expected me to give up easily?

He wouldn't have wanted me if I had.

I knew that with every fiber of my being.

So, when Eike appeared carrying the little azurite pendant from upstairs, I made the split-second decision to truly earn whatever punishment he had in mind.

Turning my attention to my creatures in their cubbies nearby, I said, "*When he changes me, don't hesitate. Drop through the floor. There's a relic vault. There must be another passageway down there. Go. Find Brodie. Find Fern. Find Cass. Lead them here.*"

I felt their agreement, more than heard it.

All save my mermaid. She was uncanny—she looked exactly like me but with golden eyes and much longer hair, floating in the watery cubby on the second level, as if it was her own private bathtub.

"*Can't swim here,*" she said.

"*I know,*" I told her. "*But could I borrow your heart for what comes next?*"

She offered me a small nod, and I felt her heart's coldness numb the rest of me moments before Rav pressed that azurite stone to my raven's body.

The pain was sharp, but muted faster, and I could feel my mermaid's heart *fighting* that pain, almost spitefully. Gnashing her teeth against it.

And when my human form ripped my raven's body apart, I felt my creatures escape out of me through the corridor floor one after the next.

It was enough. It had to be enough.

Especially because Rav had something else when I sat up on the castle floor and covered my naked form with my hands and hair.

He held the jet-black choker in his hand, although I didn't recognize it at first. It was looser and longer, with great wire gaps between the beads. He waggled it at me impatiently before spreading it wide with his hands.

Even though my mermaid's chill made me not care, I tried to argue anyway, "Come on, Rav."

"Enough," he snapped quietly, not even looking at me as he raised it over my head and brought it down around my neck. "You're lucky I don't make this permanent. Although, if you keep misbehaving, it may be necessary."

Someone behind me pulled my hair out of the way moments before Rav waved his hand and the necklace tightened back into a choker, drawing a veil across my inner sanctum, my fleeing animals, and my mermaid once more. At least her coldness remained with me.

It made it almost bearable when Rav rose to stand and said, "Ready the prisoners. We'll carry out her punishment at dusk."

CHAPTER 10

Prisoners.

No single word had ever filled my heart with that amount of dread before.

And no mermaid's cold heart had ever fought so hard to keep that dread at bay.

That sensation—that unease—sat at the back of my chest, pressed against my spine, like a curled-up hedgehog, protecting my heart from feeling actual pain at Rav's threat while simultaneously prickling the rest of me with discomfort.

I didn't know which to wish for—a quick rest of the day so I could get through whatever he had planned as soon as possible or for some catastrophic external thing to happen to maybe—*maybe*—prevent him from doing anything at all.

I was put back in ropes and left on a couch to stew in my own uneasy thoughts for hours.

Then guards carried my restrained body to the dining table where Rav watched me not-eat as if he both wanted to force feed me *and* thought it was fitting that I couldn't.

Eventually, he broke his silent treatment to warn, "Not eating won't change what happens tonight."

And I responded, "Who do you have?"

We both fell into silence once more and I stared at the sinking afternoon sun through the window until Eike entered and whispered that things were ready and waiting for us outside.

My mind spiraled as Eike untied the lower half of my restraints so I could walk.

"Is it Scarlett?" I whispered at her, hoping she wasn't such a miserable loss of a human that she'd give me some tell to prepare me.

"Is it Yasmina? Corby? Is it Fern?"

She didn't respond, and although I had half a dozen additional names I could have asked after, I didn't want to, in case it wasn't them. In case naming more people just fed into his cruelty more, gave him a *longer list* of vulnerabilities to exploit to keep me in line in the future.

But the restraint forced me to carry my dread alone, with each step I took as Rav laid a heavy hand on my shoulder and guided me through the castle to the patio.

I...didn't know what I was looking at, at first.

Three cameramen were set up around the periphery, and one came forward to us immediately as we exited the castle. Another was stationed about fifty feet away from the castle, right at the edge of the statue garden, where someone had erected two...lightning rods? Hitching posts? Two giant stakes had been plunged upright into the earth with a six-foot gap in between.

The third cameraman stood by a third stake, which stood at the bottom of the patio stairs, facing the others. Eike tethered me to that one, then turned and walked away without looking back, as Rav waved at the cameramen and said, "Remember, frame everything so Natalie can be removed, if necessary."

I turned to Rav. "What is this?"

"Your second warning," Rav said cryptically.

"I don't need another warning, Rav!"

"Yes, you do!" he almost roared, as he backed away to face me. "Stealing the azurite was betrayal enough... But using it?"

"I didn't!" I shouted back. Off his scathing disbelief, I added, "I didn't steal it! I found it! And of course I used it, Rav, of course I did. And we both know you're proud of me for using it. Don't act like you're not!"

He stormed toward me at that, and the cameras veered away. His hand wrapped around the front of my throat and pulled me toward him, crashing our lips together. I could feel that spark of magick as well as need in them and anger, frustration and so much desire, it nearly bowled me off my feet.

"Of course I am," he whispered, tapping his forehead to mine. "Some part of me is in awe of you, *min skat. I wish* it was the biggest part. It's some sick divine joke, what's happening between us. Since the moment I learned you went to the witches and asked how to undo a mating bond, it is as if you have become the mate I always wanted. The way you fight. The way you hide. Even the way you *run* from me. Every bit of defiance in you calls to the structure in me. You're everything I've ever dreamed of."

I had to try again. I just had to.

Staring him down, I spoke as calmly as I could. "Rav. Listen to me, please. I didn't go to the witches to break our bond." Then I took it one step further. "*I promise you* I didn't."

I watched the darkness in his eyes lift momentarily as he recoiled an inch while still holding my throat, eyeing me as if he expected me to explode right in front of him at any second.

When I didn't, he pushed. "Then why did you ask that?"

For that I had to lie, but...only partially. "For Scarlett! Josh is a coward and a traitor and *completely unworthy of her*! You think I wouldn't do anything to give her a way out of whatever you thought you were doing when you sent Josh to alter her? And to convince her to mate with him before she even knew what she was doing?"

The words came spilling out of me, but as I said them, I realized I meant the accusation. It made perfect sense. Josh had betrayed the location of Arachne's Revenge to Rav. Rav had acted too casual when Scarlett arrived for his holy day with Josh by her side. Rav had also trusted him to just...not tell all our secrets to Scarlett while she was still human and they were staying in this very castle with us earlier this year.

But it went deeper than that, although I doubted I knew or would ever know the full extent of it.

Rav had been playing me since last summer—since he'd taken that silver-tipped arrow that had pierced my body and used the wood impregnated with my blood to work some love spell on me somehow.

How hard would it have been to find out who my best friend back home was, learn who her boyfriend was, and cozy up to him for whatever reason?

If that was it, I had no doubt Rav played some part in why Josh sprung the alteration on her. He might have even told Josh to trick her into mating with him, and it might have worked if I hadn't warned her on Rav's holy day not to use the m-word unless she absolutely meant it.

All at once as I stared Rav down, a small part of the larger puzzle of everything that had happened in the last year fell into place for me. And I felt so much lighter for it.

Especially when Rav didn't speak afterward. Didn't deny it. Didn't deflect. His mouth simply opened and closed again, and my eyebrow rose dangerously high.

"I didn't mess up by going to the witches, Rav. *You* messed up by not believing me. *You* messed up by not respecting me from the start. *You* pushed to get closer to me, then complained I was getting too close. This is *your* doing. And you're still messing up now by acting like any of this—" I motioned to the stakes, to my ropes, "—is for anyone other than yourself."

"No," he countered, leaping forward. "This is for us."

"Wrong again," I said, staring him down. "This is for you. You're showing me how you wish I'd fight for you while doing everything to guarantee I never will. You need to stop making mistakes while you're already behind."

Again, I saw a look in his eyes that suggested he was actually listening. That he could actually hear me this time. I was getting through to him.

"You can, Rav," I said so gently. "Make a different choice, get a different outcome. You can choose."

Opportunities like this just never seemed to last very long.

Two seconds later, a noise interrupted his self-reflection and popped it like a bubble. He turned to stand beside me with his hand on my shoulder as the cameramen fell into position and we all watched Eike and several guards lead two exhausted, weary people out and tie them to the stakes.

Two people I had never actually met but knew well.

Two people who broke my heart to see.

Long ago at Hrafnagud during my very first days in the Raven Court, a wine bar owner and his obnoxious neighbor who swam naked in the pond where all the bar owner's customers could see had come to Rav to settle the dispute between them.

Later at Hamingja, Rav had mentioned they'd come to him again, complaining about each other, and Rav had been tempted to put up a fence between their properties in the dead of night just to get them to stop squabbling. I'd told him they just needed to go on a date—that all that aggravation and annoyance was actually a front. They liked each other. They just didn't know what to do about it.

Henry. Guillermo.

I still didn't know which was which.

I only knew one was billowy and unkempt like an artist. The other carried himself like a prim, dignified sommelier.

"What did they do?" I asked, almost sneering in confusion. "This seems a little extreme for a…a…property dispute…"

But the snark in my voice died as a soft breeze blew my way…and I realized what this really was.

One of them smelled of fresh-cut wood, leather, and vanilla—a beaver.

The other smelled of peat, watermint, and chamomile—a swan.

They were different forms.

I'd…done this to them.

I'd…outed them without realizing that them being together would break the law.

I hadn't meant to, but it was my doing all the same.

Even my mermaid's heart couldn't fully numb the raging ache of guilt that slammed into my heart.

I jerked my gaze to Rav. "Rav. What is this?"

He didn't look at me. "You saw what I did not see, *min skat*. You saw to the heart of the matter. You brought their intent to break our most important law to my attention. Thank you for that."

I recoiled in anger. "They aren't together. They haven't done anything wrong."

He didn't reply.

"Rav. That law is *pointless*. You know that. It's unsustainable too, now that everything's out in the open. I was planning to get rid of it as soon as—"

"It's a good thing I found you in time, then." Off my confusion, he added, "It is our most sacred law. It is what minimizes the risk of beasts being born."

"But you know that's not true! You know everything ever said about beasts is a lie. They're not made that way, and they're not dangerous either. Hell, you're trying to become one!"

But his next words caught me entirely by surprise.

"And two is enough. Our early reign will be fraught with difficulties as it is. We don't need competition as well."

His tone was…gentle. Patient. As if he was doing me a favor, trying to prevent others from becoming beasts.

I hated it. It wasn't just condescending. It was manipulating the truth to defend cruelty and control.

"These two people won't create *anything*, Rav."

"But they can inspire others who might. If everyone breaks the rules, soon there are no rules. Then what do we become but animals? They are an example. A gentle warning. It's a loss of two over the loss of many. And it will be a sanitary story of execution to share with the humans. To reassure the fearful that we can police our own. Their sacrifice is justified."

It was so gross. So…unforgiveable, what he was saying. It wasn't enough to punish them. He needed an audience. He needed a narrative. Just like every tyrant before him.

To my surprise, though, I wasn't the only one picking up on it.

Out of the corner of my eye, I saw a flicker of movement. Eike took a tiny step forward.

"Maybe this is unnecessary, my king?"

I think Rav and I both did a double-take at her in surprise. Her body language was tight and strange, unlike I'd ever seen it before…except when she was feeling vulnerable. I'd seen glimpses of this in those rare moments she'd let her guard down around me in the past.

Her raspy voice broke as she added, "You are about to wage an anti-propaganda campaign to convince people beasts are saviors, not monsters. This goes a little against brand, don't you think?"

"They will need a reliable king," Rav countered. "Consistent. They will respect that more than one who treads water in nuance and accomplishes nothing."

He motioned to the cameras to follow as he set off for the prisoners and my mind whited with panic. I yanked and *yanked* and *yanked* at my bindings, letting my mermaid heart numb the cutting bite of the ropes against my skin and muscles and bones.

"Rav, if you kill them, you'll *never* have me!"

Rav turned on a dime, his eyes ablaze. "You'd give me up to protect two people you don't even know? Two criminals who intended to break the law?"

I laughed, in rage. "There are a thousand and one cruelties in this world protected by the law. Just because a cruelty is *legal* doesn't mean it's right!"

Rav laughed too. "Welcome to politics, *min skat*. But, fine. You feel so morally superior, let's do this your way."

I stopped struggling, trying to wrap my head around how exactly any of this could be done my way, or how he would warp it to justify killing them.

I watched Rav strut confidently toward the two prisoners, as if he was joining a couple of friends for a day in the park, rather than gallows' men. He clapped a hand on the sommelier's shoulder and smiled at the other one.

"Henry. Guillermo. I'm sorry to see you again under these circumstances. My mate over there let something slip a few weeks ago about the…inappropriate relationship…you two share."

The men eyed each other, and even from this distance, I could see regret and longing on their faces.

The artist spoke first. "My king, we bicker and we drink. That is most of our relationship."

"We were dumb to bother you with our problems," the sommelier chimed in.

"My mate disagrees," Rav said.

And I couldn't help but shout, "Don't you DARE use me for this!"

Rav ignored me. "She says you are in love with each other, which isn't just inappropriate. It flies in the face of the rules that have kept us safe these thousands of years. You know that, don't you?"

The two men eyed each other again, and I wished more than anything that I'd thought to shut off my honesty gift while I'd had access to my inner sanctum. There'd just been too much going on! And how could I have known?

All I could do was shout again, "Don't try to lie! Talk around the truth! Don't admit anything to—*hmmmft*!"

But there was suddenly cloth in my mouth, gagging the words I wanted to say.

Rav glared at me, then once I was silenced, turned the full force of his focus on them.

"I could legally end your lives tonight, my friends, but I would prefer to offer you mercy," he said. "I don't want to have to punish you. I will pardon you if you make me a promise."

Oh Goddess, a promise.

I screamed at them to draw their attention. Shook my head frantically hoping they could understand not to do it! Not to trust him!

"W-What sort of promise?" the artist asked.

"A very easy one," Rav said. "You must simply say, *I promise, before king and kind, that I hold no love in my heart for—Henry, you say Guillermo, Guillermo, Henry—nor will I seek it, speak it, or shape my life around it, in thought or deed, now or evermore.*"

It was a trap. I knew it was a trap. I hoped they would see it too.

But Rav laid it on thick. "I know this would require you both to move away from each other, but I would pay for this. I would help you settle elsewhere, away from temptation. This does not need to be the end of the story for either of you. I can also repeat the promise, if you need. However I can be of help, let me know."

Again, I screamed. Again, I raged against my restraints.

Again, I hoped they could read between the lines!

And for a moment, I thought they did. They exchanged a lonesome, loving glance and I heard the sommelier say, "I can't let this happen to you, Gui. I'm sorry I ever summoned you to Hrafnagud in the first place."

"I…don't want to say this thing, Henry," the artist said. "I like our fighting. It brings me joy. You…you are my best friend."

"And you're mine," Henry admitted.

I saw the shine in his eyes from where I stood. I knew the exact moment I couldn't save him.

The sommelier took a deep breath and turned away from his friend. "I promise, before king and kind…"

"No, Henry, please."

"…that I hold no love in my heart for Guillermo Maes, nor will I seek it, speak it, or shape my life around it, in thought or deed, now or evermore."

I raged and tore at my restraints until the last word left his mouth. I hoped my muffled screaming might…might…*cancel out*…his words. Might mute them or something!

But for a moment after he finished his promise nothing happened. And I fell quiet hoping my struggle helped, hoping it didn't work.

Until Henry let out a relieved shaggy exhale and turned to smile at Guillermo and his humanity burst in a bright red second, painting his friend—and Rav—in the color of lost love.

CHAPTER 11

Guillermo's scream split the air like a siren.

So did the sound of his stomach emptying, when the absence of his friend beside him and the blood across his body sickened him.

Then he began to scream again.

And Rav dismissed his entire existence to come to me, his face half-splattered in my shame, bypassing Eike where she stood cradling herself, unable to look Guillermo's way.

I stared him down, accepting the sight of that viscera. Accepting my part in it. I had to. It's all I could do. I wanted to scream, too, and never stop screaming. Instead, I swallowed my tears for later and squared my shoulders and ignored the tremor in my fingers.

Rav knew I had a lot to say. I knew he did too. I could sense it across and around him, like a straitjacket of discomfort—one I wore myself and called guilt.

"I don't want to hear it, Natalie."

I didn't speak. I stayed quiet, knowing it would bother him far more than anything I could say.

"This changes nothing between us," he said, undoing the knot that held me to the stake. "You'll marry me anyway and forgive me eventually."

Again, I didn't speak. I didn't need to. And in the silence, I felt his discomfort spike higher.

"It's easy to seem brave when there is nothing at stake, but you won't be able to fake it when the time comes to break your own promise, *min skat*. There's no point even pretending you can."

I wasn't faking bravery—I was practically catatonic with fear.

But I was also done. Done thinking I could reason with him. Done thinking I could pretend my way into being his conscience.

Done considering him *at all* in any way other than as a threat—to me and to others.

Because the truth was, he hadn't done this just to remind me of the consequences of breaking my promise to him, or to have footage he could edit for the humans later. Or to reinforce old rules he didn't even believe in.

He thought this guilt would make me surrender. He thought the threat of more would make me docile. This was more manipulation. More coercion. Even I, with my limited experiences in love, could see how wrong it was.

Had there ever been hope of us finding a way forward together? Finding balance and partnership and building upon a fated love worth all the compromise those things would have taken? The Goddess had once told me that hope always existed, but…

I realized how dangerous it was to *surrender* to the crazy notion that we had no control over who we loved. Like it was some destined chain around our neck we had to carry forever, or risk being seen as ungrateful or unworthy or doomed to be alone.

"Fated love" was a trap.

A lie we'd picked up along the way—maybe one that had been fed to us so often we believed it was a Universal Truth or something—that guilted us into trying harder or looking for things that were wrong within ourselves to save something we thought was supposed to last forever rather than accepting it as a lesson and moving on.

That's what Rav was for me. A lesson.

In those moments as he paced around me, anticipating a response that I literally couldn't verbalize, I released any lingering doubt in my mind about what Rav was to me.

He might be my mate, in another version of my life where I wasn't as capable and I wasn't as caring and I wasn't as sweet-hearted as he accused me of being.

He might be my leader, in another version of my life where I didn't trust myself enough to know what was best for me and where I refused to admit that other people, creatures, and magicks deserved to decide what those were for themselves.

But to choose him—to choose his way of interacting with the world—was to choose death.

Death of the soul slowly over time as I became smaller and smaller and smaller to make room for the overinflated largeness he desperately seemed to need.

Death of the mind sooner than that, as he stormed off during any conversation he didn't like and kept me from my friends and family and all the people who were different from us that we could possibly learn from.

Death of the spirit as he cut me off from my creatures, from me.

And Death in the very real sense because men like him always made the fatal mistake of taunting the universe by declaring themselves immortal. All while doing the terrible things that stacked the scales against them until they were "worth more dead" than alive.

To choose Rav was to choose apathy.

To choose Rav was to choose fear.

To choose Rav was to choose total annihilation.

I deserved better than that.

We all did.

So I took a step forward, ignoring the turn of Rav's body.

Ignoring, "*Min skat?*"

I took step after step until I reached Eike and walked past her. She just watched me with a skittish expression in her eyes, which couldn't quite meet mine.

I walked to Guillermo, feeling some strange hollowness as he stopped screaming.

"The silly idiot loved me," he whispered, almost whimpering.

"I'm sorry," I told him, even though I didn't think he actually heard me.

Then I turned away, using the hands tied behind my back to begin undoing the ropes that held him to his own stake. It wasn't easy. I never thought it would be. Feeling the tough rope rubbing and cutting my skin as I blindly clawed at the knot trying to undo it was some sort of small penance. A replacement for the fact that my mermaid heart was working overtime to keep me from falling apart.

I didn't care if I had to work at it all night to free him. Rav didn't stop me either way.

But then I heard a voice, "You're taking forever. Let me."

It was Eike. She unhooked that curved blade at her back and began sawing through Guillermo's rope. Such a small gesture two minutes too late, but it was something I'd never seen in her before—an act of heart. An act of soul. It didn't absolve her of not acting soon enough, but she'd momentarily removed the Rav blinders I thought were permanently affixed to her eyes.

It was a start.

And I…?

And I took the chance I might never get again.

Instead of watching her work, I waited until the blade was fully supporting his rope, sawing upward, and I pulled my wrist restraints taut. And when she was focused on sawing, I threw my hands back over the blade and yanked as hard as I could. The blade slid out of her grasp under Guillermo's knot, slicing into the narrow loops of my rope along my wrist, slicing my wrist too.

I felt the blood pour.

Felt the sting of physical pain which had nothing to do with my mermaid's heart, although triumph pounded through it as I felt my restraints grow loose and slack.

"My queen, don't!" Eike shouted an instant before my ropes snapped entirely and I turned and caught the weapon before it could fall.

My hands were slick with blood; I couldn't even look at my gushing wrist. But I brought Eike's curved blade to my own throat a half a second before I heard the guns of the armed guards cock in all directions around me.

"Hold!" Rav shouted, taking several loping steps toward me.

"That's close enough," I said, stepping in front of Guillermo. "You too, Eike. Back away."

She did, this time wearing some expression I liked to think was half admiration.

"Shameful, Natalie," Rav tried to scold. "I'll have to kill Gui for this."

"You'll go back inside with your men now," I countered, "Or I'll slice."

Rav tried to call my bluff. "At this distance, any cut would heal instantly anyway, just like your wrist."

He was right, my wrist had already healed. Still, I laughed at him and pressed the tip of the blade to the side of my throat, until I could feel a tiny puncture.

"This is insane, Natalie!"

"I agree. You're insane."

He took another step forward and I pressed the tip deeper until I felt a ruby red drop of blood slide down my neck.

Rav paled as bright as the moon. "All right! All right! Men, go inside!"

No one moved.

"NOW!" he roared.

This time, though, no one had *time* to move.

Because in the total silence that followed his roar, a new sound cut in from the forest behind me. Rustling leaves. Snapping twigs.

Panting. Snarling. Thunderous footfalls upon the ground.

And then...*howling*.

First one, then two, then *hundreds* all harmonizing together until the sound reverberated through my head as if I was standing inside some great metal bell.

I didn't dare turn around. Wasn't willing to risk it, in case it was a trick.

But I knew it wasn't the moment a guard staggered. The butt of his rifle lowered in surprise, in fear.

"*Good God,*" was all he had the chance to say before a streak of silver struck him like a moving car and he vanished from sight.

Vaguely, I heard Eike shout, "Intruders! Fire!"

Then she was gone, too, in a blur of silver.

Shots fired far off to the right, then again off to my left, until the world sounded as if it was made of gunfire. I would've taken the howls of wolves over that any day. *Brutal.*

Everywhere. The screams of men, the *bangbangbang* of quickly emptying rifle magazines, the crashing of windows as Rav's men were struck like bowling pins and sent flying all over the place. Into the castle's stone. Into its windows.

And everywhere around me, a blur of silver...*things*...speeding past like a flood.

A flood that smelled of bonfire...and blood.

Some of the guards were quick enough to sidestep the rushing tide. My gaze snapped to one in time to see the silver blur slow and double back for him.

A tall wolf.

A tall wolf the color of moondust with eyes as red as flaming coals. Towering. Staggering. Legs bent on elongated ankles as if he could never quite stand straight. A bushy silver tail. A slightly serpentine neck. A torso rippling with so many muscles he seemed partially carved from stone. And razor-sharp claws, which he slammed right into the guard's chest like a pitchfork before tossing the man over his head.

Off to my right, another silver tall wolf with flaming eyes was taunting a guard, appearing and disappearing just long enough to get the guard to fire his gun, killing his own fellow guards with each ill-placed shot, until he ran out of bullets, and the tall wolf was there, clamping his muzzle of sharp fangs down on the man's neck.

Off to my left, half a dozen more wolfen "abominations." All silver, all red.

They were everywhere. *Everywhere.*

So many, there was nothing I could really do but focus on myself. And Guillermo.

I bolted back to him and sliced through the last bit of rope binding him to the stake.

"Run!" I begged, motioning back toward the forest, even though I didn't know if that would be a safe place for him. Then again, *anywhere* seemed safer than this.

"Are you coming?" he countered.

I nodded, sliding my hand into his—

Only to be torn right out of it.

A hand landed on my shoulder and yanked me back, knocking the curved blade away. I watched as Guillermo turned on a dime and bolted for the woods ahead of me; I couldn't blame him. But…I was surprised in that split second to see the tall wolves paid him no mind. No that wasn't true exactly. They let him go; they cleared a path for him.

Then the hand on my shoulder turned me. Rav was there, not even really looking at me, but holding me close to him protectively. His great golden wings were extended behind and around us, flicking away tall wolves the moment any tried to rush us.

"Come, Natalie," he said, reaching under my arms as if to scoop me up and fly away.

"I'm not going anywhere with you!"

His hand came within reach of my mouth and I bit. I bit *hard.*

Hard enough that when he yanked away from me, it sent me tumbling to the ground.

And he reached for me again, almost chiding.

"God, Natalie! Just because you're a beast doesn't mean you have to act like one!"

I kicked, and scratched, and crawled backward before he could get his hands on me.

"Don't make me…"

His voice died as I felt a presence behind me. He stepped back, cautious and slow, and I turned to see…my creatures.

My garnet dragon.

My silver wolf.

My orange-pink raven.

My rusty-red-brown bear.

My deep-pink spiderlady.

My…

There were two new ones, and they shocked the hell out of me. Almost more than discovering I was a beast in the first place did.

I suddenly understood why Eike had whispered, "*wolverine*," over me during her interrogation. Because a wolverine had joined my menagerie…fearsome and menacing and dark blue.

And so had a bright white aurochs. So large it looked like a bull had mated with an elephant. It… It was the aurochs I had seen momentarily when I pressed my head to Asterios's chest and asked for his power. That was one helluva confirmation that it had worked.

They came toward me in a wide line, staring over me at Rav.

"How did…" escaped his mouth in confusion, before the battle around us drew to a quiet end and we both glanced around at the wasteland of dead men at the feet of hundreds of silver tall wolves, all turning in our direction.

"'*How*' is none of your business."

We both jerked at this new voice. It was deep, graveled, half wolf, half human. And it belonged to another silver tall wolf, as it emerged from between the others, its claws and flanks and face matted with bright red blood.

Rav actually stepped in front of me, to protect me. It shouldn't have surprised me, but it did.

"Get down on your knees, king," the tall wolf snarled.

"Or what?" Rav asked.

The tall wolf stopped half a dozen paces away. "Or I can have my men tear you into so many pieces no healing power could ever stitch you back together again."

"I'd decimate your army before they ever got the chance."

"Shall we test that?" the tall wolf asked.

As if his words were a command, every wolf within sight suddenly—simultaneously—dropped into a ready stance, as if a single word would send them all *sprinting* at us like a closing net of death and destruction.

"Natalie, get up! Come!" Rav commanded.

"My sovereign stays," the tall wolf countered.

"Natalie!" Rav barked again.

I didn't get up; I simply shook my head. I'd take my chances.

Rav spared me one more glance—and in it, I could see just as much frustration, amazement, disappointment, and *desperate longing* as I ever had—before he snapped his wings out and launched himself up into the sky, disappearing.

CHAPTER 12

I remained there on the ground for a long moment, shivering from a chill that seemed to come over me, catching my breath. Long enough, my wolf came to check on me, nuzzling against my head. She whimpered too, before glancing away at the others.

"*What?*" I asked in my mind. "*What's wrong?*"

But she didn't respond. None of them did.

Then I remembered. I rose to stand and lifted my head, drawing their attention to the choker around my neck.

"I'm okay," I reassured them. "I just can't hear you."

My wolf growled at it. So did my bear and dragon. My raven landed on my shoulder and delicately pecked at the beads, to no avail.

"It'll be all right. I just need a piece of azurite," I told them.

Turning to face the…the…*horde* of tall wolves around us, my eyes landed on the blood-covered leader.

It…

It was so strange.

Aside from the blood, he looked just like every other tall wolf there, and yet…

I was struck by this *trill* of joy at the sight of him and shivered again.

But there was also a…nervousness…that wasn't born just because I was surrounded by creatures who had to this point been my enemies.

I…felt drawn to him.

I took a tentative step forward, trying to remember how to be professional. Royal, or whatever. After all, I had probably just traded one captor for another, hadn't I?

But my dragon did a strange thing, then. He *nudged* my back. Pressed his head to my spine and *pushed* me closer to this tall wolf. As if I was going too slowly for his tastes.

"I'm going!" I muttered, as my feet quit sliding and I felt a scarlet blush rip across my cheeks.

Why was I blushing?

"Thank you for following my creatures," I told the tall wolf. "The king was holding me prisoner here."

Fear got the better of me as I stepped up in front of him, my neck craning to meet his eye; he was twice as tall as I was.

I added, "D-Did you come to free me o-or take me for yourself?"

Those fiery coal eyes studied me for what felt like an eternity. And I held my breath waiting to see which way this would go. Was he my salvation or just another would-be conqueror?

I couldn't tell either way as his enormous head suddenly lowered toward me and his muzzle came within millimeters of my hair, sniffing so hard I could feel tiny baby hairs rising off my scalp. Right before a sound like a whine—just the softest groan—escaped him before he jerked his head back and glanced away. I watched him for an entire minute, the way his shoulders sagged, the way his chest heaved, the way he seemed almost…beaten down despite utterly destroying Rav's private guard? It was like watching a mute man mourn.

…his hands were shaking too. Trembling like he wanted to do something more. To me? With me? I had no idea. But there was *resistance* in the tightness of his body. Like he didn't know what to do with himself now that we were alone and the conflict was over, but also couldn't leave.

I didn't know what else to do either, so…I raised my hand between us, offering it to him.

"I'm Natalie Damarand," I said. "What's your name?"

Still, he didn't speak. But I swear, as his muscles finally untensed, I could see a faint smirk across his muzzle and a raised fuzzy eyebrow, as he slid his massive, clawed hand into mine to shake.

And a magnetic tug under the skin—like coming home—slid into place between our fingers.

I think the chill of my mermaid's heart was the only thing that kept me from blubbering loudly right there in front of him. But the relief was staggering anyway. My breath blew out of me as if someone had punched me.

"Cass?"

Again, he didn't speak.

But something wondrous began to happen. Like…light refractions disappearing with a readjustment of a lens, the tall wolves around us lost their three-dimensional qualities. They flattened and darkened until they *slid* sideways *into* the tall wolf in front of me and disappeared.

One by one by one.

Faster and faster.

Until there was only him.

With his free hand, he reached into the thick fur of his chest and caught a black cord around his thumb, pulling it away so the pendants that had slid around to his back were visible…the little circular bit of green sea glass with the crescent moon that I'd given him for his birthday.

Beside the sea glass, there was a new addition—a teardrop of blue azurite.

He clutched them both and erupted in a font of viscera I could barely care about. I literally couldn't look away from his eyes as the wolf form sloughed away and that human form I knew so well emerged.

Hair of flame.

Eyes of moonlight.

Still taller than he'd been before his alteration.

Still beefy in that new way that made me dry swallow.

Still beautiful in that old way that had my stomach tightening in anticipation. No, not my stomach. Lower.

The scars were all gone, save for the two across his chest—the symmetrical claw marks from the wolf who'd attacked him in Luxembourg.

Any thought of the past, any thought of proper behavior, went right out the window.

I flung my arms around my friend so tightly I wouldn't have been surprised to look down and find us fused together…which would have been a little awkward considering he was painted from head to toe with blood and bits of fur and utterly naked otherwise.

I didn't care.

He was there! He'd come for me. Again.

I couldn't stop giggling as I said, "Couldn't get here any sooner?"

"It's good to see you again too, Natalie," he said against my hair, hugging me warmly.

"Thank you," I cooed, savoring a feeling I hadn't felt in *months*!

Gah, the relief of it. The magnetic warmth along my body. The *safety* of him, my Goddess. My creatures had found one of the three people in the whole world who might still trust me despite my beastliness. I wasn't alone! I was free!

I pulled back still smiling, filled with a gratitude that thawed my heart and left it deeply uncomfortable and antsy to belong to my mermaid again.

My creatures, too, mooed and grumbled and cawed at me for attention.

I showed him my choker, "This thing is cutting off my connection to my creatures." Motioning to his azurite, I added, "May I?"

"Oh. Of course," Cass said.

I reached for the pendant—

At the exact moment he reached to take it off his neck. My hand missed it in passing and grazed his chin awkwardly, but I loved the feel of his stubble against my skin and before I knew it, my fingers slid through it along his jawline, just marveling that he was *really there*.

"You could have kept it on," I said, laughing. "I could have just held it."

But he didn't laugh. He took a step back, out of my reach, and held the necklace out for me to take.

"No, it's all right, my lady, here. It belongs to you anyway."

Oh. I…

I didn't like the sound of that.

Not at all.

Nor the tone of his voice, how…nearly friendly to the point of acquaintance it sounded all of a sudden.

I eyed him uncertainly, trying to read him. His gait. His eyes. His flat perfectly cordial smile.

I didn't like any of it.

But…I didn't know how to ask him about it. Or what to feel if he gave me an answer I wasn't ready to hear.

He was my friend.

He'd been my friend through all of this.

That…that was what mattered.

But words fumbled their way out of my mouth anyway. "Are we…going to talk?"

"Oh yes," he said, laughing, and I almost heard the old Cass—my Cass—in the sound. "I know the wedding was a lot for you. I know…this…has been a lot. We don't need to discuss it now. We can do that once we're back in the Eighth Kingdom, don't worry."

But I *was* worried.

Especially when he offered me another flat smile and wiggled the necklace dangling between us, urging me to take it. I did…slowly. Once

I did, he stepped farther away, riling some unquiet discomfort in me. Then he turned and glanced around at the battlefield.

"Let me know if there's anything you need inside. Otherwise, I'll be…over here looking for pants that fit. Once you're done here, we'll go, all right?"

It wasn't all right.

And not just because Cass zipped away in a blur half a second later, accidentally blowing a gust of chilly wind across me that left more than my skin feeling cold.

Some colossal being could have taken all the emotions inside me, whirled them into a mighty tornado, and disoriented me less than that brief reunion with Cass had. For a moment there, it had felt like everything was finally right with the world. Like the universe was finally offering me some sanctuary after everything that had happened. A gift, for all I'd had to endure.

But, of course, as much of a gift as Cass was and had been for so long, he was a person first.

Someone I'd hurt.

I had no right to ask him for anything, really. No right to expect anything from him either.

Just because I had no right didn't mean I didn't want to catch him, force him to sit down with me, and just talk everything through now so we could…so we could…what?

So he could break my heart once and for all, like he had every right to do after what I'd done to him at Versailles? And before. Versailles wasn't the first time I'd hurt him.

I had to remember I was starting from scratch with a friend I'd hurt so badly.

And…that was okay.

That was okay!

I'd…move at his pace. I'd…let him set the tone.

Maybe with time…

My mermaid's heart tugged at me impatiently, tearing me from…whatever I was thinking. Fantasizing? Reminiscing? Some combination of the two? She didn't like any of it, ha.

My creatures, too, seemed antsy to return to my inner sanctum.

So, without further ado, I wrapped my hand around the azurite, yielded to its offer to alter me and…

Immediately crashed to the ground as a mermaid tail ripped my pants apart.

"What the…?"

I didn't even need to finish my own question because I figured out pretty quickly what was going on. All of my creatures had escaped to find help, leaving only my mermaid behind…so that's what I transformed into.

And she didn't have a narrow enough neck to slip the choker off like my raven had before.

It was a friggen dummy move.

Then again, I supposed every beast had had something similar happen to them at least once…if any had lasted long enough to mix up their creatures. So I laughed at myself as I returned to my human form, savoring the fact that I *could* laugh in the freedom I'd won for myself again, with Cass's help.

Of course, not a second later, I heard a soft *fwoomph* sound, and turned to find Cass there, washed and wearing some dead soldier's pants. And I threw myself behind my animals to shield my nakedness from him.

"Something wrong?"

"Uh, sort of. Cass, I've, uh, had an accident. Is there any way you could zip inside to the closet in the northeast top corner and grab me a clean set of clothes please?"

He was gone and back in a flash of silver, with clothes in hand.

"Oh," I added grimacing. "And there's a large seashell in that closet? Please?"

Cass eyed me with a soft smirk. "Sure."

He was there and back again with Tidebringer Rawan's conch shell in hand.

"Thank you," I said. "Could you…turn around?"

Some expression flitted across his face that I forced myself not to overanalyze before he turned away and I redressed, not surprised in the slightest to discover he'd found a mismatched set of clothes amidst the corporate princess barbie accessories Rav had purchased that actually felt like me—a pair of billowy purple yoga pants and a Moroccan-tile-patterned top, soft as a cloud.

"Thanks Cass, you're good," I said. "I'm ready to go."

Cass glanced at the ghostly menagerie around me. "Aren't you forgetting something?"

"It's not working. I'm still cut off from my animals."

"Are you sure?" he asked.

With a quick point of his finger, he drew my attention to a tiny wisp of movement I never would have noticed on my own. There, emerging out of the castle and onto the patio, was…the spider. The spider who'd brought me the azurite before.

It scrambled awkwardly across the smooth stone, toward me, as if trying to catch me before I left. And it didn't stop until it reached my feet and waved its tiny arms at me as if it…wanted to be picked up?

But it didn't. When I bent down and extended my hand to it, it waved that away and motioned to the azurite instead. And the second it took hold of the blue stone, its body suddenly *expanded* and *molted* until enormous bits of spider body fell away like a shell to reveal a naked woman within.

"Idalia?!" I almost screamed, throwing my arms around her before she was even fully on her feet again.

"Who the hell did you think it was, you *cabbage head*?" she chided, hugging me back.

"I thought you were dead!"

"Nearly," she sighed. "I would be if I hadn't had another piece of azurite on me. Stupid soldier didn't even notice me crawl out of my own mouth in that tunnel."

"H-How did you get all the way here?"

"In your hair, *corvetta*," she said, reaching for the thick bramble. "You have no idea how many strands I ripped out trying to hold on as you ran from the king through the forest. We must find you a better scalp treatment."

But…if she'd been with me in the forest. And she was there now, surrounded by my creatures…

"You're not…afraid of me?" I asked, both her and Cass. "My beastliness doesn't scare you?"

"It scares me a little," Idalia admitted. "But I like things that scare me. There is always much to learn from them."

I glanced at Cass, hoping he might be as reassuring. Instead, I found him looking away at the sky.

He sensed me staring, though. "It's nothing to be scared of. Although, we'll have to find some way to get that chain off your neck soon so it's easier for you to hide. We don't know yet who can be trusted."

"Nothing to be scared of, but you won't look at me when you say it?" I asked.

I didn't care that Idalia was there to witness how lonesome and pathetic I sounded. I just needed to know.

Cass's eyes snapped to mine, almost angry, but his voice was gentle, as if he didn't care that she was there to hear him either. "If I feared this part of you, I wouldn't have come, all right?"

Then his gaze snapped away again, and he stuttered boyishly as he added, "But Idalia *is* stark naked, so, I'll keep my eyes on the sky while you…find something to travel in."

"Fetch me a dress, would you?" she commanded, teasing.

His head bobbled for a moment and then he disappeared and returned again in a flash, handing her something before he walked off to the far edge of the patio and stood there with his back turned.

Idalia's long white smile dripped with amusement as she unzipped the black dress he'd found and stepped into it, eyeing me like we had some private joke about him.

"Well, I don't have tits or hips like yours," she said after she turned and had me zip up the dress, "but I think it suits me. Now, let's get the hell out of here before that flying brat or his henchbitch come back."

CHAPTER 13

I had no idea how to make it back to the UK without revealing my creatures to other alters, or the humans, as we passed. I thought I'd have to tell them to swim and fly ahead, across the North Sea, and I'd meet them there. But Cass had another idea.

He took us to the bed and breakfast by the water—the one run by the human Marna and her selkie partner Imi—where I had once turned to for shelter after being injured by the silver arrow last summer. My creatures waited in the woods outside while we went in and showered and Cass made arrangements for us. Then we ate dinner with Imi and Marna and I fielded a thousand and one questions about everything that had happened since they'd last helped me.

I didn't tell them everything—and spoke about Rav as little as possible. But when Marna eyed me with concern and asked, "Are you still with the king then?" I shook my head *immediately*.

"No," I swore. "Absolutely not."

I couldn't help but glance Cass's way to see how those words hit him, if they did at all. But he simply studied me with that unreadable look on his face, and nodded nonchalantly, and my stomach twisted my gaze elsewhere.

"You were right last year," I added to Marna.

"About what?"

"You told me how a man acts when a woman feels unsafe says a lot about his character." I let out a sad chuckle. "I finally listened."

She waved that away with a jagged grumble. "Hear this old woman—these types of mistakes happen. Don't dwell in them, you know? Don't…uh…how's it said? Don't make them your whole personality. Don't carry them with you either as if they're scars. Use them to tune your intuition. The stronger it is, the more you can trust yourself, the fewer mistakes you'll make."

"Besides, you have been busy," Imi added. "Even the animals have noticed the ways the world is changing. The Moon, too. Her radiance is brighter now."

"It is?"

All of them nodded at that, including Marna.

"Did you not see how bright the last full moon was?" Imi asked, in surprise.

"I…had to miss it," I said, clearing my throat. "A friend needed me."

"*So magnificent!*" Imi cooed in reverence. "Like an iceberry drifting through the Aurora."

"Three rings around it, too," Marna said. "Usually that means a storm is coming."

"But it does not feel dark, you know?" Imi added, wiggling in her seat. "Her glow reaches deeper in the ocean now. She's happy, I think. Or excited…about you, maybe?"

With that, they all fell silent, waiting for me. Obviously, they'd been watching the news, but…I hadn't really thought about the Goddess and her connection to everything that had happened, except in…roundabout ways. To blame her for things, ha.

But of course, she knew. The cult's part in all of this notwithstanding, She'd known in Greece, even before I did.

She'd warned me that hard days were ahead.

She'd warned me to trust myself.

And…I was learning how.

I didn't know what to say to the others' hopeful faces, in the moment, except, "I-I hope She picked the right person."

"She did," Idalia said, so confidently for my benefit. "You must believe She did if you hope to survive, *corvetta.*"

"Oh, she'll survive."

That…was Cass. My neck almost cricked, turning to look at him, to watch him cough on his own words and massage his throat—clearly my honesty gift had summoned that promise he wished to keep hidden from somewhere deep within him. It didn't surprise me exactly, although I didn't know how or why he said it, but it *definitely* didn't surprise the other women, who all eyed him gently, before they glanced at me teasingly, and then returned their gaze to him again.

It left us both blushing.

"I-I just mean…" he stammered, "It's my job t-to protect her. And there's an entire army waiting to do the same once we're back in the

UK."

I wanted to reach for his hand. Really, I wanted to hold out my hand for him to take, if he wanted it. But…I could see the little lapse of control had embarrassed him.

So, I shrugged to cover him, "Well thank you. All of you. For everything you've done. I am *so* ready to be home again, I can't tell you."

As the others began talking of other things, I risked another glance Cass's way and caught him watching me again, that strange, unreadable expression—some mix of curiosity, maybe, and suspicion?—back on his face.

***

"You and Idalia can take this room. Cassian, we've placed you just across."

"Thank you, Marna."

I'd hoped to have a moment alone to talk with Cass as the house wound down and rooms were assigned, but whatever fleeting curiosity he'd had at dinner seemed to disappear afterward.

He took the towel Imi offered and went into his room with a quick, "Goodnight, everyone," and didn't meet my eye once.

But I understood why he went to bed so quickly a few moments later. Our room faced a wide swath of green grass between the house and forest. As Idalia flopped into bed, I watched at the window as silver tall wolves began to appear in a literal wall outside the bed & breakfast, shoulder to shoulder, facing outward. Just beyond them, in the deep cover of the trees, I could see my creatures walking the perimeter, keeping guard too.

"That is some gift," Idalia said in the stillness.

"It is." Turning back to the room, I found a tall wolf was there with us suddenly, facing the door. "Whoa."

I crept closer and pressed my hand to its forearm; there was no magnetic tug. And when it looked at me with its unblinking eyes, I felt no snowflake chill. I walked around it in a small circle, just…examining it, I guess? Compiling more questions I desperately wanted to ask Cass, when we were finally alone.

"A little creepy," I said, as I crawled into my own bed, and the tall wolf went back to staring at the door.

"Given the circumstances, I think the word is…protective, no?"

I nodded; that it was. These copies of Cass didn't feel like Rav and his guards, smothering me, intimidating me, and it obviously made all the difference in the world. Safe versus scary. Empowering rather than threatening. I knew I was going to sleep very well with that tall hairy long-toothed sentinel standing guard a few feet away.

"I'm sure it would crawl into bed with you, if you just asked," Idalia cooed, half asleep.

I scowled playfully at her. "What exactly are you implying?"

"Nothing, of course," she teased. "Oh to be an eight-eyed spider on the wall of Arachne's Revenge. To hear strange tales of redhaired ghosts crawling into bed with our VIP guests every night."

Maybe the surprise I felt should have been greater, but… "Spying is creepy, Idalia."

"I am creepy. But! I never said I was not. Besides, this is war. Privacy is hard won in war. I am also quite capable of reading body language. The way you two look at each other when you think the other is not watching? I can read you like a book, baby. Him too."

This time, my scowl felt crooked with embarrassment and denial.

"I thought you had to touch people to know how they felt."

"It helps, but Cassian Mahon would never let me read him." She rolled toward me with a smile and held out her hand between the beds. "As for you, my little open book… You are free to volunteer your feelings so we can pretend I did not read them when you hugged me earlier."

I wanted to scowl harder, but I was already at max-glare. So I rolled away instead, grumbling, "Annnd that's the last hug you'll get from me."

Idalia laughed softly. "Liar."

***

I woke in the morning to the buzz of Idalia's soft snore and the otherwise empty room; our tall hairy sentinel had retired with the dawning sun, it seemed.

But I figured that meant Cass was up. I hoped that if I was quiet enough, and early enough, I could get a moment with him.

Nope. I was already too late. There was a quiet argument happening in the front room. Marna, Imi, and Cass were whispering, and for a good long while, I listened to snippets just out of sight, lamenting that I didn't have my wolf hearing with me.

"Dangerous…"

"…That didn't stop you from bringing her here..."

"…do you care…our lives?"

"You fool."

"We have *eyes*, Cassian."

"Who knows…could become."

"You've brought this enormous risk to our doorstep…others have already been killed."

I didn't need more than that. Maybe they'd seen my creatures lurking outside. Maybe Cass had told them about how we'd escaped the king. Maybe something else had happened and I was one of the last to know again.

I understood what mattered: me being here was dangerous for them. I was a danger for anyone who knew me.

Hell, I'd never even met Guillermo and Henry, yet mere mention from me had been enough to cost one of them their lives.

We needed to leave. That was the short of it.

And I had some big decisions to make about my future. I couldn't disappear and just live off by myself away from everyone to protect them; that option had been taken from me the moment my name left Robine's mouth during that internationally televised broadcast of our Great Secret. No, the only way forward to protect people was to *dive in deeper*. And I couldn't do that until I wasn't on the run anymore.

So I blew out a deep breath and stepped hard on a board underfoot to announce myself before entering the front room. The words, "Marna, Imi, thank you so much for helping us last night," left my mouth in a rushed breath before I realized there were more than three people in the room.

Cass, Marna, and Imi had been arguing by the door fully visible from where I'd been standing. But I found Guillermo seated in the corner, just out of sight, his arms crossed, and legs spread wide, feet tapping, as if he'd been waiting all night to speak to someone.

To me, I realized, as his eyes snapped to me, and his legs fell still.

"Guillermo. How did you find us?"

"He didn't," Cass said. "I found him wandering. Thought you would want to speak with him."

I did. I'd snapped awake with thoughts of him and realized that in all the chaos at the castle, he'd run away and I'd never sent anyone after him.

"Guillermo, I…know you must hate me. And I know I can't do

anything for Henry, but…can I do anything for you?"

It seemed like such a tone-deaf question, maybe, but…it felt like the right thing to ask. The obvious thing to ask.

Guillermo began to tap his feet again, his body language more awkward than it had been before. He shrugged and whispered, "I don't know. May I call upon you again when I think of something?"

"Of course. You're also welcome to come with us, if you're afraid of going home."

"No, I am not afraid of the king. And home?" He shrugged again, his mannerisms growing somber and manic. "I won't know until I get there, will I? It is where Henry lived, so…maybe I should go back. Maybe not. Seeing the wine bar empty may be too much. And the boat rusting in the water?…Henry liked to sail. He was always trying to get me to go out on his little boat even though he was an *awful* sailor. So tense and proper, he was like a plank of wood out there on the waves. Henry said he liked the simplicity of it—you pull a rope, you turn the rudder, the beautiful craft goes where you want it to go. But I liked it because it was the only time he swore. Not real swears, you know, but little phrases he thought were. '*Frogsticks!*' he would say. Or '*You unfermented philistine!*'"

I had no idea why Guillermo was telling me this, until he chuckled at his own memory of his friend, and I realized he might have had no one else to mourn with him. So, I took the seat beside him and listened. Just listened.

"I feel stuck," he admitted after the laugh faded away. "We convince ourselves we will always have a little more time. A few more grains of sand in our hourglass. One more night to say the things we hide in our hearts."

He gulped suddenly, and his big wet eyes met mine as he finished, "But there are no more nights, and the boat has lost its captain."

I took his hand, and relief swelled in me when he tightened his grip on mine.

"The king's promise, it was a trick, yes?"

"Yes," I told him.

"Henry died because he broke a promise he could not keep?"

"Yes. He promised not to love you, but…he wouldn't have made that promise if he didn't."

"To think he only beat me to it." Guillermo chuckled sadly again. "If only I could tell him that."

My spine straightened automatically, gleefully. "You can."

"What do you mean?"

"On Ognianima, you could speak to him again. Would you want that?"

Guillermo looked at the others. "Is this true?"

They couldn't help there. All three looked frozen at the mere suggestion.

But the moment was saved by a new voice, from the hallway, as Idalia said, "Yes, it is real, *cigno*. Although *someone* should be asking *permission* before she offers rituals she does not know how to conduct herself."

I grimaced imploringly at her, before squeezing Gui's hand again.

"However, in your case, sir, it can be done," Idalia said gently.

"Then that is what you can do for me," Guillermo said.

"You'll come with us?" I asked, just to clarify. Off his nod, I turned to Marna and Imi. "Would you come too? I didn't hear everything you and Cass were saying before I came in, but I don't want you to suffer for helping me. Cass brought me here because he feels safe here. He trusts you. So do I."

A look passed between the women, and in it, I saw reluctance.

"Come with us just until this is over?" I asked.

"I'll keep you safe," Cass added, in promise.

And I finished with, "If I have it my way, the king won't be one for long."

At that Marna laughed, but her body untensed. "You've come a long way since last year, girly."

Two hours later, after Marna and Imi had battened down the hatches and sealed their home, Cass guided us all down to the small beach below the bed & breakfast to wait for something called a coaster ship—a small cargo vessel with a large, underdeck hold with no windows, where the animals could go. It appeared a few hundred yards offshore like a bright orange safety cone. And from its side, it let down a matching enclosed lifeboat—the sort I'd seen before dangling from the sides of cruise ships.

This smaller thing—which was still the size of a studio apartment—putt-putted right up to shore and tendered everyone across, including one of Cass's copies, leaving the real redhead and me behind.

No, we had to wait for the lifeboat to come back with just the copy of Cass aboard so my animals could board both ships without being seen.

And you'd think that in that interim, he and I would have used that time alone to talk like we both seemed to want to. Well…we *did* talk after a long awkward silence. A little. About the copies.

"They're incredible, Cass," I said, trying to generate a conversation.

"They're…something," he replied.

"The one you sent with me? Saved me a lot," I tried.

"Yes, well. That was his job—to protect you."

It was *annoying*, all that…politeness. All that uptightness. I don't know what kind of delulu confidence took hold of me then, but all I wanted to do was break his rigid Englishness a little bit. I just wanted a glimpse of my friend again any way I could get it.

So I glanced away toward the ship and teased, "Ohh, he did more than protect me."

Out of the corner of my eye, I saw him do a double-take.

I kept my face as neutral as I could, but softened my voice and added, "A lot more."

Cass suddenly stuttered, "N-No, he couldn't have. I didn't give him that ability…"

And I grinned before I could help it.

Cass tsked loudly, drawing my attention to the relieved smile on his face. "Oh, you're messing with me."

"Am I?" I asked, twisting my lips, widening my eyes. Daring him to ask. "Are you sure about that? Let's ask him. Call him out."

"He isn't—" Cass coughed again, as if my truthsayer gift had him on the verge of revealing something he didn't want to, before he replaced it with a squeaky, "I'd rather not."

I won't say it didn't break my heart a little to hear him hide from me.

But then again, I hadn't earned his trust back yet.

So, I let the moment pass and normalized my voice and offered, "If you want to know what really happened, just ask me, okay? I'll tell you. Whenever you're ready, I'm ready."

Cass didn't reply to that, but I *felt* the tightness I could see in his throat as he swallowed and looked away.

I had to remember. Cass was technically another casualty of mine. Just like Guillermo. Just like Marna and Imi and Idalia were, in their own ways.

I wasn't blaming myself fully for things I had no control over. I just found myself taking stock more of how much I owed other people. For my life. For my soul. For my heart. Eike had once accused me of "collecting strays.". But they weren't strays. They were islands in the archipelago of my life. Separate from but impacted by the wellbeing, or lack thereof, of my island.

And realizing that left me with a lingering question. How could I stop others from getting pulled under by the currents swirling around me—currents I hadn't caused and couldn't escape?

CHAPTER 14

Something about returning to the Eighth Kingdom made me feel like a proper spy again. Perhaps because I had always been sneaking around it for one reason or another—to avoid chaperones, to escape tails.

This time was no different. After we spent two days traveling across the North Sea puking into bags, Cass disembarked at Hull and returned with a disguise for me and something people in the UK called an MPV or people carrier—a minivan. While my animals continued around the coast to our final destination on the boat with one of Cass's copies, our weird assortment of characters left the ship and took the shorter route. We drove for nine straight hours through places I loved and missed with all my heart. Places I wanted to *linger in* and *visit* for the good memories.

Like York, to see Jane Lakeland and maybe revisit that rain-cloaked hotel room where I'd once stolen a few intimate hours with Cass.

Like Edinburgh, to sleep in a bed that technically belonged to me.

Like half the wild places we passed as we drove deeper into the majestic, incomparable Scottish Highlands. I didn't exactly have *plans* to climb the snow-peaked mountains around us, or frolic in the golden frost-capped meadows, but it hardly seemed fair to let all that majesty go to waste.

Even grumpy Marna complained about Cass's relentless desire to take us wherever we were going as quickly as possible.

"Not even time to stop for pictures?" she asked.

But he shrugged with a quick glance back at me in the minivan's rearview mirror and said, "The quicker we get there, the sooner we can stop running for a while. I think we all need that."

We carried on to the tiny port town of Mallaig, Scotland, where a private, unassuming fisherman's boat was already waiting to take us a little farther north to a secret Cass had been hiding from me for months.

To a place called Loch na Feàirn.

"You *bought a town*?"

"Technically, you did," he said without even attempting to sound guilty about it. "It would've gone to the National Trust otherwise."

I...couldn't help laughing. *Town* was a big word for what awaited us as we stepped off the boat. *Village*, too, would have been a grandiose word for it. Between the great pine forest on the hills and the pebble beach, a single short concrete path connected a long string of white buildings topped with slate grey shingles and bright red brick smoking chimney tops to a smattering of other buildings including a church, a general store, and the boat launch with its attached gas station. So late on an early winter evening, most of the places were already aglow with golden light. And someone had gone ahead and strung naked bulbs down the full length of the "street," like some sort of emergency lighting leading us home. There was no road in other than the sea, and a *lonnng* overland hike to "civilization."

But there was still a soldier named Orla waiting for us as we disembarked, who offered to take Guillermo, Marna, and Imi to their rooms, as if we'd all arrived for a posh stay at a luxury resort, complete with in-person escorts and armed butlers. Idalia almost left too, but Cass urged her on, promising us both more surprises worth staying up a little longer for.

"It's only an hour away by boat to Kinloch Castle," Cass explained as we walked.

"Then...why didn't we just go there?" I asked.

"Because the castle is slowly transforming into a prison," Cass said quietly out of the side of his mouth. "After taking Arachne's Revenge, we had to store the prisoners somewhere."

"Arachne's Revenge!" Idalia spat in surprise. "You buried that lead, Cassian. You won the battle? You saved my library?"

Cass nodded ahead, "Not me. Them."

A door up ahead along the string of white buildings opened suddenly and a bearded man built like a truck emerged wearing something I'd never seen him in before—a plaid shirt and blue jeans. Normal everyday clothing. A stark contrast to the military gear I usually saw him in.

"Brodie, hey!"

The door opened again and Millie, Jonesy, and several other soldiers emerged, all dressed down, carrying bags of...what looked like mortar...over their shoulders.

"Well, look who decided to grace us with her presence," Brodie said. Despite the hefty bag he was carrying, he curtsied for me, "My sovereign."

Millie and Jonesy did the same.

"It's true?" I asked, after I gave them a side hug. "You saved the library?"

"Aye. Wasn't easy, but we kept the ceiling from cavin' in *and* got us a few new lags in the nick," Brodie beamed. "We've found out a bit more about the Knights' infrastructure too, but that can wait, lass."

"Why?"

"There's a few more faces wantin' a look at ye," he said, tossing his head in the direction of the next building down. "Go easy on Fern. She's had a tough time since the fight. I dinnae ken what happened but it shook her somethin' awful."

"I know what happened," I admitted. "I'll talk to her about it. But then we need to—"

He didn't mean to, but Jonesy cut me off with a sharp cheeky whistle.

"Guard your eyes, lads, before Brodie cuts them out of ya," he almost sang, his gaze drawing our attention to the beach.

Vaguely, I heard Millie ask, "Do you have to be such a pratt?"

And I heard Jonesy say, "Contractually, yes."

There, just coming out of the soft waves was…a woman I *almost* didn't recognize. Not without her golden eyes and bright blue tail.

"Rawan?"

She emerged from the loch like some old TV beach babe, naked save for her long flowing black hair, an azurite pendant dangling low by her belly button, and carrying a giant netted bag full of what looked like scallops and oysters. She reached for a pile of clothes she'd clearly left there for when she returned and when she was dressed, she joined us on the path.

"*You're here,*" I said, giving her a hug.

"*You don't want me?*"

"*Of course I do! I'm just surprised.*"

"*Yes, well, this one told me you were captured,*" she said, tapping Brodie's chest, "*As your ally, I chose to come north to…be in range if you had need of me.*"

"*Are you sure you didn't just want your shell back?*" I teased.

"*I might if no cabinet meeting is scheduled soon.*"

She spoke with a teasing tone too, but there was a look in her eye that warned I might only get a few hours of peace before the world demanded my attention again. Then she smiled playfully before she said she was off to deliver her fresh seafood to the kitchens and walked away.

It was at that point I realized Brodie had neither spoken, nor moved, while she was there. He stood rigid and stoic with his jaw set at a slight angle, as if he was more statue than man. The picture of casual indifference.

It was a front, I realized. One he seemed to hope came off as silent and strong and masculine, to hide the fact that it was actually a freeze response in the presence of a woman who made him forget how to talk.

I knew this because he couldn't tear his eyes off Rawan as she strutted away. And when Jonesy teased him, "Snap out of it. She probably thinks you're mute, man," Brodie turned beet red and mumbled some gibberish word before twisting his foot up to kick Jonesy in the butt.

It was cute to see such a big man so…flustered.

Teasing, I turned to Jonesy and the other guys, who were also staring and said, "You know, you're not supposed to leer at beautiful women. Especially not ones that could *literally* drown you for it and sleep like a baby."

Jonesy paled and scampered away after Millie, but Brodie lingered, still tongue-tied.

"Did you hear me, Brodie?" I nudged. "*She might drown you if you keep staring*."

His great big happy grin grew like a sunrise, slow and delighted.

"Ah, it's not how ye die that matters, lass. It's who's got hold of you when ye go under."

I felt my eyebrows shoot up. "Brodie!"

He leaned in, mischievous and smug. "I've been practicin' my swimming every day. And holdin' my breath." With a wink, he added, "I can go for four minutes now."

Then he walked off, too, and I turned back to Cass and Idalia with a smile. I think they could both tell that a few minutes back in this place, on this land with these people, reset something in me. The anxiety that had frothed and boiled aggressively inside me for weeks—*months*—was suddenly simmering.

"Come on, I can't wait to see the others."

"Give us a second," Cass said, suddenly darting around us both to hold the door open to the building Brodie and the others had left.

As we watched, a veritable *conga line* of Casses walked out, each carrying a heavy mortar bag over their shoulders. Like the world's most identical octuplets.

"Okay, now you're just showing off," I joked.

Cass's heart-shaped lips tipped up at the edges. "A little bit."

My eyebrow rose again. "Do they *have* to be shirtless?"

Idalia smacked me in the stomach. "Ay. Shut up and enjoy the view, eh? Ungrateful."

***

"Yessss, chica! Finally!"

"Holy hell, Nat!"

"Thank the Goddess, my lady!"

Voices that swelled my heart with joy flew at me the second Cass opened the door for Idalia and me.

It was a…café. Someone had renovated the downstairs area of this old cottage in the middle of nowhere into an *actual* coffee shop with an enormous espresso machine and a glass display case of pastries and giant everything bagels. It smelled of roasted warmth and savory bread and a scent from childhood almost ingrained in me at that point—some lemon surface cleaner. I would've recognized it anywhere.

Who knew little things like that could make you feel so at home? *So* at home.

Those, and the hugs, of course. I seemed to be a hug magnet, and I greedily accepted them all, as Corby enveloped me, then Yas, then Scar. They'd made it! I-I'd thought they did, of course, but again…it was one of those pieces of information that was different to *know*.

It hit differently. This place was a sanctuary.

One that seemed to contain almost everyone I cared about.

Which…seemed dangerous. Wasn't it dangerous to gather all my soft spots in one location like this? It riled my anxiety again before I could stop it. And for a brief moment, I felt *relief* that one person in particular seemed to be missing until the kitchen door suddenly swung open—

"*Mom?*"

"Natalie?"

She'd lost weight and her hair was up in a jumbled bun dusted with flour, which made her dark blonde look almost ashy, and there were dark circles under her eyes, but it was her! She was there!

She hit me like a brick wall going sixty miles an hour. Knocked the air right out of me as her arms tugged me in against her chest and her human scent hijacked my brain and filled it with memories. We held each other forever.

"Thank Goddess, sweetie!" she said.

"Goddess?" I asked, even though my thoughts were one unending string of thank yous to her too.

"Yeah, well, I've started…learning about all of this to prep for when I join you," Mom said, pulling back to study me. "Are you all right? Are you hungry? Do you need a nap?"

"*Mom!*" I groaned. "No. I'm okay. Are you okay?"

"Busy," she said with a smile, drawing my attention to the apron she was wearing and then to the display case of foods. "But it's been easier with more hands."

My eyebrow rose playfully. "Well, we *both* know Scarlett isn't helping you."

"Excuse you," Scarlett said, pinching my waist. "I can make ganache."

"That is true," Mom agreed. "She can make something…like ganache."

"Corby?" I teased.

He grinned and wrapped a lazy arm around Mom's shoulder. "I am your mama's number one food tester. Best job I've ever had…n-no offense."

I turned to Yas, but she waved me away before I could ask. "Don't look at me."

"Then who?"

The kitchen door swung outward then and someone I never expected emerged—another man with hair of flame, and unblinking eyes of moonlight. One who'd kept my head up in more ways than one over the last few weeks.

"Cass?" I yelped. "…*my* Cass?"

I felt a sudden lick of snowflake attention from the real deal behind me, but I couldn't stop myself when my ghostly protector turned on a dime, walked right through the café counter, and pulled me into a deep, satisfying hug as if he had genuinely missed me while we were apart.

I would never have said this out loud, of course, but it was the reunion I'd hoped to have with Cass, crashing into one another without so much baggage between us, clinging to one another proudly, intensely, unabashedly.

"I-I didn't think I'd see you again! I thought Cass would have…absorbed you already. Is absorbed the right word?"

I directed the question at Ghost Cass, then Cass, then Ghost Cass again. Of the two, Ghost was more emotive. He nodded, smiling at me warmly, while the real one eyed my arms around his copy's waist with another unreadable expression on his face.

This was…gonna be complicated, I could tell.

Especially when Ghost's arms suddenly tightened around me, and Cass's eyes narrowed, as if…as if he was scolding his copy telepathically. As if he was telling his copy to step away and Ghost was refusing.

Again, I was hit with competing emotions. I didn't want to let go. I didn't want Ghost to let me go either. For the first time in forever, I felt friggen safe *and* held, thankyouverymuch! Was that too much for a girl to ask for?!

I felt *so* safe and *so* held, I found myself asking a question I never imagined asking in a million years, "…Is there a problem, Cass?"

He opened his mouth to lie—I could literally see the embarrassed sneer streak across his face—before he realized he couldn't, and his mouth closed again as he shook his head.

"Thank you for letting me see my friend again," I added, pulling a little closer to Ghost just to punctuate the moment.

But…I quickly realized how odd this must look to the people around us. The whole crowd seemed to have parted around the three of us, watching silently. *Smiling loudly*.

Thankfully, my mom saved me.

Her hand patted Ghost's shoulder, drawing everyone's attention away. "This one is *great* at repetitive tasks. He makes baking for two hundred people seem like a breeze. Him and—"

The kitchen door swung open again and this time, I wasn't the one who yelped for joy.

"Jasiri!"

Idalia's legs pinwheeled like a cartoon character, veering around everyone between her and her man, who startled like a cat at the sound of her voice, leapt over the café counter and slammed into her like a freight train. His enormous arms engulfed her and his hand cradled her head pulling her in for a passionate kiss before they devolved into a private rapid-fire conversation in Italian and Swahili that wasn't meant for anyone but the two of them.

But…I watched anyway, and listened anyway, and admired their passion, and corrected the earlier inside thought I'd had—*that* was how I wished my reunion with the real Cass had gone.

***

My reunion with Fern went…a little differently. A couple hours after Idalia and Jasiri left for his room, and everyone else wound down together in the café before heading to their own rooms, I told my mom there was one more reunion I couldn't put off any longer, bid her goodnight, and said I had to talk with the friend who'd had zero chance to adjust to what I was before seeing me in all my eight-legged glory.

I didn't tell her that last part. Obviously. Mom—like most of the rest of my friends—only knew me as a raven. But she intuited that this talk with Fern was going to be…heavy…and wished me well before she left too.

Then it was just me, Cass, and his Ghost.

I turned to find them silently arguing between themselves, and whatever they were saying, the talk was heated. There was a lot of gesturing, glaring, set jaws and pursed lips.

I hoped I didn't look *that* crazy when I talked to my creatures. I mean, I probably looked way worse. This, at least, looked like twins in a silent standoff, whereas nobody could see who I was talking to.

Watching them argue was *trippy*. But…also fascinating. They looked identical in the face, save for the blinking, but there were plenty of differences too. Even though he didn't need one to help my mom, Ghost Cass wore an apron over his clothes. His hair was also shorter, as if it had frozen in length the moment he separated from Cass weeks ago. He also moved differently. Smoother. Silkier. As if he was more comfortable in his skin than the real Cass was.

Ghost was also happier, if copies could be happy. His eyes were brighter—closer to pearl than the stormwater of Cass's gaze. He stood straighter too, as if he wasn't carrying the weight of the world on his shoulders.

But…

They could both feel my stare.

They turned in unison to meet my bald gaze head on.

And let me tell you…the…the *ripple* of delight and something spicier that went through me as their silver eyes connected with mine? I had to almost glue my feet to the spot where I was standing to keep from lunging for them. The urge was *so* strong to close the distance between us.

My body *craved* them—*him*—with the strength of a stomach's roar of hunger. Except it wasn't my stomach telling me to cross the room and push them down on a tabletop until we found our way back to each other again.

But it wasn't just my body. My mind? *Phew*, it was *tingling*. Like a sleeping limb regaining sensation. The thoughts I wanted to share. The feelings. The whispered secrets that belonged only to them. My least unhinged way of dealing with the overstimulation was just to smile at them because just being able to see them—*him*—and *know* he was real and alive and healthy and not a million miles away made my entire soul feel like it was shining.

I had to force myself to calm down. I had to be civil.

"Could one of you tell me where to find Fern, please?"

The argument between them seemed to pop like a bubble. Cass untensed as he said, "She's in the building with the blue door—"

But Ghost's hand landed on Cass's shoulder then and shoved him toward me.

Cass glared at him, then offered me a flat smile before waving his hand toward the door. "Actually, I'll just take you."

Then Ghost shoved his shoulder again, and Cass glared at him *again,* before walking to the door to hold it open for me. I shot Ghost a smile in passing as he winked at me.

Given the awkwardness of the last ten seconds, I'd expected Cass to march ahead quickly, to get me there as fast as he could just to escape quicker. He didn't. We fell into a very slow stroll outside as I matched his pace. I could see the building with the blue door five doors ahead of us, but it might as well have been a mile away.

I thought that this might be the moment he asked me to talk. Or maybe tried to schedule our talk, considering it would take *a lot* longer than we had from there to the blue door.

Instead, he surprised me. "I know I'm not your Second anymore, but could I ask you *not* to tell anyone else what you are for a while?"

"Cass, I always listen to you. And I didn't *tell* Fern. I was forced to show her, to save her."

"I know," he said.

"You know? You've talked to her about it?"

He nodded.

"Is she afraid of me?"

"Not exactly, but I won't speak for her. I only ask you not to tell anyone else because...well...it's..."

"Dangerous?" I supplied.

"It's *wild*," he said instead as his eyes blew wide and a smile threatened to erupt on his face. "Radical, even."

I giggled—at that glimpse of the old Cass, at his choice of words, at him. Cass's gaze darted to my smile and brightened before glancing away again.

"Did you just say *radical*?" I teased. "Are you going to call me *tubular* next? Bodacious? Wicked?"

He grimaced with playful embarrassment, and I stumbled suddenly as he bumped his hip against mine. "I could update my vocabulary, if you like. But don't pretend for a second that you wouldn't have a laugh no matter what word I used."

I smirked, admiring him. "True. It is very fun to tease you."

Goddess, I'd missed this. These moments we'd always manage to steal with each other.

It just sucked that they never seemed to last very long.

Cass sobered as he said, "You're a new creature, Natalie, in a world terrified of things unknown. I'll ensure they love you before the end, but until it's safe, this needs to be a secret only a very few of us know."

"You're a new creature, too," I said, hoping he might share more.

But the smile playing at the edges of his lips faded at that, and his eyes darkened to stormwater again, and his shoulders sagged so heavily all I wanted to do was give him a hug.

I chickened out, though.

Instead, I rubbed my arm against his and said, "How does it feel to be taller?"

His smile blossomed again. "Nice. Apart from having to hem all my pants."

"I'm surprised you didn't just buy yourself a whole new wardrobe like you bought a whole new town."

"Maybe I will once you give me a raise for all my good work."

"If anyone deserves a raise, it's Ghost," I joked.

"Ghost?"

"Your copy. My copy of you."

He eyed me then, his brow quirked in what I could only guess was disbelief.

"How does that work?" I asked.

"I'm only just figuring it out myself. Took weeks to work out the details of what the gift even was, let alone what I could do with it. The first time one of them showed up, I thought I was going insane."

"That makes two of us."

Cass laser-focused on me again, and I clarified, "When he showed up in my bed in Crete, I thought I had *lost my mind*." I shrugged and added, "Didn't help that he showed up right after I realized what I was. I thought he was a sign I was already doomed. But, by the end, I didn't think so. He saved me. Literally, you know, but also in other ways."

I kept my tone light, my body language casual. But Cass continued staring for long enough, I finally had to ask, "What?"

"He didn't really try anything with you, did he?"

Again, I felt a wily smile slide onto my face, and I wore it the last few steps to Fern's front door, savoring the snowflake feel against my cheek as he waited for an answer that was *far* too fun to keep to myself.

"Go on in," he said. "Fern's at the top of the stairs."

"You're not coming in?"

"Not for this, heart."

CHAPTER 15

I was more curious than afraid as I climbed the stairs to Fern's room, knocked, and let myself in when she called out to me. Some quiet part assured me there was nothing to fear, from her at least.

I found my friend by a steaming kettle in the corner, pouring two cups of tea. Her hair was back in that beautiful seashell shape. She was dressed down and cozy in her exercise pants, barefoot and flowy around her tense body.

She didn't look at me immediately. She focused on the tea and tossed out, "Please sit."

Then she left me to sit in the quiet, twisting with uncertainty for a few moments, wishing I could read her mind. When she finally joined me and handed over a cup of citrusy-scented tea, we sat there for a few moments, warming our hands on the mugs and just studying each other. I tried to make myself seem as harmless as possible, as *at ease* as possible, so she might feel that way.

But after a moment, Fern said, "You don't have to pretend, you know."

And I exhaled with audible relief as I sat forward in my seat almost bouncing, "Okay good, because I don't want you to be afraid of me, Fern. I'm not a bad thing, I don't think. I-I can sort of prove it to you once we open the crate of Idalia's books we shipped, wherever that is. Asterios showed me some proof while we were in Italy that this isn't the bad thing everyone thinks it is. I was worried that I was going insane, too, but I don't think I am anymore—"

"I know that," she said, quietly.

"You do?"

"Yes, I was there with you in that library. I heard you tell the king you knew why he wanted you back. I saw the look on his face, all but confirming it. I saw your animals fight for you too. And I was there when you saved me. You don't need to defend yourself from me."

My shoulders fell away from my ears with that, even though I couldn't quite interpret her cool demeanor, or the tension I could still see in the lines of her shoulders.

"But…are *we* okay?" I asked. "Are you scared of me?"

The tiniest grimace flitted across her face, and my stomach dropped, waiting.

"I'm not scared of you; I'm scared *for* you," she said. "I've…spoken with my mother."

Her mother—Lady Saeli of the Asian Elephant Court, one of my equals, politically.

"Oh?"

"She more or less interrogated me. About you. About what part I played in the reveal of the Great Secret."

My stomach sank even further, until I felt like throwing up. I'd never thought about that—the consequences that being named the Knights' leader would have for my friends. Fern was one of my Seconds and her mom was the ruler of another court halfway across the world. How traitorous did Fern seem after that announcement? After all, no one but Rav and my allies knew I had nothing to do with it.

"I'm sorry," I said. "You know I didn't know they were going to do that."

"I told her that, but…politics and gossip are two sides of the same coin. And both are fed by incomplete truths. If people only hear part of a secret, they tend to fill in the gaps in dangerous ways. My mother told me the other Alter and Sovereign Supremes are demanding answers, and the longer those take to appear, the more their imaginations are running wild ahead of you."

Oh.

"You're warning me," I said gently. "I can't hide anymore."

I knew that, and Fern already knew that I knew that too. But she was doing her job, preparing me for this next leg, and it felt right to assure her understood her advice this time, especially given how much of it I'd missed at Hamingja.

"You think staying silent protects you. But in politics, silence doesn't buy you time. It sells your story to someone else. Whether they'll tell your truth or their own is anyone's guess, but in your case, my lady? With the king and the cult motivated to own you, the only person you should trust to tell your story is you."

It was a good warning, one to take to heart in a big way, but…it also sounded like a goodbye.

"Are you going to be there to help me do that or are you leaving?"

"My mother called me home."

Fern glanced away, obviously torn. She'd stayed with me since the announcement, while our little team recalibrated, but that'd been before speaking with her family. I couldn't expect her to choose me against them, nor was I asking her to.

"I understand. Really, I do, Fern."

Fern gritted her teeth, still looking away. "What need does the world have of a hundred new kings and queens when they could simply look to you? She's afraid of losing her authority. They all are."

My mouth opened and shut at that.

"Fern, you don't think I want to be some weird dictator or something, do you?"

Her gaze snapped to me. "No, of course not. But it may not be your choice."

"I should hope it is," I said, almost defensively. Then, when I saw her studying me again, I declared, "It is, Fern. I decide what kind of queen I am. I'm not a cult's public sacrifice. I'm not some king's consort. I'm not a Goddess and I don't want to be. The Secret's out. That genie is *free*. Now's our chance to start something brand new. Something good."

"Good for whom?" she asked, her shrewd eyes unblinking.

And there it was—the real question that would determine whether she threw her faith behind me or went home to help her mom.

I couldn't be flippant; I couldn't be cocky either. This was a promise I was making, to her, to them. And of all of them, she'd keep me very honest.

So I took a breath and said, "Not just for me. Not for the knights. Not for the king."

Fern didn't reply; she just waited.

So I plunged along, "I don't think any of that handful of powerful people has any right to say what better looks like, least of all me. But I know I've been given a lot of power for one person—the kind of power that destroys people…and empires. I also know I can't just sit on it. If I do, other people will misuse it. You're right."

Her eyes narrowed, and I figured she was probably wondering whether I was buttering her up or not. I wasn't. I met her gaze head on.

"Asterios shared a story with me at Arachne's Revenge about how the relics first came to be. It was just a handful of powerful, greedy alters who decided they wanted to rule everything, and then changed the story to claim they'd been given the right to rule by the Goddess after the fact, to make others afraid to question them."

Fern chuckled. "It's not just the alters who do that."

"No, it isn't," I said. "We have *a lot* of examples where a handful of people—usually the loudest, richest weirdos—reshaped the world, forcing the rest of us to just...live inside whatever they build. And wouldn't you know, that never seems to work out. Not a single one of those assholes built a utopia people were happy to live in, did they."

"You can see why you—the *idea* of you—makes people nervous."

I shrugged at her, "Maybe I was chosen because I don't want that job."

"But it's yours anyway," she countered, still prodding.

"I don't think control is the way to lead. If being around the king so much taught me anything, it's that control reeks of insecurity more than authority. We might wear a crown or a sash, we might sit in a throne, but we're supposed to be public servants, you know? We're supposed to listen first, talk second—and even then, we're supposed to serve the people we listened to."

Fern's lips twisted with curiosity. "What does that mean to you?"

I smiled at that, because I knew exactly how to describe what I wanted. "A table. A long, messy, frustrating Gathering Table where *everyone*—great court and lesser family alike—has a seat and the conversations are hard and slow and necessary. But the goal isn't greed or monstrous unquenchable growth—it's kindness. It's happiness.

"We've already been doing this, Fern. On a smaller scale, sure, but it'd work on a larger scale too. Our audience hours. We ask people what they need and we find solutions for them.

"Obviously, I don't know everything, but I know that most of the systems we already have don't actually fix problems. They fix the symptoms of those problems without digging a little deeper to figure out what's really wrong. We can do that.

"I spent my entire childhood living a struggle life. People are scared and angry and they make cruel choices because they're trapped in survival mode all the time. '*How am I going to feed my family?*'... '*How am I going to keep the heat on?*'... '*Is this other person that has nothing to do with me taking something from me by existing?*' One thing I *know* is that we have the resources to make this world better. Not in terms of ideologies or anything like that, but from the base up. We can help the world *thrive* rather than just survive. That's not crazy or impossible or idealistic. It's *literally* just resource management."

"And you think people can actually work together like that? Without someone at the top pulling the strings?"

"They already do. Every day. People solve problems. They share meals. They protect each other. When someone's struggling, nine times out of ten I believe someone would give if they had something to give."

"But what about that tenth person? There *are* bad people in this world. Exploiters. Conquerors. Grifters."

"Well, for one thing, we hold them accountable. For another, we improve the baseline of everyone's lives to the point where they push out those bad actors too. Then we look at the gap or loss or weak spot those people were exploiting and we fix it so they have to run off and try to exploit something else. Then we do it again when they get there. They're not proof of failure. They're tools we can use to tweak our strategies and build a better world."

I leaned forward then.

"We make sure our kind are protected, their rights are ensured. We keep them from being exploited and we punish those who do harm. We reassure the humans, the witches, the wild magick, the Goddess. We ask people what they need and we actually listen. We make decisions for the common good without ever claiming to know the greater one. We work every day to make this place and the people in it happier. All people. All alters. All witches. The animals too. This world could be *incredible*, Fern. The magick is all around us. And we know that because we all get glimpses of it from time to time. Hell, we've seen it in our team. Happy is different for everyone, but there's enough to go around without deciding what it is for anyone."

"But they're going to put a crown on your head anyway. Even if you tell them not to."

"Then it's my job to redirect them to that table, baby. Again and again until they get the hint. And if that crown gets too comfortable on my head, you have my permission to knock it right off. Not that you need it; I know you'd do it anyway."

I paused for a moment, waiting to see if she would speak. She didn't, but I could see it in her dark eyes—a spark of belief.

"It's not going to be perfect. And it's not going to be easy. But it *will* be kinder. More representative."

A tiny smile turned up the edges of her lips as she whispered, "Not a throne. A table."

"With a seat for everyone. Even the ones who don't trust me yet…like your mom."

A skittery breath escaped her then as if she had been holding it the entire time I'd been speaking. "She would like that."

I nudged, still wondering if she would stay. "I hope you will too. Whether you're here or…ten thousand miles away?"

Fern smirked and sipped her tea. "I think I'd have a hard time knocking your crown off from all the way over there, my lady."

***

I emerged from Fern's room a little wiser and a little wearier but cautiously optimistic.

It was real, what I'd said. It felt real. Maybe I was idealistic in some ways, but…I genuinely believed everything I'd told her. This world *could* be incredible without a heavy hand looming over any of it.

There were still miles to go before we got there, but we would.

I'd do everything I could to lay the foundation for a world like that.

After I slept.

A yawn stretched my cheeks almost to breaking as I stepped onto the concrete path outside Fern's blue door and realized…I had no idea where I was supposed to go. Orla had handed out room assignments to my guests, the others had had theirs assigned before I got there, and…well…I realized that this was the first moment in a *lonnnng* time that I'd truly been alone. I couldn't hear my creatures; there were no guards in my eyeline, even though I knew they were there patrolling the entire area. They were, or the Casses were; either way we were safe. And since someone had shut off the "street lighting," there wasn't even much light pollution to make the world seem small around me. Instead, the Milky Way lit up the far south horizon like a white string of paint splattered against an indigo canvas. And the partial moon offered me a Cheshire Cat grin. I *could not wait* to see what the night sky looked like there during a full moon. If I got my creatures back in time to enjoy it, of course.

"Is that you, my lady?"

I turned to find Millie walking down the path.

"Yeah, do you know where I could find Orla?"

"Orla? Why do you need that stroppy cow?"

I raised an eyebrow at her in surprise.

Her face twisted with embarrassment. "Sorry. She owes me fifty quid from poker. Hence the insult *stroppy cow*."

"What would you call her if she owed you a hundred?"

"She'd be a right thieving mare but trust me she'll *never* see another pound out of me."

Laughing, I replied, "Well, I need a room assignment, and she seemed to assign everyone else's so…"

"What?" Millie's nose wrinkled as she grabbed my wrist and wrapped my arm in hers. "You don't have a *room*, my lady. You have a whole house just over there. Here I'll show you."

Ten minutes later, we came to the tail end of the house row and veered away into the woods, down a dark eerie path around some rocks…

I stumbled to a slow stop at what awaited us. It…was a cottage. White plaster over brick. Shutters that looked sort of green in the dark. Golden with light from within. Through the window, I could see a wood stove, a little kitchen and table, a living room, a bookshelf-staircase leading up to a second floor. It was more than inviting, more than cozy; storybooks had been written about less.

Millie left me to push inside on my own, which was probably a good thing. The scent of woodfire was so strong from the wood stove, I literally began salivating…which…was embarrassing, considering the thoughts that leapt to mind along with that automatic bodily response.

"Mom?" I called out as I shut the door behind me and glanced around.

The first level held exactly what I'd seen through the window, plus a small bedroom, a bathroom, and a little hallway that looked like it went to a mud room, but it was otherwise empty, and all the lights had been shut off for the evening.

Sounds drew me up the stairs to the bedrooms. Someone was talking.

I knocked and pushed the cracked door open. "Mom?"

But it wasn't her. Cass stood by the window in all his spy-ish glory talking on one of those box satellite phones. Goddess, he was shirtless, his nearly scarless skin on full display. In dark grey sweatpants that hugged every unignorable part of him. Those ruined any chance I had of being semi-normal.

The best I could do was half-whisper, "Oh, sorry," as I jerked my indecent gaze away.

I was already backing out…when Ghost stopped me. His hand landed on the door and kept me from closing it, motioning me to wait and listen.

Cass, too, motioned for me to wait. "Yes, I understand…And Eike's there too?...Okay, call me when they move on…Yes. There's a reason he hasn't gone home again yet. Find out what it is. Thank you."

He dropped the phone into its cradle and turned to me.

"Sorry, that was one of our spies," he said. "He's been following the king and his Second since they left the castle. I anticipated him trying to follow us, but he didn't. He went to the south, to Oskar Lange's estate in the Black Forest. I thought he would at least have sent Eike back to the castle to check on his staff, but she hasn't and they've scattered."

I nodded. "Thank you for telling me."

"Of course," he quirked, as if it was a given. "We keep 'minutes' now. They all go into an encrypted account, so everyone's kept up to date. I'll show you how to access it tomorrow."

I nodded awkwardly again, still staring. My brain had interpreted Ghost and Cass gesturing for me to stay as…permission to gawk, apparently. How could I not? Both were shirtless. One was so magnetic that even from across the room, a core part of me was clawing at me to*…just…walk…closer and touch the living piece of art, for Goddess's sake!*

Then, Cass bit his lip.

Holy hell.

That, plus him, plus the smell. Mmm. I'm sure I looked insane standing there, staring at him for half a minute before anyone said anything.

"Are you all right?" he finally asked.

I was *not*. Felt like I was on fire in the best way.

And the worst, because I couldn't do anything about it!

"Uh, sure. Um. Millie said I was assigned to a room here?"

A smile curved up half his face. "Not a room. The house. This is yours."

But…it wasn't *just* mine. This room wasn't a spare he was using for "communication purposes." The closet door stood open, displaying racks of clothing—men's clothing. The bathroom door, too, was open and I could see a toothbrush in the holder. The bed was made-ish. And there was a dark green battered journal bent in half laying on the desk surface nearby.

"Mine?" I asked.

"Yes, well, there was an extra room."

"You put me with you?"

It both surprised me and didn't. Just like the words that came flying out of his mouth before he could stop them.

“I can’t be away from—” He reached for his throat, massaging, and hacked out a cough to cover whatever he was about to say. “It’s safer this way. I can surround you…i-if something happens.”

It wasn’t a lie; he couldn’t do that. But it was definitely an excuse.

“A-huh, okay,” I offered, savoring the little flutter of…hope?...of wishful thinking?...that ran through me.

“N-Next door’s yours,” he said, striding forward quickly past me, throwing open the opposite door.

I walked across and stood in the doorway, sort of…trapping him in the room for the moment. Just for fun. Just to watch him squirm a little as his eyes slid down my body, taking in my position, realizing what I’d done, before darting upward to meet mine again.

No, I didn’t want to make my friend uncomfortable per se. I just…missed him, even while he was there with me. I didn’t want him to go. Yet. I wanted these moments with him, as many as I could have, even if he was still angry with me. Or disappointed in me? Ugh, my heart squeezed with pain at the thought.

“Do you like it?” he asked.

I’d taken in the room at a glance a moment before he became my focus, but…looking again, I noticed details this time. Someone had put a purple comforter on the bed, and little paintings on the walls that…were like the ones Cass had sent to me in the mail. A vase of wildflowers—heather and purple little pompom things and the brown seed heads of what I knew were thistle—sat on the dresser, alongside a…

“Oh! A book nook? Mom brought one of my book nooks here?”

I darted forward, reaching for his forearm to pull him in again when he tried to step back. I wanted him to see this part of me.

“Do you remember I told you I used to make these?” I asked, picking up the little art diorama I’d spent *literal days* putting together with gorilla glue and fake moss. The scene inside was very fitting of this place—a magickal cottage in the woods, complete with billowing chimney smoke made from cotton balls and a tiny black cat sitting on the porch step.

“I do,” Cass said quietly.

“The lights in the house used to work, but it’s an old battery,” I said, flicking the dead switch a couple times anyway. “I made this one when I was thirteen, I think. I was super into the Brothers Grimm…and look at me now. In a magickal cottage of my very own.”

“You knew what you wanted even then.”

"And you gave it to me," I offered gently.

"Yes, well, it isn't what it ought to be. No rain room."

His tone was so muddled. He sounded lonesome and hopeful and resentful and friendly. Again, I had that powerful urge to just, like, *shove* him back on the bed and...and...sit on him until he stopped being mad at me. Or, more likely, *actually* got mad at me so we could have the argument I knew was coming.

I just wanted to start it myself. I wanted to just have it out with him so we could blow everything up and see what was left after he didn't hate me anymore.

But that was Rav's way, not mine. I couldn't force this. I didn't want to. Cass and I had never needed that. And in the aftermath of the chaos and pain and panic of the last few weeks, I had to find peace.

We were so close. Not touching. But we didn't need to. There, in the millimeters between us, so much energy sparked and flowed it was like standing just under shelter as a hurricane passed by.

At least, it was like that for me. It was a new intensity that I'd felt only once before—at Rav's wedding. When Cass had crash-landed out of nowhere in that suit, not looking at me, *my Goddess*. The urge to go to him then? It was a fraction of this.

Maybe something had happened between then and now to crank it up to this level?

Whatever it was, my heart hadn't stopped going a mile a minute since I'd opened his bedroom door and saw him standing there shirtless. And when he turned to me? I didn't need animals inside me to feel like one, ravenous for something other than food.

And here? In this quiet moment with him? I glanced up to find his eyes already on me. I wanted to reach for him. Pull him into me. Get back to that space we'd once shared, where it felt like the world would wait for us.

I don't know what expression I wore on my face, but, as quiet as a breath, Cass asked, "What is it?"

Words couldn't do it justice.

I put the book nook down and raised my hand. As if he knew what I wanted, he held his out, palm up. The tip of my middle finger connected with his, and energy shot between, all the way into my arm. But I didn't rush it. I let the rest of my fingertips brush against his, feather soft, giving him the chance to pull away if he wanted.

He didn't.

Cass's glance lowered to our hands at the exact moment I realized his chest had stopped moving. He was holding his breath, waiting to see what I would do.

So I ran my fingertips over the inner sides of his fingers—the pads, the curves—savoring the bright energy between, and the silent little intake of breath Cass took the moment my fingers glided across his palm. The moment *he* touched me back. His fingertips slid across my palm to my wrist, teasing the skin there in little figure eights the way he had done in the ruins in Luxembourg.

"Your heart is racing," he whispered after a moment.

The thought that he could feel it only made it race faster. Until my head felt light and woozy. Until I just wanted to touch more of him.

"What's wrong?" he whispered, as our fingers continued their gentle caresses between us.

"Nothing. I…" I didn't want to hold anything back from him. "I missed you."

I'd said that to him so many times at this point, it felt almost like another secret code between us. An organic one, instead of one we chose. One that, to this point, had always been followed by a kiss.

Not this time. Cass dry swallowed as his gaze returned to mine.

"In what way?" he asked.

So many ways. Too many to say all at once. Too many being beaten back by an aching fear that he would reject me. Punish me for hurting him. I was painfully aware that I deserved that.

But my mouth ran away with me and what escaped was, "I thought you died."

And once they were out, my throat tightened with tears that geyser-rushed for my eyes.

"I watched you die. I watched my m—" The wrong word almost escaped, but I pushed it down with, "—m-my best friend die."

A spectrum of expressions rushed across his face before his brow bent. "I asked for grace."

I laughed at that, and his gaze darted to my lips. "*A lot* was going on, Cass."

But then sincerity trickled into me and I added, "Thank you for saving me. Again."

"It was the gentlemanly thing to do," he murmured.

And I groaned. "Take the friggen gratitude, dude."

A half smile crept up his cheek again as he murmured, "You're welcome." But then he added, "And thank *you* for my alteration. Both for…what you did in Versailles…and later at the full moon."

"Fern and Yas told you about that?"

"They did, but I knew. I've never felt pain like that. I don't think I would've made it through the night without your help."

I'd honestly forgotten I'd done anything at all, but I teased, "What's a medium amount of pain between friends?"

"A medium amount?"

"Yeah, you're a lightweight."

His thumb swept across my wrist, scattering sparks.

Cass didn't say anything. He just watched me. With an intensity that made me shiver, but…watching seemed to be all he wanted to do. A moment later, some pang of sadness burst in his eyes and he released me altogether, and moved around me toward the door.

Taking his warmth with him.

Robbing me of his magnetic touch.

"We should rest. Goodnight, Natalie."

He said it so coolly as he walked away.

And that anger—that weird physical anger I'd felt in Versailles—revved back to life with a vengeance. It was as if some…some…*brat* inside me came out to play. I spun on a dime and followed him to the door.

Cass turned when he realized I was there just behind him.

"Where are you going?"

My eyes landed on Ghost, who was still standing in the doorway to Cass's room. I didn't know if he'd watched from there or what, but there was a wide-eyed almost-smile on his face. "Ghost? You coming?"

Ghost didn't hesitate. Not one second.

He walked right past Cass, right past me, into my room like he owned the place.

"Coming?" Cass's deep voice almost yelped. "Coming where?"

"We've got a routine now," I said. "Goodnight."

"Uh, he sleeps in my room."

"Does he."

I didn't say it like a question. And Ghost didn't take it as a command. From his place by my bed, he crossed his arms and stared at Cass.

Cass didn't say a word, but he stepped back and motioned to his own room with a snap of his fingers, like he might to a dog; Ghost only smirked and shook his head slowly.

"You done?" I asked after a moment.

Cass sputtered, flustered and unsure of what to say. When he finally spoke, it was with an exasperated sarcastic tone. "He can't do anything,

Natalie. I *know* he can't."

"Are you sure about that?" I teased.

Cass—my old cunning friend—reappeared for a moment as he leaned down into my space, glaring playfully.

"Yes. Because I didn't give him the equipment for that."

That was news to me, but it summoned a cheek-aching grin to my face, and I narrowed my eyes at him in return as I reached for the door.

"Because you knew he wanted to."

"N-Not exactly."

"Weren't *you* the one who told me all you needed was ten minutes, two fingers, and a tongue?"

The moment Cass's mouth dropped open, I waggled my fingers at him, sang, "Goodnight, Cass," and closed the door in his shell-shocked, blush-red face.

I turned to find Ghost there wearing a grin as big as the one on my face felt. And when he shut off the lights and pulled back the covers, I crawled in and accepted the arm-pillow he gave me.

It was *so* weird. All of it was so weird. But it was *fun*. The first bit of fun I'd had in ages!

I mean...it wasn't *exactly* the type of fun I wanted, but…

"Do you think he's still by the door?"

Ghost nodded at the exact moment we heard the wooden floor creak outside.

"Do you think he'll come in?" I asked, hoping he would.

But at that, we heard his door across the hall close. Ghost gave me a reassuring frown.

"It's okay," I said. "I didn't think he would. I know he's still angry at me."

Ghost didn't argue with me on that one.

"Why hasn't he absorbed you yet?" I asked.

His answer surprised me. He first covered his ear with his free hand, then covered his eyes, then his mouth.

"…Hear no evil, see no evil, speak no evil?" I guessed, adding when I realized, "He doesn't want to know what happened while you were with me?"

Ghost nodded.

What a power. Not only could Cass be in multiple places at once, and have his copies move about independently, but he could then absorb their experiences afterward. It was the sort of ability any spy or general might sell his soul for. Incredible.

In this context, though…

"So he's *really* angry at me," I said.

But in response to that, Ghost shook his head. He pointed his thumb at himself and jerked it toward his chest.

"He's mad…at himself?" I asked.

Ghost nodded.

Trippy. And sad. I hated the thought that Cass was mad at himself.

"Why?"

Ghost's expression told me there was just too much to say through charades, but it didn't matter. I'd find out eventually. I'd earn Cass's trust back one way or another, even if it was the last thing I ever did.

But Ghost ran a finger across my cheek to draw my attention back. He held up his hand and gestured with it like a mouth—as if encouraging me to just speak with Cass.

"I *will* talk to him, don't worry."

He shook his head and pointed at my heart before making the talking gesture again.

Oh.

"You want me to tell him what I told you while we were on our own," I said, to clarify.

He nodded.

I rolled my eyes and nuzzled into my spot under his head, murmuring, "Easy for you to say."

CHAPTER 16

I wasn't trying to make a point with Ghost. I wasn't trying to pressure Cass into opening up to me before he was ready either. Although, it kind of ended up looking that way from the outside.

Over the next few days, Ghost went everywhere with me. He opened doors. He brought me snacks. He seemed to anticipate my small needs and satisfied them. Like getting me toiletries from the general store. Like rewarming the mocha Mom made for me when my little ragtag team of grassroots world-changers got together in the café to make big initial decisions—like sending reinforcements to Italy to resecure it for Idalia, *finding out what happened to Giselle and Rolfe*, and scheduling my first official meetings with the Sovereign Supremes, the King of England and his Prime Minister, the Taoiseach of Ireland and his President, the human leaders who had demanded meetings, and so on.

I knew I was overusing the word, but it was just…trippy…for *everyone*…having Ghost and Cass wandering around, doing their own thing.

Cass made copies of himself for tasks all the time—for security, for construction, even for unloading supplies when a boat arrived with new plants and fertilizer for my mom's garden—and people were used to those versions of him. They were blank. Or….simpler? Maybe that was the right word for it. They only did *the task* they were assigned before disappearing again. Really, they *could* only do the task before disappearing again. Asking them to do anything else resulted in a cute sort of glitch where the Copy-Cass looked woefully confused but nodded helpfully before getting back to their pre-approved job.

Ghost was different. Cheekier. Unabashedly on my side. Not affectionate in any over-the-top way, just…dutiful. Generous. Devoted. And very, *very* public about it.

He drew attention to "us" in ways that made me nervous...but *especially* in ways that made Cass nervous. Because it took a hot minute for people to figure out that it wasn't Cass. And Ghost made a point of taking on more of Cass's mannerisms so some people never realized.

Until gossip began to circulate that Cass and I might have something going on.

I...didn't stop Ghost from doing this.

I know, I know. Maybe I should have.

I never *commanded* him to do anything, at least.

But the one time I pulled Ghost aside and said, "You're spending a lot of time with me. You don't want to make Cass uncomfortable, do you?" Ghost grinned and waggled his eyebrows as if to say that was *exactly* what he wanted to do. And when I added, "Okay, well, I don't want that," Ghost booped me on the nose and stayed by my side anyway.

In private or public, it made no difference.

Every evening, Ghost made a show of picking my bedroom over Cass's. And Cass lingered outside the door longer each time listening.

And every time Cass and I ended up in a room together where there was seating, Ghost would pull a chair up for Cass right beside mine. He'd only take it if Cass veered away, and if he did, Ghost dropped into it proudly, glued to my side, drawing everyone's eyes to us in ways that made my cheeks heat and my shoulders shrug.

Fern, Yas, and Scarlett, especially—they glanced between Cass and I with a palpable frustration I shared.

I didn't really know what Ghost was trying to pull, but I knew he *was* trying to pull something. He just didn't seem to understand that he was getting in his own way.

I knew Cass.

Better than his own copy did, apparently.

He moved in the shadows. Preferred it.

Cass was never going to come talk to me with Ghost hovering around all the time.

Which was frustrating because aside from those tiny moments together that first night, Cass had been distant with me. Watchful—ever watchful—but distant. I'd feel his snowflake attention in random gusts from random directions no matter where we were and look up to find his piercing silver gaze on me from across the room or through a window in passing, or from all the way down the concrete path.

It was strange. Before, he'd been the one telling me I stared at him too often. Now? I was always shivering.

I loved the anticipation of it. At any given moment, a frosting of snowflakes would blow across my hair, my face, my neck, my calves, and I just knew I'd find him watching if I looked up.

When I worked with Idalia, Jasiri, and Brodie prioritizing Italian strongholds to secure…

When Fern, Yas, Scar, and I worked with Corby to prep him for his grand debut—since I had *every* intention of putting him back to work as our Reassurance Liaison, helping new and prospective alters transition into their new lives…

When I sat down with everyone to narrow down candidates for my cabinet, experts with decades of experience in Foreign Affairs, Justice, Science & Innovation, Climate & Environment, Health, Housing, Food, Labor, Arts, and Indigenous Affairs, along with Magickal Affairs, Biological Diversity, Multispecies Culture, and Magick Ecology…

None of these processes were quick—some meetings quite literally lasted *for days*—but Cass attended every single one, raising goosebumps across my skin constantly with his random attention.

He tore his mercurial gaze away the moment I turned my eyes in his direction, of course, but I got into the habit of smiling before I looked up so he would see in that split second that I liked his attention.

I liked being seen by him.

But…not more than actually being with him. He ripped a piece of my heart out every time his gaze diverted like he was ashamed of his…attraction to me, if that's what it was. I wondered how many pieces I'd have left by the time one of us finally broke.

He didn't withhold kingdom business from me; he overshared most of the time, until I was *fatigued* with updates, trying to keep track of the movements of our soldiers and enemies alike. He talked to me just like everyone else when business was on the table.

But he didn't seek me out in private like he once would have. He didn't try to be near me like before.

He was hiding from me.

That was it.

I'd damaged his trust the way Rav had damaged mine, so he'd retracted his personality privileges from me. And all I could do was the opposite of what Rav did—give Cass the space to decide what we would be to each other moving forward.

There was just one problem with that.

And it wasn't until a solution arrived for that problem that I realized what I might have to do to set things right between us.

***

A week to the day after we landed in Loch na Feàirn, the tiny tucked-away town was caught up in a tizzy by two sudden arrivals.

One was expected.

The other, not so much.

Cass came to get me for both. He knocked on my door and said, "Are you decent?" in a way that made Ghost and I grin.

"Come in and find out."

Snowflakes blasted into the room the moment he entered, blowing across my back as I finished brushing my teeth. I met his moonlit gaze with sunshine in mine.

"Hello there."

Even when his gaze darted to my smiling mouth? Who needed peppermint gum with a winter blast like that?

"The ship's arriving."

The…ship.

The ship!

"My creatures?" I almost squealed. He was already wearing his coat, so I reached for mine. "Okay. I'll come with you to meet it?"

"Later. It's still a few miles out. And we can't move them ashore until nightfall anyway."

"Oh, all right."

"But there's something else you should see."

Ghost and I followed him down the concrete path to the point where the row houses ended and the individual buildings began. In this in-between spot, there was a dirt path leading up the late autumn hills—which were really just small mountains—that sheltered the town from Scotland's harshest northern winds.

"We a-b-b-bsolutely need to do a supply run for heavier coats," I told him when we walked high enough that the icy wind could smack me in the face.

"It's already on the schedule," he said, holding out his hand. "Come on, up here a little farther."

Off the path, the ground was misshapen rock disguised by tall grass. I took his hand, letting that magnetic snap do half the work of keeping me on my feet, until we reached the very tallest part of the hill before it became nothing but near vertical stone. There, someone had built a small lookout shack—little more than a windbreak made of wood and glass warmed by a woodstove. Inside, we found Brodie waiting, using a pair of binoculars to gaze out across the rocky wilds that separated this place from the rest of the world.

"Doin' some exercise, my lady?" Brodie asked at the sight of me.

"I need it to keep warm," I grumbled.

"And ye call yourself a Scot."

"Scots don't get cold?"

"Our blood runs hot. If all else fails, that's what whisky's for."

I grumbled again, rubbing my red stinging cheeks as I turned to look out across the landscape around us.

"So is this an initiation or something?" I teased. "You bring all the young high ladies up here to test our mettle?"

Brodie's expression was still teasing, but his tone was softer, when he turned to me and said, "I think you've been tested enough for several lifetimes, lass. No. There's a stranger comin'. Havna spotted her yet, but we got word from our lookout in Glenfinnan that she's on her way."

"At this time of year?" Cass asked.

"Aye, she must really want to be here."

She must really want to be here because the only overland route to this town took three days to travel…if you were already used to walking up steep trails.

Once my mind thawed, all manner of possibilities came to mind about who it could be. Dream of all dreams, I wanted to see Giselle walking across the highlands with her strawberry curls bouncing and her cheeks pink with healthy exercise. But it wasn't likely to be her, if she was alone…unless something had happened to Rolfe.

Nightmare of all nightmares, it was Eike.

"Ah! There she is."

Brodie handed me the binoculars and pointed, drawing my attention to a tiny speck of a figure in the far distance. One who, even without the magnification, looked…unique. Odd, in the face of the rugged wilderness surrounding her. She was wearing heavy skirts for one, kicking up her feet to get them out of her way as she walked. Her chestnut hair was up in a giant bundle on her head. And…

"No way," I murmured, using the binoculars just to confirm.

"What?" Brodie asked.

Cass echoed, "Do you know who it is?"

I did.

And I was *so excited* to see her!

But she had miles to come, so I took my time explaining.

Handing the binoculars to Cass, I said, "What's that beside her? Can you see?"

"Is…is that what I think that is?"

"Yep."

"But how—"

"Let me see, lad," Brodie said, snatching the binoculars and taking a look. "Does she have a *floating suitcase* with her?"

"Yes, she does."

I couldn't believe it. The witch Belina Saldo had said she would come. She'd told Yas that she would find me 'after dawn.' Well, dawn had risen, and the sun beat down on her floating suitcase and the witch's bag she carried across her chest, and her dark voluminous hair where it peeked out of a red scarf.

"Radio ahead to Orla," I said. "We're going to need a room assignment for her."

Two hours and a whirlwind of bustling preparation later, Cass, Ghost, Brodie, and I met her where the trail crested the hill and began its descent into the town.

She didn't stop; there was no sappy welcome fanfare.

She motioned to us all to join her as she trundled past, saying, "Hello-Hello, thank you for having me, yadayada, coffee first. And warmth. You and I need to talk."

I didn't know if word had spread or they could smell her unique cheese and parchment scent or there was just something in her aura that told everyone we passed that she was different from the rest of us. But they all stared as we walked by.

Especially Scarlett.

Scarlett *came out of the building* she was in as if…well…as if she could sense her arrival.

Belina didn't seem surprised. The moment she spotted Scarlett, she sighed as if some great nuisance had befallen her and whined, "You and I will speak soon, *sorellina*. Don't worry. The timing's just not right yet, okay?"

"O-Okay." Scar's voice leapt high with surprise and uncertain hope, as if she had no clue why Belina had singled her out but was relieved she had.

I realized why a few moments later when Belina motioned me to walk beside her and chided, "You have not told her yet, have you?"

Oh. She meant about the magick I'd taken from her.

"N-No. There's been a lot going on."

"*Che stronzata!*" she swore at me. "Excuses are double lies—one to the other person and one to yourself. No more of those, understand? Tell her. Before it's too late."

I tried to ask her 'too late for what?' but she suddenly veered away to a door, tore it open, marched down the hallway to the back of the house, and popped the next door open too, bringing us all into my mom's greenhouse.

It was a new addition; one Cass had had built within days of Fern and Yas relocating Mom there. It sort of hung off the back of the house like a weird frozen glass fart, larger than the house itself, with a pond and wood stove for temperature regulation set off to the side. I didn't like being in there, but for selfish reasons. The plants had been there long enough to explode with growth; some were even flowering already. They were a reminder that I'd uprooted my mom's life *again* and forced her into even more danger this time, and there she was making the best of it...*again*.

But Belina seemed to feel at home there. The tension in her body dissipated with a loud sigh as she located my mom at the back of the room and walked right over to her.

Her hand shot out between and a smile appeared. "Mrs. Damarand?"

"Rebecca, hi," Mom said, shaking her hand.

"Rebecca, I am Belina Saldo, the new resident witch...for who knows how long. I have need of a place to plant. Would you mind if I grew in your garden? I would need to begin planting tonight, for my purposes. I promise nothing will die while I'm here; in fact, I can guarantee a bountiful harvest for you, in exchange."

Mom's eyebrows rose nearly to the sky. "A real witch? Witches are real?"

Belina scowled at me, grumbling in Italian, "This *is why I am here, cara.*" Then she replied in English, "I am quite safe, I assure you."

A dazzling smile erupted on Mom's face. "Oh, no, that's amazing! Please, plant away. I have *so* many questions."

Belina looked momentarily caught off guard, then flattered. "Humans are usually terrified of us. But I suppose with a daughter like yours, this is just another Tuesday for you."

To that, my mom said, "It's my new normal, I love it," and a tension I hadn't even known I was carrying melted away. She meant it. She loved this. I supposed I knew she would, but again, it was different to *know*.

It was different to live life openly. Proudly.

To not have to hide our identities.

To be surrounded by people who loved us for who we were.

My eyes sought out Cass's from across the room, wishing I could share that simple epiphany with him. Wishing I could offer him that proud open life…with me. Wishing I knew whether he might ever want that again.

A lick of joy went up my spine when I found I already had his attention.

But…not for the reasons I wished. He suddenly stepped forward and cleared his throat. "Rebecca, would you mind giving us the room please?"

When Mom finally left, he came to stand next to me, and Ghost moved closer, sort of…shielding me…as Belina eyed them, and Brodie at the door, then me, with amusement.

"Go on," she said. "Begin your interrogation."

My eyes darted to Cass, expecting denial. Instead, I saw the set of his jaw, the square of his shoulders.

"No interrogation, yet," he said. "But we must know how you came to know of this place. There's nothing tying Natalie to this location. Nothing."

Belina's eyes narrowed with play. "Perhaps you were followed here."

"We weren't."

"There is a cargo ship—big as a village—headed this way."

"Registered to a commercial shipping company, with no ties to her."

Belina smirked. "You think the Raven King will be distracted for long by the false paper trail you laid, pretending Natalie went east to Romania?"

Cass twitched with surprise.

"Even if his people follow that path to its conclusion, they will find a new one leading even farther away from here," he replied. "The only way you could have known about this place is through magickal means…or someone told you. Since everyone who knows is already here, barring a handful of people, I thought it prudent to ask whether we're compromised…or you're gifted."

Belina grinned. "Natalie might use that word to describe me. She knew I was coming."

I nodded confirmation. "She told Yas she would find me."

That wasn't enough for Cass. "So magick, then?"

"Witch magick, in fact," she replied, staring him down. "Jane

Lakeland sends her regards, by the way, Lady Damarand. She's been expecting a call from you for some time."

I winced with guilt. "I know. Things…kept getting in the way."

"What did I say about excuses?" Belina scolded. "She spent many days seeking out the information you requested. The least you could do is take it from her, to free her from that burden."

The information I requested.

About mating.

About how to break a mating bond.

I'd asked the witches for help untethering myself from Cass.

I hissed with regret when that little memory came back to me, attached to the many, *many* other unpleasant ones that had happened as a result of asking for that.

It had accidentally become the most important, life-altering question I'd ever asked.

Ghost was there a second later, with his hand on my shoulder and his brow furrowed with concern.

"I'm all right," I said.

But Cass's attention was on me too, and despite being Ghost's spitting image, he was harder to look at. Harder to lie to. Especially about that.

"Belina, I'll call her today. I promise."

In response, Belina pulled a strange sheet of silver paper from her pocket, barely larger than a picnic napkin, and held it flat in her palm.

"Yes, you will," she said. "Because the Witches Council can't wait any longer to speak with you. The European cohort have called a session tonight knowing I would be here with you to deliver this invitation. Will you accept it?"

I hesitated—more out of surprise and suddenness than reluctance—but she saw it.

"This is a rare offering, girl," Belina warned. "Once in a lifetime for most people. It's been years since another alter was invited."

"Y-Y-Yes, of course, I'll attend," I spat out before my accidental freeze could cause an international incident.

"Wonderful."

She snapped her fingers and the silver paper in her other hand began to move. Began to *fold*. Before our very eyes, it bent itself into…a moth. A tiny silver *moving* moth, glowing with witchspeak symbols across its wings.

"*Beautiful!*" escaped me like a prayer.

Belina grinned and walked the delicate creature to the nearest window, releasing it into the air without a second thought. It fluttered for a few moments on its brand-new wings before it sped away and disappeared, heading southeast.

"Jane will speak with you at the meeting," Belina said, turning back to us. "Midnight. We cannot be late."

"Right." I chuckled in fear.

Then Belina nodded at my neck. "If your man is done with his interrogation, perhaps I can prove my trustworthiness in other ways? That chain around your neck. Have you had an encounter with another witch recently?"

My hand rose to the choker Rav had collared me with.

"No?" I said honestly. "The Raven King put it on me."

Belina motioned to me, eyeing Cass. "May I approach?"

I quirked at that. "Why are you asking him? Ask me. Yes. Please. Help, if you can."

Belina's gaze darted between Cass and I again, and a small smile tipped up the edges of her lips. She murmured, "*Interesting*," and strutted forward, reaching for my neck.

I felt her nails skim the jet-black beads before she said the word, "*Interesting*," again, this time in a tone that was much darker.

"This is a *Ligatura Animæ*. A very ancient witch's tool. We call it a soulchoke today."

"Okay. What is it?"

"It's what it sounds like. It's a tool of suppression of something spiritual."

I opened my mouth to tell her everything, but stopped myself, remembering what Cass had asked of me—I couldn't tell anyone else about my beastliness yet.

"I can't talk to my animal. She can't reenter my body either."

Belina hummed at that, still examining it. "This is…bad. Very bad."

Maybe I was just used to terrible news at that point and it barely fazed me, or I had just enough faith in her to believe she'd get me out of it somehow, but Cass took those five words *way* worse than I did.

He was there behind me instantly. His hands landed on my waist, and through them, I could feel his heartbeat *raging*. Then he raised one hand to my hair, pulling it tenderly out of the way to…give Belina better access to my neck, I guessed?

"Anything you need to get it off her, we'll do it," he swore quietly. "Anything. Magick or otherwise, ask it of me—*us*. Say the word and

I'll hunt the king down and deliver him to your feet myself."

Belina and I opened our mouths in surprise, I thought, but Cass continued.

"Or there's a ritual place I've found only a few miles away. I can pour myself into it. If a sacrifice is required, or additional magick, I have copies of myself to spare. Pieces I hardly need."

The words burst from his mouth like a flash flood. Ghost "spoke" in his own way, nodding emphatically with everything Cass said, as if he too would sacrifice himself at the plinth of my freedom without hesitation.

And I peered up at them both from below, struck silent with…some emotion that took my breath away. Before Cass's alteration, his eyes had gone completely black when emotions overtook him; after, that strange bodily response seemed to have mellowed. The whites were still white, but the silver was almost as dark as the stones around my neck. And his brow? His beautiful brow was bent so sternly, it twisted a hook in my gut and pulled. He looked ready to go to war.

"Supplies. Herbs. A cauldron. I could have them here tonight if—"

"Easy. Easy, *guardiano,*" Belina whispered soothingly, cutting him off. "It is not dangerous for her beyond its purpose, okay?"

"You're quite sure?" Cass asked, bringing his hands back to my waist.

"Oh yes. So long as we don't try to cut it off, she will be fine," Belina assured him, her voice soft and slow.

But considering how hard I'd tried to yank the thing off back at Rav's castle, I couldn't help asking, "What would happen if we did?"

Belina glanced at Cass, then at me, and waffled, "Let's not attract the evil eye, okay?"

Cass's grip on me intensified suddenly and I glanced up again to find fire in his gaze and that need again that made me want to comfort him.

Belina added quickly, "I simply meant the Raven King should not have the ability to create such a thing. This is stolen magick. You see here? Where there should be witchspeak symbols carved into the stones, there are runes. He's made the spell his own."

She manually tilted my head to show him.

"The witches will want to know about it. They'll demand an investigation."

"On their heads be it," Cass said, pushing on, "In the meantime, how do we free her?"

"I don't know the north runes," she said, shrugging. "There might be witches there tonight who do. We'll ask them."

"But—"

"I'm okay, Cass," I whispered, reaching for his hands. Covering them with my own seemed to settle him a little. "Belina will help."

Cass stared at me for another long beat, as I felt his heart settle and his chest calm. Then all at once, his eyes shut tightly and he pulled away, robbing me of his touch again.

"Apologies, I don't know what came over me," he said. "Make a list of supplies you need and we'll see you sorted. For now, we have rooms for you. Hot coffee. Sweaters if you didn't bring any."

"That is very accommodating of you, but, if it's all right, I brought my own rooms with me."

***

Belina was a force of nature. I'd known that since the first night we met in Italy. So I wasn't surprised when she walked us outside again, took a right, gathering curious followers like the Pied Piper, and headed to the far end of the concrete path, away from the other houses, where she picked a flat empty clearing in the woods and claimed it for herself.

What *did* surprise me were the rooms she'd brought with her.

From her witch's bag, she pulled…the tiniest miniature of a cottage I'd ever seen. Small as a walnut, detailed to perfection—it looked like a dollhouse you might put in a dollhouse.

With a barked, "Everybody stand back," she set the tiny thing in the center of the clearing and…snapped her fingers, leaving us all to *marvel* at her magick as the cottage began to stretch and fatten. It grew and grew until eaves popped from the rounded building and the roof groaned and chittered as shingles clattered into place. Until the foundation, which was split and jagged, did an incredible thing, reaching outward like fingers before plunging into the soil like roots, cementing it to the earth. I doubted a great quake could move it.

Just for the flex, I think, smoke began to billow from the chimney and the lights inside snapped on, inviting and *established.* As if the town had encroached on her land, not the other way around.

I was tempted to ask Belina if she really needed my mom's greenhouse at all—surely, she must have brought one with her in her magick bag—but just as quickly I let the temptation pass. She welcomed everyone who'd come to watch in for coffee, but left the front door open. She offered to make cough syrup for a sick guard, then made it in front of him, explaining each herb as she put it in the small pot on the stove, while she chatted with everyone. She pulled my mom over to her apothecary cabinet full of exotic seeds and offered to grow anything she wanted.

And everywhere I looked—in little spell jars on her shelves, in paintings on the walls, and in her grimoire, which sat on its own podium in a little vestibule—a particular turn of phrase kept jumping out at me. So many of her spells ended with the line: *an it harm none, so mote it be.*

Hell, the fact that she let me peruse her book of spells at all?

She was endearing herself to us. These were her bids for connection. Her ways of showing us that she meant no harm.

I wondered if it was in a witch's nature to be so inviting…or if these were protective measures. Cass had told me this world had an unfortunate history of fearing things unknown. I wondered if this was her way—befriending before fears could spread.

And then I wondered if this was why she'd come, to lay the groundwork for my team to trust others like her.

To protect her people.

To prevent them from being *othered* again.

To ensure the witches found their fair place in this bold new world I wanted to build.

Let's just say I got the message loud and clear.

Especially when I peered through one of Belina's windows and saw my entire team, save Scarlett, standing out on Belina's front lawn, talking quietly between each other while the impromptu housewarming party raged on.

I took a deep breath before I stepped out to join them, prepared for anything. And I accepted the spot Yas and Ghost opened for me as Fern finished whatever she was saying with "…Midnight doesn't leave us much time."

"Much time for what?" I asked.

"To debate whether to let the witches join us moving forward," Cass said.

"Surely, that's their decision," I said. "They might not want to reveal themselves."

"Assume they do," Fern said. "They can do that with or without us. But only you can decide whether to let them fend for themselves or have them as your allies."

I opened my mouth to speak, but Yasmina cut me off before I could.

"It's no easy decision, my lady. If they become our allies, they become our responsibility. To champion in times of joy…and to defend in times of trouble. The word 'witch' comes with a lot of baggage."

I opened my mouth to say I knew that when Corby interjected this time, "There's a reason witches live in the shadows with us. Some cultures are cooler with brujas than others. There are still places in this world where suspected witches are put to death, evidence or no."

"Sounds like a reason to help them, not abandon them," I said, but they pushed on.

"Alters don't have that reputation yet," Yas added. "Throwing our lot in with them will risk fanning the same fears. They might see us the same way before we have a chance to prove otherwise."

"It will be challenging enough to safeguard our rights, before demanding the rights of others as well," Fern said. "And we know nothing of witches. There are parts of their culture we'll *never* know, which they will hide no matter what. You will be declaring our collective loyalty to a group of people you can never be sure will be loyal to you, if you're in danger and need help."

"Not to mention the history," Cass added. "There have always been rumors about why the witches and alters stopped working together centuries ago."

I waited to see if they had more to say before speaking, but when I did, it was Cass's contribution I latched on to first.

"History's rumors are against you and me too," I told him.

Cass's eyes widened in surprise. "No one knows that. The witches, on the other hand? Every culture has an opinion about them."

"Probably wrong opinions," I pointed out.

No one had a response to that. And I…felt a heavy sadness tug on my heart. Belina had come here in good faith; she was trying to bridge a gulf between our two people that had existed for centuries. That was as dangerous as it was brave.

I thought of Idalia, too. Since coming to Loch na Feàirn and reuniting with Jasiri, she'd dangerously and bravely decided to walk tall beside him despite the wayward glances from my soldiers and the other alters who knew they were breaking Rav's most powerful law being together. I'd noticed that during each public display of affection, the others were all watching me, mirroring their reaction off mine.

Including Brodie, who had watched me not-react to Idalia and Jasiri and then woken up the next day with the courage to ask Rawan to teach him better underwater breathing techniques "for water defense and combat purposes."

But it was another memory that really asserted itself in that moment.

I thought of the run-in Jonesy and I had under the Domus Aurea in Rome. The cultist had called Idalia's hybrid spiderlady a monster. He had spat the word at her like a slur, despite being part of a collective full of hybrids.

For some reason I'd probably never know, that man had believed himself better than her. Different enough that it was okay he didn't treat her as someone worthy of respect.

That's…how it started.

Small things like that built up over time.

Small erasures.

Small dismissals.

Small indifferences.

They'd called me a monster too, when I transformed into a spiderlady to save myself and Fern at the Battle of Arachne's Revenge. They'd fired so many silver bullets at me, I'd had to drag my tattered wings behind me across the foothills of the alps like destroyed Kevlar. Without them, I wouldn't have survived at all.

Just like I wouldn't have survived without Rawan, another hybrid who'd put herself in harm's way for me in Alexandria.

I'd been silent only a few moments as those thoughts marched themselves neatly through my head before Cass asked quietly, "Any thoughts, my lady?"

I had too many.

With a deep breath, I glanced at Fern. "A messy table is better than a half-empty one. And we aren't worthy of anything if we'd sell out other people's rights to secure our own."

Fern's mouth popped open with a, "But we'd have to defend them—"

I shook my head. "Then we defend them, and we hope they defend us. And if they don't, we readjust then. We don't preemptively assume they won't…otherwise they have every right to assume the same of us."

"They're different," Yas began.

I shook my head again. "We're all different. Different doesn't mean harmful."

"But they might be," Corby countered.

"They might be, I might be," I said. "We don't accept them blindly. We all meet with them tonight in good faith. We listen to their words and judge their actions. Go back in there and look through her grimoire.

Every single spell ends with the line *an it harm none, so mote it be*. Every. Single. One. We owe them an open mind. Especially since we're asking for that ourselves."

"None of us can read Italian," Corby murmured.

I…didn't either. At least, I hadn't before. I wondered if this was another of Asterios's gifts I'd inherited after his death, not that this was the time to bring it up.

"You trust me that I read it, don't you?" I asked instead.

Everyone glanced between each other in concern…save Cass, whose snowflake attention scattered shivers through my body.

I couldn't help but ask him, "Would you still support me if I chose to work with them?"

The pride I could see on his face? More shivers.

"I would, my lady," he said, his bright moonlit eyes beaming.

"Would you?" I asked the others.

They hesitated, and I knew their nerves were getting the best of them. But I could also see Corby and Yas were waffling, watching Fern to see how she might sway. She was silent, stone-faced while her eyes swiveled, considering.

To her, I said, "It's not idealistic. It's necessary. It's fair. There's room at the table, Fern. At least for tea, right?"

She sighed at me for half a minute. "That's another cabinet seat. More, probably."

"A lot of potential allies too," I pointed out. "Powerful ones."

Corby and Yas nodded their reluctant willingness to run with me on this and I took it. It had to be enough for now.

Then I turned and walked back into the cottage, leaving them to gossip and fume and decompress without me, however they needed, knowing I'd see them all there again at midnight.

CHAPTER 17

Six minutes after sundown, Cass pulled me from another exhausting meeting and led Ghost and me down to the pier. The cargo ship had anchored offshore. The bright orange rescue boat we'd used to ferry my creatures to the ship had arrived at the pier to pick us up.

"We'll go get them and then tender just to the north so they can run into the woods there," Cass told me as we boarded. He eyed Ghost and added, "You can stay behind."

Ghost didn't and Cass didn't hide his frustration as we stepped inside the boat's cabin to stave off the wind. He took a seat apart from Ghost and I, almost pouting. It was funny, in a way, but it was more of what I didn't want. More distance that Ghost didn't seem to understand he was causing.

"You know, it's weird to watch you argue with yourself," I said, as generously as I could. Trying to keep any toney-tone out of my voice.

"I wouldn't have to if he'd just listen the first time," Cass replied, staring daggers…at himself.

"Why doesn't he? Why is he different from the others?"

Cass winced. His eyes darted in my direction, then to Ghost beside me, then away again. "It's a long story."

I made a point of separating myself from Ghost then. I stood up and joined Cass on his bench. Not touching him. Just open. Just nearby. Leaning in and giving him my full attention.

"I have time."

His breath blew out of him, but eventually, he spoke. "Natalie, that first night? So much happened. You know *a fraction* of it."

"I know you told me you didn't want this without me." I said it softly. I meant it as an offering, an opening.

Cass's eyes slammed shut, in pain.

And pain tore at my stomach. I regretted saying it *immediately*.

"I'm sorry."

"It's not you," he said, as if he genuinely believed it.

But clearly, it was me. He looked like he was in agony at the thought. His hands were trembling, and all I wanted to do was reach over and take them. But I couldn't. I was terrified he'd pull away.

"I didn't mean to hurt you. You know that, don't you?"

"I…do." He forced the words out. "But there was pain. A lot of it. I thought I'd lost you forever. I thought I was turning into a monster. I *did* turn into a monster. A nightmare. I saw the fear in Fern and Yasmina's eyes and then I saw my reflection and I thought I was…"

"Doomed?" I supplied.

He exhaled at the word and finally opened his eyes, nodding.

"Me too," I offered.

But again, pain shot across his face. He jumped to his feet as if he wished he could be anywhere else.

"Cass, you're not doomed," I almost barked. "You're not. You're just a different creature. I promise."

"I'm *not* a different creature," he countered, almost panicked. "I'm three creatures. I have three animals, Natalie. They combine when I alter but they're separate inside me. I'm a beast, of some kind."

"So am I," I said defensively. He already knew that.

But again, he shut his eyes. In pain? In disgust? Whatever it was, he still couldn't look at me.

"Beasts aren't what we've been told they are, Cass."

"I know you say that, but…"

"But what?"

From where I sat, Cass looked like a bomb about to detonate. His hackles were raised. His shoulders were shaking. And a growl, deep from within his chest, sounded with cavernous resonance. I knew if he turned around, his eyes would be black again.

Ghost rose from his seat, then, and laid a reassuring hand on Cass's shoulder.

It didn't calm him completely, but the shake became a simmer. And eventually, Cass found his way back to himself.

"I'm sorry. There's a lot to say. This may not be the best time for some of it, Natalie."

"Okay."

"I'll share what I can."

I nodded when he glanced my way.

"*A lot* happened that first night. It didn't happen the way I was told it would. It wasn't how everyone else had said it was. I wasn't a passenger. I was a part of the collective—my three creatures and me all in possession of my body. A wolf from my mother. A bear from my father…and a dragon, like you'd thought there might be.

"We hid ourselves away in the woods while I tried to make sense of it. While they tried to convince me that everything would be all right. But…I was so angry. So…*alone*."

That broke my heart to hear.

"You were never alone," I swore.

"Things ran from me," he murmured.

"Only because you were running," I rationed. "My raven stayed with you, didn't she? She wasn't afraid."

Cass nodded stiffly, admitting that one little thing.

"She was the one that reminded me to pray."

"Pray?"

He nodded. "I did. And when I did…She appeared."

A shiver ran through me as he said it. Relief came with it.

But he looked away again. "The Goddess…told me a lot of things. But eventually, she explained that the suffering I'd experienced was…unfair. Unfair but…special, she said. She swore I wasn't forsaken."

"You aren't!"

He didn't reply to that. "Eventually, she asked me what gift I wanted. I told her I wanted to be useful…to carry the burden and…make up for lost time. At that, a dark figure left my body and stood before me. It introduced itself to me."

"Ghost did?" I asked for clarity.

"Not exactly. She simply said it was an extension of me. I would make of it what I willed. So I did. Even that first night, my…ghost…did things I could never imagine. It went places even I couldn't go. Then, once I was human again and stopped trying to…"

He caught himself, but I knew what he was going to say already. Fern and Yasmina had told me he tried to hurt himself after that night.

"Once I'd gotten my impulses under control, I started experimenting. I came to understand that these copies *are* me, but only what I give of myself. I decide what they are, what they can do. If I need them to speak, if I need them to think. It's an exercise in existential control."

"And Ghost?" I asked, drawing us back to that original thread.

Cass shrugged. "Let's just say I've learned not to make them when

I'm…emotional."

Emotional because I was in danger. Emotional because he was angry at me but still felt responsible for saving me.

"Ghost is special," I offered.

"Ghost is a pain in my arse," Cass confirmed.

"Then, why don't you just reabsorb him already?" I asked, just to see if he would tell me the truth.

He didn't answer. He kept his mouth shut as his eyes swiveled, trying to talk around what he so clearly wanted to lie about.

It was torture watching him try to hide from me.

And when I couldn't take it anymore, I shifted the conversation myself, "What about the one that died at Rav's wedding?"

"*Rav's* wedding?" Cass asked.

My eyebrow rose and I held his gaze as I said, "It certainly wasn't mine."

Cass hummed at that.

"Did that copy pretend to die and then come back to you later?" I asked.

"That was the plan. Didn't work out that way."

"What do you mean?"

He opened his mouth to tell me, but the driver of the boat drew our attention away, and his answer was lost as we navigated the cargo ship to the hold, where another one of Cass's copies was standing guard. We did what we had to do to pull focus so my creatures could climb into the orange boat without being seen by the crew, and then we reboarded the spiritually crowded boat silently. Ghost took the wheel and veered us away to the coast, as Cass and I ducked inside to keep warm.

There was no room. None. Just because my creatures were bubble forms of their animal namesakes…it didn't mean they didn't take up space. Especially like this, unable to reenter my body. I'd never actually *felt* them before. They'd always just gone in and out of my body like breaths of air or splashes of water. There, they buzzed against my skin like energy incarnate.

They filled the confined space on that boat almost to bursting. My aurochs, dragon, and bear were pressed shoulder to shoulder, awkwardly wrapped around each other so my aurochs's horns wouldn't peek through the hull. The others were crammed in everywhere else, leaving only a tiny bit of space, a foot or two for Cass and I to stand in.

It was better than the biting wind.

And I didn't mind being this close to Cass. I stood with my back pressed to the wall, and he stood in front of me, sort of sheltering me from the press of my creatures, with his hand against the wall beside my head, to keep him from crushing me.

"Sorry," he said after a while.

"Why are you sorry?"

"I just realized I could have done this myself. There was no need to trap you in here like this."

"I wanted to come," I said softly.

But that answer made him uncomfortable.

So I turned us back to that incomplete conversation from earlier. "You were saying before, about your copy at the wedding?"

"Uh. It…died."

He said it so bluntly, I quirked in confusion.

"What do you mean it died?"

"That part of me. I think the silver bullet did something to it. I felt the shot. I felt the disconnection. Later, when I went to dig up what they buried, I found a body there. My body. I tried taking out the bullet, but that didn't change anything. It was simply…dead."

I felt my mouth drop open without my permission.

"Cass…"

"It was only a small part. Nothing important was lost."

"Nothing important was lost? *Nothing important*?"

"The other pieces of me got away just fine. Ghost attached himself to you. It was worth the sacrifice."

But…that was his rational side speaking; I could see that plainly on his face. Something *had* been lost. That version of Cass had been able to speak. To me. To Rav. It had smelled of him. It had shared some part of his magnetic tug.

He'd made it in his likeness.

"You sent yourself."

"I was too slow, so my copies attached to your raven. She flew like the wind."

"But you sent yourself," I pushed. "You wanted to save me."

His gaze snapped to mine, almost in offense. "Of course I did. I *hated* that I'd pushed you at him. I *hated* that I'd made so many mistakes with you. I *hated* that I couldn't be there when you needed me most."

"You *were* there for me," I tried to assure him.

He scoffed, almost to himself. "I failed you so many times. I shouldn't have taken you to the Raven Court. I shouldn't have turned down the offer to become a dragon with you. I regret wasting so much time being the bigger man when I was only ever your man."

Oh Cass.

My breath burst out of me at gale force, as if he had sucker-punched me. My body heaved with release, with joy, with hope. *My man.* I couldn't properly qualify how right those two words sounded to every part of me.

There were so many things I wanted to tell him. So many apologies I wanted to make too. When we got to shore, we could stand there all night in the freezing chill, hashing this twisted thing out between us until we found our way back to each other again. I wanted that. More than anything.

This felt like an opening.

This felt like a breakthrough.

Until he suddenly groaned, "This is killing me."

Annnd…all at once it felt like a nightmare.

Those four words caught me so off guard. What he'd said before had set my heart soaring…and those four little words cut it right out of my chest.

"What is?" I asked.

"Being here with you like this. Altering changed me in more ways than just my form. My dragon thinks of nothing and no one else…but you. At all times. Like I have no mind of my own anymore."

I took an accidental step back, which was no easy feat considering how little space there was, but the motion? Cass latched onto it with a hyperfocus that set his heartbeat raging again. And I knew that because I could literally see the *beatbeatbeat* along the curve of his neck.

His eyes darkened.

He took a step toward me too, until I was staring straight up at him, *wishing* he looked excited by the sudden closeness. Instead, he looked burdened by it.

"And my wolf? He *yearns* for you. He howls incessantly hoping you'll answer the call. Hoping you'll admit your mistake and come back to me. And he mourns knowing you can't hear him."

I opened my mouth to tell him that *every part of me* wanted to answer that call, but he spoke before I could.

"But you ran from me at Versailles. You *consumed* some essential part and abandoned me and even though I know you did it for me, you still chose him and this new version of me can't rationalize it like I could before. I *understand* why you didn't stay with me, but what does that matter when the wound of betrayal is still bleeding?"

Abandoned me. Still chose him. Betrayal. Those words lashed shame through my entire body.

I could feel my heart breaking.

It was breaking.

"I'm so sorry, Cass."

He was suddenly closer, pressing his forehead to mine. "I'm the one who should be sorry. But if I told you why, you'd never forgive me."

"Try me," I begged quietly.

I waited. I stood there in the silence feeling my heart shred itself, waiting for him to speak.

But he didn't. I watched him fight with himself, watched his mouth open and close exactly the way Rav's had done that night in Hamingja when I'd asked him to be honest and he'd chosen to stonewall me instead.

I knew Cass wouldn't attempt to sedate me or anything. I knew this night wouldn't end the way that one had.

But the same frustration roiled in me, bringing with it a new revelation that was bigger than either of us.

"You know, the whole time I was on the run, I felt really guilty for yelling at you over the phone in London. I felt awful that the last words I'd said to you before you died were so angry. I felt guilty for...other mistakes too..."

I gulped, admitting, "Like choosing Rav."

Cass tore his gaze away from me, his expression resentful and angry, but I reached for him. I cupped his cheek and forced him to look at me again.

"Yes, I chose him for a little while. I'm sorry about that. I chose him because everyone—including you—was telling me how incredible soulmated love was and I saw Giselle and Aldric's bond and wanted that for myself. I chose him because I was scared that if true love was possible and I could only have it with one person, I might miss out if I didn't claim it with my whole heart.

"But since the beginning, *I've been working with the information I had.* I made choices based on what I knew, what I was *allowed* to know at any given time, and look at how that turned out. Aside from your alteration, which I already explained had to be kept from you, everything else is a chance to share with me, Cass. I can't know everything, but if you keep things from me, why are you surprised that you don't like the decisions I make? How can you hold it against me if I make the wrong ones?"

"I'm not angry at you. Not exactly."

I ignored that. "Rav hid from me, now you're hiding from me. Everyone and everything in this alter world *hides*."

Cass's brow furrowed. "We've had to."

"Yeah, but *that* is our true second nature. The 'turning into animals' thing? That's a cool fringe benefit! It's awesome! I'd be surprised if half the world doesn't sign up to alter before the year is up.

"The secretive thing is the problem. We feel unsafe, so we hide. But in doing that, we tamp down the best parts of us. We don't show up correctly. It makes us inauthentic. We can't be ourselves. We can't be free. Again, if it were *only* for protection, I could almost understand it. But it's not. Because we're not safe even when we hide. No, it infiltrates every other part of our lives, until we can't show up correctly even for people we should be able to trust!"

The moment the words left my mouth, I felt like a coward and a hypocrite...because as much as I meant what I said, I also knew I was hiding from him too. I knew it felt safer to hide the fact that I was already mated to him than risk the possibility of his rejection if I told him.

But I also couldn't risk him embracing our mating bond while still hiding from me.

That would ruin any chance we had of something good.

It would.

I reached for his hand. Interlaced my fingers in his.

"Tell me your truth, and I'll tell you mine. Tell me, so I can carry it with you."

Cass sighed with his whole soul, shaking his head.

"I choose you," I told him.

"For now..."

"I *choose you*, Cass."

"I can't live like before. I can't have you for a moment and lose you again. I won't survive it."

"And I can't promise myself to someone who hides from me. *So don't. Please* don't hide. You know you can trust me."

Again, his mouth opened and shut so stupidly.

And whatever courage I might have had gave out on me. I had to leave. It hurt too much to stay. I couldn't be in there another moment with him. Or with my raven, who I knew was yelling at me even if I couldn't hear her.

The biting wind would hurt less.

So, I moved past him and reached the door to the boat deck as fast as

I could. And before I stepped out, I made him a promise.

"Don't worry. I-I'll fix it. You won't have to feel like this for much longer."

CHAPTER 18

Sour with frustration wasn't *exactly* the best headspace to walk into a witches' coven meeting in, but it kept me focused. It kept me clear. And what I'd said to Cass was a good jumping off point for whatever might happen in this meeting.

After all, I meant what I said. We hid to feel safe—but there was no more hiding. For the alters, at least.

It was time to find out whether the witches were ready to step into the light too.

Five minutes to midnight, I knocked on Belina's front door. Yas, Fern, Corby, and Scar were with me, so I wouldn't have to repeat whatever I heard to my team. Ghost was there with me too. Cass's silver blur arrived a few seconds later, but I didn't turn to welcome him, and I ignored the snowflake attention that dappled my head.

I didn't need the distraction.

Or rather, I preferred to alchemize it to my benefit.

Fern had warned me that silence wouldn't protect me. And both Cass and Rav were walking examples of how much harm silence could do. They were warnings—proof that hiding can betray you, no matter how long you cling to it for safety.

I knew I had my own work to do in that department but…

Eventually—probably far sooner than I would like—people would find out about my beastliness. That was inevitable. And that didn't scare me like it maybe should have. The fear of being seen was being overtaken by the fear of being defined by someone else. More and more, I was coming to terms with that version of myself I could see in the future, living my life out in the open. I loved her. I wanted to meet her. To build a world for her to stand in proudly.

So when Belina called out, "The door's open!" I twisted the knob and led my team in, ready to fight for her. For anyone who wanted that for themselves.

Belina seemed to sense that resolve in me. She eyed me, then her gaze diverted Cass's way, and for a moment I wondered if she could read minds. She didn't tell me either way. Instead, she shifted, wrapping one of her arms around me in welcome.

"Lady Damarand," she said. "Your light is stunning tonight. Thank you for coming on time."

"Thank you for setting this up. I hope it's okay that I didn't come alone."

She eyed me with a teasing glint. "Eh, my sistren know that where one walks, the shadow follows."

She led me to a far interior wall that…stood out from the others. Where all the other walls in the cottage were crowded with drying herbs and photographs and certificates and shelves of strange objects I figured were witch shinies…only this wall was bare.

Well, nearly bare. There, right at the center, was a stone. A thick square of slate, no more than a foot wide and long, had been affixed to the old, faded wildflower wallpaper behind it.

Belina guided me to a spot on the floor, maneuvering me into position.

"Right there in front of the viewing stone." Then she hummed and squeaked, eyeing me with concern. "So young. My Goddess. It's fine. Just be yourself. Be the…most mature version of yourself."

My lips twisted in amusement. I doubted it would be the last time someone snap-adjusted their encouragement for me. I let it roll off my back like rain.

But my team was quick with their responses.

Corby murmured something in Spanish under his breath I hoped she couldn't understand.

Scarlett yelped, "She's so mature!"

"She has held her own this far," Yas chastised.

"You called this meeting," Fern echoed. "They either respect her or they don't."

Cass didn't speak, but Ghost gripped my shoulder in solidarity for a moment before stepping back.

I nodded at Belina. "I'm ready."

It was all the reassurance I could fit into the moment, but I hadn't had enough time to overthink this. This wasn't my meeting, after all. It was theirs. All I had to do was listen.

That, and remember who I was.

"Ope, they're here."

Belina stepped into position beside me and gestured with her head toward the wall as the slab of slate started to shake…and then divide. Layers of stone slid sideways across the wall one by one by one until a grid took form and the stones began to glow. The dark grey gave way to blue to smoke to glass, until I was suddenly peering into dozens of different spaces, greeted by dozens of new faces, and a handful I recognized.

I almost chuckled.

I didn't; I showed that much restraint.

But…it was a video call. A magickal video call. It was amazing, don't get me wrong, but…we held half a dozen of those each day using good old-fashioned wifi. Hell, this tiny village on the ragged edge of nowhere was connected to the web through underwater fiber cables; the connection was faster there than what I'd had in Rome.

Not that I was going to bring that up.

No, I focused on the people. There were more women than men, and they all shared some natural quality to them—some frizz, some tassels, a wayward curl or two—but those were the only patterns I could glean. Some were older, some were very young. Some wore suits, others overalls. One had a giant chameleon perched on her shoulder. Another, a cat. And yet another was standing at a stove, holding his baby in his arms while stirring something.

And there in the middle of them, I spotted Jane Lakeland with her floor-length mass of gray hair and Fiadh Clarke, with her wild strawberry blonde mane and giant glasses, along with the other three witches I'd met in Ireland—the ones that made up the Eighth Kingdom's contribution to the Witches Council.

But right at the center, was the leader. I knew without being told. She was older, with dark hair, dark eyes, and medium olive skin. She was also less impressed, gawking at me less openly than the rest. She also seemed to be in an *actual* courtroom, if the set dressing around her and her outfit was anything to go off.

With an accent I thought sounded Swiss-German, mixed with something more eastern, she said, "Mage Saldo, thank you for arranging this. Lady Damarand, I'm High Priestess Tiamat, the principal guardian of the European Witches Council."

"Thank you for having me," I said.

"We've heard a great deal about you, from Belina, from Jane and

Fiadh. And from others, who we don't hold in such high regard at the moment. Your story precedes you."

Fern's words came back to me as I replied, "Not my story. Someone else's version of it."

A flutter of noise ran across the slates at my response. Everywhere I looked, the witches were wide-eyed, almost cooing with delighted gasps or surprised giggles.

I glanced at Belina; she looked almost proud.

Tiamat did not. She wore as impenetrable a mask as Rav preferred to wear.

"Did I say something wrong?" I asked.

"On the contrary," Tiamat said. "The Goddess told us you might speak those words. It's a good sign for us, for this meeting. Considering you've become the face of the end of the Great Secret. The entire world is waiting for you to reveal yourself and begin this open global discourse on shapeshifters, which naturally puts *our* Great Secret at risk."

The lightness of moments before darkened instantly.

"You understand that secret doesn't just belong to the alters. Certainly not a child who's been one for all of a year."

Belina took a hesitant step forward in surprise. "High Priestess..."

Tiamat ignored her and stared straight at me. "No one reached out to us. No one asked us if we wished to make ourselves known. No one bothered to ask how many of our kind died at the hands of the humans the last time witches became the boogeymen of the day."

I waited a moment before I quietly replied, "No one asked me either before revealing the Great Secret."

Another wave of reaction rippled across the slates.

"And yet, you've been named Arch-Sovereign of all of this," Tiamat said.

I countered quickly. "Without my consent."

But Tiamat pushed. "If you were anyone else, you'd already be dead. Your own laws forbid the breaking of the Great Secret. And yet you are still alive. I simply wish to understand why. Is it because you are the Raven King's mate or something else? Last I heard, you two were set to wed soon."

I opened my mouth to respond instantly...and stopped myself.

There was a *niggling* pain suddenly in the back of my throat, and in my neck at the base. A streak of explosive shock that hit me the moment I remembered...*Rav's promise.*

I'd promised to marry him.

I'd bound myself to him accidentally.

Let's call it what it really was—*a trick.* Rav had tricked me into making a potentially life-ending promise to marry him. My body had reminded me, and the surge of gratitude then was indescribable.

But…I thought there might be a loophole for this moment. I hadn't promised to mate with him, only marry him—

My throat tightened, warning me. The magick didn't like defiance.

Still, I could thread the needle.

I drew a slow breath, tasting the edge of the spell in the back of my throat, and said, "I never promised to be his mate. But yes, he wants the position I've been given."

That answer seemed to surprise them.

Even more when Belina stepped up to defend me. "He is no friend to her, High Priestess. The king put a soulchoke on her."

And I realized why he'd put this thing on me—because he'd made a promise with *me* he couldn't break. He'd promised not to use magick to sedate or incapacitate me. He'd found some technicality to work with.

Smart.

Vile.

Belina motioned me forward, to display the choker around my neck. Again, like a little wave, the witches across the slates moved to get a closer look at it. This time, the ripple of noise from them was graveled, more worried.

Little snippets broke through— "trespass…" and "forbidden…" and "there must be a reckoning."

"Dark days," escaped Tiamat like a swear. After a moment, she asked, "How did you escape?"

"I used azurite to free my raven. She found my friends, and my friends found me."

"She is clever," Belina offered. "And her people are loyal. They believe in her. I think we should too. Especially now that she's seeking to free herself from her hellmate."

This time, the ripple of reaction was on our side of the slate.

That word, *hellmate.*

It tickled some memory just out of reach. She'd said something like that to me before, but not in any sticking way.

I glanced back at my friends. Everyone save Cass was huddled, discussing. Meanwhile he stood aside to himself, clearly talking to Ghost. Ghost was arguing some point silently that Cass didn't seem to want to hear.

Before I could ask, Belina continued, "Jane, you're helping with that, I believe?"

Jane stepped forward, and eyes across the slates gave her their attention.

"Yes, I am," she said. "Lady Damarand has recovered several grimoires for us at this point and asked very little in return. Just a bit of help with the soul bond."

"What about it?" Tiamat asked.

"She knows ravens and witches have history together. She asked for our records on how to break a mating bond, and I gathered them for her. Brought them with me tonight."

At that, she held up a strange looking…journal…made of wood and pressed felt and leaves and flowers.

I didn't know what she thought she was going to do with it, but I could sense Jane was waiting for some permission from Tiamat. When it didn't come, Jane tucked the journal back out of sight.

Tiamat turned her steely gaze back on us.

"Mage Saldo, why haven't you removed the choker yet?"

"The king's used runes to set it," Belina said. "A *seiðr* witch is needed."

At that, Tiamat's shoulders seemed to drop. The tension in them eased, as if something significant had fallen into place for her.

"Let us have an exchange then, Lady Damarand," she said. "We'll remove the soulchoke and keep it for our own examination, and in return, Keeper Lakeland will give you the information you requested."

I took a moment to respond. She wanted evenness between us. She wanted fairness. Trust. This was an easy way to set us on an even playing field, sort of the way Tidebringer Rawan had done it by giving me a shell for a shell. Why she thought giving up the soulchoke would be some sort of sacrifice for me, I didn't know, but it felt like an easy one to make. And perhaps the easiness of it *was* the point. This was another bid for connection.

"Agreed," I offered.

"I summon Freyja."

The name left Tiamat's mouth as an exhale, a chant. And as we watched, the slates began to shift, making room as Tiamat's slate split into two. The new slate's color lightened to glass, and there in the glow, a figure appeared. A waifish woman wearing antlers on her head.

We were looking at her from below. From the ground, as if that's where she'd laid the slate. Her green eyes shot to us in confusion. She snapped her fingers, and her slate seemed to lift off the ground, rising until it was level with her face, until we could see she was standing by a fire, on the edge of a frozen lake, draped in furs.

She was also painted from head to toe in long lines of white, brown, and blue. Her tangle of ice-white hair was wrapped in the antlers so tightly I doubted she could ever remove them.

Freyja was a wild spirit if I'd ever seen one. And I knew before I heard her gasp with excitement, that Scarlett *loved* the sight of her.

Heck, so did I. From a single glance, I doubted I had ever been or would ever be that free in my life.

Her eyes flitted back and forth, as if taking in the faces of everyone she could see before her gaze settled. "*Blessed be, High Priestess.*"

"You as well, Freyja…we have need of you tonight. A soulchoke bound with runes."

At that, her green gaze snapped to mine. "*On an alter? We are helping them now?*"

I stepped forward and held my hair out of the way. "*I would be grateful, if you would.*"

Freyja gasped, yanking back like a wild animal, before a beautiful innocent grin split her face, "*How marvelous. A trickster who speaks my tongue. This one is an agent of change, yes? She will unravel the cosmic order, poor creature. A dangerous, but necessary change. I do not envy her.*"

Her words sent a shiver down my spine, riling discomfort in me. It squirmed in my belly; she was telling the truth, and not just because of my honesty gift.

"*Are you a seer?*" I couldn't help asking.

"*The Goddess has made me such,*" Freyja giggled. "*But do not fear; I keep what she shows me to myself. Your fate is safe with me…unless you offend me.*"

"*I thought the Goddess didn't give people glimpses of the future.*"

"*She does, but usually only if she wishes to change it. It takes a lot of courage to know what will happen and let it happen anyway.*"

I gulped at that, absorbing. That was a clever way of thinking about it. The Goddess had told me *to know the future was to change it*. Maybe she ensured that by only giving people glimpses of things they would want to change.

"*Will you help me?*" I asked after a moment.

She tilted her head a little. "*Must I, High Priestess?*"

"Please, Freyja."

"*Very well. Come closer.*"

I took a step.

"*Closer.*"

I took another tiny step, until I was only a few inches from her slate, and I felt like I was burning in the attention of hundreds of eyes on me.

"*Closer.*"

I took one last step. But at that, hands landed on my shoulders, holding me in place. I turned to find Cass and Ghost there, almost cementing me to the spot.

"That's quite enough," Cass warned Freyja.

Freyja's nose wrinkled in delight. "*Doesn't the twin flame know he should cast no shadow?*"

"*What does that mean?*" I asked.

But Belina was there a second later. "It doesn't matter. Freyja, the soulchoke, please."

I…suddenly understood why the slates were so special, and I took back my silent joke from earlier about the village wifi being better.

Because Freyja's hand pierced the slate and appeared right there in front of me, reaching through to touch the choker around my neck. It wasn't an illusion. Her skin was soft as her fingers slid across my throat, across the stones. But I could feel the roughness of something ancient on her fingertips, and tiny bits of dirt falling away as she scraped her nails against the beads.

Her eyes grew milky and her voice rasped. "*This is polluted witch magick. Some kind I've never felt before. Powerful. Misused. The runes…they're… He's used symbols for union and love. Symbols for fate and power and protection, both for her benefit and against her. A severing. He tried to sever some part of you he feared. Some part he thought you should fear too. But that is wrong. You should not fear yourself. You should not fear your own divinity. This is rotten love. Selfish love. I hate it. It is cruelty masquerading as care.*"

Everything she was saying was awful.

"*Just get it off!*"

Freyja's eyes snapped to mine, and the teasing in them was gone. Replaced by something colder, something wiser. Something that looked like empathy.

Her gaze returned to my neck, and she began to whisper something under her breath I couldn't make heads or tails of. The words wove together at breakneck pace, into a hum, a growl loosening.

But not on my neck. The faster she spoke, the surer I became that something was wrong.

A pinch tightened under her thumb.

"It's hurting," I said, but she didn't hear me.

The pinch became a bite became a shallowness of breath. A raging heart.

"It's tightening!" I said louder.

Belina only said, "Be patient. Let her work."

But the beads were against my throat. They were rubbing against one another, making a noise like glass against glass. Tighter. *Tighter*. Maybe they would break? Maybe they would shatter. But at that moment, they were pressing against my windpipe.

I…panicked.

"I can't breathe. I can't breathe!"

I reached for the choker…but there were already hands there.

Cass and Ghost. I felt their fingers against my throat, their knuckles pressing as they wedged their fingers into the tight chain. It was better than the beads, but only slightly. There was barely enough room for me to breathe.

Still, Freyja chanted.

I heard a moan. Felt something liquid down my neck.

"What is that? What's happening?"

"It's cutting," Cass hissed. "Hurry up!"

Freyja transcended words. Her voice rushed out of her like kettle scream, until my neck felt wetter and I heard Scarlett yell something behind me before there was a mighty *CRACK* like lightning.

The pressure on my neck released. I felt the choker loosen into the long string of beads it had been in Rav's hand before he forced it back onto me.

"Remove it! Now!" Freyja commanded.

And Cass ripped it off me moments before the choker tightened again, this time into a jumbled knot of beads, as if it was angry that it no longer had a neck to cling to.

"Take the bloody thing," Cass said, shoving it at Freyja.

Then he turned to me, closing the few inches between us, blocking out the rest of the room with his looming presence. He stared with a concern and focus so intense I couldn't look away from him. Not that I wanted to. My heart pounded in time with that intensity, luxuriated in it. Felt at home in his sincerity.

"Are you all right, heart?" he asked, his deep voice low and soft. "There are marks on your neck, but it didn't cut the skin, I promise."

"I-I'm fine," I answered honestly.

But his fingers were on my throat, massaging so gently, thrumming with that magnetic buzz under the skin I could feel all the way in my diaphragm. No, lower. And I realized, *fine* wasn't enough for him.

"I'm okay, I swear," I added for his benefit. "It feels wet, though?"

"That's…nothing."

Cass pulled away and staggered back awkwardly before attempting to hide his hand behind him. The motion was unignorable; my gaze snapped to his hand, which I realized was coated with bright red blood.

"Cass, you're bleeding."

He wasn't just bleeding. His fingers were cut all the way down the inner curves of them…as if the blasted choker had started slicing into him when he only had a knuckle wedged into the chain…and he only kept shoving his fingers deeper into it to keep the chain off my neck. Even the palm of his hand was cut and bleeding.

Ghost, too, had markings on his fingers, although he seemed confused by them rather than pained.

"Cass, can I help—"

"I'm all right," he said, pulling farther away. "I'll see to it with a bit of azurite later. In private.
Just finish the meeting, all right."

Belina offered him a rag to wrap his hands, but he seemed immoveable otherwise, motioning me back to the slates.

I turned to face the witches again, this time wiping Cass's blood off my throat.

"Thank you, Freyja," I said, finding her amid the other faces like a painting between photographs.

"*A trick for a trickster,*" she said in reply, holding up the knotted beads still glistening red with blood. "*This is the way of these things. To defeat your enemy, you must first master his games. I'll return to you once I understand what kind of game this is.*"

With that, her slate fell dark and she was gone.

"Wait, Freyja. Wait…" Tiamat huffed with frustration. "Belina, please follow up with her. Ensure she *actually* shares what she finds."

Belina nodded. "Of course, High Priestess."

"Jane, she may have your research now."

Just like with Freyja, Jane's hand pierced the slate on our side, holding that strange handmade journal, and I took it from her delicately; one drop would probably scatter its pieces permanently.

"Thank you, Jane."

"It's nothin', lady," she said, stepping back. "Been so long since most of us worked with ravens, t'was nice to revisit the old ways. I'm afraid those notes won't be enough for you, though."

"What do you mean?"

"Mating bonds are cosmic connections between two creatures. S'only natural you need to be near each other to undo one. I wouldn't recommend gettin' near your hellmate again. Not worth the risk of another soulchoke."

I nodded politely and thanked her again; there was no need for her to know it wasn't a bond with Rav that I was trying to sever. And the one I was already mated to was far closer than any of them knew.

Glancing Cass's way, I found his attention on the journal in my hand, his expression closed but curious. And I made the promise again, to myself privately, that if being near me was killing him, I'd free him of that burden.

After all, it wasn't his fault he felt that way. He didn't know why he was so drawn to me. He didn't know why he was in so much pain around me. Hell, I hadn't known why either until Rav's holy day had revealed that I'd accidentally mated with Cass long ago.

But…that was a problem for later. The meeting was still ongoing. So I held out the journal to my team, and Ghost was there to take it from me. That felt fitting, in a way.

Then I turned back to face the Witches Council again.

High Priestess Tiamat had been kind enough to wait for me, but when she had my attention, she wasted no time. "Now that that's done, the difficult conversation between our people can begin."

I nodded soberly. "Yes, it can."

"I sense that even if the title was forced on you, as you claim, that you *do* plan to take your place as Arch Sovereign?"

"I do." I took a deep breath and added, "We can't wait until it's safe to exist. Safety is an illusion. It's always been an illusion. We think that if we stay silent, we'll be safe. You know that's not true, and so do I. Only you can decide whether you're ready to reveal yourselves—like you said, that isn't my choice to make. But I also can't make the world forget alters exist. So, in the next few weeks, I'll be meeting with other alter courts and sovereigns before ultimately revealing myself to the world."

I gestured with my head to Fern. "One of my team recently warned that I risk letting other people define me if I don't define myself. And I don't trust anyone else to do that, so."

"Not even these Knights who claim to speak for you?"

"Not even them."

"That's a relief. I prefer not to speak with puppets…unless they are mine."

I met her soft smile with one of my own. "Well, I'm not one of those either. But I could be your friend. Your ally, if you would have me. And I would welcome a witch on my cabinet, whether you choose to reveal yourselves or not."

Tiamat's brow rose. "All of that and you know nothing of witches?"

"If you're willing to meet me as an equal, I'm willing to learn."

Tiamat smiled. "That is wonderful news, considering I'm here on behalf of the *entire* Global Witches Council, which has unanimously decided…to join your Great Revelation. It's about time we step into the light and secure a future on our own terms. Goddess knows, it would be easier to do together than apart."

I smiled. "I couldn't agree more."

CHAPTER 19

We stood in Belina's cottage until dawn brightened the windows, listening to Tiamat's introductory lesson on witch culture and history. Going over all the "baggage" Yasmina mentioned. It was what I imagined going on a blind first date with someone recently out of prison must be like, listening to the lore they clearly thought would scare me away from working with them.

I won't claim there weren't details that shocked me—especially when they showed me how certain single-word mistranslations in mainstream religious texts had led to *hundreds of years* of executions and persecutions for their people.

I won't say there weren't moments when I found myself wishing I could be a witch instead of an alter either.

But I walked away from that first meeting feeling more sonder than I knew what to do with, and a deep knowing that we'd barely scratched the surface of what the witches had been, were, and could be.

To me? They were…marvelous.

Strong. Savvy. Capable. Balanced between their hearts, minds, and spirits.

Terrifying, sure. But Idalia words from Fylgja Castle came back to me: "*I like things that scare me. There is always much to learn from them.*"

They were inspiring. Afterward, I, too, wished to be terrifying.

And among and between the shades of glory displayed across the various slates, in rooms across this continent, in bright eyes and brighter hearts, I could see…hope. Joy. Kindness. Gumption. Cooperation. Community.

The witches had something the alters did not—a shared nonjudgmentalness that radiated into how they spoke with each other, how they made space for each other's weirdnesses. They *assumed* from the get-go that they were all vastly different from one another. Being open-minded was the starting line, not something that they had to work at or grow into.

They didn't tolerate cruelty or excuse harm—and more than one used that phrase '*an it harm none*' as a sort of filler disclaimer when speaking to us—but otherwise, they were free to be entirely themselves.

And they extended that grace to my team too.

Throughout the evening, they made a point of asking everyone on our side at least one open-ended question and actively listened, just absorbing. Again, with an absence of judgment that was almost too much for my team to believe. It made Fern especially uncomfortable.

But it also set them all at ease the longer Tiamat's history lesson went on. Especially once Tiamat transitioned from her general historical overview to talking about the history between our two people. Again, she only scratched the surface—that's all we had time for—but she made a point of listing events, skirmishes, and outright fights that the others knew of, explaining the witches' versions of those historical accounts before giving my team time to ask questions about them. I think she was giving them homework. Things we could verify ourselves or which might lead us down research rabbit holes that taught us something.

It also helped that the witches never painted themselves as great heroes or completely helpless victims either. They took accountability for past mistakes and failures. And they were very up-front about what they wanted to see from working with us, what their political priorities were. Environmental safeguards, freedom to practice their religion, anti-discrimination protections—none were unreasonable, and all were in line with what we wanted too.

The only bump on my team's side was their final request. They made it clear they wanted more than a promise of loyalty from the alters this time. They wanted there to be real consequences if the alters betrayed or abandoned them in their time of need.

What that would actually look like? They said they'd get back to us.

But the fact that "we" (really me) were willing to entertain that possibility at all? Priceless.

I was just relieved when Tiamat asked Belina to become my Educational Liaison. It was a start. A bridge. A bid for connection I readily accepted.

So did Scarlett. *No one* walked away from that meeting happier than she did.

She had a dreamy skip in her step and awe-brightened eyes that made her look like she was made of light, babbling excitedly about details she wanted to know more about, "once Belina has time to talk to me."

No doubt, she'd have a thousand questions for me, too, when I found the right moment to tell her what I'd taken from her.

And I felt awful keeping my mouth shut, as I walked everyone back to town, given my talk with Cass on the boat about truth and the dangers of withholding.

I knew I was a big ba-gawking chicken. One ignoring the *intrusive voice of guilt* in my head that was loud enough to drown out my animals' running mental commentary that had started the moment I left Belina's cottage.

But I wanted to wait until Belina and I met in private for our first session, when I could ask her how to fix what I'd done to Scar. That way, when I went to Scarlett with the truth, I could offer her a big steaming Cup of Solutions alongside my Scone of Betrayal.

***

Instead of ripping that band-aid off, I ran. The moment I knew my friends were safely off to their rooms, I exited stage left and skedaddled into the woods like some mythological creature with seconds to find somewhere private before morphing back into a human.

I was gone so fast even Ghost couldn't catch up with me.

And once I was alone, I tuned back into the voices in my head that I hadn't heard since escaping Fylgja Castle. I beelined for that spot along the north shore where Cass and I had dropped my spirit animals off yesterday afternoon.

My creatures. My saviors. My friends.

Without Rav's choker around my neck, their cacophonous choir sang out in my head like brunch rush hour at a fancy restaurant.

Two were arguing.

Two were having a quiet discussion off to themselves.

The aurochs was humming pleasantly while rubbing his massive horn against a tree and scratching his butt against a bush simultaneously.

The dragon was horny.

The wolf was trying to hold back a howl.

But the noise stopped the moment I cut in with, "*Ah, I missed this.*"

All at once, they squawked out my name in relief and anger and annoyance, asking if I'd fixed whatever had kept us apart.

"*Where are you?*" my raven asked, her voice bursting forward when the others quieted.

"*I'm coming to you. Just a few more seconds, I'm almost there.*"

I expected rejoicing. I expected camaraderie. Heck, I expected a stampede of oversized ghost animals to crash into me—through me—on a direct line to their cozy cubbies to rest and leave the transportation up to me for a while.

Instead, they surprised me with, "*Cass with you?*"

"*No, he's back in town.*"

"*Get us. Go to him,*" my raven commanded.

"*Tell truth,*" my wolf echoed.

I snarked, pushing through some brush. "*What truth?*"

"*Mates!*" they all shouted at once, nearly giving me a migraine.

"*Whoa, chill! One at a time, please!*" I shouted back, clinging to a tree until my equilibrium stopped warbling.

"*Tell him,*" my wolf said again. "*No Jane book.*"

It took a moment to realize what she meant. "*You mean don't use the research Jane did for me? Don't break the bond?*"

"*Yes!*" they all shouted again.

This time, I swayed so suddenly, my stomach rose into my throat. "*Oh Goddess, I'm gonna be sick.*" Once my mouth stopped watering, I added, "*You heard him hide from me in the boat.*"

"*He loves you,*" my dragon countered, his voice like an alligator's guttural purr.

"*I know he does,*" I admitted. "*But love isn't enough. He's scared of being honest with me. Just like I told Rav, I won't mate with someone I can't trust.*"

"*Can trust,*" my raven scolded.

"*You know what I mean,*" I snapped back. "*Do* you *know what he's hiding?*"

The silence in response was deafening.

So I pushed on, both physically by flopping over a giant piece of driftwood, and emotionally. "*Besides, you heard him. I'm hurting him with my love.*"

But to that, my raven swore, "*Wrong.*"

"I named him my mate accidentally last year. It was an accident. Now he's suffering for it. If he were free, he could be happy."

This time, they all said it. "*Wrong!*"

"*Mate doesn't want freedom,*" the dragon growled. "*Mate scared not enough.*"

That shocked me. Anger coiled around my spine like a spitting cobra at the *suggestion* of that.

"*Cass is more than enough!*"

"*Tell him!*"

"*I have!*" How could I make them understand? "*Look, it can't just be me emotionally laying myself on the line. If he told me whatever truth he's hiding and it wasn't as horrible as he thinks it is, I would tell him everything. I would gamble my heart and risk him...*"

Ugh, my stomach rolled as the words bullied their way out of my mental mouth.

"*...I would risk him deciding he didn't want to keep the bond on his own.*"

"*Would never happen,*" my aurochs chimed in.

"*But...if he wanted to bond with me, for it to mean anything, he has to trust me with the truth. Not just the pretty parts. The painful parts too. I want Cass—Goddess, I want him—but only if I can have all of him. He has to* choose *to tell me himself, not out of fear of losing me but because he chooses to walk into this bond with his eyes, heart, and mouth wide open.*"

They didn't have anything to say to that. And when I finally reached the clearing where I'd left them, they re-entered my body in a relatively somber line, shooting me sad "puppy dog eyes" as they went. They also brought with them a whole range of emotions and needs and *urges*—mostly related to *that man* who I could tell was only a few hundred yards away down the coast—that nearly wiped me out again.

Those emotions shifted, though, as I turned around and began the walk back. My creatures were silent in a different way—in a *sneaky* way, as if they knew something I didn't.

Until I finally said, "*I...I'm not going to just snap the bond in half today or anything. I want to give him the chance to talk to me. I want to give him time to tell me everything. But I also like knowing I can end it for him, if I need to. That's all. That's what Jane's research is for.*"

But to that, my dragon chuckled. "*Too bad.*"

Those two little words made my skin crawl. "*What's too bad?*"

"*Nothing anymore.*"

I did *not* like that response either. I broke into a run.

"*What does that mean?*" I demanded. "*What does that mean?!*"

They didn't say…and my run became a *sprint*. Something was wrong. I could sense it. Then…I could see it. As I hit the far end of the concrete path, a commotion up ahead caught my eye. Right there on "Main Street," someone was fighting in front of everybody.

Two identical someones.

Hair of flame.

Eyes of moonlight.

Fighting on a bit of pavement, on the scattered, tattered remnants of Jane's research journal.

CHAPTER 20

Confetti. All of Jane's work was literal confetti blowing in the wind around two brawling bodies I knew better than my own.

I arrived in the circle of gawking onlookers just as Cass landed a left hook to Ghost's face that sent the apparition flailing back against—then through—the building wall behind him. Ghost reappeared a second later and drove the wind out of Cass with a hard kick to his stomach before pouncing on him and wrapping an elbow around Cass's throat.

But no sooner was Cass yanked back against Ghost's shoulder, he grabbed Ghost's ear and pried him off like some sort of parasite that really didn't want to let go.

Somehow before I'd arrived for the show, Cass had lost his coat. His shirt was torn. His eyebrow and lip were bleeding. His eyes were dark and…muddied with confusion.

Ghost looked…the same as always, save for the desperate and desperately determined look on his face. Every time Cass landed a blow, he took it. He took it like punishment. Physically, it obviously did nothing to him. Emotionally, he looked devastated. Devastated but relentless.

He was trying to wear Cass down.

I could see it plain as day.

Cass was putting up one helluva fight, brutal and precise, calling out, "Would you just *stop?!*" and "Enough of this!" which went completely ignored.

It wasn't enough for Ghost. He didn't stop either. He let Cass pummel him. Let Cass shove him back. Let him yank him away each time he managed to grab on…because he was waiting for Cass to drop. To founder.

But…

“Why are they doing this?” I asked Corby as Cass did his signature move, grabbing onto the scruff of Ghost’s neck before *hurling* him away fifty yards or more into the loch where he skipped across the surface like a stone before going under.

“Dunno,” Corby said. “They were doing that silent yelling thing and then…this.”

This was obviously absurd. Neither could win. They had to know that.

So why were they…?

In the few seconds of rest Cass got while Ghost waded out of the water, Cass’s exhausted gaze snapped to mine. Chest heaving. Eyes melancholic. He glanced my way with…longing and regret and anger.

Right before Ghost’s silver blur crashed into him, got him on the ground and began to…

Well, I suddenly understood why they were fighting.

Ghost pinned Cass to the ground and *jolted* toward him at a speed shy of fired bullet. A speed I wouldn’t have even been able to see, if Cass hadn’t caught his neck moments before Ghost’s face could crash into his.

“No!” Cass growled, tightening his grip around Ghost’s throat as Ghost just tried to push through it. “I said *no!*”

Ghost was…trying to force Cass to reabsorb him.

And Cass was desperately resisting.

My heart *leapt* with panic.

Before I knew it, I was shouting, “Stop! Stop it! Ghost! Stop!”

He heard me through the din of cheers and jeers and gossip from the soldiers and gathering guests. Ghost didn’t want to listen to me, but he heard me. So begrudgingly, he stopped pinning Cass to the ground.

And I rushed forward to help Cass up. Lent him my shoulder, wrapped my arm around his waist to keep him upright.

“Are you okay?”

“I’ll be fine, thank you,” Cass said, before he barked, “Show’s over. Back to bed, the lot of you.”

“Aw,” Jonesy moaned. “But this is better than telly.”

“Now.”

A choir of groans and grumbles filled the air, but they all slowly retreated…until it was just me, Cass, and his ghostly copy—both of whom looked like they were just taking a breather before going at it again.

In the lull, I stood there watching the last few tatters of felt and parchment of Jane's journal flutter away into the pebbles and waves, lost. And when they were gone, I turned to Ghost.

"What the *hell* were you thinking?"

I didn't care that he couldn't answer me. Cass commentated for the both of us as Ghost gestured futilely between us.

"That's *rubbish* and you know it!" Cass spat. "I told you I'd do it when I'm ready. Why isn't that enough for you?"

Again, Ghost gestured between him and me.

"If she wants to break the bond between her and the king, why on earth would I try to stop her?"

But Ghost frantically gestured to me this time before he dropped to his knees before me. Pressed his hands together, praying. No, he was begging. *Begging* me to…

"*He can't tell Cass I'm mated to him, can he?*" I asked my creatures.

"*No,*" my wolf replied, so lonesome. "*Can give memory of you saying it.*"

"Ghost, stop trying to force it!" I snapped. "You can't cheat this. You shouldn't want to. He has to choose it for himself!"

"Choose what?" Cass asked.

I ignored him. So did Ghost, as he suddenly jerked to his feet again and jolted toward Cass again, as if he was ready to go another round.

I stopped him. Pressed my hand to Ghost's chest. "You know I can just call Jane and get another copy of the journal, right? She's a smart woman. She didn't make just one."

I thought that tame threat would knock some sense into him, which it sort of did. Ghost gestured once more from me to Cass and then disappeared in a blur, headed somewhere else far away from us.

And I turned to my friend hoping I wouldn't see that look from the boat again—the one that suggested I was killing him. I didn't. I saw only exhausted curiosity, and a face that made me want to grab him by the cheeks and plant a long hungry kiss on him.

Goddess, he was gorgeous all sweaty like that. Especially radiating that bonfire scent.

Don't judge me for drooling a little; you would too if a beefy, caked-out Michaelangelo sculpture came to life in front of you.

But I remembered myself and said, "I'll talk to him when he's calmed down. I don't think he'll try that again."

"No, I'll handle him."

"Okay…Goodnight, Cass."

I turned to give him space, when he surprised me. "Would you want me to?"

"Want you to what?"

"Reabsorb him?" A cheeky smirk curved up half his face before he hissed and touched his split lip. "Seems an awful lot of guff to put me through for the memories of a fugitive...unless they're really, *really* good ones."

Despite all the teasing I'd done to him, it was my turn to be taken aback by the suggestion.

"Uh, well, you'd be disappointed there. He didn't actually try anything with me. I mean, don't get me wrong, when I thought the Goddess had gifted me your ghost, I absolutely thought about taking *full* advantage...but all he did was lick me."

Cass's eyebrows shot sky-high at that.

"Innocent!" I almost yelped. "Pl-Platonic licking. When I was crying one day."

Cass nodded, but fell cozily silent at that, gazing at me, then off to the loch, then back again.

I wanted...to touch him. Just to touch him.

"Does it really hurt you to be near me?"

His silver eyes locked with mine. "Yes...and no."

"What does that mean?"

"It's difficult to explain."

I risked it. "Do you...want to explain?"

"More than anything."

I took a tentative step closer. Then another. He didn't stop me. Not even when I was right there below him, back in that almost-space where millimeters divided us. Where I could suddenly feel the bellow of his chest where it barely grazed me again and again.

He could feel it too.

"Ugh, Goddess," he purred suddenly. "It's...complicated. Being away from you? Every part of me hates how it feels. But being near you?"

"Tell me what it feels like," I offered. "The physicality of it."

Cass blinked at me, considering. "The resentment is...like a brick pressing down on my heart. *That* I understand, but the rest of it? You know when your stomach is paining you and you think it's hunger, but it's not? It's thirst. It's anxiety. It's...something deeper. A need unfulfilled."

I nodded. And Cass followed the movement of my head like a bouncing ball. His tongue peeked out from between his teeth as if they were keeping the wayward organ at bay.

"I feel that too," I whispered. "All the time."

Cass murmured, "A craving," and I shivered.

We lingered in that quiet moment until…

His free hand rose, as if it had its own mind, and hovered there for a moment, almost dancing just above me before it swept forward and slid into my hair. The pads of his fingers struck like matches against my scalp. They reached the curve of the back of my skull and I felt his nails drag softly—

My eyes rolled back. They *rolled back into my head.* Little traitors. Totally without me.

I felt something touching my forehead suddenly and opened my eyes to find I had my head pressed to the center of his chest.

I jerked back. "I'm sorry."

But Cass wasn't sorry at all. He lingered, watching me with an intensity that made me shiver again.

Until he whispered, low and graveled, "I want to chase you, heart."

I winced. "But I'm already here."

He shook his head slowly, staring. "That's what the craving is. To satisfy my desire to unite with you once and for all. My human nature *craves* the connection I only have with you. The intimacy, the friendship, the love I still feel like a brand across my heart. But my animal nature? It wants to chase you. Capture you. Claim you. I want to make those woods our playground."

I…I almost took a step back just to see what he would do.

But the part of me that had been chased across the continent knew better. The chase was only fun when both parties consented to it.

"Tell me the truth, and you can," I told him.

His hand left my hair as he looked away and said, "It's not that easy—"

But I leapt at that. "I know. When you're ready, I'm ready. That's all. Take the time you need."

He stared and stared, but his eyes brightened and I knew it wasn't hurt he was feeling anymore. There was hope in his beautiful moonlit gaze.

In answer, his hand returned to my hair and gently swept around to the back of my skull, pulling me in again. His lips landed against my forehead, planting the softest, fleeting kiss, and then he released me altogether.

"Goodnight, Natalie."

"Goodnight."

He took that aching pull in me with him, leaving *the most delicious* frustration in his wake. My Goddess, his restraint was admirable and infuriating.

So, too, was the fact that Ghost didn't join me in bed that night, so I only had myself to hold onto. Couldn't sleep no matter what I did. Until finally, I had this…strange inkling that I needed to do something. A small correction I needed to make.

I climbed out of bed and went to the dresser, where I'd hung the necklace with the bit of green sea glass I'd once given to Cass. The azurite teardrop beside it buzzed against my skin as I scooped it up and crept to the door, opening the old creaky slab of wood as delicately as I could.

I tiptoed across the hallway to Cass's room and leaned against his door, listening.

"Cass?" I tried, but he didn't answer.

Maybe he was already asleep, or maybe he'd had enough of me for one day. Whatever it was, I threaded the necklace around the doorknob and left it there for him—a token, so he knew it was his and I still wanted him to have it.

Then I crawled back into bed and finally fell asleep and dreamed of walking cottages and chases through the forest and the night Cass finally opened himself up to me again.

Because I believed he would.

I hoped he would, anyway.

When I woke to dappled sunlight filtering through the windows, I was surprised to find I wasn't alone. There, seated on the floor by the door, was Ghost…with my wolf curled up in his lap, contentedly wagging her tail as he ran his hands across her beautiful silver coat.

Yes, I could feel every brush of his fingertips over her, like phantom breath across my skin.

Trippy.

And he stared at me with an apologetic look on his face that seemed so…individual. Not a copy at all, but his own expression.

"I think I need to ask you what you are again," I teased him, as my wolf rose to her feet, pressed her forehead to his, licked his face, and then reentered me.

He simply rose to his feet and pressed his hand to his heart before drawing my attention to…the book nook on my dresser.

It was bright with light.

Someone had come in, replaced the old battery, and left it on for me to find in the morning when I woke.

"Did you…?"

Ghost shook his head as he opened my bedroom door for me. I didn't know if he knew about the gift I'd left Cass the night before, but a whistle of relief blew through me when I saw that the necklace I'd left Cass was gone.

It was such a small thing, but it meant the world to me.

I turned right around and yanked open the closet to get dressed as I asked, "Is Cass awake? Is he still in the cottage?"

I couldn't even see Ghost as I asked, too consumed with sweaters and wool-lined pants, but it didn't take long for me to realize Cass wasn't in his room, or in the cottage either.

And this time, when I asked, "Do you know where he is? I want to thank him…" Ghost met my enthusiasm with gentle warning. "What is it?"

I found out a few minutes later when I stepped into the café to the scents of rich coffee and warm pastry and Yas told me, "He's gone off with Brodie and the others on a scouting mission."

"A scouting mission? Where?"

"I don't know," she said. "But they took Idalia, Jasiri, and the water nymph with them."

So, something sea-based in Italy maybe.

"Did they say when they'd be back?"

"A few days."

Ugh. I guessed I'd just…stew in my own hormones until then.

At least it explained the *absence* I felt inside myself. Amidst the activity of the rest of my animals, it'd been harder to tell one was missing. My raven had left with Cass, the obsessed little weirdo.

"Ey, what is this sad face for? We have plenty to do here in the meantime," Yasmina chastised. "Like sending off the supply list to be filled. Finally. Today. Salty snacks are *nonnegotiable* for me in stressful times. If I don't get *flint* soon, I will turn into a real monster, I promise you. Make sure you put down everything you need before ten. Tell everyone else also."

Yasmina glanced at Ghost then, eyes narrowed. "Do ghosts need anything? If you do, put it down too, I guess. Natalie is made of money."

"*That's* definitely not true," I grumbled playfully, adding my needs to the bottom of the supply list.

I…should have waited until she left. Without a crumb of shame,

Yasmina glanced down at what I wrote, and a wide teasing grin blossomed on her face.

"Birth control?" she said so loudly I shushed her, even though we were the only ones in the room. "Someone's feeling optimistic this morning. Would it have anything to do with your man fighting himself in front of everybody last night?"

"Yasmina!" I shushed again. "I just need to get back on it after being without it for so long. Couldn't refill a prescription on the run, could I."

She didn't buy that excuse for a second.

"Whatever. I don't change diapers anyway, so what's good for you is also good for me. One of us should be getting laid at least."

"Yasmina! My mom might hear you."

"She went to deliver pastries to somebody. Hopefully somebody energetic for her own purposes. We all deserve that. Heck, I wish I had a hot sweaty man to keep me amused during these trying times. One who doesn't talk so much, you know. I prefer my men like statues—hard and silent."

"Holy hell," I laughed and rolled my eyes simultaneously.

Yasmina grabbed her coffee and headed for the door, but not before tossing out one final parting word of wisdom. "If I learned anything from the war in my own country, it is that the spirit matters as much as the body. Any little joy you can find makes a world of difference, especially when most other comforts disappear."

"And that means what, for me?"

"Man. Crisps. Chocolate. *Indulge*, my lady."

The moment she left, I turned to find Ghost smiling at me. *Beaming*, actually. Like an obnoxious post-pubescent boy.

"What?"

His eyes darted to the list in my hands. To my addition at the bottom.

A blush as hot as brushfire ripped across my cheeks as I realized why he was smiling.

"Please don't make this weird!" I begged.

He shrugged and looked away, too proud of himself. The smile on his face didn't disappear, though, and I caught myself almost wiggling with hope and anticipation that Cass might be that excited too...when we got there.

And then I added chocolates and a few of my favorite snacks to the list, realizing that it had been so long since I'd had any little comforts that my creatures had to remind me what some of them actually were.

CHAPTER 21

To my surprise, all the soldiers I was on a first-name basis with had gone on Brodie and Cass's mission, save one. Millie had caught "a rotten cold overnight" which had left her hacking her lungs out and going through box after box of tissue like she was trying to beat a world record.

"It's nothing, my lady," she claimed before chugging an entire mug of boiling hot tea. "Just a stuff. Be better before you know it. Thanks for checking up on me, though. I know you have better things to do."

I'd come to see her at the tail end of her sickness, three days after the soldiers left.

"This is definitely not some Princess Diana moment for me," I joked, standing across the room from where she was lying in bed surrounded by so many crisp and biscuit wrappers it looked like she was building a nest out of them. "I actually wanted to ask for your help with something."

"Anything."

I'd been doing a lot of heavy thinking about my ragtag team's collective future since Cass left. *Worrying,* I guess most people called it. I liked to call it *future-chess*, because some deep part of me knew that just because we'd found a small break between skirmishes, it didn't mean the war wasn't going on all around us. This was a lull. This place—this peace—was an exception. A calm before the storm Marna had warned me was coming.

Each morning since arriving, a "debriefing packet" had been delivered to me. It included a schedule of my responsibilities (mostly meetings) along with news highlights from the day before. Anything of critical time sensitivity was delivered as it happened, but these were more...summaries of alter news from around the world so I didn't become one of those lazy politicians wearing blinders who couldn't tell you the price of bread or whatever people were freaking out about in the moment.

These packets made it so that I could walk into talks with Brodie, with the lawyer Vanessa, and the accountant Neville, and half a dozen other trusted connections *outside the loch* who routinely reported to me so I could actually make relevant decisions as they were needed.

And let me tell you…the demands of audience hours *before* the reveal of the Great Secret when I was just the Alter Supreme of the Eighth Kingdom were *nothing* compared to after.

Because I was suddenly *everybody's* Alter Supreme. Our online scheduling site broke down the day after the Great Reveal and had to move to a much more powerful server to accommodate the insane number of random requests for help that were pouring in from all over the globe—from alters who had genuine needs, from people who wanted to *be* alters, and from celebrities, rich people, and absolute *freaks* offering to pay well for the "exclusive privilege" of having *me* alter them personally.

Bleck.

No, we couldn't just ignore the real requests for help until everything else was sorted.

No, we didn't have enough time to help all of them either.

But I set aside a couple of hours a day and started holding "group audience hours," so I could address a bunch of people with the same issues in bulk.

Which…led to the first real issue of my "Arch-Sovereignty." *Goddess, that title was a mouthful.*

No, the real issue was that people all over the world seemed to be having the same problems. So many of them had already gone to their leaders for help and been turned away, and now that "they knew who was really in charge," they were asking me.

They were hoping I would be different.

It got old fast reminding them I didn't have authority in their kingdoms, but that I could reach out on their behalf to their Alter Supremes.

It would mean more meetings; this time, super awkward ones with people who felt threatened by my mere existence and already defensive at the thought that I was calling on behalf of *their people* and the complaints they had.

But all of that I could handle, even though most of the calls were either heartbreaking or boring. It was good to hear grievances and have my team start sorting them into Big Issues we might actually be able to help fix once I made my debut.

Those things were only half of my daily debriefings.

The rest...had to do with that pesky "invisible" war going on. With Rav, this time, rather than the Knights.

Rav had essentially *vanished* after I left Fylgja Castle. He'd gone to the south, to the Deer Lord's estate in Germany, where he'd been holed up ever since.

Thanks to our spies, I knew every visitor he received.

I knew every movement of his people, too. Particularly in Italy where we'd managed to force them away from Arachne's Revenge but not out of the country...which Cass suspected meant they were plotting some new attack.

I also knew that Sorina's people were hunting for me in Romania where Cass's trick trail had led them.

And I knew that Archer Mahon, Ulric Garand, and Oriol Savall had visited Rav three times in the last week. *That* was a combination I did not like.

On top of all of that, Giselle and Rolfe were still missing...but I didn't know if it was because they were hiding, they had been taken prisoner, or because they were already dead. I *hated* not knowing which.

The counterweight to all of this was that the threats and fears that the cult were going to attack us or others had dissipated by, like, 100 percent since the Great Reveal. Robine gave television interviews occasionally. So, too, did "select middlemen" in various countries. But they all said they were stand-ins for me, that I was busy "working behind the scenes to ensure the continued safety of our people" and would appear shortly. And in the meantime, everyone could call the Knights' hotline for more information.

Outing myself was the tipping point, I knew. Stepping onto that bright world stage was the point at which all hell would break loose.

But I couldn't do that yet, and not for the reason any of the others probably thought.

It was the reason I'd come to Millie.

"I need you to teach me how to alter at will."

Millie's eyes popped a little at that. "*Teach* you. Dunno if that's even possible, my lady."

"I taught Jonesy how to farsee with his water buffalo. If I can teach him, I think you can teach me."

My creatures had told me it was more than possible, too, but she didn't need to know that.

"Well, I can try," Millie said after a moment. "But I'm not even sure how I learned to do it."

"What do you mean?"

Millie shrugged so casually and said, "It's a trauma-response, isn't it."

"What trauma?"

"A while back, before you put in all them nature reserves for us, my cousins and I ran into a spot of trouble. At a farm. We...got caught eating some of the farmer's feed and he...well...he strung us up in his barn. Strung up my cousins, I should say. Hung the boys from hooks."

I flinched at the thought.

"I'm a sow, so he put me in a pen. Guess he thought he could breed me? As if that's flattering. Anyway, I almost shit a brick panickin' because I knew he wouldn't keep the others, and I heard this quiet voice in my head asking me what I needed in that moment."

"The Goddess?" I asked.

"Nah, I wish. It was my animal, wasn't it. First time she really spoke to me, so it was a bit of a shock, but she knew we were in danger, and she talked me through it."

"What did she say?"

"It was weird. She told me I had to *remember what it was like to be human.*" Millie shrugged and gave a quiet snort-laugh. "How was I supposed to forget that? That was back before I asked my cousins how they felt when they altered and found out there was barely a unique thought amongst the lot of them. When they were boars, they were *boars*. Whereas I was always both."

"So what did you do to make it happen?"

An embarrassed half-grin rounded her apple cheek. "It's silly, but...did you ever see *Kill Bill*?"

"The movie?"

"Yeah. Remember that scene when she wakes up from her coma and it's been so long since she moved that she can't feel her legs?"

I nodded. Of course, I remembered that.

"She's just killed that bloke in the hospital and she steals his truck and sits in the back for hours staring at her big toe verbally commanding it to wiggle. That's what it was like. Took a *helluva* long time, but I sat in that pen for hours remembering individual parts of my human body until the boar part of me retreated and the human emerged."

She snorted with delight and added, "Sounds so *profound* when I say it like that, doesn't it."

"It does," I agreed. "So…I just…have to remember my humanness."

"Yep. And be patient. Or in life-threatening danger. One of the two."

"Oh great. So, easy then."

***

After borrowing Millie's azurite, I pushed my way through the forest to a spot far enough from town I thought no one would find me. I needed the distance to attempt this, considering my raven was gone and I'd have to transform into one of my other forms in the meantime.

I found a small glen in the woods where a little stream covered by a thin film of ice so late in the year sat quiet and peaceful. There, I tried to sit down on a stone, until the frigid chill poked through the thick lining of my pants and I realized I'd need to remove my clothes so they weren't wrecked if I actually managed to transform at will.

I almost threw in the towel the second I took off my jacket; I'd picked a windless day, but there were zero clouds in the sky and the cold hovered in the air like invisible knives, pressing their tips to every part of my uncovered body as I shivered and shook and tried to generate *some* sort of heat.

Which I did, when my wolf suddenly asked, "*What doing?*" in a tone that suggested she thought something was wrong *with me* for spazzing out, and I laughed some warmth into myself.

"*I'm freezing. Can you help?*"

I hadn't expected anything to actually happen, but I really needed to stop doing that. No sooner were the words out of my mouth but I was *hot*. Roasty-toasty and mostly naked, heated from within.

"*Is this you*?" I asked my wolf.

"*Us too*," my bear and dragon replied.

And I smiled, a little awed by the fact that asking and receiving something I needed was so simple. Maybe it shouldn't have surprised me, but it did. It felt like a secret perk of this beastly gift of mine; to be able to use their various physicalities to my advantage. Maybe not just their physical stuff, but their other strengths too.

I…realized the extent of my powers might only be limited by the breadth of my imagination.

Such a terrifying and wonderful thought.

But I put it to the side and forced my mind to concentrate.

I didn't just need to be able to change into a human at will; I needed to be able to do the reverse as well.

So, I didn't use the azurite.

Instead, I stood in that clearing focusing on…my wolf. Her form. The softness of her fur. The bent of her ankle. The tail. The haunches. The ears.

I stood there for at least an hour, in the frigid white wilds, waiting for something to happen while my creatures ran commentary.

"*Don't imagine*," my wolf said.

"*Feel*," the aurochs echoed.

"*Feel good*," my dragon snickered.

"*Quiet please*," I begged.

"*Pick part. Focus,*" my wolverine grumbled.

Don't get me started on the fact that her voice sounded like Eike's. Not enough to torment me, thank Goddess, but enough that it was like that woman was haunting my brain.

I did as she commanded, though. I closed my eyes and focused on my toes. On my wolf's toes. The way they'd felt when I first transformed at the wedding. How they'd kicked off as we ran down the slope. How the earth had felt between my claws.

And there…just on the periphery of my senses…was a twinge of connection. A tickle of one as I felt the sensation of *dirt* under my claws.

…Which disappeared the moment I got excited about it.

I opened my eyes and found no difference in my feet that I could see.

I tried for another hour before the alarm on my phone told me I had other places to be, but the twinge never came back. Still, it had been there, and I was honestly excited by the promise of it.

Especially when I went to redress and noticed tiny bits of fur around the place where I'd been standing and saw that there were claw marks where my toes had made impressions in the ice-cold soil.

***

"My Goddess, you're hot as a coal."

I arrived at Belina's cottage for our first session together a few minutes later and stepped in to the scent of bergamot and vanilla and a teapot shaped like a round of parmesan sitting on a small end table between two comfy armchairs.

"Come in, sit down," she said. "Get comfortable. We're going over *types* of witchcraft today."

I pushed my shoes off and left them by the door as I aimed for the cozy arrangement she'd set up, but I only made it a few steps before a sound stopped me in my tracks.

Someone was humming Chappell Roan; I'd've recognized that voice anywhere.

"Scarlett?"

I heard the creak of a chair pushing back and then her blonde head popped out of an open doorway down the hall. "You rang."

"Hey. What are you doing here?"

She pivoted a little and waved a massive book at me. "Just readin'. She has a whole library here."

I glanced at Belina, and she motioned for me to take a look.

It was more than a library. It was some sort of…tesseract? Shelves stacked thick with books crowded every wall, with seating at the center. Ordinary, it seemed at first; but as I watched, the room shifted. Books pulled back and disappeared before others replaced them and the shelves themselves narrowed or grew to accommodate tomes large and small. Objects popped up and then sunk away at random too, as if offering themselves briefly before making room for the next. It gave the room a living, breathing quality…and a faint, seasick sway that forced me to focus on Scarlett's face to stay grounded.

Until I saw how happy she was in there, and my gaze shot away to a small desk covered in books with a notebook and pen sitting off to the side.

"Been here a while?" I asked.

"Try three days," Belina grumbled, appearing in the doorway.

Scarlett didn't deny it. Instead, she shrugged and said, "You said it was okay."

"Before I knew you were a homeless miscreant little nerd who would eat all my cookies and leave crumbs on my books!" Belina chided, but with the voice of an annoyed older sister.

"God, that was *one time*, Belina," Scarlett countered. "Besides, that cookie was the only reason I didn't lose my spot."

Belina eyed me. "Cookies as bookmarks. You see what I have to put up with?" Then she snapped playfully at Scarlett, "And that's *Goddess* to you, little miss. You have a lot more reading to do. Back to it. Natalie and I will be out here doing our lesson so I'm going to seal you in until it's done. If you come out, you'll have to sit through it too."

"No thank you," Scarlett said, dropping back down at the desk. "Wait, what's the lesson, maybe I want to—"

Belina closed the door with a flick of her fingers, and a lock audibly *shunked* into place.

"She will learn this anyway, but not today. Not until *you* do the right thing and return her truth to her," she said, taking hold of my shoulders and gently guiding me back toward her living area.

"I will," I swore. "And I wanted to talk to you about that."

"Oh yes, I have no doubt you do. Sit."

I sat.

I sipped the tasty bergamot-vanilla tea.

I waited for Belina to take the other seat, groaning loudly as the chair cushions contorted around her body, hugging her. Then she turned to me with a grin, "I love magick."

"That makes three of us, I think."

"Yes, it does. But magick isn't a toy and it isn't a birthright. It must be respected, or it will chew you up and spit you out, honey. Believe me."

"It's not a birthright?" I asked.

"Not the way you think. Can you be *born* a witch? Absolutely. Do you get to keep your powers *just because*? Not necessarily. It's why in the last century or so a lot of work has been done to codify the learning of the craft. So we teach our kind to be careful first, powerful second."

Belina sat up then and glanced in the direction of the library. "You can't wait much longer, pet."

"I know."

"You know-You know, but you don't do it."

"Because I wanted to ask you how to fix it—if I *can* fix it—before I tell her."

"And if you can, would you?"

"Yes."

"You would take another decision away from her?"

I blinked. "No! I'd do anything she wanted to make it up to her."

"Well, that's the spirit, even if it's a reckless one. Unfortunately, there isn't much literature on undoing something like this. Most of it just says, *wild magick is wild and assuming anything is ill advised*, which seems ridiculously vague to me, but I could look for more…if you actually tell her."

"I'm here to listen to you, Belina. If you advise something, please do. The magick went into her when she was unconscious. I made a mistake because *to that point* all I knew was that I wasn't allowed to tell her what had happened and I didn't want her to suddenly, I don't know, *erupt with witch powers* at the full moon and be scared witless trying to figure out what was wrong."

"Why not? You would've been there to help her through it."

"I…just didn't know."

"Yes, you did, but because the choice was taken away from you, you didn't want it taken away from her. So you took a different choice from her instead. I get it. I'm not judging. I'm just warning that you're running out of time."

My spine tingled with uncertainty. "What does that mean?"

"I've…heard from Freyja," she said, sighing. "She did not tell me what was going to happen, so don't ask. But she did say that we all need to tie up loose threads before tomorrow. Tomorrow brings…bad tidings."

"Bad tidings."

"That's what she said." Belina sat forward then and reached for my hand. "She also told me what she discovered about the soulchoke. She wanted to wait to tell you *and* your mate when he returns but I think we should tell you now. The choice is yours."

I felt my shoulders tighten automatically. "What do you mean *mate*?"

Belina scowled at me. "Baby, you know what I mean by that word."

I didn't. Was she saying she knew about Cass or was she saying Rav was on his way here? One was frightening; the other was *horrifying*.

"Are you saying Rav's coming—"

"No! No," she swore. "I see the problem. When you have two, I must specify. Not your hellmate. Your chosen mate."

That word again. "What's a hellmate?"

Belina's mouth opened and shut in surprise, before some understanding registered in her eyes as she studied me. "I shouldn't be surprised you don't know what that is. He would never have told you about that possibility."

"Who? Rav?"

Belina eyed me with pity. So gently, she said, "A *hellmate* is not your soulmate, not really. They might share many qualities you seek or mirror your complexities or match you in ways no one else has. It might feel as if the universe is conspiring to bring you together. You might even feel truly seen and understood for the first time in your life.

"But eventually, the cracks show. Your ambitions, your boundaries, your sense of who you are become threats. Attempts to improve yourself become accusations. And your successes trigger their insecurities.

"Hellmates charm, excite, and confuse. They give…then take in ways that corrode the parts of yourself you once cherished. Soon, they demand more than they give. Their expectations shift, and you are asked to accommodate a version of them you don't recognize. They become…ruiners, not saviors."

She leaned in then and added, "A hellmate is the person you think will complete you, but they only hollow you out."

"You're saying that's what Rav is to me?" I asked quietly. "But we can share gifts. The Goddess said I *could* mate with him."

"It might surprise you to know the Goddess is an optimist at heart. Perhaps you were once a good match. Or a good match if you had made the choice to shrink yourself to keep him. Or he learned to appreciate you rather than feel threatened by you. But somewhere along the way you grew and chose to be your full self and he did not and you were no longer compatible. And what might have worked for who you were becomes toxic to who you are now. In the end, hellmates are…"

"Lessons," we both said together.

I sort of sat with that for a solid minute. I deserved that, didn't I? At least one minute to absorb before something else knocked me off balance—

"I am not surprised someone like you has two mates, honestly. When your choices hold such weight, and your mind is so crowded, it's only natural that she would give you options. Especially one like *il rosso*. You've woven your fates together tightly without even trying, honey. There is a natural rhythm there many of us spend our entire lives trying to find."

Il rosso. The redhead.

Even though seconds before, I'd been okay with the possibility of her knowing about Cass, hearing her voice it so casually made me feel suddenly unsafe. I couldn't speak. I didn't know what facial expression I was making, but it obviously wasn't subtle.

"Easy, easy, Natalie," she cooed, rubbing my arm. "It's okay. Nothing has happened."

But her soft words didn't help. And half a second later, a silver blur arrived beside both of us and stopped on a dime, blowing leaves off her houseplants and doilies off her tables. Ghost's hand landed on my shoulder in concern, his steely eye on Belina in warning.

"I'm fine, Ghost." It was a half-truth. He landed on his knee beside me, and his hand turned my chin gently, forcing me to look him in the eye. Gah, it was *uncanny* how much he looked like Cass. "I swear, I'm okay. She just surprised me."

"*Tranquillo, Ombra. Sta bene,*" Belina echoed to him. "But this is good. The best of both worlds. He can listen on your lover's behalf."

"Cass isn't…I-I mean, he *was*."

"He *is*," Belina said gently. "And I know that because the soulchoke would not have come off so easily otherwise."

"Easy. Easy?!" I almost yelped. "It almost cut Cass's fingers off."

"Exactly. *Almost*."

I waited for her to continue, but the dramatic side of her forced out another sigh before she spoke.

"I summon Freyja."

Again, spoken like a chant, low in her throat, it held a power that was palpable even before the single slate across from us on the wall began to tremble and lighten to glass. The view was dark for a long moment before light appeared above us and I realized Freyja had been carrying her slate in a pack. She lifted us out, revealing herself by a wilder coastline this time; I could hear ocean waves crashing against rocks nearby.

"*I am not on call all hours of the day, Belina*," she chastised.

"*She's here, Freyja*."

Freyja's intense blue gaze snapped to me as if she hadn't noticed me at first. "*Dear one, lucky to still have her pretty head. I knew we'd speak again.*"

Belina had no time for her, it seemed. Very drolly, she said, "*You told me to call you when she came, Pazzarella.*"

Freyja blinked. "*Perhaps I did. It's been a long day tracking the one who made the soulchoke.*"

"*You're tracking Rav?*" I asked.

"*Not him. The traitor who helped him make this*," she said. "*He could not have done it alone. But I am near them, in Norway. They will answer for their crime.*"

I knew where she was—somewhere near Hamingja.

"*Don't go in the building, Freyja,*" I said. "*It's dangerous. And powerful. I barely escaped the last time I was there*."

She giggled, her head tilting. "*I do not take orders from you. Give me another one and I will tell you how many children you are to have…and how many will make it to adulthood.*"

My spine tingled at the threat…and Ghost leapt forward, placing his hands to either side of my head as if he intended to cover my ears if Freyja made good on her threat. This made her giggle again.

"*Not an order*," I said. "*A warning. There are many alters there.*

Powerful alters loyal to the king. Please, just be careful."

"*Tell her what you know about the soulchoke, Freyja,*" Belina pushed on. "*So we can let you go.*"

"*It wasn't just severing you from your divinity,*" she said. "*He bound it with his blood so that only your mate could remove it. If anyone else attempted it, the cost would have been your head.*"

I felt sick.

"*It had a self-destruct mode?*" I asked to clarify.

"*Don't sanitize his betrayal. No. He told it only your mate could have you, and if he couldn't then no one could.*"

The threat of sickness rose into my throat; my mouth began to water, and I didn't know what to say.

Almost extraneously, Freyja added, "*Lucky you had another one of those so close at hand to free you or* I *might have taken your head off. Unintentionally, of course.*"

Well…there was that too.

"*Thank you, Freyja,*" Belina said for me. "*Blessed be.*"

"*Blessed be.*" And she was gone.

We sat in the silence afterward for a long moment, while Belina studied me and rubbed my arm and Ghost stood on my other side, petting my head. For reassurance, I knew. But it was only enough to keep me from screaming. The betrayal I felt at the thought that Rav would rather kill me than let anyone else have me? I didn't know what to *do* about that, but I knew how it made me feel—*rageful.*

Without Belina's touch, without Ghost's touch, to steady me? I don't know what I would have done.

But it simmered down a little as Belina tried to help. "I think that is also why the Goddess allowed you to choose a second mate."

"Why?"

"So that if one's cruelty threatened to shatter your faith in love, the other's devotion would remind you what love truly is."

CHAPTER 22

Love.

It seemed so easy to dismiss it as unimportant in the midst of…everything else. And yet, that deep knowing part of myself I was only just learning to listen to knew better. Giselle had said, "*How we love is how we change the world.*" That statement hadn't just rung through my body, my mind, my spirit, as one of the truest things I'd ever heard; it staked a claim in my soul.

So much of what I'd gone through since joining this world had only confirmed how true it was. So much of the cruelty I'd seen dispensed by others confirmed it too.

Rav's choker was blasphemous proof.

So were his laws about not mixing—Henry died because of a rule forbidding love.

Hunger and poverty and war and *scarcity* were the direct result of choosing not to lead with love, of not transforming the world with love.

Fear and hate and greed prevented the world from changing for the better. It was as simple as that. And it only reaffirmed the 'how' for me—the way in which I wanted to be a leader for my people.

It lit a fire under my feet when my meeting with Belina ended. I went right to Scarlett in the library, and I didn't mince words.

"Hey babe? Can you cut your study session short today? There's something I need to talk to you about."

Scarlett blinked her baby blues at me, reading me like a book. "Sure."

I knew Belina was happy to have her house to herself again—the way she sort of lightly slammed the door behind us as we left confirmed it—but she also seemed proud of me. In those last moments as she wished us a happy day, she shot me a shy smile with a raised eyebrow and whispered, "Good luck."

Ignoring Ghost where he walked silently behind us, I looped my arm in Scarlett's and slowed us to a soft stroll through the woods.

"Are you okay?" she asked. "I know I shouldn't've crashed her house like that, but I literally didn't look at a clock once until you called my name. Like I seriously haven't eaten since she brought me snacks initially. And the cookie thing was her fault. She made them from scratch and they friggen sparkled with magick, Nat. Like, actual magick."

"No, it's not that. Belina's just dramatic; she likes having you over there." I took a deep breath and plunged on, "I...need to tell you something that's gonna hurt, I think. I'm scared you're going to hate me, which is why I've been a big chicken about it."

"Well, we both know you've always been a chicken, so you've already set the stage, my friend."

I pinched her. "Jerk."

"Seriously, it can't be that bad."

I winced.

"Is it?"

"I...don't know. Scarlett, I know you know that we aren't allowed—or we *weren't* before the Great Reveal—to tell anyone we're alters."

Scarlett hip bumped me. "Keepin' secrets from your best friend—for shame."

"It goes a little harder than that," I told her. "There are...punishments attached to breaking that law. A thousand lashes is one of them."

"Geez," she said.

"The other...is having anyone who finds out force-altered against their will. Friends, family, strangers, kids, it doesn't matter."

"What?! How can that be legal?"

"The people who make the rules decide what's legal. That one, I had nothing to do with."

"But...Marna's still human," Scar said.

I sighed. "The way I had it explained to me was that *officially* anyone who knows should be altered but *unofficially* so long as the human keeps our secret they can potentially remain human. But that's for cases like Marna, where they're married or related to an alter. She wouldn't put Imi in danger by outing her. And if they broke up, it was sort of implied that she'd be forced to alter to give her a reason not to put *herself* in danger."

"Not force-altered into a seal, I hope," Scarlett said. Off my surprise, she added, "Marna's terrified of the ocean."

I blinked. "How do you know that?"

"She told me. She said you guys sailed across the sea to get here and she hid how she felt for Imi's sake but swore if you tried to make her go back the same way, she'd sue."

I laughed softly at that. But…that explained why Marna had never chosen this life, even after getting together with Imi.

"Anyway," I said, pushing on. "Do you remember Luxembourg?"

"Of course."

My fingers were starting to tremble. "Do you remember falling in that ruin Cass took us to?"

Scarlett grew quiet, but nodded.

"Something happened after you fell…*Magick* entered your body while you were asleep. Wild magick. I think I've explained what it is a little bit and how it's different from our magick?"

Again, she nodded.

"When we got back to Rav's castle, you started sleepwalking and talking to the magick at night, and I got scared that you would have the choice to be one of us taken from you like it was taken from me. I'd been working with Belina by then and I knew how to…take the magick out of you. So I did."

Scarlett drew to a soft stop, her face an unreadable mask of neutral curiosity. "You took the magick? What does that mean you took the magick?"

I held my breath and said, "I asked you to give it to me and you did because you didn't know what you were doing."

I expected anger.

I expected confusion.

What I got instead was heartbreak and despair. While I held my breath, Scarlett's breath seemed to blow right out of her like a tempest gust; she exhaled heavily and stepped out of my grasp, looking anywhere but my face.

"Is that why I felt so empty?"

"I'm sorry."

"I thought I was going crazy. It felt like something was missing. I thought maybe I was depressed but it hit *so* hard so fast I didn't…" Her voice faded away before realization seemed to set in. "I was supposed to be a witch, wasn't I."

She didn't ask it as a question. Not really. I shrugged because I wasn't sure. "Maybe. You would have decided during the full moon."

"But I didn't get to. Because you stole it."

I bore the sting of discomfort that prickled my back, my spine, my conscience.

"I planned to find a time later to tell you about it and *offer* you this life, so you could make the choice for yourself. I wish I had just told you but I couldn't—"

Scarlett blew a raspberry, interrupting me. "Don't give me that. *Couldn't*. You're the friggen queen of the world, Nat. No one would've whipped you. *You're* one of the rule makers."

It wouldn't have done any good to say she was right, but that I hadn't thought of myself like that back then.

"Did you keep it?" she asked.

"No. I gave it to someone else."

"Who?"

"...Yasmina."

Scarlett spun in the direction of town, peering through the woods as if searching for her.

"She doesn't know," I said. "She doesn't know where it came from. It was an experiment to see if the magick transfer could be done."

"So you didn't even know if whatever you were trying to do would work?"

Again, I shrugged; the tension in my shoulders made it painful. "I was still learning. I guess I'll always be learning, but...in that case, what mattered most was not trapping you in a life you had no say in. That was my first priority, but..."

"But what?"

"I was also trying to help Yas and Cass alter. They'd never been able to before and...eventually I figured out how to force it for them."

"So you forced it on them, but took it from me?"

"No! I forced it a different way. They always wanted this. They just couldn't make it happen for themselves. I helped them."

"By hurting me."

I took a step forward and froze when she stepped away to even the distance.

My voice squeaked. "No! I didn't want to hurt you. That was the *exact opposite* of what I wanted. I was scared you'd wake up and freak out and be stuck in a life you didn't want."

Scarlett sneered in disdain suddenly. "Well, that happened anyway, didn't it."

And with that, she shoved past me, headed toward Belina's house, and didn't look back.

***

I found a random log of old driftwood on the beach and claimed it for a good long while after that, just…pondering…while Ghost sat silently beside me and my animals ran a semi-muted but endless stream of reassurances through my mind that she'd forgive me eventually, and that the hardest part was over.

Maybe that was true; I still wanted to feel bad about it anyway. It didn't matter that Scarlett might forgive me. I shouldn't have done it to her to begin with.

Yes, a part of me knew I never could have helped Cass finally alter if I hadn't run my wild magick transfer experiment, but that was a limp justification. I think I would've figured it out eventually, even without taking Scarlett's magick.

I'd made a bad call.

I'd made an ignorant mistake…

In the end, that's what it was. Most people got to make at least a few of those in their lifetimes; this was one of mine…but…

A mistake.

My mind tickled at that word. *Mistake.*

Something came back to me then that I hadn't thought about in weeks. My call with Robine back at Arachne's Revenge. She'd finally answered the question "why me," by claiming it was because I'd never robbed anybody of their magickal future by eating a false sacrifice. But she'd also said I'd made mistakes. Ones I had to fix before I could be the leader they all wanted me to be.

Was Scarlett one of them?

Maybe robbing her of her magickal future by taking her magick was sin-adjacent?

Would Robine know how to help her if I called back?

Belina swore she would research, but I didn't want to wait if I could help it. If I could give Scarlett a choice, one she could make on her own about who she wanted to be, I wanted to.

"*You know*," my wolf spoke up.

"*Know what*?"

"*Know fix.*"

"*No, I—*"

But before I could finish the thought, she countered, "*Mate.*"

"*Ask Cass*?"

She shook her head. "*Good for mate, good for friend.*"

Oh.

Ohhh.

"*Are you saying I can just find another bit of wild magick and give it to Scarlett? Would that work now that she's an alter?*"

"*Ask,*" was all my wolf said in reply.

I just had to ask the wild magick. Sounded so simple when she said it…as if I could just pick up another little one of those sprites from the nearest Tesco's. As if shadow men in sandals and melting technicolor goats were a dime a dozen.

But…

There was more wild magick out there; I knew there was.

And if that was what Scarlett needed, I'd find it for her…

…once we handled the *bad tidings* tomorrow would bring.

As Belina's warning came back to me, I rose from the log, left the beach, and went to warn the rest of my team.

CHAPTER 23

"They should be here by now, right?"

"Should be visible any second, my lady."

Time had flown by since the warning from Belina. I'd told the team, who told everyone everywhere to gird their loins and be careful in a strange game of secret telephone. It gave me a great birds-eye view of the whole operation and how pyramidal the entire system had become, disseminating to a select group of trusted connections who then shared it with their trusted connections, down and down and down to our runners and soldiers and scouts as far away as Serbia and Portugal, so that our little nuclear intelligence center remained unknown to all but a handful of diehard loyalists.

The warning message had, of course, reached Brodie, Idalia, Cass, and Rawan first, who'd informed us that their secret mission was complete and they were already on their way back to us, using the circuitous route Cass preferred for safety.

And Cass had ended the message with, "We're bringing a gift, my lady."

It left me with something to look forward to, once we were finished warning everyone to prepare for "bad tidings" to happen. And while everyone else was scouring the internet, marathon-watching the only television in town, and checking with our contacts every hour for updates, Millie, Ghost, and I went to wait on the pier for signs that our friends had made it home.

Really, they came to act as security for me. Because *the moment* I told them to prepare, my entire team swarmed me as if they expected an ambush at any second—Rav's magick was still at work in all of them, compelling them to protect me at any cost, even to themselves. It took a long conversation to get them to unguard me. Even then, Millie and

Ghost never left my side, joking that they'd come along "just in case less-friendly fish-tailed women wanted to pull me into the loch."

I wondered how shocked they'd be when they saw me with my own fish tail one day.

"There it is—the signal, my lady," Millie suddenly said, pointing to a guardsman standing on the very lip of the far coastline, where the loch gave way to the sea. "They should be right…there."

The bow of the ship peeked from beyond the point, followed by the rest of the tiny shuttle boat, carrying so many people, there was barely any room across the deck for anyone. But there by the bow, like Rudolph's red nose guiding everyone home, was Cass.

It isn't dramatic to say the sight of him made my entire body *thrum* to life like an idling engine suddenly given gas. Nor is it unfair to admit that *every* part of my body felt awake in his presence…including my creatures who swished their tails and purred their delight, immediately at ease in a way that felt difficult to qualify given that he was still a quarter mile away.

"*Everything okay?*" I asked my raven, who I could see tucked inside Cass's coat.

"*Heart racing*," she said.

"*Oh, yeah, I guess it is—*"

I felt the shake of her head from afar. "*Not yours. His.*"

Yes, I blushed, but... "*He can tell me that.*"

I hadn't been able to look away from him since the moment he came into view, so I knew he was staring straight at me with an intensity that nibbled at my skin and a snowflake chill that made me desperately want to hug him for warmth. Well, I suppose "hug" is a great euphemism for the certain four-letter word that actually came to mind.

But it was his eyes that did it for me. They were pearl. No darkness at all as he gazed at me.

I wanted to just…reach for him as he came off the boat. Just intertwine our fingers and hold his hand openly the way I could see Idalia and Jasiri holding each other's at the stern as they waited for the boat to dock. Hell, even Brodie and Rawan were standing closer to each other than ever before.

It was a parade of wishful thinking as the soldiers disembarked, followed by my friends.

But they didn't come alone, and unfortunately what they carried with them robbed me of that fantasy in my head of a gentle, romantic stroll back to town with the redhead who made me hot and sweaty at the sight of him.

I say *what* they carried with them. I really should say *who.*

Four copies of Cass disembarked the boat carrying a man tied to a chair, completely swaddled in spider silk. He looked like a mummy. He smelled like dry grass. And he wriggled frantically to really emphasize that he hadn't been brought there of his own accord.

"Who's that then?" Millie asked, as Cass finally stepped down the plank and opened his coat, letting my raven fly right into my body.

"An old frenemy of Natalie's," he replied. "One who weighs as much as an elephant and required just as many tranqs to put him down."

We unwrapped our newest guest in the café, with me standing behind him and my truthsayer gift at full power. Idalia ran her nail down the silk, splitting it, until a dark head, a tweed sweater, and the scent of an old once-friend emerged.

I actually recognized him from behind; I'd spent so many afternoons staring at the back of his head while he taught me lessons at Fylgja Castle.

A man I hadn't seen since London many months ago when I threatened to decapitate him in the elevator of our building after I'd found him with my mom.

Mom…

Her face twisted with surprise and heartbreak at the sight of him. "Baruti?"

"Dr. Sanga," Fern echoed a moment after.

The discomfort across my mom and friend's bodies at the sight of him was palpable, even though from where I stood, I couldn't tell if he acknowledged either of them.

"This is *absolutely* inappropriate," Dr. Sanga said. "I am an educator, not a prisoner."

"You can be both," Cass replied.

Dr. Sanga stared at him for a long beat. "I recognize you."

"Really? By academic reputation or just from your nightmares?"

"You're the Bear Lord's brother. The traitor."

A smile as sharp as broken glass split Cass's face. "The Bear Lord is long dead, long live the Raven Queen."

"Is she here?" Dr. Sanga asked, turning to my mom. "Is she the one who had him *ambush* me, who had him *wrangle* me into submission like this, Rebecca?"

"Our lady had no part in it," Cass replied. "But she's the reason you're here instead of in prison. She may deign to speak with you eventually, but what matters now is why you were visiting the king at the Lange Estate."

Dr. Sanga remained silent for long enough that Cass continued. "We went to Italy, expecting to find Rav's forces retreating. Instead, they were embedding themselves in little coastal towns all over the place. Preparing for something. Rav came and went from an estate in one of these towns—one Lady da Carra identified as belonging to her rival…"

"…Dino Costa…" Idalia murmured the name like a curse.

"And then he left and returned to Oskar Lange's estate in the Black Forest, where you visited him."

Cass waited again for Dr. Sanga to say something. All while I, with a view of my old mentor's back, watched him tug futilely at the silk bindings on his wrists, until the brown skin there was taut white and red, and I thought he might dislocate something trying to break free.

"Do yourself a favor and speak, sir," Cass said after a while. "We watched you enter the estate and leave on multiple days. You weren't staying with him, but you were trusted enough to return again and again before he finally left for Norway. The king summoned you, did he not?"

"Of course, he summoned me. I've known the king since he was a child. There are few people who've spent more time with him than I have."

Dr. Sanga suddenly coughed; I watched his throat distend a little as he negotiated the feel of my truthsayer gift. He hadn't meant to say so much.

"Excellent," Cass said. "You're a prize prisoner, then. Dare I say, one of our VIPs. We'll have to keep you close at hand for the foreseeable future."

Even without seeing his face, I could *feel* the scowl there as Dr. Sanga stared Cass down. Then, he turned to Jasiri and switched into Swahili.

"*For shame, Jasiri. Helping these people? Do you know what the Elephant Court will do to you when they learn of what you've done to me?*"

Jasiri didn't flinch. "*Probably tell my court to promote me, once I reveal what* you *have done.*"

Dr. Sanga turned his head just enough for me to see the sneer on his face as he said, "*A house does not collapse unless someone inside pulls it down.*"

Jasiri snickered. "*You didn't go there to undermine the king from within. You went there to help him, even though you know that Golden*

Bird thinks only of himself."

"*He would be our ally, if we negotiate with him. He trusts me. He respects me. He desperately needs guidance. And he's poised to become the most powerful alter in the world. If we're in his ear when he takes control, we become players in the new order of things.*"

"*Only if you play by his rules.*"

"English, sirs," Cass said. "If you would be so kind."

"*I will speak whichever tongue I prefer—*"

"Dr. Sanga," Cass interrupted, speaking slowly. "Why were you summoned?"

"Because he is preparing…"

His tongue seemed to catch on the words as they escaped his mouth clearly without his consent; he made a gurgling noise and tucked his lips between his teeth tightly, to keep the rest from getting out.

"Preparing for what, Dr. Sanga?" I asked, stepping around to join my team.

I wasn't surprised by the glare of mistrust on his puckered face; but the fear I saw there? That caught me off guard. He looked at me with such…disappointment.

"Something's happening today, isn't it," I pushed. "Is he going to hurt people? Is he going to kill them? Can he be stopped?"

His mouth opened and shut before his resolve weakened and he said simply, "No, this cannot be stopped."

It was a non-answer.

"Dr. Sanga, if he hurts anyone…if he does something unforgiveable and you don't help us try and prevent it, that makes you an accomplice. You know that don't you? Could you live with yourself if he—"

"No one is going to die today, Lady Damarand."

"Then what—"

"BBC World News."

I blinked. "Excuse me?"

"BBC World News. 3:00pm today. You should be watching."

Just the way he said the words—the way his shoulders sagged, the exhausted tone of his voice—rubbed me the wrong way. It was an announcement, whatever Rav was doing. A personal announcement, if I read the droopy-eyed guilt on Dr. Sanga's face correctly.

"If he ignored my advice like I suspect he did," Dr. Sanga added after a moment, "we should *all* be watching."

***

"Move, man. I can't get comfortable like this."

"Keep it down back there."

"My knees are pressed to me tits."

"Jonesy! Deal with it!"

The town only had one television, mostly because we'd been too busy to put in more and nobody had added more to the supply list. It was an old, but large-ish flat screen, which Brodie brought outside, threading the cord through a window, so we could all watch. Thank Goddess the sky was a bruised storm color, or we wouldn't have been able to see anything anyway.

Copy Casses had rushed around grabbing chairs and couches until the concrete path looked like an outdoor theater, crowded around the screen.

I was sitting in a…throne…for all intents and purposes. One of the Casses had found an old, ornate purple armchair and set it apart for me, and I hadn't had the heart to tell him I was too anxious to stay seated. The moment my butt hit the chair, all I wanted to do was stand up and start pacing.

Ghost tried to stop me. He came to stand behind me and put his hand on my shoulder in reassurance, but it wasn't until Cass did the same on the other side that I finally settled down. Which maybe was a little pathetic, I don't know, but…that magnetic tug made me feel safe. So did the fact that he didn't pull away when I tucked my fingers around his.

He knew I was nervous.

And he knew why. Right after Dr. Sanga had told us to watch, I'd pulled Cass aside and told him about what happened in Italy, during the Sovereign Supremes meeting—when Rav had…had…practically bewitched everyone. When he'd commanded them to protect me even at the expense of their own lives. When he'd commanded them to hunt me down and return me to him.

I told him about how Asterios and I had to rip the cords out of the walls to prevent our own team from listening to his second command…and I warned him that the reaction to the first command had been intense. Even after all this time, my team became self-sacrificial the second they thought I was in danger.

"That has very little to do with the king," Cass pointed out.

"I'm just saying he might do something like that tonight," I said.

"And with the whole world watching? What if he turns everyone against me?"

Who knew how powerful Rav really was? I'd been closer to him than almost anyone and only seen glimpses. And those glimpses? They'd turned my world upside down.

"No one will ever harm you, I promise," Cass said.

"It's not me I'm worried about," I countered.

"I know, but at the first hint of trouble, we'll end it."

He motioned to the window through which Brodie had threaded the electric cord. One of Cass's copies was kneeling just inside with his hand on the outlet, ready to pull the plug if we gave the command.

"If we'd had more time, I would've gone to London," Cass said. "I would've stopped the broadcast…not that that would've held him back for long."

No, it wouldn't have. This was inevitable, which is why I suspected Freyja had only given us the 'bad tidings' warning, rather than telling us what was actually going to happen. This wasn't a moment we were meant to change.

Belina knew that too. She stood across from where I sat, waiting for the broadcast to begin, beside Scarlett, who refused to acknowledge my existence. Or Yasmina's, when Yasmina attempted to join them.

It was like watching a weird little silent play. Yasmina and Belina's eyes darted my way, in commiseration, before Yasmina backed off and went to stand with Fern. Belina shot me a flat-lipped smile, as if to say '*stay strong, she's just angry.*'

I'd fix it. I knew I could fix it.

I had to. Because I could feel the absence of Scarlett's affection the same way I could feel Cass's, when he was angry at me and wouldn't look at me. Couldn't, maybe.

"It's on. It's on!"

The noise around us dropped away in a rush, leaving only the soft hush of the loch waves and the voice of the BBC's anchor audible.

"Good afternoon. It's been just three weeks since the world learned that magickal creatures called alters who are able to shapeshift into animals—long thought to belong to myth and legend—are, in fact, real, and living among us. Tonight, in a BBC exclusive, we speak to His Majesty King Rav Elivagar, alleged ruler of the European alters—the first public interview ever granted by a leader of their people. Your Majesty, thank you for joining us."

The perspective pulled back into a split screen, revealing Rav in all his imperial glory, dressed in another one of his preferred haute couture suits—red tonight—with his hair pulled tight and his fiery blue eyes unwavering, and seated in an actual throne.

One I recognized—the lightning scorched chair from Hamingja. Although…it looked like he'd changed it in some way. He'd…cut into the sides of it? Where the back of the chair had once been rectangular and normal, it was now shaped like a vase.

"Norway," I whispered to Cass. "Power."

Rav's deep voice pulled my attention back to the television. "Thank you for having me. It is an honor to be here."

"Now, I mean no disrespect when I say this—most of our viewers will never have heard of you before today, but you call yourself a ruler of Europe, is that correct?"

Rav's eyes narrowed and a smile played at the corner of his lips. "Many people recognize me that way. Millions, in fact, and that number is growing every day, now that there is so much interest in joining our community. But as you mean it, yes, I am the alter ruler of the European continent. I am also the king of my own kingdom, which extends from Greenland to Finland—what you call the Nordic countries we recognize as the Raven Court."

"You're saying you turn into the bird, yes?"

Rav's grin grew. "Yes. Each alter takes after a single creature—one form, one nature. That is how it has always been until now."

The camera suddenly zoomed out as Rav leaned forward and *fwoomph*—his golden wings erupted behind him at full span, spreading to either side of his throne in grand display.

The anchor didn't speak for several seconds, his mouth agape, his eyes swiveling to take it all in. It would've been comedic, how fast it smacked the snark out of his mouth, under different circumstances.

But Rav and the rest of it settled like a sharp stone in my belly. The vision of him and those undeniable, angelic wings would be on every newspaper and magazine cover by morning. By next week, he'd be on t-shirts and posters. By next month, he'd have his own superhero in Marvel. Rav knew that. He relished in it. Especially the way his wings tucked into the new grooves in the throne behind him. Clever man had cut it to fit them before the broadcast; a detail the audience couldn't have known.

The silence on the BBC's end embellished the effect. The anchor sat there slack-jawed, in awe until someone off-screen hissed, "*You're still on!*" and he coughed and blinked trying to compose himself again.

"Well," he squeaked after a moment. "That is quite a sight. Although, many of our viewers today will be wondering why we're speaking with you instead of Lady Natalie Damarand when so many of your people have identified her as the true ruler of the alters."

Rav took that in stride. "Natalie will reveal herself when it is safe for her to do so."

"By safe…?"

"Humanity is still adjusting to our existence. Only two nights ago in Poland, an alter family was attacked in their home. A few days before that, more despicable hunts for shifters were carried out in Alabama in the United States. And we've all heard about the incident in Saudi Arabia by now. She will remain hidden until the time is right for her to come forward. Her safety—*our* safety—must come before all else."

"You sound very protective of her."

My spine tightened in warning. "He wouldn't dare…"

Rav's grin grew again. "No one is more so. She is my fiancée, although that word doesn't do our connection justice. We share a bond blessed by the Gods—we're soulmates. She is the heart of our people, and I am their hands. One without the other is meaningless."

Soulmates. The effect of that word rippled outward, like a spell cast over every viewer listening. Everyone except Cass. The moment that word left Rav's mouth, I felt Cass's grip on my shoulder begin to lighten. I felt him start to pull away—

And I held on for dear life. My fingers tucked around his tighter, held tighter. I looked up at him and shook my head, hoping he'd believe my silent swear that Rav was lying. Anger and resentment swelled in Cass's eyes, darkening his silver gaze, but I kissed his wrist. I kissed it gently, still holding onto him, still shaking my head, until the darkness receded. Until the tension in him eased. Until his grip resettled on me and his magnetic touch grounded me once again.

I turned back to find the reporter almost chuckling. "Are you saying soulmates are real?"

"Very real. For alters, at least. Well, for the alter forms lucky enough to have them, like the ravens," Rav teased, as he added, "For all of you thinking of becoming one of us, be sure to ask which animals have them if you would like to receive a divine union as well."

"That…diabolical prick," escaped Brodie like a compliment and a threat. "Clever git probably just doubled his numbers in a single sentence."

Rav continued. "And I promise you now, our wedding will be one to remember. Mark your calendars—November 11th."

The anchor's eyebrow rose. "So we'll meet Lady Damarand then, or…?"

Rav's eye twinkled as he stared *through* the camera. At *me*, as he said, "That is our official wedding date; all the arrangements are made. My mate wouldn't miss it for the world."

The back of my neck tightened to pain—magick bit at my spine in warning.

Official wedding date.

She wouldn't miss it for the world.

He…

I…

No one around me understood the gravity of what he just said, of the countdown he'd just set for me. Or the promise he'd tricked me into making months ago.

Diabolical prick was an understatement.

Ognianima was only six days away. November 11th was eleven days after that.

In seventeen days, I'd have to either marry the king…or I'd die.

Ha! As if he wouldn't kill me *the moment* he discovered I couldn't mate with him anyway.

Do not pass go. Do not collect two hundred dollars.

I'd been given my execution date. Despair crept right into my belly and hollowed me out until I could feel my head shaking in denial. The magick didn't like that; pain bit at my spine again, forcing me to stop.

But that wasn't the worst of it.

Oh no, Rav had more damage to do.

The reporter chuckled, drawing my attention back to the screen. "Well, we do love a royal wedding, don't we."

"Not just royal—divine. The Gods will descend to Earth to bless our union, and everyone is welcome to watch."

"These…Gods…will officiate your wedding?" the reporter asked politely, despite the skepticism clearly written across his face.

"In a manner of speaking. All soulmate unions are blessed this way, but our union is very…unique. We are destined for great responsibilities, as the Arch Sovereigns of every altered person on this planet."

"Holy hell," I murmured, sitting forward.

The planet. He'd just…claimed dominion, not just over Europe, but the entire globe. He'd called me the ruler of the world.

No, not me. *Us*.

And there was still more, I could tell. I could see it in the sharp glint of Rav's eye that he was going to say something else.

Something worse.

Inside me, a collective horror rose from my creatures, as if they were all holding their breath and clawing lightly under my skin. They could sense it too.

And then Rav said, "You see, she and I are different from other alters. We have been blessed with the greatest gift the Gods can bestow upon someone. Natalie is a…Crownshift."

He paused, letting this new word hang in the air.

"She can change into any animal form she so chooses…and once she and I are mated—" his grin could've swallowed the sea "—that gift will be mine as well."

CHAPTER 24

Intuition is a funny thing. It can guide you, it can scream at you, and yet it can't make you actually do anything. You have to listen and put it into practice to reap the benefits from it.

Damn it, I'd *known* the secrecy thing would come back to haunt me. All of Fern's warnings, all my monologuing at Cass, all my frustrations about how the hiding was our greatest problem as a collective…and yet I'd still hidden. I'd still kept secrets.

Nevermind the fact that Rav had just issued my death warrant…he'd laid my most private secret bare.

I'd hoped I'd have a chance to establish myself first before throwing *another* live grenade at people for them to catch.

Instead, I'd left space for Rav to run down the clock for me.

"She's a beast?" I heard the soldier to Jonesy's right whisper.

"Shut up, she's not," Jonesy said, his voice unsure and defensive. "King's lying. He's a liar—that's what he does."

They were all staring. The fifty or so people who'd come to the edge of the world with me to hide, to defend me, to help me "rise to power" and reclaim my throne and be the great leader they believed I could be, were all staring at me, frozen, uncertain.

Among them were the ones who already knew. Fern. Idalia. Cass. Ghost.

Between them were other friendly faces that took the news in stride. Brodie. Millie. Belina. Rawan. My mom. Marna and Imi. Even Corby seemed more curious than suspicious.

But the rest? They were scared. Of course they were. Most had been raised on stories of monsters like me. Feral creatures like me tearing through livestock and teenage girls on the hillsides of France and Ireland.

And Scarlett. She looked betrayed, even worse than before the broadcast. I…couldn't quite interpret why, but…I could see the hurt across her red face as she stared at me and tried to hold back tears.

It broke my heart.

It forced me to my feet to go to her, but the second I stood, she turned abruptly and walked away into the growing dark without looking back.

"Is it true?" a soldier barked. "Are we out here freezing our bollocks off to protect a monster?"

Cass's voice roared like thunder. "Call her that again, I dare you!"

There was a silence for a moment until someone murmured, "Monster lover."

Cass's lips curled back, exposing his canines—

I grabbed his hand before he could attack in a blur.

Then they were all talking; their voices rose like an approaching mob, until it was so loud, I felt surrounded by their noise.

"*Insane…*"

"*What if it's contagious?*"

"*Just wrong idn't it?*"

"*Too dangerous to be here.*"

It gave me a headache. First a small one, then a migraine when I thought of how many people beyond this village—how much of the pyramid of people out there working on our behalf—were thinking the exact same things at this moment.

Worse than that, though, was the look on Cass's face as I glanced his way. He looked like he was in pain. *Physical* pain as the cutting words enveloped us. He cringed every time someone used the word *monster*. He flinched as if they were using actual sticks and stones to wound him, rather than words. Eventually, his eyes shut and his grip on my hand tightened to the point it felt like he was holding onto me for dear life.

And when he finally opened his eyes again and his gaze met mine? There was so much guilt there. *So much.*

I hadn't seen that look on him since he'd told me about killing Lilla in London, or when he'd spoken of Marix and her daughter Mael.

I didn't even care what they were whispering anymore; I just wanted to know why he looked like that—like he hated himself.

Until Brodie's voice cut through. "All right! All right! Shut your holes for a spell, you fair-weather miscreants." He took several steps toward me despite the uncertainty I could sense across his body, then turned to face the team. "At least give her a chance to explain."

It was something. An opening.

As they all turned to me, I took it. "The king isn't lying. At least, not about me being a beast. The rest of what he said was nonsense, but…I *can* change into more forms than my raven."

The noise swelled again, and this time, a voice rang out from someone whose name I didn't know. "So it *was* you—that spider-thing that stopped the battle cold in Italy."

I opened my mouth to speak but Fern beat me to it, "She saved my life, turning into that thing."

More noise, this time as grumbles, until someone admitted, "Mine too, if that red dragon was yours. Pried one of the king's men off me."

"It was," I said.

"The bear saved me," another chimed in.

"How many forms do you have, my lady?" Corby asked, surprising me. "Can they all come out?"

Internally, I opened that question to my creatures. My mermaid and spiderlady stayed back but one by one by one, the others stepped out of me, forming a line for my team to see—my dragon, bear, wolf, raven, aurochs, wolverine, and my…

There was a new creature again. This time, a serpent grey and slender with a rainbow sheen like gasoline. It slithered under the feet of the others and coiled around itself into a little ball, yawning harmlessly despite the massive fangs I could see in its mouth.

Interesting.

Very interesting.

Not that it was the time to discuss its sudden appearance or what it might mean.

The noise from the crowd this time was hushed and awed. Curious in a good way, I thought.

So I admitted, "They're incredible. Every single one of them."

As the words left my mouth, I felt a squeeze of surprise through Cass's hand and found that look of guilt on his face had taken on some shade of disbelief I didn't quite understand.

"They don't confuse you?" Jonesy asked, pulling my attention away.

"Confuse me?"

"Like, we're told beasts are confused, you know? Their animals get mixed up and then they go feral."

"They help me keep track," I said. "I can also turn into a mermaid and the spiderlady, but only when the conditions are right. They don't let me lose control. Believe me, I spent a long time thinking I was losing my mind, but before he died, the Aurochs Lord showed me that beasts aren't what they seem."

"And how *exactly* did he die?" a soldier was quick to ask.

Idalia was just as quick to respond, "He was killed by one of the king's men while defending the queen at the Battle of Arachne's Revenge—put some respect on his name."

I pushed on. "I can show you old documents proving beasts aren't what you've been told they are, if you want to see them."

These soldiers didn't seem to care about that, so I went with something else.

"Think about it this way—the king himself just said he *wants* this gift. He *can't wait* to be like me. To be a 'crownshift' or whatever word he made up for it. Why would he want this if it's bad?"

That seemed to get through to them. I could literally see their presumptions and superstitions buckling as they tried and failed to make them align with Rav's speech.

Minds were expanding right in front of me. I wished I had Idalia's crate of books with me in the moment to prove it to them, but—

A soldier rose from a couch, groaning, "Nah, man. My mum told me stories about your type, eh. The king probably just wants to trick you into giving yourself up."

Then he turned and walked away into the gathering dark. Several other soldiers trailed after him. Then the rest stumbled to their feet and went off in different directions. Guillermo went too, glancing back at me over his shoulder. Until it was mostly my core group left.

Even then, Yasmina looked frozen as I took a step toward her. Rawan glared, but…I got the sense it wasn't for the same reason.

"I'll show you, Yas. I can show you old letters between the old kings agreeing to kill beasts because they were powerful, not dangerous."

"I…believe you…" she murmured weakly. It wasn't a lie, but it wasn't a confident truth either.

"Rawan?"

"How long have you been able to turn into a daughter of the sea?"

Ah, that explained the anger. Her English surprised me too.

As for the question, it was one I'd only just learned the answer to, so I gave it to her, "Since you scratched me saving me in Alexandria."

"Scratched you?"

I nodded. "I think that's how I get new forms. A scratch. A bite. A form can be given to me, too."

"I did *not* give this gift to you."

"And I didn't take it, I swear. But the wolverine is from the woman who tried to claw me out of your grasp in the harbor. Asterios gave me his aurochs after he died. The spiderlady bit me in Rome. The serpent? He bit me at Arachne's Revenge. The vampire bit me in London. The bear clawed me last year in Scotland. And the wolf?"

I gestured delicately back at Cass, where he stood pressed to my back, still holding my hand.

"I don't know for sure if that's how I got them, but…"

"But you know," Rawan said, her tone defeated and concerned. "You said there is proof?"

I gestured to Idalia. "In the crate of books we brought back with us from Italy."

"Show me," Rawan said. "I'll need to explain you, when the other daughters ask."

"So will I, to the witches," Belina echoed. Then she teased, "Lucky for you, there are very few things my kind cannot accept."

"I will," I swore. "We'll get the crate here as soon as possible and I'll show all of you. And if that's not enough, Ognianima is less than a week away. Asterios can tell you then. A little patience, that's all I'm asking."

***

A little patience turned out to be too much for some of the soldiers. Less than an hour later, half of them appeared out of the darkness carrying their packs. They ignored Brodie's commands to go back to their rooms and made a show of walking onto the boat to go home.

It was a little dramatic, honestly; none of them knew how to drive the boat, so they sort of ended up just waiting there in protest, not looking in my direction, while one ran to get the captain.

Cass darted for the boat.

I could hear snippets of him arguing with the soldiers as I walked past the pier, to the edge of the far forest and made my way to Belina's cottage to find Scarlett. I could see Scar through the library window, sitting in a cozy armchair, wiping her nose with tissues that rose and disappeared on the moving bookshelf beside her.

She didn't look my way when I knocked.

She shut the curtains when I begged her to talk to me.

But when Belina offered to open the locked library door, I turned her down. Scarlett was angry. I had to let her be for the moment.

Instead, I dropped onto one of Belina's kitchen chairs and let the weight of that newscast settle inside me. It was quiet in her home; it smelled like cinnamon. The perfect place for a silent meltdown.

Not only had Rav outed me.

Not only had he used my authority to elevate his own.

He knew I'd never voluntarily come back so he'd…found a way to call in that toxic promise I'd made to marry him.

I had to give him credit—he was clever.

Cruel, but clever.

"Spill."

I glanced up to find Belina in the doorway. She went right for the kettle, set it on the stove to heat, and turned back to me.

"It was just a lot," I murmured.

"I'm sorry he took your moment from you."

I laughed sadly. "He took more than that."

Belina leaned in playfully, then. She propped her chin up with her hand and waited, as if for juicy gossip. I suppose it was. And…I needed to tell somebody.

I needed to do *a lot* of things if I was going to die in seventeen days.

"Rav has…a gift. A bad one. More than one, if we're honest."

"That does not surprise me," she teased.

"I suppose someone should know, in case…"

"In case, what?"

"*Uck,* it's going to sound so melodramatic."

"So what? I am Italian. I love melodrama!"

"I…might die soon?" I delivered it with a shrug.

The playful smile vanished from Belina's face. "What does that mean?"

"One of Rav's gifts makes promises mortally binding. As in, if you break a promise you make to him, you die. Not even slowly either, just *poof*—congratulations, you're a firework, your leg's over on aisle six."

Belina's next words came slow and low with worry, "…What promise did you make him?"

"He made me promise to marry him if he showed me one of his gifts, which he did."

Anger spiked through Belina's body. She hissed as if I had wounded her, so I added the obvious, "I made the promise without realizing it!"

She paused. "*Just* to marry him, not to mate with him, yes?"

My shoulders sagged. "We both know he's going to summon the Goddess to that wedding. He's going to broadcast our union, probably as some sort of recruitment tactic or something. Not that it matters."

"Why doesn't it matter?"

"I can't mate with him."

"Well, obviously not."

"No," I risked, staring her down. "I *can't* mate with him."

Thank Goddess for intuitive people. She picked up what I was putting down big time. "Because you're already mated to somebody else? *Il rosso?*"

I nodded, swallowing a thorny ball of pain at the back of my throat. "You've already seen how Rav reacts to…anything he doesn't like, especially when it comes to me. Now just imagine embarrassing him in front of the entire world. Exploding might be the better option."

I expected defeat. I expected her to pour me a cup of tea and give me a hug or something.

She didn't.

Belina marched around the kitchen island to face me, leaning down as if speaking to a kid. I hated when Rav did it, but Belina wasn't being condescending. She looked *hurt*.

"Baby, this is why you have allies. You tell us important things like this *before* they get dire. So we can help you. So we can save you."

"I…"

"No. Don't say something stupid like you didn't want to burden us. The entire *point* of community is to be there when somebody needs help. You have options, girlie. First thing's first. You're going to summon the redhead—"

I winced. "He doesn't know."

"I beg your pardon, *he knows*."

"No, he doesn't. I only realized what happened a little while ago myself. I met mated pairs at Rav's holy day and realized I accidentally mated myself to Cass my first night as an alter. It's a long story, but it was an accident."

"That explains how tangled you two are," she said. "That explains him especially. Maybe even the Raven King's obsession as well."

"What does that mean?"

"Mates are like two halves of a heartbeat. Bonded, your rhythm is strong—keeping you both alive, in a sense. Unbonded, he's erratic, beating too fast, too hard. He gives everything he has trying to fix the rhythm, never realizing that if he completed the bond, the heart would finally steady."

My sweet Cass; that explained so many of the choices he'd made. To give me away, to sacrifice pieces of himself. I hadn't meant to hurt him like that.

"If you just told him…"

"What? Our bond would save me?"

"No, it definitely wouldn't—not from a business contract like a marriage. But at least you would get to enjoy him for a little while. And he could calm down."

I shook my head. "Cass is hiding something big from me. Something he thinks will make me hate him. I haven't told him the truth because I don't…I can't imagine…"

Again, Belina understood. So matter-of-factly, she said, "You don't want to reward your mate for lying by omission, or trap yourself in an unequal bond, I get it."

"That's why I asked Jane Lakeland about undoing a mating bond, so I could free him if he didn't want to be with me. Or to free myself if he chooses not to show up right for me."

"Tough," she commiserated, her mind clearly racing behind her eyes.

"I guess if I had to, I could undo the bond and just marry Rav," I said, thinking out loud.

But Belina was having none of that. "You do not *ever* resign yourself to toxicity. Alone is better than broken. What am I saying, even when you're alone you're never alone, so you cannot be broken anyway. We just need to find a way out of that promise. I'll call the Council. We'll find a solution."

She motioned me up from the chair, grabbed my shoulders, and guided me toward the front door.

"Could you ask Jane for another copy of her research too?" I managed to ask.

"Yes-Yes. In the meantime, go to your people. Do your own brainstorming. You have seventeen days to change your fate, and if all else fails consider telling your mate the truth, all right? Goodnight!"

The door opened on its own, the rug on the floor whipped me outside, and it shut behind me without a second's pause.

The boat with the soldiers was gone by the time I arrived back at the concrete walk, and I thought it was an ill omen—that I'd find the entire village deserted as I walked through.

I didn't.

Building after building, I peered in windows to find soldiers putting stuff back in their dressers, winding down for the night.

Others were stepping out in uniform to relieve the soldiers on the surrounding hillsides. They tipped their heads at me in passing.

Millie straight up hugged me too, whispering, "Ignore the haters, my lady. Badass like you, I'd follow into hell, I would."

Their numbers were thinner, for sure, but some had chosen to stay. Cass had convinced them somehow.

As for Cass, I found him, Ghost, Yasmina, Fern, Corby, Mom, Brodie, Rawan, Marna, Imi, Idalia, and Jasiri in the café. The whole gang seemed to be holding a…strategy meeting.

I stepped in to sounds of scheming.

"If he's as much of a hound dog as you say, Idalia, Rawan and her people should have no problem luring him out of hiding."

"I could even drown him, if you prefer," Rawan added. "It makes no difference to me."

As I slipped into a seat beside Fern, I glanced Brodie's way to gauge how her words affected him and…let's just say he looked more in lust with her than ever.

"No, Costa is a pest, not a predator," Idalia mused. "But with him in our custody, I would have no problem retaking my palace."

I hated to interrupt but, "Costa? Your rival?"

Cass had a map of Italy pinned to the wall, and it was chicken-pocked with red thumbtacks.

"Apparently there was a second part of the BBC interview we missed," Fern explained. "Rav introduced the other European Alter Supremes…all seven of them."

"Seven?"

Cass laid them out. "Archer for our kingdom, Ulric for the Wolves, Oskar Lange for the Deer Court, Oriol for the Lion Court, Sorina for the Dragons…Dino Costa for the Spider Court, and a man named Eryx Pontikos for the Balkans."

"An orca," Imi said. "I don't have experience with him specifically, but he wears a fishhook earring—the selkies consider it a mark of dishonor. He belongs to a bully clan."

There were so many political nuances in that statement—I had to take it in stride.

"He chose an orca," I said. "That's intentional."

"Yes," Rawan confirmed. "Orcas are rare in the Mediterranean, although I would expect their numbers to grow with an Orca Court coming to power. No doubt the king offered him that throne in exchange for naval protection. Orcas are apex predators—to seals, to mermaids, to any enemy that enters the water."

"There's more to it than that," I told them. "If Rav replaces the

Aurochs Court with the Orcas, he'll have to remake the relics we made in Versailles. I *barely* convinced the Gathering Table to hold a fertility ritual instead of a massacre; Rav won't bother. He'll kill thousands. We need to send out a warning to *everyone* not to accept any invitations from the king."

"Well, fortunately for me, Dino Costa is an easy man to manipulate," Idalia said, motioning to Rawan. "A pretty face? A naked swim with a daughter of the sea?"

Rawan smiled. "We'll have him in chains by morning."

"But then the real work begins," Idalia said, teeth gleaming. "Too many spiders cut webs when I needed them. Every single one of them will fill my belly in time."

"As for the new Orca Lord, we can surveil and assess as we go," Cass said.

"Or," I countered, "We can ask Asterios who his true heir is at Ognianima?" Turning to Idalia, I asked, "Will you come back to help us with that?"

"You ask me to interrupt my rampage of revenge to let you talk to ghosts?"

I put on my widest grin. "Pretty please?"

Idalia grumbled. "Only for you."

"Thank you." I rose from my seat. "Because there's more. Worse. I need your help undoing a promise."

I'd spoken briefly about Rav's gift with Fern and Yasmina before. Despite her fear at the sight of me, Fern sat forward, "A promise you made with the king?"

I nodded and told them what I'd told Belina. Not that I was mated to Cass, but about Rav's promise gift. I told them about what happened in the village in Finland, too, when the cult leader Antonio's men made the fatal mistake of reneging on a promise with Rav.

And I finished with the obvious punchline: "If I don't marry him on November 11th, I think the magick will kill me."

The renaissance painting of my friends, going through various stages of grief in front of me, warmed my heart.

My Mom, especially, she came to me and gave me a hug with tears in her eyes.

"I've already told Belina, and she's gone to the witches to ask for help figuring out how to undo my mistake," I told them. "But since I only have a few days left, if any of you can think of a solution, I'd…owe you my life. Literally."

I chuckled, but no one else did.

Cass, especially. He made a noise at the back of his throat that made me think he was disgusted by my macabre humor, but when I glanced at him, I saw that brutal guilt on his face again. He could hardly look me in the eye. Ghost was beside him a second later. Despite his mouth never opening, it was obvious from the way he leaned into Cass, they were talking with each other.

It was Corby who pulled my attention away. "We could kill him."

"Kill…?"

"The king," he said. "We could kill him, no?"

My mom lit up. "Yeah. Then there's no promise to break."

I almost liked the sound of that, honestly. Cass did too. He jumped in with, "Give the command, and I'll go now, heart. Say the word and I'll bury your mate by morning."

My heart fluttered at the threat, which I did not have the emotional bandwidth to judge myself for.

"He's not my mate, Cass," I said gently. "I don't think we can kill him. If he put a self-destruct mechanism on the choker he used on me, I don't want to risk it if his gift has fine print too."

"Maybe you don't have to," Fern cut in. "That witch gave you a way to undo a mating bond, right? You *could* marry and mate with him, and we could undo it for you."

Again, Cass made that noise of disgust. "That is *not* an option."

"It might be her only option," Jasiri said quietly.

"There's a problem there," I said. "Rav also has a gift that allows him to touch people and erase them from the world. It doesn't kill them, but they're basically forgotten, or they forget themselves."

"He used it on me," Fern said.

"Add to that whatever would happen if I mated with him, there might be no 'me' to save afterward."

Cass opened his mouth to protest, but Idalia beat him to it, "Not our first option, but we'll keep it until we can think of something better."

After that, there was more brainstorming, but it widened into more discussions about Italy, the new Supremes, and what Rav's ultimate goals might be.

But Cass didn't engage like before. He retreated into his mind and only responded to direct questions before retreating again.

I wished there'd been a moment to make him swear he wasn't going to go after Rav, but when the meeting finally ended, he walked away into the night without looking back.

Again, Ghost motioned for me to go after him, but…I went to see Dr. Sanga instead. I found him in one of the rooms in a nearby building where Idalia had spun him in silk and plastered him to the wall, completely cocooned save for his face. He looked like some horrible piece of modern art. Even the guard assigned to watch him didn't like looking at him.

The way he hung on the wall; it gave him the air of a judgmental painting. His eyes followed me as I walked across the room.

"Sorry about this," I said. "I'll have you taken to our actual prison in the morning, so you…can use your own legs, at least."

He just glared at me.

And I realized something then. "We're both victims of Rav's promises, aren't we?"

Through the tight silk, I watched his body sigh. It was all the confirmation I needed that I was right.

"He probably tricked you at some point?" I offered.

Dr. Sanga sighed audibly this time. "When he was a boy. On a dark day in his father's shadow, he made me promise to always help him if he needed it."

"So he summons, and you go."

Drolly, he supplied, "Do you really think a university professor has time to tutor a single high school student for months?"

"You did a good job anyway."

"Of course I did. I'm a professional. And you were worthy of the time, in hindsight."

"High praise," I joked. But the weight of my thoughts came back to me and I asked, "Can I get out of the promise I made to him?"

"I don't know, I'm sorry."

"Did you give him the idea to call in my promise like that?"

"I warned him against it. Desperation only breeds desperation."

Well, when you're right, you're right. I didn't volunteer news of Rav's potential demise, though.

But Dr. Sanga seemed to sense the potential of it anyway. "I know you don't want my guidance, but I would urge compassion. Despite his immense intelligence and strength, Rav has a weakness born from childhood trauma. Because so many loved ones slipped through his fingers, he clenches his fist now to prevent the loss of any more."

"He's a grown man, Dr. Sanga," I countered. "He's responsible for his choices. He's done unforgiveable things. And we both know he had something to do with those "loved ones slipping through his fingers" in the first place. A boy with the power to heal doesn't lose both his parents to "exhaustion.""

"It was horrible, watching a father grow to fear and then resent his own son," Dr. Sanga said. "Even worse to watch that father use that son to punish the mother for trying to protect him—to poison that son against her. When it was too late, Tenna was gone and he was trapped with a father who no longer had to pretend he cared."

"What happened when Rav realized the truth?" I asked.

Dr. Sanga stared me down as he said, "I witnessed what happens to the body when it's struck by magickal lightning."

The sight of that lightning throne—and a great man reduced to ashes as he sat there—flashed in my mind.

"I also discovered how powerful Rav's gift of promise truly was."

"The king made Rav a promise, even though—"

"Ivar didn't know. I didn't know. Rav hid his gift from all of us."

Not all of them. Asterios knew; and he'd asked for a gift to protect him from Rav's influence—one I suspected I now had, even if it didn't seem to apply to the promise I'd already made him.

"At what point in your story does Rav take responsibility for his part in it?" I asked. "You know, after I realized he was hiding from me, I offered him a chance not to. I offered him a future in the open with me, as my friend and partner and mate. A real offer."

"I know," he hummed sadly. "Elephant alters don't have mates, so we love in the human way. The imperfect way. We imagine soulmates the way small children imagine fairies—something wonderful that might exist *somewhere out there*, but not anywhere we can go. But… soulmates or no, to be truly loved and love in return, you must allow yourself to be truly known. That is terrifying to most creatures…especially those who know they have done "unforgiveable things.""

Dr. Sanga was telling the truth; he couldn't help it and wasn't trying not to. I knew that. I *did* have sympathy for Rav. And once upon a time, there might have been a way for him to tell me his truths without those mistakes from his past being unforgiveable.

But…that was the vital, missing piece that nuked all this potential compassion I was supposed to have. Compassion didn't mean acknowledging someone's suffering and blindly forgiving repeated mistakes they made as a result. Compassion literally meant "to suffer together." It meant to face their suffering head-on and try to alleviate it with them; to intentionally change the result *together*.

If Rav had been vulnerable with me, I could have carried the burden with him.

But either way, Rav still had to make better choices on his own.

He'd had every opportunity to do so. Instead, he'd signed my death warrant.

It was so strange how…unpanicked I was at the thought. It was horrible, yes. It was scary, yes. But I couldn't feel it yet. I knew I would, eventually, and it would be terrible. I'd watched my dad go through the stages of grief with his own terminal diagnosis; I'd never forget the way he seemed so okay with it most of the time…until despair hit him at odd hours and I'd hear my parents crying long into the night together.

At the moment, I was okay. Hollow. The only terminal symptom I had was a tiny intrusive voice in the back of my mind that just kept repeating, *I'm going to die in November. I'm going to die in November.*

And I was suddenly emotionally and physically exhausted. By the day, by the conversation, by the fact that I was on borrowed time. I turned to leave—

"For what it's worth, I did like your mother very much," Dr. Sanga called out. "Befriending her was a wonderful surprise, not a strategy."

A few moments later, as I ran out into a downpour of *freezing* sleeting rain, I noted the darkened windows in my mom's building and made the decision to tell her in the morning about scaring Dr. Sanga away. She had a right to know; and I wanted no more secrets between us.

After all *I was going to die in November.*

Then I hurried on, to the wooded path, then deeper to the cottage, which was mostly dark, save for the flickering orange flames I could see in the woodstove.

Even those roaring flames weren't enough to warm me through my drenched clothing. I raced up the stairs on all fours, dreaming of sweatpants and my warm comforter and Ghost's arm-pillow.

When I threw my door open, the tiny residual light from below spilled across the bed, across Ghost where he was already under the covers waiting for me.

"Thank *Goddess* you're here," I joked, shutting the door behind me. "I *really need* a hug tonight."

My shirt, my pants—*soaked* and icy on my body. For whatever reason, I felt even chillier in this room; maybe it was too far from the fire. I didn't hesitate; I reached for my shirt and flung it off and away to who cared where before I'd even reached for my dresser drawer.

"Could you maybe keep me warm, too? I'm *freezing*."

My fingers went to my pants and popped the button, desperate to slough them off—

"Would you settle for me instead?"

I spun on the spot like a cartoon character, took in the shape in my bed again. The red hair. The silver eyes.

"Cass?"

I took a tentative step toward the bed; when I did, more of him came into focus. He was shirtless, on his side, gazing up at me with an expression I'd seen before—on Ghost, back in Italy. He'd lain in the dirt and offered me his arm, despite the look on his face that suggested he didn't think I'd accept it.

Cass looked like that now, like he fully expected me to tell him to leave. His hand ran through his hair, ruffling it, before it slid across his scarred chest to the empty bed beside him. To the covers. He pulled them back, in offering.

Then his deep whispered voice teased, "I don't know if you remember, but I'm very warm. I run even hotter now."

I...didn't know what to say in response. But my body sure did; my heart jolted in anticipation, tugging on some invisible hook in my stomach, and lower. It wasn't so much a nudge as it was an emotional *leap* inside me.

I was still frozen physically. For all that desperate desire thrumming through my body, some part of me still seemed to think this was a dream.

My voice was little more than a hush, "Let me just find my pjs—"

"Whatever you want," he said, voice as soft as mine. "So long as you stay."

I shivered at the offering under his words. I wanted *nothing more* than to stay. Well, not *nothing* more.

Staring at him, I unzipped my pants, savoring the way his eyes darted down as I shimmied out of them and left them where they lay. I watched the lump in his throat bob with...delicious longing.

And then, he surprised me again. He reached under the covers and removed his own pants, tossing them behind him.

"I'm cold," I warned him, as I climbed onto the bed and crawled toward him.

"Not for long."

There was no pause, no hesitation—nothing but his open arms, his blazing warmth—as I slid under the covers and he pulled me against him. I nuzzled into that safe place against his chest, and we just laid there together for a long beat. Like puzzle pieces finally snapped into place.

"Cass—?"

"No. Don't say you missed me," he said, pulling back with his eyebrow raised playfully at me. "We're done missing each other."

"You…still want to be with me?"

"I never stopped."

Ugh, my heart *soared.* It was almost everything I wanted to hear.

"Does that mean you're going to tell me—"

"Not tonight." I opened my mouth to protest, but he beat me to it. "You've suffered enough betrayal for one day…but soon."

Soon.

It was such a lovely word.

Betrayal, though, was not.

"Cass, you know I love your drama, but…betrayal is such a big word."

He took a moment to run his fingers lightly through my hair. "It's fitting, for this. Unintentional, though it was."

"If it was unintentional—"

"Soon," he said again, his tone gentle but final. "Tonight, I just want to hold you."

I wanted that too. Needed it. And my body fit so well against him as he pulled me in and began to run his fingers over every inch of the back of me.

Goddess, the feel of him? I was home.

That magnetic tug along our bodies? Everywhere his hands slid, it buzzed under my skin.

Don't even get me started on his smell. Fiery cedar tingled my sinuses, and there was a slight hint of something new—the faintest whiff of sherry, as if a bonfire had been fed with an old cask. The undercurrent of blood completed the bouquet, a tang that perfectly offset the richer warm notes.

"Are you sniffing me, my lady?"

"Yes." Who had time to lie? Who wanted to?

"May I?"

I pulled back just enough to admire the glint of mischief in his eyes. To enjoy his hungry expression when I bit my smiling lip and nodded at him. To savor whatever came next, and how patiently I knew he would do it.

His hand glided feather-light up my back, then swept my hair out of the way before he leaned in. I felt his nose against my shoulder, felt the softest puff of breath.

"Honeycomb," he murmured. "And alpine breezes. Wildflowers. Soil. And something even sweeter. Something I want to—"

"Oh!"

Teeth. The softest graze of them along my shoulder, the spot above my clavicle, my neck—

"Ohhh!"

A grazing nibble. A moist flick of his tongue against my skin. A resonant guttural hum of delight deep in his throat.

I was suddenly *vibrating*. Clinging to him. Clenching my legs together without even realizing.

Every. part. of. me. felt drunk and electrified suddenly.

"*Goddess*," he groaned against my skin, nibbling again. "I think I need a head examination. Every time I'm near you, I feel feral."

"Feral?"

"Ugh," he groaned. "That's a tame word for it."

I couldn't help myself. "Maybe… I just make you want to howl."

"*You're* supposed to be doing that…"

Cass bit down harder and chuckled when I yelped. I was practically panting when he pulled back to study my face. *Whimpering* when I saw the haze of lust in his eyes.

But the lust was muted…by sorrow.

"What? What's the matter?"

"Just admiring you," he deflected.

It scared me, whatever he wasn't saying. I knew him. I knew that faraway look in his eye meant he was planning something.

"Promise me you won't do anything crazy," I begged. "Promise me you'll just wait until Idalia's books get here. Maybe the answer is in one of them. Promise me you won't go after Rav. If he got his hands on you…"

"Hush, hush," he said, pulling me in again. "I won't…yet. But if it becomes our only option, he's dead. I'll rip the heart out of his chest myself."

"He could erase you," I told him. "He could make you forget me."

The softest laugh escaped him then, and his hand slid into place along my cheek, tilting me to look at him and the smile on his face.

"Impossible."

"*Very* possible."

Still smiling, he shook his head and pulled me into his lips, kissing me with a passion I felt everywhere the buzzing reached. Robbing me of breath while breathing into me simultaneously. Winter wind and the taste of him flooded my senses.

But only until he pulled back and pressed his forehead to mine and my hand to the center of his chest.

"Every beat belongs to you, heart. No one can erase the heart's instinct to beat."

I scowled gently. "No, but he *can* kill you."

"Already sick of my poetry?" he teased.

I wrapped my arms around him and tucked my head under his. "Never."

"Never's a dangerous word."

"So is impossible."

Cass hugged me so tightly then, I could feel his heart raging under his skin.

"*Impossible* is you mating with the king," he said. "That will never happen."

He said the words with a poet's conviction, and I almost told him why he felt that way. I almost gave away the truth I'd been waiting for him to earn.

But...*soon.*

He wasn't like Rav; he would tell me the truth soon.

Which meant he would know my truth soon too.

The promise he'd made to tell me his secret set me shivering again, this time with relief and anticipation. And a bittersweet string of thoughts I hadn't expected.

My friend.

My love.

My home.

My mate.

No matter what happened...I'd get to enjoy him until the very end.

I deserved that. After all, I was going to die in November.

CHAPTER 25

I fell asleep in Cass's warm embrace, but I woke alone to a bouquet of flowers from my mom's greenhouse sitting on the dresser, along with a note that read: *I've left for Idalia's library. You're right, one of those books is bound to save you. I'll return before Ognianima. Every beat, Cass.*

Ghost, it seemed, had gone with him.

So had my raven.

"*Who else went?*"

"*Many,*" she replied, giving me a view of the plane, which held Corby and Yas and Fern and Idalia and Jasiri. Rawan too.

"*They're all helping?*"

My raven ran her feathers down my spine, in consolation.

In Ghost and Cass's absence, a Copy Cass appeared—a new shadow guardian who was…definitely not Ghost. You'd think it'd be impossible to tell the difference, but it was like day and night. This one was *enormous*, for one thing. Like a version of Cass that had eaten one of Mario's magic mushrooms. He was also empty; robotic. He was there for only one reason—to protect me. He stood way too close, growled at anyone who came within reach, and ignored me otherwise.

Aside from handing me another cute little note from Cass, which read: *This one can keep you warm, too, but I didn't give him the equipment for anything else. Control yourself, woman.*

I tucked that note in my book nook for later.

Then I went to tell my mom another truth I'd withheld from a loved one to protect them.

She took the news of me scaring away Dr. Sanga *way* better than Scarlett had taken hers.

"That must've been hard for you," she said, sitting down with me over coffee and fresh bagels.

"You're not mad?"

She shrugged. "No."

"Just…no?"

"You weren't being a brat. You weren't trying to hurt me. You were trying to help me. Is this a situation in which *if you could have, you should have told me*? Yeah—you are *forbidden* from *ever* lying to your mother again, kid, I swear to Goddess. But you couldn't tell me, so you did what you thought was best. It's actually really mature and I'm proud of you for telling me."

I wished Scarlett felt that way.

"For what it's worth, he did seem to like you for real," I told her. "He said it when my honesty gift was on."

A tiny smile played at the corners of her mouth as she sipped her coffee. "Of course he did. I'm amazing."

Yes, she was. She'd have to be, to survive what was going to happen in November.

"By the way," I said, forcing the morbid thoughts out of my mind. "Fern's birthday is the day after Ognianima. Corby's is six days after that. And Scarlett's—"

"Is November eleventh."

I'd thought about that after Rav's announcement—I'd momentarily wondered if that's why Scarlett was so mad. But that didn't make sense. She knew better than to think I had anything to do with that date…or that I would ever schedule anything for myself on her day.

Certainly not this one.

My death day.

What a party pooper I'd be.

"That's a lot of celebrating we need to do," Mom said, drawing my attention back to her. I found her staring at me. "A lot of cake orders to fill, yes?"

"I'll help you."

"You bet your butt you will. Corby's already told me about tres leches cakes about forty million times…and we need a mariachi band to wake him up in the morning, apparently."

I smirked at that. "We could definitely do a Scottish mariachi band—three bagpipes, two drums, and a fiddle."

"You laugh, but I think you can arrange that."

"I can. I will. I'll find out what Fern's birthday needs too. As for…"

As for Scarlett…

"Don't even think about it, hon," Mom said, yanking me out of my thought spiral again. "You will be *right here* on Scarlett's birthday, you understand me? So help me, I will strap you to a chair and send Rav a bag of flaming shit as a wedding gift."

"Mom…if I don't go? I'll—"

"No, you won't," she cut me off. "We'll figure something out."

I eyed her gently and reached for her hand on the table. She squeezed it as if she was already refusing to let me go. I loved her so much.

***

The crate of books from Idalia's library arrived later that day. Apparently, Yasmina had tracked it down and Cass had sent Brodie to fetch it personally; the brawny Scot arrived on a boat with the massive box in tow, and Copy Cass carried it to the café for me.

Together, Mom and I spent the rest of the day, and the next, sorting and starting to read through them—our own contribution to the readathon my friends were holding at Arachne's Revenge.

We were looking for an answer.

Some magickal solution that might save me.

On the third day, I learned from Belina that witches across the continent who had spare time were searching too. She'd also told Scarlett about my deadly promise to Rav. Scarlett had spent the last two days researching anything and everything in Belina's library with her that might help me.

It warmed my heart to know Scarlett was trying to help, even if she still wouldn't talk to me.

But…after a while, our search started to feel a bit like that scene in *Willy Wonka* with all the factory workers working themselves to exhaustion in search of a golden ticket.

The updates were sparse.

A mention of magickal promises here. A reference to magickal unbinding there.

Jane Lakeland found a "solution" in her grimoire archive, but advised against using it saying, "Came from a sangromancer, lady. A blood witch. Blood magick ain't evil, but this particular witch worked with extremes. Can't even open her grimoire without pourin' out a pint of your own blood first."

"What's the spell?" Belina asked anyway.

"…Pretty simple, actually. You just have to decide which curse you can live with and which body part you can live without."

Next please, thank you.

It didn't help matters much that that third day was the first of the full moon. *Everyone* was antsy and hangry. When my friends called from Arachne's Revenge, they were caught in a full-blown argument…about cookies.

Apparently, they'd run out of snacks, lost their ability to concentrate, and fought over an oreo.

I became the voice of reason they desperately needed by telling them to take a break and just make a snack run already. An hour of reading wasn't going to make the difference.

"Buy in bulk," I teased.

But Cass stayed behind at the library to continue the search. He waited until the rest had left to tell me, "It feels like life or death to them, heart. They're not hungry for food; they're eating their feelings about you."

Oh.

"Tell them thank you for me," I said. "Tell them, my mom and I are searching. So's Belina and Scarlett. And other witches too."

"They know."

"Tell them I'm okay."

Cass remained silent for a moment before he replied, "I won't lie to our friends, heart."

***

I was actually relieved that it was a full moon.

Or rather, I was relieved I'd *get* to experience one last set of full moon nights before…*November*.

Especially in this isolated part of Scotland, where the Milky Way shined brightly even without magick.

Yes, I knew the best use of my time would have been trying to summon the Goddess and ask for her help.

I did. Those first two nights of the full moon, I released all my non-hybrid creatures into the woods. And I sat on my bed with the curtains drawn, calling out to her again and again, but she…never appeared.

No phantom fingers through my hair. No hushed sense of presence around me.

I seemed to be on my own for this.

When I realized that, I changed plans for the third night.

"*Are you sure?*" my wolf asked right before sundown, as I moved around the lower level of the cottage getting things ready.

"*Very sure. Form a queue and be prepared for anything.*"

I had blackout curtains drawn across every window.

I had plastic lining every nook and cranny of the foyer, until it looked like a serial killer's kill room.

I had *four* azurite pendants laid out on the side table, and two more dangling from the light at hip-level, as well as the one around my neck dangling from a long chain, just in case.

If this was going to be the last full moon I ever experienced as an alter, I was going to know what it felt like to *live* as every single one of my creatures.

I had nine animal forms. So late in the year and without my raven present, that gave each of the other eight a little under two hours to run wild.

I knew all this prep was overkill, and I wouldn't return to the cottage until sunrise if the azurite pendant I was wearing never got lost, but…they deserved the chance to be free.

So that's what I gave them.

At exactly 4:20 p.m., I walked down to the edge of the loch wearing flimsy clothing I was okay losing, and I waited for the sun to set.

I bathed in the purple twilight, anticipating how it was going to feel transforming into a daughter of the sea *and actually getting to explore the sea.*

And when the last remnants of sunlight disappeared and that silver moonlight snapped on like some cosmic neon light overhead, I surrendered to the flash of pain that stripped me of my humanity and released my tailed hybrid form into the world.

Turned out, her cold heart did more than just protect my emotions.

Water that had been frigid only moments before felt as warm as a bath as my body splashed down into it and my tail sped me away toward the open sea.

Cass had been right, when he described that *collective feeling* he shared with his creatures. Hybrids experienced alteration differently. I wasn't a passenger of my animal; I was one with her. Both in control and not. My gills, my eyes, my tail—they all just worked. I could breathe underwater. I could see and move underwater as if I had always been able to do so. The salt in the sea teased my tongue instead of burning.

But "we" moved together. And if "I" got too ahead of myself with a tail that allowed for hairpin turns like a Ferrari, "we" veered away from danger before it was too late.

It was like being on a never-ending rollercoaster.

One I could handle since the fear and uncertainty that the human in me might have had was muted by my chilly heart. I was braver, but more reckless too.

I didn't lose myself in her; we expanded into something bigger than both of us, in a vast inky abyss that shimmered with technicolor moonlight.

Imi had been right—the moon *was* shining brighter than she had before.

Maybe that meant the Goddess was busier than she'd been before too? Maybe that's why she hadn't answered my call?

It was best not to dwell.

Not when I became a bear and rampaged through the forest.

Or a dragon that slipped in and out of shadow like a wraith.

Or a spiderlady with a webbed tapestry to weave.

Or a serpent that slithered into the tiniest holes and climbed trees by wrapping around the trunk and elevating itself one body loop at a time.

The world became a playground. I suppose we all know in some sense that it is, but there was nothing *to do* as an animal but play, explore, follow our curiosity.

Danger existed; of course it did. And when my wolverine met it, I learned what her claws were for.

But the worries of an artificial world *intentionally designed* to be more difficult than it had to be to trap people faded away.

I felt like a child again, marveling at the world's magick. I felt loved as my wolf howled in time with the Moon's song, the one she reserved for those still connected with nature. I felt at peace when I sat back on my aurochs's haunches and watched the technicolor universe drift by.

And I no longer feared death.

CHAPTER 26

I woke the day before Ognianima *knowing* something in the world had changed.

There was something in the air. Something in my dreams.

I woke with a sense of joy that came from somewhere outside me. As if some overexcited sandman had sprinkled me with anticipation rather than restful sleep.

I knew Cass and the rest of our friends were coming home.

I knew long before any of them sent a text saying they were coming.

When that text *did* come, though, it didn't come from Cass but Yasmina, which surprised me. The message in the text surprised me too.

We're almost home. Clear your schedule. Cass needs you.

Of course, I tuned right into my raven, plunging into my inner sanctum with a fluid transition that was getting easier by the day. I no longer had to imagine the mental version of myself standing there first; that cubbied room was as much my home as the cottage was.

"*Is he okay?*" I asked.

Through the viewing windows, I could see my raven sitting on him where he lay on a bench in a boat. He looked green with seasickness, but…he also looked *haggard*. Worn down.

Absolutely unshakably asleep.

"*Exhausted,*" she said.

"*Why? What happened?*"

My raven's disappointment was palpable as she said, "*Search continues.*"

They hadn't found a way to save me.

"*He read until he collapsed?*" I asked.

"*Spread himself too thin,*" she replied.

His poetry hadn't suddenly rubbed off on her. When the boat arrived with everyone, my friends all looked tired and sorry that they hadn't found anything for me. But they also lingered, worried, as I climbed onto the boat and made my way to where Cass was still dead asleep to the world.

Normally, he looked like a Michaelangelo sculpture come to life—vital and robust.

But there, exhausted and stretched thin, he was gaunt. Dark sunken circles, like storm-ponds, hugged his eyes. His hair was tangled a bit. His new-normal beefiness was…leaner.

"Is Ghost here to help carry him?" I asked.

"No, my lady," Fern said.

Strange.

"Copy Cass?" I called out instead.

The giant sentinel tilted the boat as he stepped aboard; the deck groaned under the *heft* Cass had given him.

"Take him to the cottage."

I hadn't meant for him swing Cass's body over his shoulder like a sack of potatoes, but that's what he did. I figured Cass would forgive me for embarrassing him like this; I certainly couldn't have lifted him.

My friends didn't think anything of it. They eyed him, then me, with a softness in their gaze that would've embarrassed me under different circumstances.

"What happened to him?"

Corby tried to answer, "Uh… He said we'd never read enough in time…"

I had no idea what that meant. I turned to Yas, then Fern, then Idalia.

"He made copies of himself," Idalia said. "They're still there. Hundreds of them. Reading."

I…didn't know what to say. But "stretched thin" suddenly made sense.

My mate was clever; I'd give him that.

"We're okay. Go be with him," Yas urged.

So that's what I did.

***

The Copy Cass rolled Cass into his bed with about as much tenderness as a caveman, flopping his body down on the mattress and then leaving without another glance back.

Still, Cass didn't wake.

I didn't like that. It meant the exhaustion was soul deep. And his copies were still out there, draining him.

I closed the door softly and took my time undressing him. His shoes first, then his socks. Getting his coat off was a nightmare, and I got too impatient for the shirt; I just sliced it off with scissors.

Maneuvering his body fully onto the bed, orienting him correctly, was worse, though. My walking heater of a man—he was cool to the touch.

I didn't like *that* at all.

Then, I set pillows against the headrest and made myself at home, pulling his beautiful head and massive beefy shoulders into my lap, so he could rest against my thigh.

I just held him. Brushed the beautiful saffron-orange hair from his face. Hummed gently while I tried to think of what to do.

Memories of healing Rav came back to me, and if Cass had been conscious enough to consent, I would've given him all the magick he could ever need that way. But he wasn't, so I simply caressed him and imagined my supply of magick as a beautiful technicolor ball inside me—one that began slowly unraveling and seeping power and energy into him through our touch.

"*Am I doing this right*?"

My raven didn't have the chance to reply before Cass suddenly whispered, "*Natalie*," and a glimmer of color caught my eye. I looked down in time to see the faintest shimmer of orange-pink magick flushing away the last of the darkness under his eyes.

It was working.

That's all that mattered.

So I rearranged myself. I gave him a proper pillow and curled around him, beside him, pressing as much of my body against him as I could, hoping sheer magickal osmosis would give him everything he needed.

***

I woke bathed in soft pink twilight. Sunset had banished the blue from the sky through the window. Stars were beginning to twinkle their hello, and the wide approving smile of the waning moon was already on full display.

I woke to magnetic connection—Cass's fingers traced a delicate arc across my neck, each touch like falling snow.

I turned my head to find him staring at me. Smiling so contentedly, despite how exhausted he clearly still was. My magick had perked him up, but there'd be no leaving the bedroom tonight.

I rolled over into the crook of his arm. "You used to tease me about staring, you know. Now you're doing it."

"I was always doing it. I was just faster at looking away than you."

But he wasn't looking away anymore; the patient quiet of him said as much, as he continued to stare, continued to trace his fingers delicately across my skin.

In all the fuss of getting him into the bed, I hadn't noticed how long the hair on his face had grown in the few days he'd been away. It suited him. And it conjured lovely images to mind. Bearded Cass as an older man, in bed, as little giggling ginger and dark-haired children came to wake him up, summoning a smile that stretched from ear to ear across his beautiful face. He tossed them into the air and caught them, then snuggled them into the crooks of his arms to savor a few moments with them before the chaos of the day began.

I'd…never really thought about our future like that before. Seemed a million years away.

And there'd been too much going on, hadn't there?

But I loved that dream in a way that brought tears to my eyes.

I wanted to see that. Live it someday.

"You're crying." Despite his exhaustion, Cass pulled himself closer to me. Just that extra inch. "What's wrong?"

That dream was just for me.

"You can't misuse your magick like this," I said gently.

"There's no better use for it."

"Cass."

"Saving the woman I love from a man I hate?" he teased. "That's the stuff legends are made of."

"Cass."

I expected more teasing, or jokes.

Instead, fire blazed into his eyes. Low and graveled, he said, "Say it one more time, I dare you."

Said the man who was so tired he could barely move.

So I called that bluff immediately.

I leaned in and kissed him. "Cass."

Another kiss, another whispered, "Cass."

And a lick to his lips. "Cass—oh!"

He grabbed my butt so fast I almost thought it was someone else. His massive hand took hold and yanked me closer, until my side was against his stomach and my legs were propped over his hip. His legs curled up below me and…

He had enough energy for one part of him, apparently. I could feel its warm twitching eagerness pressed to my thighs.

But…he left it there, and his hand slid up my side, squeezing and pressing.

"What? What's wrong?" I asked breathlessly.

Cass grinned, embarrassed. "My ego bit off more than it can chew. I am *so* tired, heart."

I giggled, tightening my legs around his, until we were a little ball, entirely intertwined with each other.

I could've stayed like that with him forever.

But…I knew from experience that…*that*…was one way to help the healing process go faster for mated alters. If I finally told him the truth about what he was to me, and he was open to that, I thought I could help him that way.

It was time to tell him anyway, wasn't it?

Especially because this exhaustion was my doing, indirectly. He was depleting himself trying to help me. Trying to give and give and give to fix the broken rhythm of our one-sided mating.

And…we were running out of time.

If I wouldn't get to enjoy the reality of who Cass would become, we could get a glimpse of that magick now.

"Cass, I…have something I need to tell you. It's important. It's…why you've felt like you're not in control of yourself around me—"

His sleepy eyes snapped open. "Wait, heart. Let me go first."

Let me tell you, I fell silent *immediately*. I think my eyes widened too; I could almost feel the cartoonish stretch on my face. Even a pause in my own heartbeat.

"Are you sure?" I asked—like an idiot!

Cass chuffed out a nervous laugh. "Yes, you deserve that. And it affects…other things to come."

His hand swept up to cup my cheek, and a glimmer of fear streaked across his face.

"But first, can I have one more kiss, just in case?"

I hated his tone. The look in his eye, as if he was memorizing the love on my face because he thought it would disappear.

I nodded, though, and watched him.

Cass pulled me in, tipping his lips up to my forehead first. Their soft press against my skin felt like a blessing.

"My heart," he whispered.

His lips skimmed to my temple and blessed me again.

"I'm so sorry for *ever* saying being near you was painful. You didn't deserve that. And it had nothing to do with *you*."

He kissed my cheek. My ear. The spot just underneath. So tenderly.

"The pain was guilt. It was shame. I thought I was too broken to be worthy of you."

Even though he couldn't see it he felt it as I scowled at him.

"We've been over that before, my love," I said gently. "I told you what I needed from you."

Teeth nibbled gently at my jawline before his heart-shaped smile landed against the very corner of my mouth.

And then he pulled back with so much love in his gaze, it scared me.

"Yes, you did," he hummed. "But I had to fix myself, didn't I. And in the middle of that fixing, you gave me the greatest gift of my life…as well as my worst nightmare."

Pain tugged at my belly. I thought I knew what he meant, but he didn't leave me to wonder.

"In those days between Versailles and my first alteration, I knew something was…wrong, beyond the heartbreak. I could hear things from miles away. I could smell alters just as far. I had fur in odd places…but also scales. At first, I thought it was like your claws—some sort of recalibration in my body preparing me for the transition. But then the pain came, and when your love saw me through to the actual change, so much happened that destroyed everything I thought I knew about myself, my place in this world, my purpose."

Cass took a deep jagged breath.

"Heart, *the first thing that happened* when the shock of what I'd become finally subsided was a *bombardment* of sensations. The needs and desires of my creatures hit me all at once. Like a…bomb. One moment, I was panicking about my monstrous nature; the next, my creatures hit me with an explosion of every moment you and I had ever shared together. And three words rang out from all of them—*go to her*."

I shivered. I didn't know why it hit me so hard, but I shivered so suddenly, Cass tightened his hold on me, as if he thought I was going to pull away.

"It devastated me, heart. I'd never felt so powerless. You were in Norway with…him. I'd turned into some…*monster*. I told you before that I prayed to the Goddess. But it was more of a cry for help, really. I didn't summon her. She came because of you."

"Me?"

"I didn't know that at first. She just appeared in the midst of my pain and sat down beside me, petting my head until I calmed down. Then she comforted me for all the unfairnesses that I'd faced—some before I was even born—and all the ones that came after. She didn't make excuses for the poor choices I'd made as a result, but eventually she explained that all these challenges from my past had done something incredible.

"That was the word she used—*incredible.*

"But it didn't sound incredible when she went on to say that I now had the opportunity to live a "truly unborrowed life.""

I blinked at him. "What does that mean?"

Cass smiled. "Your guess would have been as good as mine. But I started to understand when she told me that most people lead unfulfilling lives."

"You mean *boring* lives?" I asked to clarify. "Boring sounds pretty lovely sometimes."

"It does," he cooed, brushing his thumb across my cheek. "No. That part she was crystal clear about. A garden could be fulfilling. A sailboat on the sea could be fulfilling. Taking care of friends, of family.

"She meant unfulfilling as in a life that never set their soul ablaze. Without passion. Without purpose. Without ever really discovering who they truly are and choosing to be truly themselves. They're so afraid of failure that life-changing decisions become paralyzing.

"Easy for her to say. Everything she said terrified me. But she seemed convinced that I'd received some great gift. She said rare were those who forged their own destinies in a world full of people who would resent and fear them for doing so.

"I couldn't decide if I wanted to laugh, cry, or shout at her. I thought she was saying, 'Well you've lost everything, but here's your consolation prize—a lonely tragic existence as a…freak.'

"But then she said the fact that my difference was a consequence of birth or helped along by a friend wouldn't take away from the choice to live proudly, to be who she knew I wanted to be, once I stopped being afraid."

I was gentle when I asked, "And do you? Want to be a "beast?""

"I didn't at first. But not for the reason you think."

The light faded from Cass's eyes then; the silver darkened to storm cloud.

"Her talk of fulfillment started to sound like propaganda to me, and

I finally understood what she was *really* saying—that hard days were coming. That something would happen that might destroy me, if I didn't believe I had my own reasons to keep going in the face of it.

"In the moment, in my heartache, I thought the loss of *you* was that destruction. My creatures were *roaring* at me to find you, to be with you, king be damned.

"She said that was part of the reason she was there. Because I had no one in my life who could explain it for me, she had come to tell me why every cell in my body was screaming for you."

I went still.

Had…had she told him? He'd altered before Rav's holy day. Had she told him that I'd accidentally mated with him?

I didn't know how to feel about that, about the possibility that he had known before me and not told me, while I was off with Rav at Hamingja.

But what I was feeling wasn't anger. Certainly not betrayal.

"What did she say?" I asked.

"She said that *fate had nothing on the power of free will.* She said she could make a thousand plans, arrange a thousand serendipities…and they'd mean nothing in the aftermath of a single choice."

I…didn't know what that could possibly mean—

Until Cass said, "She said I could choose you."

"Choose me? For what?"

"To be my mate," he said. "She said if I declared you my mate, she would bless our union right then and there. She made a strange joke, even—that each step of mating came so naturally for us we didn't even know we were doing it. She told me to say the word, and it would be so."

That damned Goddess.

She hadn't told him; but she had, in her read-between-the-lines way.

"But you didn't," I clarified. "You didn't say yes."

Cass recoiled with a look on his face I'd remember forever—a disdain I could feel in my soul.

Words burst from him wrapped in a sneer, "Heart, I would *never* make a decision like that without you there to decide with me."

I…

I don't know what came over me, but…tears rushed for my eyes. I tried to hold them back. I tried to swallow them down; without them, though, my sobs sounded like I was hyperventilating.

Cass panicked. He gripped me so tenderly. "What's the matter?"

"N-Nothing," I lied.

"Without you there, I couldn't," he rushed. "I'm sorry if that hurts you, but I wouldn't. Please believe me when I say I *wanted* to join my soul with yours—more than anything I've ever wanted in my life. I swear."

My Cass. I pulled him into my lips with a force that surprised both of us. But I couldn't help myself, I needed him as close as alterly possible. The only way to express the relief and joy and love and gratitude fizzing like champagne inside my corked bottle of a body was to tangle our tongues together until we didn't know whose was whose.

And all I could say in between kisses was, "Thank you."

So many choices had been taken from me. So many fateful moments had happened *to* me.

Even though I knew *my* secret might make me sound like a hypocrite, I was so grateful for his.

But eventually, when we had to stop to catch our breath, Cass pressed on, "Heart, there's more."

"I'm ready."

"When I turned her down, she told me the potential for our union would always exist—that our fates were intertwined regardless. Then she offered a gift instead. A way to hide my scent, but also carte blanche to choose something for myself. But…her words echoed in my head that I would have to *endure* the fallout of how badly I'd fumbled you. How many mistakes I'd made pushing you toward the king."

"You couldn't help it—"

"When she asked me what gift I wanted, I told her I wanted to help *you*. I told her I wanted to be useful to you, to carry the burden for you, and make up for lost time *with you*. I'd hoped she'd find some way to give me a second chance with you; instead, there were suddenly two of me.

"Over time, I made peace with who I would be to you. And who I would be to myself—I did *not* believe the Goddess when she told me being three creatures wasn't the death sentence that I'd always been told it was. How could I when an entire cult of those…tall wolves…were out there causing chaos everywhere?

"I thought I was going to die. I operated as if that was inevitable. I took risks I shouldn't have. I did dangerous things. But I thought that if I could secure your authority, it would at least settle the constant desperate roar from my animals to find you. To claim you."

I shivered again. Goddess, I wanted him to chase me. I wanted to live to next Lunasa when I could give him the chase of a lifetime.

"And then the wedding happened." Cass gulped. "My copies flew with your raven. They gave my fallen copy the chance to confront the king, for Ghost to attach to you, and the rest of them to keep the Supremes' Seconds at bay.

"I knew this because eventually, the copies that survived returned to me. I saw…everything that happened. I saw the look on your face when you realized I'd come for you *and* the horror on your face when you thought I'd died. I saw you declare that you were leaving with me.

"I saw…you transform into the wolf."

He flinched then; his eyes closed in pain.

"What?" I asked. "What's wrong?"

"I ruined you."

He said it so low in his throat, I thought I misheard him.

"Ruined me? How?"

His wounded gaze darted back to me, full of a self-loathing that broke my heart.

"I'm the reason you're a beast. That's what the Goddess was trying to tell me. We'd done everything but mate. Our fates were intertwined. I'd experienced so many signs of the soul bond around you…I was constantly pouring myself into you—even as far back as Bear Glen. I couldn't help it. Even though I *knew* there was something wrong with me, I just kept giving. You turned into a *wolf*, for Goddess's sake!"

"Yeah, I did," I countered. "*Thank you* for my wolf—she's wonderful."

"Natalie, don't thank me! I ruined you."

My eyebrow rose. "I am not ruined, *thankyouverymuch.*"

"I'm the reason you became a monster."

That word again. Anger flared in me. My hand lashed out before I knew it and grabbed his cheeks, forcing him to look at me.

"Hey! I am *not* a monster. And neither are you, do you hear me?"

He heard me, but he didn't believe me.

"Cass, I've always been a beast."

"No—"

"*Yes.*"

Cass rolled toward me again, this time with a ridiculous look of pity on his face.

"A raven makes love to a wolf—helps him *become* a wolf—and then becomes one herself? You said it yourself just a few days ago; you acquire new forms through touch. A bite. A scratch.

"The moment I saw you alter into a wolf, I knew I'd done this to you.

I've cost you a full and happy life."

I could see he genuinely believed that.

"Is that the betrayal you think I can't forgive?" I asked him.

"You shouldn't."

I knew I needed to change tack with him. He was too smart for this. His willingness to blame himself for things that weren't his fault was getting in the way of all the proof that he was wrong.

"Why not?"

Cass gaped at me. "What do you mean, why not?"

"Why shouldn't I forgive you?"

"Natalie, *centuries* of warnings and witch hunts and old fables have told us—"

"'*Beware the beast.*' Yeah, I know. Who wrote those stories?"

His mouth opened and shut as his eyes swiveled.

"Isn't it convenient that this supposedly terrible thing suddenly becomes a *great gift* if the king can exploit it for himself?"

His eyes settled on me.

"And isn't it strange that the Goddess didn't seem worried enough about it to warn you that that's what I would become? Isn't it strange that she *offered to mate you to me* despite what I am? Isn't it strange that instead of smiting you when you turned into a tall wolf…she urged you to embrace it?"

"That's not…"

"I'm going to skip over a lot because I already went through it, but I thought I was going insane. Even when I recruited new allies. Even when Asterios swore he had proof that I wasn't. Even when the Knights of the Rising Sun declared me their leader.

"I thought I'd slip into madness suddenly or feel myself leech away slowly over time until I didn't recognize my own reflection. That didn't happen. It won't happen. Because right after Asterios showed me that proof, your father showed me that this is always what I was."

"My…father?"

I nodded. "I summoned Will back from the dead, with Idalia's help. He knew. Before he ever made me his heir—he knew. Hell, that's *why* he made me his heir."

"But your first new form was a wolf…"

"All I know—what I believe with my entire brain—is that the Golden Raven King would *never* pollute himself with something toxic.

"And I know with my entire heart that you would *never* do something like that to hurt me. So. I don't want you to blame yourself for this. And tomorrow, I'll show you every scrap of proof I brought with me in Idalia's books that beastliness isn't what you've been told. And then I'll summon as many ghosts as it takes to prove you didn't do this to me.

"And if I die in a few days, you'll know it has *nothing* to do with being a beast."

"You're *not* going to die, heart. At least, not alone."

I couldn't handle the implication under his words. I shook my head and just said, "Don't say that."

I took a deep breath and nestled deeper into his arms, kissing his chest for assurance.

It was time for my truth.

"As for the wolf...*I know* I turned into one because of you."

Cass winced and looked away.

"Because long ago, before I knew better, I fell in love with a ginger gentleman and...made a mistake."

Cass's gaze returned to mine.

"One night my ginger gentleman went out into the woods to confront a mistake from his past, and that past attacked him, and I used a word I didn't understand to save him. A certain m-word with...cosmic implications."

My heart was going a *mile* a minute inside me, as I waited in silence for him to say something. But he just continued to study me, until I added, "A word I *never* would have used without your consent, if I had known how powerful it could be."

And all of a sudden, it all spilled out of me. "Your black eyes. Your over-protectiveness. Your desperate need to give me away. It's my fault, Cass. I'm so sorry. I'm so sorry you felt like that all this time without knowing why. When you said it was killing you to be near me—I felt *awful*. But please know I mated with you without realizing I was leaving you to suffer when life pulled me away. I never meant to hurt you. Never."

The tears I'd managed to hold back came back with a vengeance then, spilling down my warm cheeks like spring water.

It was a purging—and of more than just the guilt I felt for putting him through that. It was many months coming; I needed to let it go.

And when I finally purged the spiked ball of feeling in my throat too, I asked him the question I hoped had an obvious answer, "Can you forgive me?"

"...Can you forgive that I already know?"

I blinked at him. "You know? Did the Goddess tell you—?"

His hands rose to cup my face once more…but this time, when he pulled me in, it wasn't to give me a kiss.

He licked me.

Licked me.

He turned my head just enough and slid his tongue up my wet cheek, lapping my tears up as he went, before he pulled back wearing a gorgeous, cheeky smile.

"You reabsorbed Ghost before I got to say goodbye?"

"He's here," he said, bringing my hand to his chest. "Along with every version of me who loves you. You think some *accident* is responsible for my devotion? Heart, we chose each other from the beginning. We *forged* our bond again and again. Built it from our own choices."

"I made so many mistakes—"

"A battle-tested bond at that."

"Are you sure you can—"

"I think you think this is fragile," he teased, smiling at me. "But if a single choice can bend fate to its will…I choose you."

CHAPTER 27

Cass and I may not have formally joined our souls, but we joined everything else. In our exhaustion. In our relief.

Slow. Patient.

Tender.

We didn't even move positions. My legs on his hip. His arms cradling me. That lovely lower part of him connecting us as we kissed and moved and enjoyed the spark of energy that leapt between us every time he pushed our connection deeper.

And every time he did, he groaned his joy against my skin. That delicious sound alone?

Shivering.

Panting.

We savored our return to each other.

As well as the…rejuvenation…this sort of healing provided him.

It led us to a pleasure so sweet we didn't even separate when we were both satisfied. No, we just fell asleep like that—still connected.

In the morning, I woke alone to another bundle of flowers from my mother's greenhouse sitting on the bedside table. But this time, the mission that had pulled Cass from my bed wasn't a thousand miles away.

I found him in the café, surrounded by the towers of books Mom and I had taken from Idalia's crate.

I should say I found him…and him…and him…and him…and him. So many copies, they probably could've read all the books in a single day.

"Cass! You can't make more copies. It's too much strain on your body."

Cass yanked me into his lap, into his lips, as his delicious voice graveled out a wish-full of words that had me aching to drag him back to bed: "Any excuse to have you nurse me back to health, eh?"

I glowered at him. "Don't start that bad habit."

"That's a very good habit, I would say."

His flirting stopped a few moments later, though, when Fern, Yasmina, and Rawan entered, on the hunt for their first coffee.

Cass's eyes widened and he took his hands away, leaving the path open for me if I wanted to get up. I didn't take it. I wrapped my arm around his neck instead and deepened my sit on him.

"Good morning," I sang to the ladies, matching the surprised smiles on their faces with a more confident one of my own. "Cass, did you make coffee already?"

His voice broke. "Y-Yeah." He coughed and found his rhythm, his wide eyes volleying between me and them, them and me. "It's in the kitchen."

"Don't mind us," Fern teased.

"We see nothing," Rawan added.

"But we imagine *everything*," Yasmina finished, waggling her shoulders at us playfully as they disappeared through the sliding door in a fit of giggles.

And I turned back to Cass. "Did I embarrass you?"

"N-No, of course not."

"Are you okay being with me where everyone else can see?" I asked. "I don't want to live in the shadows anymore. We can't. Too much is at stake."

Cass tugged me tight against him. "It's safer to hide."

He didn't say that as if he was turning me down; he said it as if he was warning me of what we might face in the sunlight.

"Only physically, and sometimes not even that," I said. "We both know hiding only turns you into a ghost while your heart is still beating."

Some sort of luscious freakout struck his body suddenly—his eyes rolled back before their dark, heavy gaze landed on my face, his hands began their squeezing roam across my body, and he gritted his teeth.

Then he planted a kiss on me hard enough to scatter my thoughts.

"Goddess, I love your poetry—keep talking pretty to me."

I smiled and kissed him again. "It's a new dawn, Cass. I want to be *with you* until the very end."

But some dark resolve colored his face then as he set me on my feet again, "There is no end, heart. One of these books—or the ones in

Italy—will free you."

"How will you know if the books in Italy…?"

"I'll know."

Some quiet part of me got excited. "Cass…can you share my farsee ability?"

He smiled. "In a manner of speaking. I can see everything happening there through my mind's eye. I could only make that connection with one copy—it's half the reason I think I'm exhausted—but it's worth it. I don't have to reabsorb them all first for updates. I'll know *the moment* they find what they're looking for."

"Maybe that'll get easier, now that you're with me," I said, shrugging, wondering if I'd start to exhibit some of his gifts in time…if we *had* time.

***

The day passed by in a blur of crossed eyes and coffee breaks. By sundown every single friend I had at Loch na Feàirn was reading—even the soldiers.

Scarlett came too, but she was still mad. She offered me a flat nothing smile before picking a seat across the room to read.

Belina brought an entire stack of books to read in the company of others. These, she said, had come from Jane, from her archive in York, who'd passed the books to Belina through the viewing stones.

"This is how much I care about you," Belina teased, grimacing openly as she turned a sticky page on a sticky book that seemed to be *literally sweating honey*.

"Could you care a *little* more?" Mom begged. "Put a towel down, at least."

Belina snapped her fingers and the drips on the floor vanished. A towel went down too.

"Do we have a deep tupperware somewhere?" Belina asked. "The next book has ants. Nevermind-Nevermind, I'll take that one outside."

I hoped I'd have time someday to ask her how (and why) so many grimoires oozed things.

Having everyone read the books from Idalia's library had a second, more immediately beneficial perk. Asterios had picked these books specifically because they contradicted long-held beliefs of the alter community. About mixing. About beasts. About the hierarchy of the Gathering Table. Historical events that many of the soldiers told me were taken at face value had the foundations ripped out from underneath them. Critical anecdotes that some of my friends said had shaped entire belief systems in their families were rewritten.

Not because *one* new source suggested "somebody" had been lying to them.

But because *many* did.

There was anger—a lot of it. One soldier threw a book across the room and stormed off around mid-day, and when he finally came back, Brodie quietly explained to me that the man's father had basically wielded an old story from history against him and his brothers growing up…except it wasn't the *whole* story. And once he read the entire thing, the soldier realized his father had been lying to them their entire lives. Holding them to a standard that *was completely opposite* what the full story was actually about.

"Contextomy," Cass explained. "It's when something is quoted out of context in a way that changes the original meaning. It's very common."

"Can you give an example?" I asked.

"Sure. You know that old saying "*Blood is thicker than water*"? That's only half the saying. The original full saying is "*The Blood of the Covenant is thicker than the water of the womb.*" Means the exact opposite of the truncated version. It's also called proverbial shortening, for example, "*Curiosity killed the cat*" is really "*Curiosity killed the cat, but satisfaction brought it back.*""

It was…eye-opening to say the least.

Insidious too, how many people throughout history edited and snipped and cherry-picked source material to confirm their own beliefs instead of the other way around. In some cases, we could literally trace the edits through the books over time.

But that was the point Asterios had been trying to make all those weeks ago.

He'd told me, "*Questioning everything isn't the answer. It's the method for finding the answer. It will always be better to question what you think you know than to defend it blindly. But that isn't enough. You must then go one step further—dig, tear, burn through what you have been told and what you fear, and stand in what is left. That is where the truth begins.*"

I couldn't wait for my friends to hear him say that himself.

When the sun finally went down on Ognianima, Cass led us all onto the ferry boat and had the captain sail us part of the way to the altar Cass had found months ago when he'd purchased the town.

We disembarked at a loch shrouded in mist that caught the waning moonlight and lit the way for us across the honeysuckle-scented shore and into the forest beyond. We didn't exactly fit the epic image of some pilgriming group heading into the majestic unknown. We looked like a little line of penguins waddling down the trail in our parkas and hats and gloves. But our flashlights did a special thing as we approached the altar; the light caught on the tendrils of magick creeping away from that sacred place. More and more flashes of orange and pink and neon white sparked and dazzled the closer we got. That, plus the entire bright universe visible above us through the treetops, made it feel like we were traveling through the eye of some gargantuan magickal cat that was watching us while we were watching it.

Cass held my hand the entire way. Proudly.

It seemed like such a small gesture, but it had the same impact on my team as the books did—it was a tiny act of defiance in the face of *everything that had been taken at face value before.*

The soldiers especially eyed our joined hands, half suspicious, half hopeful.

You could literally see the shift of understanding on their faces—how they realized "monster lover" wasn't the slur some of them thought it was.

That it didn't impact us the way they thought it should.

You could see tiny questions taking root and spawning more. It was beautiful. Scary too. I felt vulnerable under their scrutiny; so did Cass. But that was exactly when walking proudly mattered most.

The altar Cass had found? It was beautiful too.

Sure, it shared the same arrangement as the rest—a stone plinth at the center, surrounded by two rings of circular stones—but this one sat at the center of a forest meadow of hip-high heather. As each person swayed the stalks in passing, the bright purple blossoms swirled the magick and appeared for a moment like they were on fire. *Beautiful.*

We weren't there to use the plinth. And only a few of us knew what it was really used for anyway. So it became Idalia's dais. She stepped onto the stone foundation around the plinth and turned to address our 50-strong circle with a mysterious smile on her face.

"Tonight, on this most hallowed of holy days, we will summon the dead," she said, her too-long white smile shining in the lowlight. "Clear your minds. Open your ears. The spirits bring with them the wisdom of many ages; it would be wise of you to listen."

Yes, there was *way* more theater this time than there had been at Arachne's Revenge. But Idalia and I had spoken about it before transporting everyone to that spot.

"I need them to listen to Asterios," I'd said. "How do we keep them from getting distracted by…other spirits?"

"That's easy," she said. "I'll summon Asterios, and only once he's finished with them will I tell them how to summon others. A captive audience for the lesson, and a reward of nostalgia at the end. They'll hear him, I promise you."

But there was someone else I needed to speak to as well, so Idalia made an exception with me that she'd never made with anyone else.

She taught me how to summon the dead myself.

She showed me the passage in the book that laid it out and practiced the movements with me for several hours while everyone else was reading in the café.

"Personally, I would not reopen that old wound," she warned me. "But if you must, wait until Asterios arrives and then step away into the woods to summon the one you want."

That's exactly what we did. I picked a spot in the circle closest to the forest and Cass sort of shielded me as Idalia began her tai-chi-like summoning and started to murmur the words she'd taught me.

I waited until the magick began to gather and that tear in the fabric of reality appeared before them all, shaped like a curly-haired Greek man taken in his prime, and when Asterios stepped through to greet them, I backed away and walked into the woods.

I'd speak to Asterios soon enough.

But first…I found my spot at the base of an old, toppled oak; the massive roots fanned up and around me like a wooden sun. There, I cleared my mind and began the soft movements I'd practiced with Idalia. I did them again and again until I *felt* the magick around me begin to shift.

"That is the secret," Idalia had said. "Magick is *life*—it's movement as well as intention. One without the other accomplishes nothing. You'll feel when you're doing it right."

Right was still awkward af, but soon the magick began to glow, began to gather.

And eventually I whispered, "*Magick stirs, and silence breaks, bones whisper, and spirits wake, by my will, cross the shadowed divide, rise, join me on this unhallowed side.*"

It was a spell. Obviously. I ventured a guess that it was one taken from the witches at some point, given the tempo. And I knew, since Belina had come with us to celebrate the holy day, that I'd hear an earful when we got back to town.

Offhandedly, I wondered if the spell was from the days when shapeshifters were closer to witches, or if it had been truly stolen. I was sure Belina would tell me either way.

But I focused on the condensing magick, as it sliced through this world in the shape of a woman.

I'd never met this person before; I'd only ever seen her in pictures.

So when it felt right, I called out, "Could I please speak with Tenna Elivagar?"

And a woman with dark flowing hair and Rav's fiery blue eyes stepped into my presence. She was…lovely. Sharp. Curious. She carried herself well, with her shoulders pulled back and her chin never lowered. Regal was the wrong word for it—she was, don't get me wrong, but—*wise* was closer. *Earned* was closest of all.

"Are you my son's betrothed?" she asked, stepping toward me with a disquiet gravity.

I wasn't about to trip that forsaken promise's switch accidentally.

"So they say."

To my surprise, she offered me the thinnest smile I'd ever seen—one edged in sad relief, I thought—before her shoulders dropped just the tiniest bit.

"Have you come to ask me how to kill my son?"

"What? No!" escaped me almost defensively.

Maybe…maybe that was something I'd have to think about in the future…but…that was the last thing I wanted to have to do.

"I wouldn't blame you," she said.

"I doubt you'd tell me," I replied, adding honestly, "I wouldn't believe you anyway."

"Smart. But we both know I can't lie to you."

"You'd find a way," I countered…and she didn't correct me.

Tenna took a deep breath, even though she didn't need it. "So why have you summoned me?"

"Are you…aware…of what Rav's doing?" I asked.

"It's complicated," she replied. "We're not watching you like that, but…we can sense when we should pay attention. I knew the moment he found you. I knew the moment he ruined it between you. I should say *moments*. You are…very young and kind; I could sense a willingness to overlook signs of trouble in him. To assume the best. You made the mistake many have made before you—you moved your boundaries, you questioned your own discomfort, you ignored the people around you calling out his behavior."

"Is that what happened to you?"

"Not at first. After Ivar began to court me? Yes. It seemed romantic, wining and dining me, inviting me to stay at the palace. I didn't notice I wasn't calling home as often. Even when I did, even when I made plans for my family to visit, they never seemed to come. Ivar said it was because they were jealous. He said they had never cared for me, not really. He said I shouldn't be so concerned with my old life anyway—didn't I appreciate all he wanted to give me?

"My grandmother used to warn me that evil is wily. It comes in different guises. Sometimes it is loud and fast and easy to identify…but you must be vigilant because sometimes evil comes slowly or wrapped in gold or wearing a smile. And sometimes, evil weaves a spell to entrap you."

"The wooden pieces of art in Rav's office," I said. "I've seen them—the ones carved with ravens. Ivar wove a love spell using your blood."

"Yes, he did. Used his own blood too, to be fair. But I had no idea about any of that until we were already mated. He was always borrowing witch magick. He said witches took advantage of alter magick for centuries; it was only fair to return the favor. But to do this, he had to commit sacrilege."

"What does that mean? How?"

"In the old days, female shamanic seers— *völva*—wielded *seiðr* magick through their connection with the gods. It was not the work of men. That is not me saying that—the people of that time considered it a shame for them to use these magicks. Personally, I disagree, but because Ivar truly believed it was inappropriate for men to wield them, his belief held great weight in his work.

"He said that the *völva* and witches were constrained by their own conscience—they willingly leashed their power to their principles. Every vow of humility was power left lying on the ground.

"But…a power like that wielded by someone unbound by morality would be unstoppable. So he gave these magicks to…*false priests*…who lived in the dungeons under Hamingja. Two of them. Creepy men who dedicated themselves to learning what they believed was not theirs to learn—the future, among other things."

I had met them. The two men who wore runic robes and had helped Rav throw me into the Goddess's magick for the first time. Maybe every time.

"Ivar explained it once before I clawed myself free of him," she said quietly. "Their emptiness unleashed them. Their inauthenticity gave them great power—they could wield witch and *völva* magick unbound by humility, unbothered by responsibility."

"Horrible," I muttered. "Bad actors with cruel intentions."

"Yes," she said, her voice fading. "And the more successful their bad acting was, the more power they wielded."

"How did you feel about that?" I asked.

She frowned, embarrassed. "It took me too long to realize that Ivar was the best bad actor of them all. I learned later that the love spell he'd trapped me with dulled my discretion. It wasn't until my son was born that I saw Ivar for who he really was. My love expanded beyond him and the spell's power waned enough for me to wonder how I had mated with someone so…shameless."

"What did you do?"

"I went to the library," she said, a soft smile emerging. "I think you and I share this sanctuary in common. The more I read, the more I started to wonder if something was wrong.

"And then, like a knife to the heart, I found an answer in the thousand-year-old codex of a raven alter working with a witch. That type of partnership was common then, and it was common to record day-to-day routines. Magickal happenings. Holy day rituals. Villagers who came to them with ailments and requests for spellwork.

"That was the day I learned what a hellmate was. It was the day Ivar began to make sense to me. I…hadn't been interested in him when I first met him. My intuition had warned me to stay away, but he *pushed* and he *dazzled* and I ignored my raven's warning cry that something was wrong. Ivar was only happy with me when I kept my mouth shut. Once when I was crying in front of him, begging him to let me go home, he said, "*if you didn't complain, our relationship would be perfect*."

"I scraped my knee when I finally tried to run from him and woke up the next morning…besotted. I couldn't stop thinking about him. I didn't want to be out of his sight. I forgot my home. I forgot my family. I forgot myself and all the things I had wanted for my life."

Tenna turned to me then, eyes the color of sorrow. "I wanted to be a surgeon. After I escaped with Rav, I returned to Greece and started classes. Almost finished my pre-clinical training before..."

Her voice trailed off as her attention wandered.

"I'm sorry," I said, drawing her back. "How did you escape?"

Tenna eyed me. "Not in a way that will save you. I went to the witches and asked for help. I was surprised the Council would even see me…but they did. They showed me how to break my mating bond. They even helped shield me while I plotted my escape with my son. Very kind of them, even if it was all for nothing in the end."

"It wasn't for nothing," I countered gently. "You gave Rav a chance. Many chances, I think."

"One too many, in the end." Tenna's gaze snapped to mine. "Don't make my mistake."

"I'm trying not to. I'm trying to break—"

The moment the words left my mouth, my throat tightened with panic and magickal warning.

"—I made a promise to him," I shifted. "A bad one. Is there anything I can do about that?"

Tenna stepped away from me, and wrapped her arms around herself, as if she was cold…or for comfort. She stared off toward the plinth and the bright bit of magick she could see there.

"Is that Asterios?" she asked. "Such a sweet boy. Clever too. He once tried to warn me about Rav's gift. But I didn't think he'd ever…use it against me."

"Asterios gave me that gift."

Tenna turned back, as if she didn't believe me.

"He gave me permission to eat his heart after he died," I explained. "I didn't. But I accepted his powers anyway. I have his resistance gift, a little too late, and his translation gift."

"Rav did the same to me, without my permission," she said, turning away again. "Took the very gift the king pursued me for in the first place."

"What gift was that?"

I saw her lips twitch…as the tear in the fabric of reality that she had walked out of suddenly dilated, expanding and expanding and expanding until it became a great cyclone of magick that entirely hid the fallen oak from view. I could feel its power *nibbling* at me, pulling me toward it—*luring* me toward it.

"Amplification," I heard her say before the magick dissipated again, and returned to the shape it had held moments before. "Mostly, I used it for emotions—to calm, to soothe—or to make my plants grow faster. My husband and son thought it should be used for other things."

At that she turned back to me and added, "That is why your promise to him is unbreakable. Magick isn't transactional. It's reciprocal. He gives promises with so much power behind them, you are left with two options—follow through or *give everything* to pay him back. It is why—"

I finished that thought for her, "It's why people explode when they break their promises."

"I would have preferred an explosion. Wasting away is far worse."

A few moments later, Tenna returned to the magick from whence she had come, her words echoing like a death knell.

They were heavy. No doubt, I'd be chewing them over until the very last second when I erupted in a font of blood and bone.

But I tucked her wisdom away for later and shook out the sorrow her visit had brought me.

And in those last few seconds while the tear in the fabric of reality remained, I remembered to ask for the *other* person I'd come to speak with.

"Giselle Garand?" I called out, just in case. "Giselle, are you there? Can you come through? Can you talk to me?"

I called her name for a short eternity…until the tear began to close…and the last remnants of magick flitted away like fireflies in the night.

It was the pick-me-up I needed—Giselle was alive!

No matter what happened to me, I'd make sure my friends found her. And I'd make sure they summoned me back so I could say hello after I was gone.

***

By the time I returned to the clearing, my friends were no longer gathered around the plinth. There were dozens of neon specters scattered across the meadow, each with their own little crowd. Some I could tell were just for fun—not that I could have identified him on site, but I could have sworn I saw Christopher Lee amidst a group of soldiers—but others, not so much.

My reluctant guest Guillermo stood by a far tree talking with Henry. Even from this distance, Guillermo's eyes glistened with longing and lost chances—a stark contrast to the happy-sad smile on his face.

It was so unfair what had happened to them. And maybe it was still too fresh for this reunion to be healthy for him, but I watched as some tender moment passed and their hands came together between them. Guillermo's smile deepened as tears finally fell, and I turned away to give them the privacy they rightfully deserved.

Cass was also off by himself…with Will.

I didn't interrupt but watched as Will hugged his son goodbye and then stepped back into the magick; when Cass felt my attention and turned, there were tears in his eyes. He walked toward me through the heather with his hand out, looking like a man caught in an emotional undertow, reaching for someone to pull him ashore.

I did. "Everything okay?"

His hand swallowed mine tightly. "I spoke with my mother. She was…as lovely as I always imagined. My father was an unexpected interruption. But I'm glad he came."

"Did he tell you—"

"He told me everything. More than I ever wanted to know. Again, probably for the best. I feel freer now."

"Good!" I whispered sincerely.

Cass smiled at me and stepped ahead. Guiding me around the plinth, he said, "There's one more person waiting to speak with you."

Asterios was still waiting, chatting with Idalia, while they both watched over my team like chaperones.

"…You know that isn't true, Asterios," I heard Idalia say.

"Yes, well. Dying strips away a lot of insecurities."

"Shameless looks good on you," she teased as she stepped back to let us into their conversation. "Speaking of shameless—do you see these two? *Cavorting* in the open like our great laws mean nothing at all!"

"I saw them in private," Asterios teased. "The girl had no idea he was the one who saved her in Crete."

I blinked. "What does that mean?"

Cass glanced away shyly with a smile.

"Talos," Asterios said. "My friend in Crete who told me an injured alter girl had washed upon the shore, he said Talos—the great bronze one—had led him to you. His twin helped hold your legs down when we pried the bullet out of you, too."

"Yes-Yes, the *romance,*" Idalia grumbled. "This isn't a Celestial Temple. We only have until the magick runs out, so don't waste it on a telenovela I watch every day."

With that, she walked away and Asterios stepped in front of us.

"She's right. I don't have much time, but the time I *do* have, I'm taking. There is a choice I've made that affects both of you, but…to earn it, I must ask a favor of you both."

"Anything," I said. I owed the guy my freedom. That wasn't

something I'd ever forget.

"You say that..." He, like Tenna, blew out a breath he didn't need. "It's important for me to share my history with you. One story in particular that shaped many of the choices I made. One story I wish you to *carry with you* once you acquire this—" he laughed awkwardly "—rather *large* gift I've given you."

"Asterios," Cass said, patient at ever. "*Thank you in advance*, we understand."

"It's not about thanks...nevermind. You will understand. Please, let me introduce you to my guests."

Guests? He stepped sideways and magick began to gather in new shapes—two of them. One enormous, one rather tiny in contrast.

They almost matched Cass and me. Or, they would have if he was in his tall wolf form. The larger of the two was behemoth, at least ten feet tall, with horns that made him even taller. With a snout. With hooves.

"Is that a minotaur?" I breathed.

"*The* Minotaur," Asterios said just as quietly. "The *Bull of Mino*. My ancestor, Asterion. He's been the one person I've turned to again and again for guidance."

Cass balked. "The Minotaur is a myth, Asterios."

Asterios smiled. "No. He was *mythologized*, as so many of us have been."

"How did you meet him before?" I asked. "I thought Idalia hadn't taught anyone else how to summon—"

"Oh, she didn't," Asterios laughed. "She refused to teach the king's best friend how to do this ritual, even though I swore I'd never tell him. But she would occasionally take pity on me for my birthday...when I begged."

Idalia's voice suddenly rang out from nearby. "Eh! I am a very giving person! Discerning, but giving. Don't fill their heads with nonsense."

Asterios smiled. "No nonsense tonight. Lady Natalie, Lord Cassian, please let me introduce you to Lord Asterion and his mate Lady Lysandra."

They stepped through the magick together, holding hands. Despite his bullish features, he was handsome. Rugged, muscular, with thick golden-brown hair that grew like a mane across his head and merged seamlessly with the brown sideburns and beard on his face. She was human as far as I could tell, with long dark hair and full lips that made her look like she was pouting even when she wasn't.

"*Hello, Asterios*," Lysandra said, her voice quiet and her accent thick.

The Minotaur eyed us before his gaze held on Cass, then slid away to Asterios. "*Is this the one?*"

"*Yes.*"

The Minotaur studied Cass again—the gaze felt sharper, just the tiniest bit, as if assessing him.

"*What does he mean 'the one?'*" I asked.

The Minotaur ignored me, turning back to Asterios. "*We must be quick, pai. There is finite magick left here.*"

"What are they saying?" Cass asked.

"It won't matter in a moment," Asterios said. "They're going to show you the past. Their past. It is better this way, for you to experience it rather than being told. But only if you're willing. It is not for the faint of heart. Their stories were…tragic."

"*Only in the beginning, pai,*" Asterion countered.

Asterios's brow quirked. "*All of it was tragic to me. But…yes. Quick. Please.*"

It *was* quick. They wasted no time at all stepping toward us, the Minotaur toward Cass, and Lysandra toward me. Their hands rose toward us together.

I'd expected the same thing that had happened when Will showed me my past—for her hand to simply drop onto my head—but instead they showed us tenderness.

Her hand brushed hair out of my face before settling along my cheek. His hand went to Cass's shoulder affectionately—

And all at once, in a camera flash of blinding white, we were somewhere else. I was, at least. I was standing in a dark space again, peering through Lysandra's viewing windows. Her eyes.

It took a moment for me to understand what I was actually looking at, there were so many limbs flailing. So much screaming.

She was in a room…being beaten. Being pinned. By soldiers, I thought? And then one landed a brutal hit. The viewing windows went dark…and soreness crept into her, into me.

When her eyes opened again a moment later, the room had changed. Where the space before had been stone, this was wood. Creaking wet wood moving in great nauseating swells.

She was on a ship, chained in the hold.

As she peered around, other prisoners came into view—thirteen others, seven young men, six young women.

"*What is this?*"

"*The King's shame*," one of the men said. "*We are being sent to Crete to feed the beast*."

Lysandra began to tug futilely at her chains. "*I thought that was only every nine years*."

"*I heard rumors he sends anyone he wants to get rid of to the Minotaur*," another woman said.

"*Sure*," a man said. "*What beast eats only once every nine years? What king's shame is not infinite?*"

"*But I am a good person!*" Lysandra almost growled. "*My goddess, please! I did* nothing *to the king!*"

"*Wait...I know you*." A woman's dark narrow gaze fell upon her—us. "*Lysandra from Athena's temple, yes?*"

I felt Lysandra's body stiffen.

"*Oh yes,*" the woman cooed with venom. "*I heard about you. How poetic and petty the king is to send you with us. 'You did nothing to the king.' Weren't you the one who asked him why the Gods don't come to claim the sacrifices he says they demand? If it were truly for them why is the Minotaur necessary at all? That was you, yes?*"

Lysandra fell silent. "*It was just a question*."

"*And I was just hungry when I stole bread,*" the woman laughed. "*It makes no difference to a king who cares nothing for his own starving people or the enemies he feeds to beasts*."

At that, Lysandra hung her head to weep and the viewing windows went dark again.

When they brighten again, the ship was *rocking* violently.

So violently, it even made me sick inside her.

Water poured into the hold. Beams cracked as prisoners tore against their chains until blood trickled down their arms.

Shouting. Screaming. Thunder.

And in one violent moment, the ship broke in two in a great roar that drowned out Lysandra's voice as she fell into the sea.

Saved by luck, she was. A beam hit the thing holding her chain to the wall and snapped it, leaving her with shackles and chain links, but free arms nonetheless.

She swam. She swam and swam and swam toward the debris-covered surface, as the sun shining beyond. Her lungs hitched. Pain welled. Then fresh air tore into her body so fast I felt the shock of it in mine.

But even then, it wasn't over. The storm raged. Men shouted for help that wasn't coming.

All she could do was swim. In the open sea, toward who knew where.

Toward an island to the far south—a destination.

When Lysandra's feet staggered onto the shore, I saw myself in her. She laid down in the sand in a little ball and cried herself to sleep.

When she woke, all I could see…was skin. Dark brown skin in the growing dusk.

All I could hear was…snorting.

She tilted her head just enough for me to see she was being carried in the arms of…the Minotaur.

There was plenty of fear in her, but…that wasn't what made her heart begin to dance when he turned his attention to her and said, "*Rest against my chest. We have miles to go.*"

Emotions fought inside her like toy soldiers. She stilled and awakened while she stared at him.

"*Please.*"

"*Please what?*"

"*Please will you kill me before you eat me?*"

The Minotaur snorted in derision. "*Drowned maiden is hardly edible. And you're skin and bones anyway. Perhaps I could use you for a toothpick.*"

A flutter went through her when she focused on the tiny smile playing at his lips. "*Maybe you should feed* me *instead, then.*"

At that, he set his full attention to her and said pointedly, "*Perhaps a vegetable stew? Would that satisfy you*?"

"*…Yes.*"

He carried us into the deep system of a cave, to a spot I recognized—the stone cottage Asterios had shown me on Crete. Only this one was in pristine condition with white-washed walls and a thick thatch roof, blooming with flowers. The pond at the center of the sky-open cave was more lagoon than puddle then, too. It was much deeper then too.

And there, on the embers of an afternoon fire, was a pot of soup.

He set us down and disappeared into his home, returning with a chisel and hammer, as well as a bowl and spoon. He made quick work knocking the shackles off her wrists—as if he had freed more prisoners than we would ever know.

"*There, you're free,*" he said, motioning to the soup. "*Fill your belly and go. The exit is back where I showed you. I would not recommend returning to Greece, unless you wish to die. You got lucky—once. Don't give that puny king a reason to make an example of you.*"

He went back inside and Lysandra eyed the way out, then the soup, then the cottage, in a little loop that made me dizzy.

Until he finally re-emerged and saw she hadn't moved.

"*You're not a princess, are you?*" he grumped. "*You do know how to serve yourself, yes?*"

Again, she didn't move, but her voice warbled, "*Would you like some?*"

The Minotaur blinked, surprised. His dark brown eyes studied us for a long moment before he said, "*Not yet. Not until it's over.*"

"*Until what's over?*"

A noise caught then, faint and sharp—shouting. Begging.

It was coming from overhead. From…a prisoner we both recognized from the ship.

"*Please don't do this! Don't do this! Even Poseidon didn't want me!*"

"*Shut up, you. You can go in dead or awake with a fighting chance.*"

Lysandra saw the prisoner, saw one of guards with him—a man we also recognized, one of the men who'd come for Lysandra originally—and ducked back suddenly.

She tucked herself behind the Minotaur, peeking over his shoulder where he sat by his home, as another great scream rang out…and the prisoner fell from above, shoved, into the water below.

"*Now the rest of you!*" the guard shouted.

One by one by one, four others were thrown down—the few who had survived.

No, there was one more. As we watched, the bread thief walked quietly, easily, toward the hole, where she paused.

The guard didn't. "*Go! I've had enough of you!*"

"*Yes, of course, sir. Of course. I just thought you might like to come with me.*"

It happened in a flash. She grabbed the man by his waist and *heaved* herself backward, taking him with her.

They fell like stones. Splashed like anchors.

I didn't expect her to surface, but she did. So, too, did the guard. All the arrogance drained from his face. He scrambled out of the pool and withdrew his dripping sword with terror on his face.

"*My gods, the beast itself!*"

The Minotaur sat easily beside his cottage.

Two of the prisoners ran immediately, straight through the far tunnel. The other three seemed frozen there.

"*Go on,*" the Minotaur told them. "*Freedom lies that way. I have no problem with any of you. Get out of my home and leave me in peace.*"

"*Lies!*" the guard barked. "*You feast on them for the king.*"

Through Lysandra's touch on his shoulder, I felt him flinch.

"I *am a king*," he bellowed. "*I do* nothing *for any other. Not the one in Athens. Not the one on Crete. Petty childish cowards who cannot handle their own problems, so they send them to me. Idiots so sheltered they've dreamed up flesh-eating cows, apparently.*"

To punctuate his point, he took a giant loud chomp out of a carrot.

"*You will not chase us?*" one of the remaining prisoners asked.

"*No.*"

They bolted. On bare feet across sharp rocks, without looking back. Until it was just Asterion, Lysandra, and the guard, in a lazy standoff—one in which Asterion seemed entirely unmoved from his little seat by the cottage.

"*You set all the offerings free*?" the guard asked.

"*This one's surprisingly clingy...*" Asterion grumbled.

"*But...this is who you are!*" the guard demanded.

"*I do not concern myself with the opinions of cowards*."

The guard began to shake—*literally,* he looked like a little overheating engine about to blow.

He took a wide step back and readied his blade, his face growing redder by the second.

"*Then I shall end you once and for all,*" the guard declared.

"*You can try.*"

"*In the king's honor! He will reward me for freeing him from this burden!*"

"*He will slaughter you for taking away his excuse.*"

The guard ignored that and turned his suddenly unctuous gaze on Lysandra—us. "*Perhaps he will let me keep you, little reward—*"

Lysandra's voice rang out in her head. "*My goddess will protect me!*"

The guard laughed. "*I doubt that very much. Temple maidens must be virgins, no?*"

"*I...that is what I am, sir.*"

"*Not anymore.*" He turned to the Minotaur then with a shrug—as if he had suddenly become "just another man" to him. "*What kind of man would let it go to waste?*"

Her heart froze. Ice crystals spread across the dark room in her head around me; and the soreness I felt in her body before broke my heart. Lysandra took her shaking hand off the Minotaur's shoulder. Panic swelled like steam in a kettle.

Lysandra suddenly roared. *Roared.*

Her hand landed on a sharp, jagged stone. She hurled it at the guard, her aim true. Hit his head with a thud that might have hobbled him, if he'd been a little closer.

Instead, he just laughed and wiped the blood away. "*I prefer you asleep.*"

She reached for another—

But Asterion rose to his feet, casting his long shadow across her. He partially raised his hand, staying her anger.

Then he turned back to the guard. "*Her goddess would not forgive her for seeking revenge...but mine would. You want to 'free your king from his tithe?' Do your worse.*"

The Minotaur suddenly shifted position. Dropped into a statuesque lunge that flexed his muscles until he looked made of stone, mythic in proportion—even crouched, he truly looked like a king.

Lysandra backed away as the guard shouted and charged…and the Minotaur responded.

He took three sprinting steps and dropped his head low, catching the guard in his gut with the tip of his horn. The man's body didn't fly off and away. Oh no. The bull's head pivoted, swinging him up and over and down on to the ground with thunderous power that shook the cave walls and gored the man deeper.

The guard moaned as blood trickled from his lips, but…the Minotaur wasn't finished. He ripped his horn clear, grabbed the man by his pinned arms and *charged* the cave wall. They struck together, crushing the man's body and the wall behind him in one blow. There was a new tunnel suddenly leading away in that direction, deep enough we couldn't see them anymore.

Then silence.

And a random thought—I'd walked through that very tunnel with Asterios to reach this cave in modern times.

When the Minotaur reappeared, he emerged dragging the still alive body of the broken guard behind him. Asterion's eyes landed on Lysandra, and I saw an expression on his face I knew well—presumption that she wouldn't want anything to do with him now.

"*Would you like to see something pretty, lady?*" he asked, surprising the both of us.

"*...Yes,*" she said.

He motioned for her to follow…and we did. Out through the very tunnels through which he'd carried us. He even found one of the prisoners lost and confused, and motioned them to follow him as well.

Until we finally emerged back on a beach, and the other prisoner fled, leaving them alone again with the twitching man behind them.

"*We must wait for nightfall,*" he said.

But…no sooner was there nothing to do but Lysandra's mind started to wander. I could feel it, the sorrow seeping back in. Especially when the guard moaned again, in agony, and she glared at him.

"*Don't carry the king's shame,*" Asterion said, pulling her attention. "*What was done to you is his to bear, along with the rest.*"

"*But I must live with it,*" she countered, her voice pained and soft. "*I cannot go home now. The temple would not have me; my family would not have me. No husband would…He's done worse than kill me—he's left me alone in the world.*"

She sat on the sand then and began to cry again. So hard, I couldn't see the ocean anymore as the last light of day left the sky and darkness descended. With it, came firelight, as the Minotaur built one nearby—to keep her warm, it seemed.

And then finally, he held his hand out to her. "*Come. The pretty thing is here.*"

She took his hand and rose to stand. She didn't let go when he reached down with his other hand and grabbed the wounded man's foot.

Together, they dragged him down to the water's edge…and there in the darkness, I saw a flash of pink. Then purple. Then bright blue.

I saw wet heads with golden eyes.

A dozen of them.

Lysandra's grip on him tightened as she realized, "*Nymphs? Beautiful!*"

Asterion ran a gentle thumb across her hand before he turned to the approaching mermaids.

"*Lady Thalia, thank you for coming,*" he said.

"*You don't call often, Lord Asterion. We were beginning to wonder if you still lived.*"

"*Only for now,*" he said. "*We've had another cruelty from the king. This man has ruined this lady's honor. I thought you might want him.*"

"*Want him? No. But I am happy to punish him,*" the mermaid teased.

Something in her tone told me this was an old joke between them. So did Asterion's response, "*Enough?*"

"*Not half as much as he deserves, but…enough. More than she could imagine.*"

Asterion glanced at Lysandra. "*Can we get rid of him for you? You will never have to look upon his face again.*"

Lysandra didn't know what to say.

"*Because it will be eaten, child,*" Thalia offered flatly. "*His face—clean off, I promise you.*"

Lysandra gulped—half in awe of her and half terrified. "*By you?*"

Thalia laughed, her voice like pebbles on a wave-swept shore. "*Not me, no. We know where the sharks dwell.*"

Asterion left the decision up to her, but after a few moments, Lysandra nodded and Asterion tossed his broken body into the sea. The man's garbled, salty scream rang through the air for half a second before the daughters of the sea dragged him under for good.

And then, it was just the two of them in the firelight. Asterion guided her back over into its heat and they sat beside each other, as if they were old friends.

"*Nymphs,*" she said.

"*Yes. Pretty, aren't they?*"

"*Yes.*"

Asterion paused for a moment. "*Would you...like to be like them?*"

Lysandra's gaze whipped in his direction. "*This is possible?*"

"*Yes. They are very kind to women who have been...robbed of things.*"

She glanced away.

Asterion added, "*They can make it so you don't care. It is one option for your future.*"

"*Could I stay with you until—*"

He cut her off *immediately. "No. There is no staying with me.*"

"*Not even until I grew comfortable as a nymph?*"

He stuttered. "*Uh...no.*"

"*Why?*"

"*Because.*"

"*I could earn my keep. I might have been a temple maiden, but I come from a fishing family. I could fish for you.*"

"*I don't eat fish.*"

I felt her smile. "*No fish either? Well, I can garden.*"

"*No.*"

"*Why?*"

"*You have no future with me.*"

"*That's not what I asked.*"

"*I mean—you can't stay because I don't have a future.*"

"*In what way?*"

"*I'm the last of my kind. The best I could do for you is take your shame from you, carry it with me when I go. And you can go on and—*"

"Are you the last of your kind by curse or by choice?"

"Choice."

"Why?"

Asterion rose then and started marching back toward his cave. Lysandra was on her feet just as quickly, following.

"It's not your burden to carry."

Lysandra disagreed. *"You save me, you play the monster to show mercy, you carry shame that was never yours, you call yourself a king, the nymphs call you a lord—my arms welcome some of that burden."*

"We cannot always have what we want."

"Do you carry shame for your entire family? Is that why you wish to die—"

Asterion turned on a dime and Lysandra ran right into him, bounced right off his stomach. It was comical how far back she had to tip her head to stare him in the eye.

"Quit following me," he said.

I felt another soft smile on her face. *"You know the guards did not take me willingly. I fought until the very end."*

Asterion considered that. Turned away and kept walking.

And Lysandra followed. *"Maybe you are the last of your old family. That does not mean you cannot be the first of a new one."*

Asterion stopped cold again, but this time, he didn't turn back. Lysandra walked around to gaze up at him, at the look of surprise and uncertainty on his face.

"I do not have a future either," she said gently. *"Perhaps...we could figure this out together? Perhaps I could stay until we know for sure that that is a choice we must live by?"*

She waited for a response but when it didn't come, she turned and walked back toward the cave, leaving him to follow.

And after a moment, I felt him there, walking behind us. In a tone so dry, it brought a smile to my face, he grumbled, *"What exactly did you do to piss off the king?"*

"I asked a question he did not like."

He hummed. *"Mmm. A hobby of yours, I see."*

I felt the start of a blush on her cheeks and the viewing windows darkened again.

This time, we found ourselves back in the meadow in Scotland, standing across from Asterios and his ancestors—the unmonstrous monster and the drowned maiden. They were still holding hands, so tightly; and as they gazed away to their descendant, I could see so much kindness and sadness there, from both of them—Asterios was the end of that new family they'd built together.

"Thank you for sharing that," Cass said.

"You are welcome," Asterios said. "But as I warned, this is a responsibility, as much as a story. It's my history. I made the choice long ago never to marry. To end the line of aurochs—no one should suffer the loneliness of being the last of their kind."

I didn't know if I should ask, but I wanted to. "You didn't *have* to be the last, right?"

"Aurochs were eaten to extinction, and then replaced with cattle," he said. "My teams intercept shipments of illegal leather every day. I needed a better reason to keep us going."

"Did you hope you'd find your own Lysandra?" Cass asked.

"Yes, of course," Asterios said. "But only if it happened by chance, like it did for them. I never wanted to fill my own emptiness by dragging someone else into it. I regret that now."

My eyebrow rose. "You regret not forcing—"

"No, no force," he interrupted. "Death showed me you must fight for the things you claim you want. You cannot sit in your solitude and ask why you are lonely. Nor can you remain the same and wonder why nothing is changing. I was too passive, for reasons that were half my doing, half my family's. I could have been a great man for a great woman, but I didn't rise to the challenge and so…"

He shrugged, glancing at his relatives.

"*Tell them, Asterios*," his many-times-great grandfather said. "*We took too much magick for ourselves.*"

Across the meadow, I could see spirits beginning to fade where they stood, holding onto the precious seconds they still had.

"Yes, your responsibility," he said. "Cassian Mahon, I have named *you* the heir of the Fourth Kingdom."

"You what?" Cass said.

"Call my lawyer, Eleni Kittas, in Athens. She has the paperwork—the notarized will, the certificate of inheritance, all that."

"But why?"

"You don't say thanks for this—?"

"*Thank you!*" Cass almost laughed, leaping forward to shake Asterios's hand with both of his. "But…why?"

"So many reasons. I witnessed what your father put you through—I know how far you went to try and be the son he wanted you to be. I saw the better version of me in your struggles, and so on. The Wogon

Kingdom deserves a leader who truly cares."

Asterios smirked, glancing at me, before looking back. "I am also a romantic. This new age is as much for the heart as it is for the soul of our people—those that were, are, and will be. The politics and law may protect them, but you two will inspire them. Rav cannot do either of those things."

Asterios, Asterion, and Lysandra suddenly flickered like dying neon lights.

"We must go, but I hope we see each other again, when you've both carried us through to better days."

I gave Asterios a hug and Cass shook his hand.

But Cass had one more thing to ask. "Wogon?"

"Yes, uh, a half-wolf, half-dragon?"

Cass winced. "Are you…set…on that word?"

Asterios smiled. "I am sure you'll come up with something far better."

And with that, Asterios followed his kin back into the light and disappeared.

CHAPTER 28

Asterios's lesson in propaganda had an *immediate* impact on our team. After the last of the spirits faded away and the last of the magick in the meadow dissipated like morning dew, everyone gathered around Cass and me, much more closely than before. They made jokes. They apologized for their fears. Or they acted like they'd never been afraid in the first place.

Mostly because Asterios came with receipts. Cass told me that Asterios had referenced books and exact pages, in some places, and when my people asked questions, he was happy to give answers. He dissected narratives for them. He suggested additional reading too.

It was difficult to argue with a truly confident ghost—even the soldiers who Cass had reluctantly convinced to stay walked away from the experience promising to call back the friends who had already left to go home.

Yasmina, too, was completely altered. She gave me a huge hug and told me which of the old Ukrainian superstitions had kept her so afraid before. She also said she wanted to "get ahead of the propaganda" and put together a reference guide, so we'd have sources to show when people inevitably accused me of being a monster. She got right on it; when we returned to town, I found her (and a few of the soldiers) in the café reading late into the night.

Belina was pissed about the stolen spell. She waited until we got back to confront Idalia about it, and their argument got so loud we could hear them shouting in Italian all the way down the concrete walk. But when I finally went to check on them, I realized all that shouting was friendly. Basically, bickering between cousins over the book Idalia had taken the spell from, which resulted in Belina saying the spell was outdated and Idalia grumbling that she could, you know, *fix* that if she was feeling generous. The last thing I saw before I left them to it was Belina rolling her eyes and motioning for Idalia to follow her to her cottage so she could show her a better spell.

The surprise of the night, though, was Cass.

I'd expected *elation.*

I'd expected the boy equivalent of jumping up and down and squeeing.

There was a little of that…until he asked me whether Tenna knew how to break my promise to Rav. When I told him she didn't, he grew quiet. Introspective. He held my hand, kissed my head, enveloped me to sleep, but…I knew he laid awake for a long time, just thinking.

And in the morning when I rolled over and kissed him, he said, "Let's wait to tell people about my new position until we confirm with the lawyer."

I knew what he was really saying—*let's keep everyone focused on saving me.*

***

We were lucky that the day after Ognianima was Fern's birthday, rather than one of the others. She was definitely the chillest of the three people we had to celebrate. No early morning traditions needed to be upheld, no strict schedules needed to be enforced.

I'd learned that Thai people often celebrated much the way western cultures did—with cakes and gifts—alongside a couple traditions unique to their country.

'Merit-making,' or simple acts of kindness, was a big one. They often did this by giving alms to Buddhist monks at temples. The closest one of these was in Glasgow, but given the danger, I arranged for a portion of our 40,000-strong private civil service to clear their calendars, ready to do random acts of kindness across the kingdom and deliver donations to the temple on her behalf.

The second tradition—the Thai tradition of 'life release'—was easier for us to achieve in Loch na Feàirn.

Before dawn, Cass, Jonesy, and Millie left on the boat to go retrieve the supplies, while the rest of us either kept Fern distracted or baked her a cake. Her favorite flavor was pandan, and Yasmina made a special call to one of Fern's sisters to get her favorite recipe before most of us piled into the kitchen with Mom to make it.

All while Corby, Scarlett, Rawan, and Belina kept her distracted with breakfast in bed and a long walk…and dolphins, which Rawan called in from the sea.

The only real problem we had was convincing Fern to take the day off from trying to save me.

She hated the idea of it, even when I told her it was okay.

"We can't spare the time," she urged.

"Yeah, well, I don't want to spend the last few days I have doing research," I replied.

"They're not your last few days…"

"You're right—so quit arguing with me and tell me what you want for your birthday."

It wouldn't have done any good to explain to her that I couldn't stand the idea of robbing any of them of their happy days, considering they were out here on the ragged edge of nowhere because of me. Because they were putting their lives on hold for someone who might be on her way out.

It was like pulling teeth, trying to coax the word "karaoke" out of Fern, but I finally did.

And in the end, it was a perfectly lovely day. Cass, Jonesy, and Millie returned with a full tank of lobsters from a nearby restaurant, and we each released one back into the loch's salty waters. Then we surprised Fern with her cake, which was insanely delicious considering Mom had never made it before, and then we set up a makeshift "karaoke machine" (really a microphone, some speakers and a laptop) and we all took turns embarrassing ourselves, singing Chappell Roan at the top of our lungs long into the night.

But…I also put myself out there.

I picked my moment and got up in front of everybody to sing "Count on Me" by Bruno Mars. I didn't even pretend to be cool about it—I told Scarlett it was for her and sang it directly to her.

She looked *so uncomfortable*, but by the end, there were tears in her eyes and she smiled shyly at me. She still didn't talk to me, but…she wasn't as angry as before.

It was a start, at least; I couldn't stand the thought of her hating me until the end.

***

The next morning, it was time to say goodbye. To Idalia and Jasiri, as well as Rawan, Brodie, Millie, Jonesy, and a few other soldiers. They were headed to Italy, to Dino Costa's house to…lure him into a watery honeytrap…and take Idalia's kingdom back in one fell swoop.

They promised once that was done to go to Idalia's library and continue searching.

I reminded them that dozens of Casses were scouring the library's books at that very second, and had been for days, but my friends were all convinced they'd be the one to find that golden ticket—that "get out of death free" card.

"Saving you is good motivation, lass," Brodie said as he gave me a hug. "More the reason to grab this Costa fella in two seconds so they can move on to more important things."

I caught a longing glance from Brodie to Rawan and teased, "I think you're more worried about Rawan falling for that guy's charms than getting to a library."

"You wouldna be saying that if you heard her talk about gutting him like a fish."

I laughed…but I knew she was serious. I didn't know if he did.

"Brodie, has she…told you about her past?" I asked delicately.

"You mean her ex?"

Ex was one word for it. I nodded.

"Aye, she did."

"That didn't scare you away?"

Brodie's brow quirked, almost offended. "Scare me away? I'da killed him myself, given half the chance." Then he leaned in with a great wide grin. "Did she tell ya she asked a cookie cutter shark to tear the heart clean out of him?"

"I didn't think she needed a shark."

"Need's got nothin' to do with flair, lass."

I knew he didn't mean anything by it, but those words echoed in my head for a long time after they left.

Need has nothing to do with flair. There was a lesson in there somewhere—or a suggestion? I didn't feel the Goddess's presence in those throwaway words or anything, but I felt…inspiration.

A dark inspiration related to saving myself.

I just didn't know what it was yet.

***

The next day, it was back to the grind of keeping me alive and unmated to the king. I spoke with the witches—they'd found nothing yet. At least, nothing reasonable. I wanted to keep my legs, thank you. And my eyes. And my decent luck.

But that was the nature of magick—every spell came with a cost, and the more dire the spell, the larger the price.

"While it doesn't help free you from your situation," Tiamat said, "that balance also applies to the king's powers—especially with his mother's gift of amplification. Every intention cast into the world summons an equal, answering force. He's put a lot of energy into this promise with you. If you can break it, I dare say it'll have cataclysmic repercussions for him."

"*If I can break it* are the important words in that sentence," I mused.

"Well, Freyja's found those "false priests" you told us about," she said. "The ones who twisted our magick to ensnare you with the soulchoke. She's watching them at Hamingja and searching for a way into that cave underneath. Their days are numbered; you mustn't lose hope."

"Thank you for your help," was all I could say…because my days were numbered too.

***

No, before you ask, none of this was taking place in a vacuum. Sure, I was scrambling to find a solution at the edge of the world with my team's help, but beyond the loch, hundreds, if not thousands, of others were combing through old books, manuscripts, and grimoires.

We'd shut down audience hours.

We'd postponed meetings with kings, presidents, and sovereign supremes…just in case they weren't necessary.

We'd even called Robine again, although the talk was short and cryptic.

She simply said I didn't need her help, that the solution to my problem was already inside me, and that this was one more mistake I had to fix before I could take my rightful place as Ruler of the Alters.

"Perhaps it's time you take a page out of your enemy's book," Robine said.

"You're as vague as the Goddess," I grumbled.

"And for the same reason."

"Have you heard from her, at least?" I asked.

I was surprised that she actually answered. "Strangely, no. But I am not worried yet."

“I am,” I admitted, hoping I’d hear anything like sympathy from her.

Instead, she gave me the tiniest crumb. “You’ll want to watch the news tonight…and every night, until your last.”

Cult leaders, man.

***

“Are you sure we shouldn’t have everybody watching—”

“Not this time. We’re not risking them losing their nerve again.”

Instead of carting out the town’s sole television for everyone to watch, my team and I squirreled ourselves away behind closed curtains to see what new horror the news would bring us.

Cass sat beside me, his hand on my thigh, his body language reassuring, while his intense eye remained glued to the TV as he flipped through channels. A copy of him waited, crouched by the outlet again, ready to pull the plug.

“There he is—there he is! Go back!”

Seeing Rav again struck my solar plexus hard—a punch of fear and revulsion rippled through my gut and up into my throat. I wanted to run away and spit on him and throw up all at the same time.

But I pushed through it to listen, to absorb this new version of him.

He was dressed down. Cosplaying academic chic in a professorial couture suit with his hair down. This interview was a sit-down talk with some European host I didn’t know, much more informational than his splashy BBC debut had been. Intentionally so.

And when we turned up the volume, I realized why.

“How did you feel when you uncovered this new information about your fiancée?” the host asked.

“I was nervous, of course,” Rav said so casually. “Our community relies on simplicity—one person, one animal—to function. But my father, who was a beloved king to his people for five decades, knew things aren’t always so simple. He kept an extensive collection of rare historical texts, so…now, I do. But there are libraries across the world with information about our kind as well, and these contain millions of books going back thousands of years—some printed on gold, on stone tablets. So, I went looking for reliable accounts of alters with gifts like Natalie.”

“And you found them?”

“Oh yes. Crownshifts are rarer than I ever imagined—anointed by the gods themselves to rule over the world in times of great transition.

There has never been a more momentous period of change than now, post Great Revelation."

He went on and on and on about these "great historical texts" and what they revealed about "crownshifts." He reinterpreted myth as history. He implied alters won continent-shifting battles. He ignored any story about 'beasts' like he was allergic to them, and instead straight up created his own, claiming he knew of "two crownshifts so far" who had risen to great and celebrated power in their day, including a pope from the fifth century who saved Europe from a terrible invader and an emperor from India who conquered his empire and then ushered it into an era of great moral transformation.

It was…more hype. That's what he was doing. Wooing people with epics tales of crownshift glory. Maybe he *had*, in fact, found proof of crownshifts in positions of power…but he was only saying this to shift public opinion in my favor.

Under different circumstances, and on my terms, it would've been the most romantic gesture in the world.

But there was no real romance in his words, only politics.

And I knew that because when the host asked whether all of this was the reason the Knights of the Rising Sun had chosen me as their leader, Rav suddenly grew very serious.

"We must be careful there," he said.

"How do you mean?" the host asked.

"Natalie and I are natural choices to rule the shifters, to guide them into a better future. A brighter future. A more prosperous future, but…certain forms come with obvious risks…"

My spine stiffened.

"Forms—you're referring to *animal* forms."

"Yes. One person-one *animal*. That is the natural order of things, with the obvious exception of a gods-given gift bestowed upon the deserving few, of course. But the gods do not just make *anyone* an alter. Some alters force the issue, or sometimes things go wrong, and *incomplete* transformations are the result. Some people were simply never meant to be alters and many of the Knights…well…we can discuss that at another time."

The host was hooked. "Are the knights *dangerous*?"

Rav shrugged so casually. "Look, most shifters contribute so much to our society—they're good, law-abiding citizens in every sense of the word, but… Take these tall wolves, for example—have you *ever* seen a tall wolf naturally in the wild?"

"N-No, I haven't."

"Some forms with naturally unstable transformations, well, their instincts run a little wilder and caution is needed—for everyone's safety, including theirs. I'm not saying they're all dangerous, only that we must be vigilant to ensure they never become so."

***

Cass left the building as soon as the interview ended. And I followed him out into the softly falling snow. Of course I did; I'd felt every twinge and flinch in his body through his touch throughout the entire horrible hour of television.

"Cass, it's theater," I said.

"I know," he said quietly. "Dangerous theater."

"It won't hold. The Knights will put out some statement. They'll issue some response."

"It doesn't matter because you aren't speaking for them."

"…I…could make my debut early?" I offered.

"No, heart, he's counting on that," Cass said, beginning to pace. "He wants to know where you are. He wants the world to think you're part of his theater. And you have bigger issues than what happens to a bunch of tall wolves because the king suggested they were dangerous."

I balked. "Excuse me. You say that as if I shouldn't care about your people."

"They're not—"

I stepped toward him, until I was almost looking straight up at him. Until he stopped physically pacing, and his eyes began to swivel in time with his overthinking.

"Yes, they are. They're mine, too. He attacked my people tonight, too. The question is why. Is it just to undermine them?"

"Absolutely. But…I think it's worse," he said. "I think he needs a villain."

"A villain?"

He nodded. "Some…easily villainized group nobody cares to defend, but who everyone will have an opinion about. Someone to blame if anything goes wrong."

"Well, we can fight that. I don't want to stand with the Knights, but you'll be by my side—you'll be an example of how wrong he is about the tall wolves."

Cass bit his lip angrily and glanced away. "We need more than that.

I'm nobody. I'm nothing."

"You take that back right now!" I almost barked.

Cass's clouded gaze snapped back to me.

"I'm not joking. Take it back, *Lord* of the Fourth Kingdom. *Savior* of the Arch-Sovereign. *Beloved Mate* who can *literally* turn himself into a one-man army. Take. It. Back."

The spark in his eyes, the smile threatening the corners of his lips—they made me want to shiver and shove him into some private place immediately. But this was more important.

"Cass..."

Cass's strong hand slid into place along my neck as he leaned down over me and sealed his lips to mine, pressing so hard I thought he might topple us both. I had to grab onto his waist just to keep us from going down.

"Cass!" I growled.

"I take it back," he said, his lips still against mine. He pulled away smiling at me. "I just mean I have no importance—"

I almost tweaked his nipple in frustration, I swear to the Goddess.

He twisted away to stop me, laughing, "—yet! I have no importance yet."

"Everyone has importance—Goddess, you've turned me into a kids' tv host over here. Maybe that's *your* purpose. Maybe *you* are the one who's supposed to *make people care*."

CHAPTER 29

We spent every waking moment when we weren't eating or meeting, tearing through more potential solutions to my "end of life" situation. More books arrived from the witches and from Idalia's library with each passing day.

It was super overwhelming, I won't lie.

Like a slow-motion neverending avalanche of books.

One I was grateful for, of course, because I *didn't* want to die *or* mate myself to a monster but…I was terrified I might lose the last few days of my life to searching for something that couldn't be found. Even more scared that we were all losing precious time to hang out together—my friends, Mom, Cass. Every time I saw them, they had a book in their hand or they were squinting into the bright lights of their laptops, trying to help me.

Again, *super* grateful. I loved them so much it hurt.

Especially in those dark moments when my mind became self-aware of its own ticking clock. I went dizzy, I became short of breath; my heart felt like a greyhound chasing a rabbit. They were like mini-freakouts, invisible panic attacks that only Cass could sense.

Every time I had one, he appeared out of nowhere in a blur. He kneeled beside me, put his hand on my chest, told me to mimic his breathing. And he stayed there until my heartbeat calmed—me saying I was okay wasn't enough.

"Heart, you helped me through my panic attacks," he said. "Let me pay you back."

"I don't need you to pay me back," I said.

"Maybe not this way," he teased. "Might I interest you in some private physical therapy…in my room?"

The dude was slick, I'd give him that. And his private physical therapy was the best I'd ever had. Especially after we'd cleared the air between us; his face became my throne.

I needed distractions. *Needed* them.

Especially when each new evening brought more of Rav's new persona to our television screen. He was *everywhere*, talking with Graham, talking with Oprah and Stephen. His social media numbers skyrocketed overnight to nearly one billion people.

To be fair, I had higher numbers on the accounts Yasmina started for me. But I doubted I would for long, with how much exposure Rav was getting.

But it wasn't just Rav appearing on our screen. Oriol debuted himself as the head of the Lion Court and talked about Rav's exceptional leadership and how he "couldn't wait to be part of the royal wedding party" of a queen he could barely hide his hatred for. Sorina appeared to introduce the vampire court…and steal some thunder for herself, offering the "full Twilight experience" to anyone who chose to join the Dragon Court. And the Deer Lord Oskar Lange gave an interview in which he solemnly recounted how "a vicious group of tall wolves rampaged through his private guard, killing hundreds."

But nothing quite prepared us for Ulric's appearance. Someone had spiffed him up; he and Violette looked as if they were living in the rockstar version of some Jane Austen novel. And he introduced the werewolf court with *rehearsed brevity*—as in, someone was absolutely whispering responses into his ear as the host asked him questions.

Which he clearly needed because every time the host asked about the difference between the werewolves and the "tall wolves," his brow furrowed as if he was pouting, and he grumbled some boilerplate response about the wolves being of ancient royal lineage and the "half-breeds belonging to a different court."

There was just one problem…most people liked the half-breed look of the tall wolves more. And when the interviewer told him that, it pissed Ulric off big time.

He lacked the social grace to be diplomatic, or even still, when the topic came up. His leg bounced, he slouched, and anger crept into his voice as he said, "I've met hundreds of them. I don't see what all the fuss is about. They're normal people. Becoming a tall wolf is nothing—*nothing*—anyone can do it. Hell, I could do it, if I wanted to. Maybe I will."

Which, of course, was like catnip to the interviewer.

And to us.

“Grab the phone real quick,” I said to Yasmina, motioning to the huge box phone in the corner. “Call in. Ask about Giselle.”

“Ooh, yes,” she purred.

It took a few seconds to find the right number, to dial it and wait for the satellite connection, but…a few credentials later, and Yasmina’s voice boomed over the television, “Hi, yes, I just had a question for Master Garand…well, it’s just…the only European Wolf Court I know is led by your mother, Giselle Garand, who nobody has seen or heard from in weeks—”

Ulric lurched forward in his seat. “End the call. End the call!”

Yasmina pushed. “What have you done to your mother, Ulric? And your brother Rolfe. He’s missing too—”

Click. And the line went dead.

So too did the interview. Ulric tore from his seat almost growling and slammed his hand over the camera lens to get it off him as he stormed past.

It was petty, maybe, but…it put a big smile on my face.

It did something else too—it forced Ulric into hiding and Rav into doing damage control. He had to back track on his “anti tall wolf” schtick.

It bought us a bit more time. Well, it would buy Cass more time.

He’d need it, considering he was expending so much of his energy trying to save me.

***

Corby’s birthday was another fresh gust of air through the monastic book-in-nose atmosphere of Loch na Feàirn.

Unlike Fern’s day, this one required getting up at the crack of dawn. No joke, I went to bed at two in the morning after going half-blind reading and woke up at six. I bundled and waddled myself over to the soldiers’ rooms to wake the people I’d already tapped for our impromptu Scottish mariachi band. And then, I went to wake the rest of our friends.

We crept into his room together and just as dawn broke through the eastern window, we broke into a loud, horrible, fun Scottish Mexican version of the song “*Las Mañanitas*” that had Corby smiling ear to ear before he was even fully awake.

My mom already had Corby’s tres leches monstrosity waiting for him when we got to the café. Well, she made *two* cakes—one to smash Corby’s face into when he went to take *la mordita*, his little birthday bite, and one for the rest of us.

He loved it all.

But…as he'd told me back at Hrafnagud…Mexican birthdays were *all-day* affairs. And I was no quitter, so I had a couple other surprises up my sleeve.

I made a deal with Belina to help her with spellwork for a week (if I survived November), in exchange for her conjuring a beautiful 7-pointed piñata into existence for Corby to destroy. Bless her, she'd even gone a step further and stuffed it full of Central American candies for him.

And as a final flourish, we splurged on a projector and played one of his favorite comedies, *Nosotros los Nobles*. He knew the dialogue by heart.

The fun of the day almost helped me ignore the awkward pauses between activities. It almost helped me forget how many tired eyes I found watching me each time I turned my head, the guilt I could feel from my friends that they should be searching. There was a sadness none of us could shake, running like a current under everything and I felt sorry for that…

I felt even sorrier when a horrendous yawn tore out of Cass and I discovered he'd made even more copies of himself, who scoured the internet nonstop while he kept a sliver of himself present with us.

Worst of all, I felt so guilty whenever I looked over at Scarlett and saw her trying her damnedest to seem happy, despite some storm of emotions roiling inside her. I'd always been able to read her like a book; I just couldn't tell if that book was a drama, a horror, or something in between.

I just didn't know how to explain that I had three days left before my wedding; I wanted to make the most of them, no matter what happened.

And what mattered most was finally fixing my mistake with her all those months ago.

***

The answer for how to help Scarlett was so pathetically simple, I wanted to smack my own head when I figured it out.

Instead, my mind tore me awake in the middle of the night.

Cass woke too. "Wha—What's wrong, heart?"

"I'm an idiot. An *idiot!*"

I was out of bed, hunting around for pants before Cass turned on the light.

"Natalie?"

"I'm okay. Go back to bed."

"Where are you going?"

"To wake Yasmina and Scarlett."

"Why?"

"Wild magick, Cass. I need to introduce her to the wild magick while I still have time."

I heard him stumble out of bed just as I shoved my socks on.

"Do you…know where some is?" he asked, reaching for his own pants.

"I do. I can't believe I forgot about it."

"Where?"

"Glengarriff."

"Ireland?"

It seemed so hokey, maybe, but in my dream, I'd heard the whistle—those beautiful hollow notes made by the wild hairs of magick still left in the world. I'd heard them at Galdere, and we'd heard them at Luxembourg…and in all the chaos of the last few weeks, I'd forgotten someone else had heard that eerie whistle recently.

Fern in Glengarriff.

That's why she'd picked that spot for our Lunasa celebration in the first place. She told me she'd heard whistling in the forest. She'd taken us out there on the hunt for it, in fact—me and Eike and Scarlett.

There was wild magick in Ireland.

And if I acted fast, I could give it to Scarlett before my time ran out.

"Heart, I don't think we can spare the time to go to—"

"Yes, we can."

"I know Scarlett's angry with you—"

"Exactly. I need her not to be."

"—I think she'd care more that you lived."

I cupped Cass's face and pulled him in for a quieting kiss. "Just in case, I'm gonna do it now."

I tore open the door and headed for the stairs, adding, "I'll go and come back. It'll only take a few hours."

"Famous last words," he grumbled, following me. He grabbed my coat and his own before opening the cottage door for me. "But we're coming back *tonight*, all right?"

"We?"

Cass pursed his lips impatiently at me, motioning me out the door with a swift smack to my butt. "Always *we*, heart."

Then he grabbed my hand in passing and hastened us along. "I told you; I'm done missing you."

***

Turned out, it was more than a whistle that tore me from my sleep. Some deep intuition had woken me in the nick of time.

"Scarlett, wait. Wait!"

I heard my mom shouting from all the way down the concrete walk when we emerged from the wooded path. Then I saw her, physically trying to block Scarlett's path where the concrete walk led up and away into the highlands.

Scarlett had a pack on her back.

She was trying to zip around my mom and take the 3-day trail that led to the nearest village over land, and Mom was stopping her.

"Please. Please! Just calm down, honey, you don't need to leave."

"Yes, I do, Mrs. Damarand. I need to go home."

Their eyes darted in my direction a moment before Scarlett veered left around Mom and marched away, heading for the trail. Mom caught her faster than I could blink.

"You can't, sweetheart. You're too important, too special. Someone might recognize you, hurt you—"

"To hurt *her*?" Scarlett sneered in my direction. "Yeah, I know. My whole life is bullshit now because my best friend's destiny turned me into a fugitive. I hate this!"

Scarlett veered again and marched out; Mom motioned to me.

"Nat, help!"

"What happened?"

"I don't know. I got up to make bread, and I saw her trying to leave."

"Scarlett, wait," I said, running to catch up with her. "Wait! Wait! Please just tell me what happened!"

"Like you care."

Outrage flared in me and I leapt in front of her. "Hey. You might be angry at me—but be angry at me for a *real* reason, okay?"

Scarlett just laughed and veered around me. "I have one of those, don't I."

"Look, don't go. I meant what I said—I can fix this. Just let me fix this!"

She rolled her eyes but paused long enough to say, "Fix it how?"

“I’m going to go get wild magick—the energy I took from you in Luxembourg. I know where to get more. I can go and get it and—”

“What? Keep it for yourself?”

“No! Give it to you, you friggen jerk!”

I shouldn’t have said it, but damn it, she knew me better than that. She used it as an excuse to keep marching anyway.

“Scar, stop! I think if I give the magick to you, you can make a new choice, okay? I hope you can, anyway.”

“Oh yeah, experiment on me again—that worked out *great* the first time!”

I shrugged dramatically. “I’m trying to give you what you want! Don’t you want that?”

I expected more anger, more accusations.

Instead, she suddenly yelped, “I don’t know what I want!” Her eyes welled with tears as she stared at me. “I just…I’m sad that all my firsts with this stuff ended up sucking, you know?”

“Huh?”

It rolled out of her like a swell of waves. “Josh tricked me into becoming an alter. Probably never even loved me to begin with. You took my choice away. I found out last night that my parents are splitting up, too, and I can’t even go to college because everything’s crazy and someone might attack me at any moment just to hurt you. Even if I did go to school, I don’t know what I want to study.

“It feels so unfair that you get to make all these choices for yourself, for the world, while I’m over here, forced to…roll with the punches. Stop punching me! I don’t want to be punched anymore.

“How do I deal with all of this if I lose you too?! My Goddess, I’m freaking out, Nat!”

When she finished, she shook for nearly a minute, catching her ragged breath. The rant was obviously long-coming.

But I was relieved by it. By her words, and how she sort of walked closer to me as all of that came pouring out of her. She wanted me to comfort her, so I did, I threw my arms around her and gave her a hug she seemed to desperately need.

And I sagged with relief against her when her arms wound around me too.

“This is why you shouldn’t hold back on me for so long,” I said after she calmed down a little. “I thought you were just angry at me, not…about everything else.”

She sobbed. “And I’m sorry you might explode.”

Goddess, I loved her.

I love her even more when she added, "But don't do that on my birthday, okay? I can't lose you too."

I pulled back just far enough to scowl at her. "Please, I would haunt you *so* much."

"Really?"

"Duh-doi."

She pulled me in for another hug, and we just held each other for a bit until her raging heart finally settled.

"I'm sorry about your parents too."

"I'm not," she giggled sadly. "Long overdue."

"They waited until you left home?" I asked.

"Yep. Such a cliché." After a few moments, she added, "I'm mad at you."

"I know."

She shook her head against my shoulder. "Do you swear you didn't take my magick to…turn into other animals?"

"What? No!" I pulled back to look at her; doubt hugged her like a jacket. "I wasn't being selfish. I genuinely thought I was doing the right thing. And I meant it when I said I wanted to wait for the right time and offer it to you again."

I waited until the doubt dissipated just enough to add, "Like right now? My creatures are telling me that we—you!—can ask the wild magick to turn you into whatever you want to be. I don't know for sure that it'll work, but…let's try? Let me try? I know where to find more wild magick. We can go *right now* to meet it. If you want."

Scarlett stared and stared…until finally, "I want."

Two words had never set me more at ease. Until she added…

"But I want someone better at experiments—like Belina—to go with us."

CHAPTER 30

"You've got strange priorities, girly. *Sei una rompiscatole!*"

That was Belina's response when Scar and I showed up at her cottage door five minutes later begging her to join us on our Irish adventure.

"What did she say?"

I didn't have the heart to tell Scarlett what she really said, so I went with, "Uh…she said you're like a little sister to her."

"Oh yes," Belina chuckled, motioning to her floating suitcase to follow her out the door. "A little sister who's a complete pain in my ass. You know, I did not agree to babysit when I joined your revolutionary commune in the middle of nowhere."

Scar's eyebrow rose sky high. "Puh-lease, you are barely older than us, Belina."

Belina's hand landed on the doorknob and waited. "Well, if you can do this without me…"

"No come! Please!" Scarlett squealed.

"I think I better," Belina said, shutting the door and motioning us to follow. "You two chasing wild magick alone is about as good an idea as setting sheep loose in a field of tigers."

"Excuse me," I teased. "I did pretty great with the two I've encountered so far."

"Yes, you lucked into easy ones. Who knows? Maybe the third will complete the set." From the tone of her voice, she clearly doubted that. "Summon the Elephant Princess and your wolfman, too. They should come as well."

I smirked. "Cass is getting Fern now."

Thirty minutes later, Corby volunteered to come with us as Belina, Scar, Cass, Fern and I hopped aboard the boat headed out. An hour after that, we were flying in a private plane toward the southwest, and another hour after that, we landed at Bantry Aerodrome, a tiny airfield just nine miles outside Glengarriff.

It took longer than that to arrange a rental car and grab a late breakfast at the hotel where we'd thrown our Lunasa celebration only two months ago. Gah, it seemed like another lifetime.

So did walking through the Glengarriff Nature Reserve. The forest was *gorgeous* so late in the year, bursting with gold and red and orange leaves and purple and white and yellow flowers peeking out everywhere. The air smelled of wet darkness and peat. And the early winter sunset was already smothering the forest in lightest pink.

Which made it all the worse that there was still Lunasa party garbage everywhere I looked.

I was *fuming*, considering I'd told Brodie to handle that problem weeks ago.

Cass tried to calm me down, "We'll fix it. I'll call a clean-up crew the second we're back home, I promise."

But… "It's embarrassing, Cass. The stuff's *everywhere*."

Seriously, there was confetti hanging from trees. There were plastic solo cups hidden in little nooks and crannies everywhere I turned my head. And the beautiful handmade resin tiles Cass had arranged for the main walk were still mostly there, now scratched and half-drowned in winter rains.

"Things kind of fell apart when Ulric crashed the party," Fern said in apology.

"I know, but we have to do better," I told her. "I have to do better."

"You're doing a lot already," Cass said, nudging me gently.

"Not enough," I admitted. "I spoke with Robine while I was at Arachne's Revenge. She told me I wouldn't be ready to lead until I fixed the mistakes I've made. Freeing myself from Rav seems like one. Doing this for Scar is another, but who knows how many others I've made?"

I was surprised to find anger on Cass's face, which only grew as he spoke.

"Heart…who cares what *Robine* thinks are mistakes? She ruined your life, just like the king has. If she hadn't told the whole world you're their supposed leader, he would never have revealed what you are. If anything, you should be *furious* with them. You should be asking me to hunt them down and bring them to you to answer for their crimes against you. I wouldn't even blame you if you asked me to take their lives for you—"

"Cass, Cass, it's okay," I said, reaching for him.

My hand slid into his, snapping that magnetic tug under the skin into place. Then I raised his hand to my lips and kissed it, just to soothe him. It did, thankfully. He tightened his hold on me and his thumb swept across the back of my hand like a match striking, as the anger faded.

I knew what he was really angry about.

"You know it's not your fault if we can't save me, right? You've already done so much—"

"I can't think about that, I'm sorry," he barked quietly, his voice clipped.

"I understand. But honestly? I'm sort of grateful to Robine *and* Rav for...outing me, in a twisted way."

Cass made a noise in the back of his throat—a skittering scoff of disbelief that paired strangely with the anger still on his face. But he fell silent after that, staring down at our clasped hands, and stayed that way until we came to the clearing I'd once visited, where I'd left an apple for the wild thing that lived in these woods.

The apple, to my surprise, was still on the stone where I'd left it months ago. Completely unblemished, unnibbled, unbruised. Preserved.

So, too, was the electric honeysuckle scent of wellspring magick; it hung heavy as mist around us. And in that mist?

"Can anyone else feel that?" Cass asked.

The magick held a charge of knowing. Sensing. Something was out there; it just wasn't whistling at the moment.

"Electricity," Belina said. "Be careful—"

As the words left her mouth, a new sound reached us. Phantom hooves clopping; they sped by in the brush off to our left, heavy and thunderous and tetchy.

"It seems angry," Corby yelped.

"It *is* angry," Belina said, widening her stance a little.

"How do we befriend it, then?" asked Scarlett, her voice still hopeful.

"I don't know if you do," Belina warned.

But Scarlett's downtrodden face was enough to make anybody promise the impossible.

"Listen," I said. "In your mind, listen for it. The wild magick I encountered before spoke to me telepathically. Does anyone hear anything?"

No telepathy was necessary. There came a sudden loud *braying* from our right, and something launched at us out of the forest so fast, all we could do was step back before the projectile hit the ground beside us.

It was...a trash can. A *literal* trash can.

Belina barked out a laugh. "Well, she isn't subtle."

"It wants us to clean?" Corby asked.

I smiled, picking the can up. "Spirit of the forest is pissed at us." I set the can in the center of the clearing. "Split into pairs. Let's fill this bad boy up."

Was cleaning the Glengarriff Forest anything I ever expected to be doing in the last three days of my life? No. But it was a small price to pay to make amends to Scarlett. Hell, it was something I wanted to do anyway!

Cass joined me. He grabbed pieces of trash out of my hands as soon as I picked them up. My creatures got in on the action too—everyone but my hybrids spilled out of me and went to collect litter.

All while the wild magick huffed and puffed in a wide circle around us, watching.

Cass put himself between me and that unseen creature at every turn, like a little dance between him and whatever was out there. So casual, you might have thought he wasn't doing anything at all. Unless you noticed the raised arches of his shoulders. Or the way his unwavering stare pierced the ruffling foliage, on high alert, *daring* that thing to come near me.

My protector.

My love.

He was so cute when he caught me watching him; a soft smile grew across his face before the creature's wild braying rushed in from my other side and he stepped between us again, whispering, "If you keep staring at me like that, the magick won't be the only wild thing in this forest tonight."

I kept staring.

How could I not? Cass bent down to grab a stray piece of litter…and that sea glass pendant of mine slid out of his shirt.

Goddess, the sight of it.

What a whirlwind of emotions it evoked.

Oh, there was *plenty* of lust, sure, but…there was also so much desire to mate with him, it was insane. I didn't even really know what that *meant* or what it would feel like! I just knew it felt as if someone had put a woodstove in my belly, and kept tossing in logs, flaming the fire higher, pulsing it hotter, each time he showed me how much he cared.

That connection, that sense that we belonged to one another, had grown stronger every single day since I told him I was already mated to him.

Stronger and increasingly impatient.

As if revealing that truth had kicked another cosmic countdown into play. One which seemed to be speeding up the closer we got to Rav's wedding deadline. To my potential death day.

As the wild magick brayed and stampeded past again unseen, I let it distract me from those unhelpful thoughts. The creature sounded like a horse. Maybe that was its form? I couldn't wait to see it.

Scarlett, too, was just as excited. She stood about fifty paces away with Belina, and every time the braying noise drew near, she turned toward it, eyes wide and hopeful rather than scared.

I would have spent the rest of my short life cleaning up garbage if it meant she could meet it.

***

Three hours in the dark spooky forest and one overflowing trash can later, we found ourselves in the clearing again, waiting to see if we'd done enough to meet the ghostly creature still haunting us.

Everywhere it ran, leaves shivered.

Everywhere it trotted, it dragged magick with it; after sundown, little pops of fluorescent color sparked in its trail.

But…it didn't come forward like we hoped. It only whinnied and neighed.

"Does she want more?" Scarlett wondered.

It couldn't hurt to ask. I pushed my thoughts outward, searching for it. *Her.*

"*Do you need more? I'll ensure the forest is cleaned anyway. Properly. I promise. But we came for you. To give you a home. Would you like that?*"

I didn't hear anything for a long time, except snorting and thunderous footfalls.

And then a sound grew around us…as she began to whistle. No, not whistle. Not exactly. Her noises…became music.

She sounded like a fiddle, maybe? Braying, galloping, neighing—each were notes played on an instrument of pure magick.

The forest, too, sang around us. And her percussive hoof falls set the beat.

It wasn't a peaceful score.

She wasn't calling for war either, but…

There was mischief in the melody as it grew and grew, until it swelled as loud as a concert in a music hall.

"Oh yes," Belina purred. "I like this energy for you, *sorellina.* Prepare yourself for anything."

"O-Okay," Scarlett squeaked. "I've got this."

She did not, in fact, "got this."

A sharp squeal sounded behind us, and we turned in time to *leap* out of the way as a massive form of green-gold magick barreled right through the clearing, scattering my friends.

Cass's hand landed on my shoulder as I picked myself up, and he was suddenly pressed to my back protectively.

And I marveled at the wild magick, as I'd done every time I'd encountered a piece of it before.

The melting technicolor goat. The tulip-sized shadow man. Now this…musical creature.

The weird, whimsical ways they expressed themselves were features, not flaws—to lure in their match, someone equally weird and whimsical.

They were as unique as fingerprints. Wholly themselves.

Wonderfully theatrical in their own ways.

This one, especially so.

"It's here!" Corby shouted.

"I'm ready!" Scarlett screamed.

Just as that blast of green-gold shot toward her again, she held her arms wide for it, to catch it—

It disappeared in a poof of mist the second she swung her arms shut.

Whinnied laughter cut in off to our left…and a smile as beautiful as the sunrise dawned on Scarlett's face.

"Here!" Fern shouted, pointing at the colorful trail of magick rushing by in the forest…right before a tiny green-gold ghost cat emerged from the underbrush.

The little creature gave a melodic meow that grew into a violin's wail…before the brush across the clearing suddenly rustled and a green-gold goat emerged and bleated at us, the noise becoming a bagpipe chord of orchestral proportions.

The leaves rustled again to our right and a rabbit hopped out, thumping its back foot against the ground, pounding bass into the percussive beat of the horse's hooves.

"Music," Scarlett breathed. "She wants music."

Almost in confirmation, one more green-gold creature shimmered into existence among us—a beautiful wolfhound. It found its spot, sat back, and *howled.*

The craziest thing happened then. Deep inside me, my wolf began to howl too.

And the green-gold dog's attention snapped to me as if he could hear it.

"Scarlett, howl!"

"What?"

Heck, I just went with it. I tipped my head back and, "Awwwoooooooo!"

My wolf howled with me.

And then *Cass* did too. He looked at me as if he'd never been so turned on in his life. His large hand slid into place along my spine before he tipped his head back and a perfect low howl soared out of his mouth.

"Everyone! Come on!" I shouted as soon as I caught my breath. "Now! Awwwooooooo!"

Thank Goddess for good friends (and goofy ones). Half a dozen heads threw themselves back and filled the crisp night air with wolfsong, clapping along to the beat.

And then my creatures emerged too, adding their sounds to the score.

How our contribution didn't *ruin* the beautiful music, I had no idea.

Well…it was magick, after all.

But the music swelled as the forest *came alive* around us. The misty magick began to glow, the leaves shivered and shook. And the wild creatures at our feet ran around and between us, trailing magick behind them, until the entire floor of the clearing glowed green and gold in the dark.

Until Cass's hand landed on my arm and spun me in place. He reached for my face, pulled me onto my tiptoes before I even stopped howling…and kissed me like it was the climax of the song. His tongue slid across mine, in offering. Its tip flicked across my canine and he pulled back to bite my bottom lip, teasing it between his teeth, before doing the whole thing again—only deeper. Until I could feel every needy part of myself pulsing in time with the music.

Despite the *actual magickal concert* raging around us, he'd managed to steal my full attention.

It was a perfect moment, one I'd savor forever…even if my life ended in a few days.

And when we ran out of breath and nature's song reached its crescendo…the wild magick finally revealed itself to us, stepping into the clearing as a song in physical form.

"…a pony!"

"A púca…"

She was dark as moonless night…sort of. The gold-green magick hugged her darkness just enough to let us see that her squat little body was covered in flowering bark, and her mane and tail were woven moss. And her eyes were drops of morning dew.

Beautiful.

It took me a beat too long to realize she was walking straight toward me.

"*You're offering me a home?*" Her inner voice was just as much a serenade as the rest of her. "*You would keep me?*"

"Nat?"

Scar's voice was so soft and unsure; it broke my heart when I looked over and saw fear on her face—that I would take this from her.

"Scar, come here. Hurry up!" I pulled her right up alongside me. "Talk to her in your mind. Just say hello."

Scarlett shifted her weight nervously, staring the creature down, but after a moment, all the tension in her body erupted in an excited little wiggle. "She's saying hello!"

"I know," I said. "Talk to her. Offer her a home."

Scarlett took a tentative step forward, waffling nervously as the pony nickered. But it only took another silent beat or two before Scarlett offered the creature her hand…and she accepted. The stout pony stepped forward and pressed her forehead to Scarlett's palm. There was a flash of magick and she was gone.

No, not gone.

A musical giggle of surprise and surrender escaped Scarlett as she staggered back and turned to face us, her blue eyes ringed in green-gold.

"I can feel her," she said, before her head tilted. "I can see her."

"Good," Cass encouraged. "Just accept her."

Scarlett did. She shivered and smiled and threw her arms around my neck.

"Nat, I…"

"I know."

She deserved this and so much more and I was happy to have given her this experience, even if we both knew that these joyful moments were fleeting and the sorrows of tomorrow might overshadow them.

That was what made them so important.

"I'm sorry—"

"I know. Just enjoy this. And talk to her. Tell her what you want for your life. The choice is yours—it's always been yours. Screw Josh. He's a blip in your story."

I expected anticipation, or insecurity from her.

Instead, she said, "You gotta stick around to enjoy this with me, babe. I don't want this without you."

I tightened my hold on her. "Don't say that."

"She's not the only one, heart," Cass said behind me, helping in *no way* whatsoever.

Not when I could *feel* the adrenaline pouring off him, mixing with my own. That and his snowflake attention as I pulled out of Scarlett's arms to find him staring at me with that dark desire still in his gaze?

My Goddess, he said so much without saying anything at all.

"Fern?" I said, my eyes locked on Cass. "Would you take everyone back to the hotel, please? I'd like to speak with my mate in private."

Mate. It still felt like such a dangerous word, but so lovely to say. So lovely to attach to *him*—my ginger gentleman who couldn't stop staring.

I didn't even hear her reply, or anything the others said as they backed away and disappeared down the trail.

Oh no, my body had other priorities at the moment.

His touch and kiss during the concert, the lingering magick—I couldn't look away from him.

But I waited until our friends were gone, and it was just the two of us, to finally sink into my own adrenaline at the sight of him.

Cass did, too; he exhaled and let some feral darkness creep into his eyes as he stared at me.

"That was glorious," he said.

"I know. I can still feel it."

Cass's eyes darted to the raging pulse in my neck, and he groaned under his breath.

When his intense gaze met mine again, I was already smiling.

"What's gotten into that head of yours, heart?"

I took a step back—

His eyes snapped to my feet and his lip curled back, "Are you sure you want to do that?"

"You promised me a chase, remember?"

"If I recall, it was *you* who promised me a—"

I took another step back…and raw instinct strangled his polite British flirtations.

He stepped forward as if he couldn't help it.

His hands wrenched his coat off his body as if he couldn't stand it touching him anymore.

But then something delicious happened.

He realized his own impatience and some other instinct kicked in. His fingers crept to the top button of his shirt and undid it so gracefully before reaching down to the next, and the next.

Each movement was deliberate. Slow. Teasing. My pulse raced as I watched.

"You have time for that?" I teased, taking another step back. Savoring the way his entire body flinched, at war with whatever part of him was keeping the rest so calm.

"You should be doing this for me."

I shook my head; he followed the movement. "I'd just rip it off."

"Like this?"

Cass's hands gripped either side of the button line and wrenched, tearing the last of the buttons away, exposing those scars on his chest, and the heave of his gorgeous, chiseled body—how fast he was breathing for me.

And then he smiled hungrily, licking his canine tooth.

Ugh, Goddess. He'd always been beautiful—gorgeous, really—but the might and muscle of his bear, the graceful narrowness at the waist of his wolf and that hair drawing a veil to either side of his face darkening the intensity of his vampiric stare in between?

He looked…possessed.

He looked…beastly.

He looked…like everything I'd ever dreamed of last year at Lunasa.

I didn't even realize I was biting my lip until he growled, "That lip belongs to me."

Cass's mercurial gaze narrowed. "Those eyes? Belong to me. That pulse in your neck and the one between your thighs?"

I shivered. "Let me guess—yours?"

He nodded, weathering his own shiver in anticipation.

"You have no idea what I'm going to do to you once I catch you."

Desire flashed through my body as I stepped back again almost to the treeline.

"Yes, I do. You're going to claim me."

Gah, it felt like such a stolen *luxury* to be able to say that out loud. To savor the perks of a bond we wouldn't get to keep.

His eyes fluttered shut as he bit down on his lip and a low purring growl escaped his chest.

"More than that, now. You called me your mate. You shouldn't have done that."

The words confused me just enough. I stopped where I stood, even though my legs were *shaking* to go. No, I waited until his eyes fluttered open again.

"Why not?"

He raised his fist to his chest and pounded on it. "Because the animals in here are roaring for me to make it official."

My heart fumbled. I hadn't expected him to say that.

"They're what?"

"Don't look at me like that," he said. "*The moment* you confessed that you had already chosen me, I wanted to summon the Goddess and take you as my mate right then and there. Bond with you. Declare myself your husband. Make you my bride."

I…didn't know what to say. Thoughts of chases retreated to the back of my mind in favor of…this. Whatever *this* was. I'd confessed to him and he'd seemed happy about it, but…

"You never said anything."

"Whether it would or wouldn't, I didn't want you to think I was only offering that bond to save you."

"It wouldn't save me," I told him. "But…you want to marry me?"

Cass walked toward me then and slid his hands into place along my cheeks, coaxing me up onto my tiptoes. "More. I want to join our souls. I want to walk beside you forever, my equal, my partner. I want to be your peace…"

Then he brought his mouth to mine. With a sensual peck, he flicked his tongue against my lips, and added, "…and your pleasure."

I wanted that too. More than anything.

But my head shook as visions of Giselle wailing by that river after Aldric's death flashed in my mind—I couldn't do that to him.

"If we mated, you'd only have me for a few days. I've *seen that loss*. That despair. It's torture."

The softness disappeared from Cass's face. "You're not going to die. I won't allow it."

I opened my mouth to try and make him see reason. "Cass."

"If you go, I go."

The words stripped my defenses—the chase, the lust, the magick—until only the raw heart of my love remained.

"Don't say that!" I almost yelped.

"Why not? It's the truth."

"Cass, there might be nothing you can do—"

His head shook decisively. "I told you; I refuse to miss you again."

"Cass—"

"That's three," he interrupted, releasing his hold on me. He robbed me of his magnetic touch so fast I had to orient myself.

"Huh?" I stammered.

"That's three. Our intermission has concluded." As I watched, he slid each of his shoes off and set them to the side, his toes flexing against the soft soil underneath. "You have thirty seconds to run."

"That's not…important…right now. We need to talk about this."

"Talk about what? I'm already yours. You're already mine."

He didn't even look at me; instead, he undid his cuff buttons and began to roll up his sleeves.

"If anything, you should let me free you," I tried.

"If anything, you should let me give you plenty of reasons not to die, starting with a chase you'll never forget."

Still, I didn't move, my mind torn between his dark promise of a hunt and that panic in me that I only had *this moment* to convince him I wasn't worth all of this. To convince him an accidental mating bond wasn't worth sacrificing anything for.

Until he finally turned his moonlit gaze back upon me. The intensity there? *Holy hell.*

"Go, heart. Or I can summon the Goddess early to watch me claim every inch of you."

CHAPTER 31

Was he joking? Probably.

Was I so switched on I ran as fast as my hummingbird heart would let me? Oof, *definitely*.

My feet pounded the earth so hard I felt the reverberations in my calves, my thighs, between them.

My hands were up in front of my face, guarding it from the branches I pushed through as I cut a path through the dark forest. I ran over boulders. I tumbled over fallen logs. I flung myself down an incline on my butt and got up running again.

As I heard a distant molasses-dark voice said, "Let's make this a little more fun."

A flash of something caught my eye to the right, but it was gone when I turned my head.

I heard footsteps off to my left…but also behind me…ahead of me…right on top of me.

It was quiet, in the forest.

Save for the sound of his footsteps.

Save for his panting.

Thc wild magick's music had tickled my soul.

This music—his music—tickled somewhere else entirely.

Did part of me want to stop and let him catch me? Oh yeah. Most of me, honestly.

But that would be no fun and…I needed time to think up some argument that might keep Cass from making some drastic choice he couldn't take back.

As I leapt over an old rock wall, I came to an animal trail and took it.

"*Which way is he coming?*" I asked my creatures.

"*All ways*," my dragon replied…and his tone told me so many things.

They weren't going to help me, for one. I could feel them all in there watching with amusement—with whatever the imaginary creature equivalent of popcorn was.

"*Popcorn,*" my raven teased.

"*He's not serious, is he?*" I asked.

"*Deadly serious,*" my aurochs joked.

"*Not funny.*"

"*Not meant to be.*"

More footsteps flitted into the brush to my right, so I veered left and ducked behind a large boulder to catch my breath.

"*We have to save him,*" I said.

"*Save* you," my raven countered.

"*Duh. That too.*"

My wolf shook her head. "*Two birds.*"

Those two words lit up inside my head like a neon sign.

"*Two birds one stone? Saving me will save Cass?*" I rolled my eyes. "*No doi, you walnut—how do we do that?*"

But she surprised me then. Her head tilted for a long beat before she said, "*Three birds.*"

"*Oh come on, what does that mean?!*"

She didn't answer. Instead, my bear chuffed, "*Incoming.*"

I turned to run but—

A silver blur shot toward me like a bullet. Stopped inches from me, wearing a grin so sexy, it was all I could focus on as Cass crooned, "Is that the best you've got?"

I tried to run again—

His broad hand was on my hip before I could blink. He spun the fight or flight right out of me. I froze, pinned against the rock.

Trembling. My whole body was vibrating, with surprise, with need.

Especially when he leaned down-down-down into my space, aiming for my lips…only to pause inches away.

Like a tease!

I could feel my eyes widen with impatience.

A tiny mewl crept off my tongue…and he answered it with a tsk of his, slow and indulgent over the low animalistic growl of one of his animals.

The smile on his face was exquisite poison for my rational brain.

And when he suddenly purred, "I am going to lick you for hours," any remnants of worry inside me melted away. It could wait. My Goddess, it could wait!

Cass reached for the button on my pants. Popped it with relish.

His hands went to the edges of my waist. Tugged my pants off my hips—he loved that part best.

But as he knelt and coaxed my jeans off without removing my shoes, I seized the few seconds of awkwardness while he was on his knees. If he wanted a long chase, he could have one.

I bolted and ran.

And I heard him laugh behind me—

Right before a force hit me so hard from behind, it knocked the wind out of me as it sent us both flying toward a tree!

When I felt bark against my hands, I waited for what I knew must come next. I waited for the slam of my body against the trunk. To splat against it like a cartoon coyote.

I didn't.

There was a hand cradling my face.

And an arm wrapped around my belly, the hand at the end of that one splayed across my thighs.

Cass had stopped me just in time.

Stopped me…just to pin me there off my feet. He had me pressed against the trunk, held aloft so that his curves fit to mine. So that every inch of him was pressed against me.

Including a few against my butt that twitched with warmth and delight and delicious anticipation.

"*My Goddess,*" I yelped when he claimed the shell of my ear between his teeth, tugging and sucking until the entire side of my neck was prickly with sensation, and I was shivering with desperate need.

"Yes," he growled against my skin, nibbling, licking. "Call for her, heart. I'll bond with you right here, right now."

I tucked my lips between my teeth instead.

And Cass laughed again.

My feet landed on the ground. His hand splayed across my back, keeping me pressed to the tree.

And then he was suddenly on his knees behind me. His mouth—his tongue, his teeth—landed against the curve of my cheek. Nibbled with a frenzy that had met screaming that blasted Goddess's name again!

I could only squirm as he dragged his teeth across my skin, setting it ablaze. Down, down, down to the place where my butt met my thighs before he suddenly veered right between.

His tongue burrowed.

Licked.

Teased.

Tasted.

I tried to hold onto the tree, the smooth bark…

All while he dragged his nails across my skin, setting me to shiver.

All while he moaned with equal satisfaction and need—Goddess, I wanted to eat that sound.

The stimulation. It was… It was…

"Too much!" I begged, almost crying, as every part of my brain screamed for him to do more. To keep going. To go deeper.

Cass disagreed that it was too much. He always did.

He rose again, lifting me *again*, so that my curves fit within his, and he panted, "You want too much? I can give you that, heart. Right now. But you'll have to trust me mind, body, and soul."

Goddess, was he really asking to mate with me right here? Like this?

I didn't want to do that to him. Not without a future. I couldn't imagine anything crueler. Would he get over me eventually? Y-Yes, right? But why go through all that pain, all that heartache—

"Heart," he barked softly, impatient for an answer.

But how could I give him one that didn't ruin this?

"Cass, I would bond with you in a heartbeat. I will always choose you."

Cass groaned. His hand crept around my front and landed against my sensitive bud, patiently stroking.

"But I don't want to rush this. I don't want to hurt you."

His stroke hastened deliciously. "Heart, I told you already—I will *never* bond without your consent."

"O-Okay…?"

Then what was he asking for?

"I just want to show you something." He nibbled my ear again, "You trust me, don't you? Don't you?"

"Y-Yes, I d-do," I admitted.

"Good, because you're going to feel me…*in there*."

I expected those fingers on that little switch to hasten their pace. Instead, his nose pressed to my temple—to my mind.

"What do you mean—ah!"

Every hold he had on me suddenly intensified. *Every hold.*

Face against bark.

Curve against curve.

He pressed his head to mine and…my mind *whited.*

I felt *invasion*, but not an unpleasant one.

It was a request. Like someone was knocking on the door in my mind.

Like someone was flicking all the switches for my powers on and off at once.

A poltergeist—it felt like a poltergeist. A polite one. A sensual one.

So I surrendered to it.

I released the last bit of fear and reluctance in my mind, yielding to him completely…and weathered the full body tremble that followed.

"Open your eyes, heart."

My eyelids were fluttering so fast, it was hard to do what he wanted. But when I finally got them open…

"What the…?"

There, just a few feet away…was a face I recognized. One I'd had to stare down in the mirror every day of my life.

A copy of me.

A Natalie.

She was pressed against a nearby tree, just like I was, almost mirroring me.

And Cass was pinned to her back. A Copy Cass, kissing her head-her temple-her ear.

"That's me," I whispered, in awe, in wonder.

"Yes," Cass said, kissing my shoulder before his teeth landed against my skin and bit softly. "I've suspected for some time that if your side of the bond could affect me, my side—as unstable as it still is—might be able to do the same for you."

"Am I doing this?" I asked, wonder and awe swelling even through the rush of everything else.

"Almost," Cass said. "You're doing it with my help."

He licked my ear suddenly and added, "I know the exact switch inside you to flip to make this possible. I'll show you how to make it happen on your own."

Holy moly—what a gift that would be.

But I didn't have long to think about it. Cass had more to show me. "Turn your head."

I did, reluctant to take my eyes off the pair of us across the way, how tenderly that Copy Cass clutched her, kissed her.

But I found another pair of us on our other side.

This pair…Cass was pulling no punches. They were making love in a little clearing off to our right, him on top, her pulling him in to kiss, running her fingers through his hair as they stared at each other and joined again and again. Patiently. Indulgently.

The sight of that? I shivered again.

"You wanted me to see that?" Reaching back, I ran my fingers through Cass's hair, pulling him tighter against me.

"Yes, but more than that, I wanted you to *feel* this."

I was still staring at "us" across the way when his lips landed so tenderly against my cheek and our copies suddenly flattened, darkened, and zipped toward us in a blur.

They reentered our bodies as easily as breath…but they hit as hard as a wrecking ball.

They brought with them the sensation of what they'd been doing. What they'd been *feeling*.

It melded with the desire I already felt, with the delight of what Cass was already doing to me; the sensations across my body grew and *grew*.

"Holy hell. *Holy hell!*"

I clung to Cass as the stimulation rippled through me in waves, amplifying. Until I couldn't see straight. Until my center threatened to mutiny.

And then I turned my head the other way, saw the other pair of us flatten and zip toward us and—

I screamed so loud as the pleasure tore through my body, all I could do was cling to Cass and listen to his groans of pleasure in my ear as stars burst in my vision and my center exploded.

I'd *never* experienced anything like it.

Nor had I thought about that copying gift of his and whether I could borrow it.

It made sense, though, didn't it? So many of the mated pairs I'd met had said they could share gifts long before they formalized their bond. Heck, it was one of the ways they could tell they were meant for each other in the first place.

Like my wings with Rav.

Like Rav's healing gift with me.

And I suddenly understood why my wolf had said, "*Three birds*."

"Cass, I think I know how to free myself from Rav."

"Seriously? My parlor trick did all that?"

It was more than a parlor trick.

I twisted and kissed Cass, laughing. "Seriously. Put me down."

My feet landed on the earth. I turned to face him…only to find him on his knees in front of me, guiding my legs up onto his shoulders.

"Cass—"

"Is it something we can do in the next hour?" he asked, eying that place between my legs with a hunger that twisted a hook in my belly and tugged.

"N-No?"

"That's what I thought," he said, a crazed smile blossoming on his gorgeous face. "Later then. I won the chase, and now this…this is mine."

CHAPTER 32

I had never been more satisfied…or covered in more dirt in my entire life.

Literally, the dirt was everywhere across my body, where I laid at the center of a little forest clearing, wrapped in Cass's coat, tucked in the crook of his equally filthy arm and kept warm through the night by his radiator-hot body.

He hadn't been joking when he threatened to lick me for hours.

Nor had the realization that I knew how to beat Rav at his own game stopped Cass from claiming me.

I screamed the Goddess's name so many times, I was honestly surprised she hadn't materialized out of nowhere to tell me to knock it off already, she heard me the first time.

Tree to tree, clearing to clearing, it had become more than sex almost immediately.

It had become a surrendering.

A prayer for our future.

A manifestation ritual for how close we wanted to be if we actually got to complete our bond before the Goddess and join our souls together.

A manifestation I took more and more seriously when I realized it *was* possible to free myself from the king.

Or, it might be.

I had a shot, anyway. I wanted to take it.

Because the more I thought about, the more I liked what it could do for not only me…but our entire movement going forward.

"Cass?"

"Yes?"

"We need to talk about the wedding."

"Which one?" he teased. "Ours? Or the one you're going to skip?"

"I can't skip it, you know that," I said gently, sitting up to face him.

He was up like a shot, sitting across from me. "Yes, you can. You can't possibly think you'll—"

"We have a couple options," I said. "Option A—the worst option—I undo my bond with you, mate with Rav, and you guys come and rescue me. Hopefully before I'm completely brainwashed and there's nothing to rescue anyway."

Cass sneered in disgust. "Vetoed and struck from the records. *Option B*—you marry the prick with one of my copies in tow, and the second Rav says "I do," I cut the head clean off his body. No muss, no fuss. You're a widow with an empire by morning."

I didn't hate that idea—at least the part where I got spirited away before Rav could force me to mate with him.

But...

"The wedding's televised. Millions—maybe billions—will be watching."

"All the more reason to put on a show," Cass teased.

I scowled. "You'd be an assassin."

"Your assassin."

"A villain," I said.

"Your villain."

"Cass, there'd be *no* coming back from that."

He smiled, pulling me into a tender kiss. "Villain or not, I'll always be your man. The shadows will always protect us."

I shook my head. "I want you to be my man in public. I want us to *live proudly*, Cass. Together. I want to call you my mate, my love, my H-word I can't say for risk of exploding."

Cass sobered. "I want that too."

"Good."

"How does that happen with either of those options, heart?"

I took a deep breath. "It doesn't. But...Option C is promising."

"Option C."

"A-huh. It's risky. Reckless. I'd need you to help me pull it off, and we don't have much time to prepare. But it's flashy; it might be the only way we beat Rav at his own game."

Cass winced preemptively, and I added, "It might work, it might not. I might go free, I might die."

He tore his gaze away in concern, in dismissal.

But I reached for his chin and forced him to look at me again. "Option C could free me from the promise *and* completely knock Rav off course.

He'd be dealing with the fallout for ages, and it would give us time to debut on our own terms. And no one would *ever* think I'm on his side again."

"It's not that terrible witch hex that would cost you your legs, is it?"

"No, not my legs."

"Natalie," he snapped, reading me all too well. "Then, what would it cost?"

"…You'd have to trust me."

I watched the reluctance soften in Cass's eyes, until he exhaled like a deflating balloon, and he grumbled curiously, "…Out with it, then. What's Option C?"

CHAPTER 33

I barely slept those last three days.

I had to be reminded to eat.

While my team reached out to Rav's people for my own wedding schedule and arranged everything I needed, I focused on only one thing—training to attempt this crazy way out of my promise with Rav, one that might leave me dead or broken or both.

Until the sun rose on my death day, and I climbed aboard a private jet bound for the home country of my would-be conqueror.

The man who had threatened everyone and everything I loved.

The man who had killed for me…and killed to punish me.

The man who had strapped a magickal tripwire to my throat and set it to go off if anyone else tried to claim me.

Eike was waiting for me when I landed.

She patted me down. Took my phone. Eyed me with that cool distrust that would've scared an older version of me.

Not me, though—not now, about to give up a part of myself I never wanted to lose.

If you couldn't be brave on your death day, when you were poised to send a very loud, very flashy message to a man who couldn't take "no" for an answer, when else could you be?

We drove in silence to an unassuming farm near Fylgja Castle where the prep team and my dress were waiting—another golden princess ballgown. No, not a princess—a queen. Rav had pulled out all the design stops this time with an enormous sheer collar that didn't just frame my face, but my entire head, and sky-high shoes, and a hairstyle to match.

The makeup was dramatic.

The entire look was dramatic.

A post-modern royal look no one would ever forget…mostly because it intentionally looked like a costume. Not a gaudy one—not something for Halloween—but a look meant to set the trends for a new millennium, not follow old ones.

It was beautiful on me, all things considered.

And that was the first word Rav said when he stepped in the room, "*Beautiful, min skat.*"

I turned to him without a speck of fear on my face. His bespoke suit matched mine this time, a sort of pale gold embroidered to match. His hair was partially braided. The tattoo behind his ear was on full display.

As a little treat for myself, I'd finally looked up its meaning. *Ingwaz*—a symbol of prosperity, fertility, new beginnings, and the cyclical nature of existence.

Boy, was he in for a new beginning today.

One that would hopefully smack the victorious smile off his face and bring everything a little more "full circle" for us both.

He kept things surface level as our prep teams buzzed around us both, finishing final touches. A purple flower in his pocket. A purple flower in my hair.

But once we walked out to the gold convertible Rolls Royce waiting to take us past the excited crowds to Fylgja Castle where the ceremony would take place, he tried to engage with me.

"*Min skat*, I want you to know, I know you're brave for coming here today. I don't take for granted the courage required for you to fulfill your promise to me. I know this isn't the way this should have happened. There isn't enough…romance? Feeling? But…mark my words, this is for the best and the rest of our lives will be very different. I am committed to making things right between us. I will show you how to love me again."

Any snark I might have unleashed, any disdain I might have purged from my body at his expense, drained right out of me. I couldn't dwell on the insane things he'd just said. I couldn't risk breaking my focus on the plan ahead.

"Do you have anything you'd like to say?"

Oh, there was plenty. But I knew I had to say something, something that sounded like me, to keep him from suspecting anything.

"I hope you're right, Rav," I said, keeping my voice as steady as possible. "Because revealing me to the entire world makes me your responsibility. Part of your legend. You'll have to live up to the image you're creating."

He leapt forward to grab my hand and ran his fingers across my skin.

"It's not just an image. I promise. We had something real once and we will have it again. And when we do, we'll be the Arch-Sovereigns this world deserves. Together."

I nodded at that and turned away, feeling his fiery attention against the back of my head as he held onto my hand, and squeezed when it was time for us to wave to people.

The crowds weren't just massive. They were sprawling. The entire countryside around the castle was packed shoulder-to-shoulder. The lawn, too, was overrun with spectators…at least until we reached a certain point where fences and more deer guardsmen were keeping the public at bay.

We stepped out of the car to cheers from the crowds and leers from those guests privileged enough to have a spot inside.

Beyond the fences and guards, the estate had been transformed. He'd turned his home into a fairytale castle for a fairytale wedding, full of TV cameras Rav reminded me not to look at, dignitaries he wouldn't let me talk to, and fellow Supremes who smiled at me despite the deep look of suspicion in their eyes.

Funnily enough, my silence made them more suspicious than anything—there was power in it they didn't like.

Although, I didn't know why they were surprised that I had nothing to say.

There were no friends present.

No Idalia.

No Giselle.

No Asterios.

Even Archer, who'd once spared no opportunity to ask me about Cass, didn't even deign to glance my way.

Honestly, I wished I could stick around long enough to see the look of shock and awe on their faces after what came next, but…either it would matter, or it wouldn't.

Either I would succeed or I would fail.

There was a wonderful simplicity to that—life or death.

Just like there was a simplicity that came with being on display for the whole world to see.

Was that intimidating? Yes.

Was it also liberating because I'd soon have nothing to hide? Oh yeah.

I was looking forward to it.

To popping out of Rav's life for good before he even knew what hit him.

And with that fantasy playing on a loop in my head, the wedding planner pulled me out of the rabble and situated me inside, just off the patio, while the guests took their seats and Rav went to take his place near the altar.

Near the two *false priests* I could see standing there in their runic robes, holding a tome and two blue azurite stones between them.

When the orchestra began to play and the planner motioned for me to walk down the aisle, I was honestly surprised by the music Rav had picked.

I…loved it.

An epic instrumental version of "Blinding Lights" that made me seem like some mythical figure come to take my rightful place in the sun. To rise. To shine.

I didn't rush it.

I even found a soft, triumphant smile to wear that distracted from the shake of my hands where they clutched my bouquet of marguerite daisies at my chest.

I walked in time with the music, as it soared across the open lawn and swelled for the cameras, letting it bolster me in the countdown to Option C.

And as I stepped up beside Rav and the epic score softened to a dirge played by a single violin and horn, I found a quiet peace I hadn't allowed myself in my last few days of relentless training.

"We are gathered here today to witness the sacred bond and marriage between his royal highness Arch Sovereign King Rav Elivagar of the First Kingdom and his mate Lady Natalie Damarand, Arch Sovereign of Earth."

Rav's priests paused momentarily then, glancing at me. So too did Rav.

And I remembered that was the point at the last wedding when we'd been interrupted by Cass's rescue.

He wouldn't be coming today.

So I raised my eyebrows at them, goading them on, ready for a new make or break moment.

"Today, you pledge not just to stand by one another, but to move through life's endless transformations together.

"Do you, Rav Elivagar, take Natalie Damarand to be your wife, your mate, your home, through all forms and faces, in joy and in sorrow, in shadow and in light, for all your days?"

“I do,” Rav said so confidently.

"And do you, Natalie Damarand, take Rav Elivagar to be your husband, your mate, your home, through all forms and faces, in joy and in sorrow, in shadow and in light, for all your days?"

There it was. That stupid damned promise that had caused so many problems, laid bare before me.

And there was Rav, the biggest stupid damned problem of my entire life.

My biggest mistake to fix.

I was honestly proud in those last few seconds when I felt a smile creep onto my face, as genuine as the words I’d been waiting to say to him all this time.

Without further ado, I took a deep stilling breath and said, “No. I do not.”

THE END

Continue reading Natalie's story in

FIERCE

Book Seven of *The Garden of Beastly Delights* series

The final installment

CHAPTER 1

Pain welled at the back of my throat as the magick attached to my cursed promise to Rav realized what I'd said.

It hesitated and recoiled, as if it wasn't sure it had heard me correctly.

I realized that the repercussions of breaking my promise weren't immediate. They hadn't been with Guillermo, or Antonio's men either. It was as if the magick was *giving me just a few seconds* to make a different choice. To choose a different path.

It was surreal to feel the thwarted magick *grow angry* inside me at the betrayal.

Doubly so to hear the wedding party gasp in horror…echoed by a louder shriek from the faceless crowds outside the fences.

Rav gripped my arms so tightly I thought he might rip them off, spinning me to face him.

"*Min skat*. Do you take me to be your husband, your mate, your partner? Yes, right? You do, *right*?"

I savored the panic in his voice. The way he was still acting like little ole me couldn't understand the ramifications of what I was saying. As if he was doing me a favor by drawing attention to that cursed promise again.

The smile on my face only grew.

"I will *never* marry you, Rav. I will *never* be your mate."

His grip on my arms tightened.

"Natalie!" he almost yelled. "Take it back. *Take it back!*"

I felt the anger of the magick begin to rise inside me.

Even though it only took seconds, I let myself experience it "slowly." Thoughtfully.

The way it felt like a coal had begun to burn in my stomach, and that burn began to spread.

The way my neck continued to pain me. Growing sharper. Biting.

Until it wasn't just in my throat anymore, or in my stomach.

It wasn't just in my body either. No, the pain slithered through me, inside and out. A serpent unraveling me at the seams, cell by cell.

"Please, *min skat!*" Rav roared, beginning to shake me in his terror. "Say you do! SAY YOU DO!"

Continue reading in the final book…

RECEIVE A FREE PROLOGUE FOR *THE GARDEN OF BEASTLY DELIGHTS*

Building a relationship with my readers is one of my favorite things about writing. It feels like magic, connecting with someone through worlds created and stories shared.

I offer those on my mailing list a free bonus chapter or selection of free stories from other exciting new authors each month as well as details about new releases, special offers, giveaways, art reveals, and other bits of news about *The Garden of Beastly Delights* series.

You can join my enchanted circle of newsletter readers and receive *The Garden of Beastly Delight's* **free** prologue by signing up at my website www . sierraprynne . com.

IF YOU ENJOYED *SAVAGE...*

Reviews are insanely powerful for a self-publishing author like me because they help me draw attention to my stories. Someday, I might be lucky enough to have the financial might of a big wig publisher on my side, but for the moment it's just me.

Committed and loyal readers are an amazing gift. Honest reviews help me find other passionate readers, which in turn makes it possible for me to keep writing stories for you all.

If you've enjoyed this book, I would be eternally grateful if you could spend just five minutes leaving a review (it can be as short as you like) on the book's Amazon page.

A GIANT THANK YOU TO MY PATRONS

Antonia Martin, Melanie Ansley, Jenni Appleseed, Donald and Cristy Trippeer, Allison Buckmelter, Liz Luu, Xian Xian, Naman Gupta, Tarek Tohme.

Thank you so much!
Xoxo Sierra

If you would like to become a patron or name a future character, please visit my website www . sierraprynne . com.

ABOUT THE AUTHOR

Sierra Prynne is a cheeky little pen name inspired by a run-in with a lovely drunk lady who told me: "You can wake up ten years from now living the life you have or the life you want."

The women in my family have a tradition of using their middle names and Sierra is mine. Prynne is a gift to a certain complex and self-possessed literary character who deserved better. I'm learning about who I want to be as I write these stories and I think she'd respect that.

As for who I am, well, I'm a hopeful romantic who believes you can find true love if you're brave enough not to settle for less than extraordinary. Also, I probably like fantasy a little too much for my own good and when I'm not writing, I can be found wandering through theme parks, national parks, and book parks…those are a thing, right?

You can check out more of what I'm up to at
www . sierraprynne . com or email me at sierra @ sierraprynne . com

And, if social media's your style, please support me with a follow or facebook or Instagram.

COPYRIGHT

A LURING PRESS book.

First published in the United States in 2025
by LURING PRESS LLC

Cover art designed by the glorious Lisa Amowitz.

www.ingramcontent.com/pod-product-compliance
Lightning Source LLC
LaVergne TN
LVHW041115080826
845145LV00007B/1822

* 9 7 8 1 9 6 4 6 4 0 0 8 2 *